Joyce Ravid

Colin Harrison is the author of six novels, including *The Finder*, *Afterburn*, and *The Havana Room*. He lives in Brooklyn, New York, with his wife, writer Kathryn Harrison, and their three children.

ALSO BY COLIN HARRISON

The Finder

The Havana Room

Afterburn

Bodies Electric

Break and Enter

COLIN HARRISON
MANHATTAN NOCTURNE

PICADOR

St. Martin's Press

NEW YORK

www.picadorusa.com

Picador® is a U.S. registered trademark and is used by
St. Martin's Press under license from Pan Books Limited.

For information on Picador Reading Group Guides,
please contact Picador.
E-mail: readinggroupguides@picadorusa.com

ISBN-13: 978-0-312-42762-7
ISBN-10: 0-312-42762-X

First published in the United States by Crown Publishers

First Picador Edition: April 2008

10 9 8 7 6 5 4 3 2 1

For Lewis

MANHATTAN NOCTURNE

The night is the corridor of history, not the history of famous people or great events, but that of the marginal, the ignored, the suppressed, the unacknowledged; the history of vice, of error, of confusion, of fear, of want; the history of intoxication, of vainglory, of delusion, of dissipation, of delirium. It strips off the city's veneer of progress and modernity and civilization and reveals the wilderness. In New York City it is an accultured wilderness that contains all the accumulated crime of past nights . . . and it is not an illusion. It is the daytime that is the chimera, that pretends New York is anyplace, maybe with bigger buildings, but just as workaday, with a population that goes about its business and then goes to sleep, a great machine humming away for the benefit of the world. Night reveals this to be a pantomime. In the streets at night, everything kept hidden comes forth, everyone is subject to the rules of chance, everyone is potentially both murderer and victim, everyone is afraid, just as anyone who sets his or her mind to it can inspire fear in others. At night, everyone is naked.

—LUC SANTE, Low Life

I SELL MAYHEM, scandal, murder, and doom. Oh, Jesus I do, I sell tragedy, vengeance, chaos, and fate. I sell the sufferings of the poor and the vanities of the rich. Children falling from windows, subway trains afire, rapists fleeing into the dark. I sell anger and redemption. I sell the muscled heroism of firemen and the wheezing greed of mob bosses. The stench of garbage, the rattle of gold. I sell black to white, white to black. To Democrats and Republicans and Libertarians and Muslims and transvestites and squatters on the Lower East Side. I sold John Gotti and O.J. Simpson and the bombers of the World Trade Center, and I'll sell whoever else comes along next. I sell falsehood and what passes for truth and every gradation in between. I sell the newborn and the dead. I sell the wretched, magnificent city of New York back to its people. I sell newspapers.

The mayor reads me at breakfast, and the bond traders on the train in from New Jersey have a look, as do the retired Italian longshoremen sitting on their stoops in Brooklyn, chewing unlit cigars, and the nurses on the bus down from Harlem to Lenox Hill Hospital. The TV guys read me, and steal the story sometimes. And the Pakistani sitting in his cab outside Madison Square Garden, who, intent on figuring out America, reads everything. And the young lawyers on their lunch breaks, after they've checked the ads touting the strip clubs. And the doormen in the apartment buildings on the East Side, looking up from the pages as the professional women storm past each morning, rushing brightly into their futures. And the cops—the cops all read me to see if I got it right.

Three times a week my column appears, often teased on page one: SHE DIED FOR LOVE—PORTER WREN, PAGE 5; PORTER WREN TALKS TO KILLER'S MOTHER—PAGE 5; BABY WAS FROZEN SOLID—PORTER WREN, PAGE 5. It's a wonderful job. Very pleasant. Many happy people in my line of work. I talk to detectives and relatives of the victim, to reluctant witnesses and whoever happened to be standing around when the bad news arrived. I ask them to tell me what they saw or what they heard or what they imagined. In the middle of my column is a box with my name and an outdated headshot of me—clean-shaven, full of cheap confidence in a suit and tie, a certain wry lift to one eyebrow. I appear to be a genuine idiot. The managing editor chose the photo, saying I looked like "a regular guy." Which I do. Regular haircut, face, tie, shoes. And regular appetites, although it has always been my appetites that have gotten me in trouble. My life, however, is not regular; I get calls in the night and then dress in the dark and leave my sleeping wife and kids to go wherever it happened: the car, the bar, the street, the club, the store, the apartment, the hallway, the park, the tunnel, the bridge, the deli, the corner, the loading dock, the peepshow, the rooftop, the alley, the office, the basement, the hair parlor, the offtrack betting parlor, the massage parlor, the crackhouse, the school, the church. There I gaze at the slackened faces of men and women and children who might or might not have known better. And upon my return, as I stoop down to kiss my two children good morning, as they wriggle in my arms, I am not protected from the thought that one soul's exit from life that night will be converted by me into another soul's entertainment. And that, precisely, is what the idiotic photograph of me promises: *I got another crazy story for you, pal. See if you believe this one.*

There are, however, certain stories I can't tell in my column. The crucial information is doubtful or incomplete, or one of the other papers or TV stations got there first. Or it's dull. Or old. Or *Get the fuck outa here, Mr. Reporter. I see ya here again Ima fuckin' shoot off your nuts.* Or the story is about a friend of mine. Or somebody has an acquaintance high up in the mayor's office or the police department: *Hey, look, ah, Wren, listen, this thing, I hear this guy was telling you something, some kind of story that's fucking full of shit.* Or the complexity of the story is irreducible, can't be pressed into thirty column inches. The paper's readers want a quick hit of news and celebrity gossip, and then on to the sports section, the car ads, the stock page. They don't have time for me to parse the human heart, shave one motivation cleanly off from another. They expect a commodity of cheap ink and cheap sensation, and they get it.

There is, of course, one other kind of story I can't put into the paper: a story that involves me. I mean really involves me. My readers would find it strange; for them I am no more than a voice, an attitude, a guy asking questions. The fixed expression in my little black-and-white headshot is uncomplicated, a smooth mask of certainty and cleverness—not a face that by turns is surprised, clenched in lust, slack with pleasure, frantic, violent, and then last—always last—furrowed by remorse.

HOW DOES ANY TALE of misfortune begin? When you're not expecting it, when you're looking elsewhere, thinking of other problems, the *regular* problems. At the time, last January, the city lay under drifts of dirty snow, garbage trucks groaning through the slushy streets, people buying tickets to Puerto Rico, Bermuda, anywhere to escape the coldness in their bones, the hunger in Manhattan life. It was a Monday, and I had a column due in the next morning's paper. I needed to get *up*, to pop the story like one of the Knicks' guards from thirty feet out. I generally chew a lot of bubble gum, drink liter bottles of Coca-Cola, and try to ignore the pain in my hands, which are burned out from years of typing. You've got to keep proving yourself in this game, keep getting access to the main players, keep beating the TV guys, keep showing you have something the regular reporters don't, especially since many of them want a column and think they can do it better. (I certainly did, when I was a young reporter.) A guy like Jimmy Breslin, he's an institution, he doesn't have to worry anymore. Me, I'm nervous, generally, and don't take anything for granted. At thirty-eight, I'm old enough to be on top, young enough to screw it all up. My rule, for life as well as work, is this: avoid the obvious fuckups. It's good advice and I wish I followed it more often.

All that I have to tell here began later that evening, and I could well start there—a setting of wealth and social standing, of tuxedos and ten-thousand-dollar wristwatches. A place of attractive people who are pleased to discourse on the most recent mumblings of the chairman of the Federal Reserve or the inner politics of the ABC news division. But this gathering was a far step from my regular haunts. I toil, for the most part, in New York City's saddest and most violent neighborhoods. Places where working men open their electricity bills and stare at them disconsolately for long minutes, where a parochial school uniform is purchased with great hope. Where young children accrue disturbing scars on their bodies. Where the kids carry toy guns that look real and real guns painted like toys. Where the people have vitality but no prospect, ambition but no advantage. They are poor and they suffer mightily for it. It is these people with whom I'll begin, to show where *I* began that day, to explain why I approached that evening's social frivolities with a certain alienated exhaustion, with a willingness to drink too heavily—with, in truth, a propensity to allow myself to be tantalized, cheap and stupid as that sounds, by a strange and beautiful woman.

I was working the phone at my desk in the paper's building on the East Side. It was just after one P.M., and many of the reporters were not in yet. When I was younger the newsroom rivalries and intrigues interested me, but by now they seemed petty and banal; all organizations—newspaper staffs, pro football teams, whatever—throb in deep patterns of formation and decay, formation and decay; the faces change, the executives march in and out, the pattern persists. In thirteen years of tabloid reporting, an eternity, I'd seen buyouts and lockouts and union strikes and three owners. My goal had become simply to do my job, and if that aim was a meager one, then at least it was based on two hard-won observations: The first was that my work had no useful function other than providing for my family. How could I believe that what I did had any importance? No one *really* learned anything, no one was wiser, no one was saved. Do newspapers even matter anymore? My second observation was that the degraded setting we identify as American urban civilization was in fact merely another form of nature itself: amoral, unpredictable, buzzing, florid, frenzied, terrifying. A place where men die the same useless deaths as did the tortoises and finches noted by Charles Darwin. A gridded battleground where I stood to the side with my paper and pen, watching the cannon fire and the flash and roar, recording who fell, how they writhed, and when they died. There was a time when I sought to use my limited skills to tell the stories of those who suffered unfairly or who were not worthy of the powers entrusted to them by the public, but these aims had been leached out of me (as they generally have been from the American news media, which, as the twentieth century draws to a close, seems to sense its own clamoring irrelevance, its humble subservience to a pagan culture of celebrity). Or maybe my attitude was the tattered cynicism of a man whose senses had become blunt and corroded, no longer thankful for all that he had. Yes. I was, I see now, an asshole who wanted to roll the dice.

I was also a guy who needed a column idea, and after lunch I finally got a call from one of my contacts—a Jamaican dispatcher at the Emergency Medical Service who believed I should be writing solely about the imperiled children of the city. In a breathy wheeze, she gave me the details: "You see? God, he *still* perform miracles! The lady who call nine-one-one say she never *seen* a man do that before . . ." I listened, then asked a few questions, including had she called any TV stations. She hadn't. You get a feeling that this is going to be the one, and it was, a routine shooting and fire but with a sad twist, enough to squeeze out a column for the next day. My standards aren't high—I'm not making art, after all—but the story has to have something about it, a wrinkle, a little kick to the heart.

So I headed over to Brooklyn in my work car, a black Chrysler Imperial. Years ago, when I first got started, I drove an old, repainted police car, which had a heavier suspension and a bigger engine. Then I had a little Ford, to get in and out of parking spots easily, but one night in Queens a thirty-ton mob garbage truck ran a red light and drove up and over my front end. The driver jumped down from the truck, arms lifted to fight, and when he realized I wasn't getting out of the wreck, he pulled a shovel off of the truck and started whacking my door in anger. I got a column out of it, but I swore off the smaller cars. Lisa and the kids don't use the Chrysler, are never seen in it, in fact. She drives a Volvo—leased, so I can change cars quickly, which I had written into the contract with the dealership. We decided a while back that we needed to take certain quiet precautions—an electronic security system at home, an unpublished phone number. The school our daughter attends doesn't list our address in the parents' directory, and we've given the teacher a picture of Josephine, our baby-sitter, in case there is any question on the afternoons when she is picking up our daughter. I have two extra phone lines into the house, with a device that triggers each time a call comes in or goes out, records every number. The paper has a daily circulation of 792,000, more than a million on Sunday, so there are readers out there with stories. Angry readers. Readers claiming to know the real deal, which they sometimes do: cops buying drugs, where the body is, what the school principal is doing with the eighth-grade girls. Rat calls. Or sometimes a complaint: "I see that you neglected to mention the race of the defendant! What—you love niggers?" People figure I can do something for them. Maybe I can, but it's on my terms. The Wren family doesn't have a home address. All of our mail is delivered to the paper, where it goes through the mailroom. Anything strange—a big box, a dripping envelope, whatever—is dealt with by the guys in security. I've been sent items both ominous and pathetic: guns, bullets, a chocolate cake, a condom full of dog teeth (the significance of which I didn't understand), a damp purse with old baby pictures inside, the usual dead fish, a stack of Chinese money, a gold wedding ring with a dead man's name engraved inside, the severed head of a chicken, various pornographic photos and devices (most notably a huge, double-ended dildo), my column (torn to shreds or blacked out or covered with curses), a bag of blood (from a pig, according to the police), and, on three occasions, the Bible. I suppose I should muster a certain nonchalance about this kind of stuff, but I can't. Deep down, I'm just a kid from the country. I've always scared easily. So I take as many precautions as I can think of. Maybe they're unnecessary, but then again maybe they're not. New York City is a landscape of bad possibilities.

Which I was driving through twenty minutes later—passing the hunched brick buildings, the girls pushing strollers, the bodegas and newsstands and flower shops, discarded Christmas trees frozen into the snow, the old women carrying groceries, worrying each step. I headed toward the Brownsville Houses, a well-meant act of architectural savagery carried out in the 1940s by some wealthy white New Yorkers who decided that poor blacks from the South might enjoy living in squat, faceless apartment buildings with cinder-block walls and sheet-metal doors. The Houses sat a couple of blocks off East New York Avenue, and I eased the car along, watching for potholes. The sun was out, the temperature close to thirty. A few teenaged boys on a stoop (who should have been in school but were probably safer as truants) checked out my car. When it was new the kids didn't mess with it because they figured that a black Imperial could only belong to a detective or a politician. By now, however, the car had been rammed and scraped and sideswiped and impounded; it had been sprayed with graffiti and broken into and pissed on and had the bumper ripped off. But only stolen twice. I tried to discourage interest by letting a lot of junk wash around in the front and back seats—empty Coke bottles, food wrappers, crumpled pages from reporter's pads, block maps of the city. I once kept a Club on the steering wheel but the kids sprayed aerosol Freon on it, freezing the steel, then broke it with a hammer. I suppose I could have driven something prettier, a Sentra perhaps, but it would have been on a container ship to Hong Kong in three days.

I found the Houses. They were identical six-story brick buildings, and above the loopy scrawls and stylized threats and nicknames appended with RIP rose window upon window with bars on them—to prevent the young from falling out and the criminal from climbing in. Rap music pounded outward from all directions, cut through by the sound of dogs barking across the snowy mud at other dogs in other buildings. Elsewhere mattresses hung out like tongues, or the windows were decorated with old Christmas lights, some on, some off, or more graffiti, or rotting shelves of flowerpots, or riggings of clothesline from which flapped socks or panties or babies' pajamas. The scene was bizarre and ominous and in no way unusual.

Then I spotted the police and the firemen and the kids on bicycles. It's the kids that tell you whether the scene is still hot—they lose interest quickly, especially when the gore is not as good as what they see on TV, and if they're milling around, starting to argue and roughhouse, then the situation is getting cold, the bodies gone, the witnesses hard to find. This scene looked like it had only about ten minutes left in it. I stepped through to get the story and was glad to see no TV vans around. The regular cops don't usually recognize me, but when somebody's been killed, a homicide detective is there soon, and often we've talked before. (I should admit right here, early on, that I've been sewn in with the cops for a while now—one of the deputy police commissioners under Mayor Giuliani, Hal Fitzgerald, is my daughter's godfather, which is good and not good: You start trading favors, you forget what the sides are, you forget you're playing on opposite teams. This was another obvious fuckup that I didn't avoid.) The captain in charge, a tall guy with red hair, told me what had happened: a young father living on the fourth floor of one of the buildings had not paid his cocaine tab; some nice people had forced their way into his apartment to scare him or to whack him—it wasn't clear—and ended up setting the place on fire. The captain recounted the incident duly, his eyes holding the brick horizon, thinking, it would seem, of anything else—his children, his wife, his boat—anything other than another case of what cops sometimes call "misdemeanor homicide." You got anything more? I asked. Maybe there was a fight, he shrugged, or one of the bullets hit the gas stove. Or maybe the two shooters lit the fire on purpose—the details were as yet unknown, since the girlfriend was in shock and had been taken to the hospital, and of the three other adults who had seen what happened, two were nowhere to be found (probably nervously drinking in a bar in another borough by now) and the third was dead. What was certain was that after the shooters left the apartment they had jammed an old bed frame between the blue metal apartment door and the hallway wall. The door opened *outward*, in violation of all relevant New York City public-housing codes, and thus the woman had been trapped in her burning apartment with her baby and a shot-up boyfriend.

I walked into the project's common area and scrounged around long enough to find one of the neighbors, a woman in her late twenties in a black winter coat. She lived across from the apartment in question. The interview wouldn't take long, just a few questions. So people will know what happened, I usually say, accompanied by some scribbling in a notebook (only rarely do I use a tape recorder—it scares people into silence, and besides, I always remember the good quotes—they stick in your ear). The woman held a baby in a snowsuit on her shoulder, a baby most interested in this man who was a funny color. The black eyes in the tiny brown face searched mine, and for a moment the world was redeemed. Then I asked the woman what she had witnessed. Well, I wasn't expecting nothing to happen, she said, 'cause it was still morning and usually things like that don't happen in the morning, everybody be sleeping. She possessed a handsome face with strong features, but when she lifted her gaze up to the apartment, the windows of which had been shattered from the inside by the firemen's axes, I saw that her eyes were rheumy and tired. The fire had smudged the brick wall of the building, and the firemen had hurled charred household items out of the window: a kitchen table, clothing, a few chairs, clothes, a baby's crib, a television, a box spring. Flung into the snow, the blackened wreckage looked like some of the assemblages you see in the galleries in Soho, an artist's pessimistic statement about whatever age we now live in.

Did you know the family involved? I asked the woman. Yes, I be in that apartment a hundred times. How did you find out what happened? I didn't need nobody to tell me, 'cause I saw the whole thing myself. I be washing the dishes and I seen the smoke and everything out the window, and I told myself that don't look good, that look like Benita. So I call the emergency, and then I went downstairs. The woman glanced at me. She had more to tell me, and I waited. I don't usually press. People will say what they have to say. But when they get stuck, you can go back to the chronology. What time was this? I asked. Almost twelve o'clock noon. Okay, you were washing the dishes; what did you do when you saw the smoke, were you surprised? I was so surprise I drop a dish, matter of fact. What happened when you got outside? I was looking up at the window hoping that the fire department gonna make it pretty soon and then I'm looking up there when Demetrius, he come jumping through that window. He on fire, burning like, all over his shirt and hair and pants, and he holding Benita's kid, uh, Vernon, he only four months, and then Demetrius *fall*, he just fall and fall and *fall*, and I can tell that he gonna land *on top* of the baby, and I was worrying about *that*, and then just before Demetrius land, then he like, he do this little kind of *flip*, and he land on his back holding the baby *up*, like, I could see he did that on purpose so the baby be okay. Like, that was the last thing Demetrius ever did in his life, do that little flip and hold that baby up, 'cause then Demetrius, he land on his back, just like *that*—and here the woman slapped one black hand smack flat on top of the other—and he lay real still like, and I go running over and pick up Vernon 'cause I see Demetrius, *he* not gonna make it, and I check that baby over *good*, and then I thank the Lord, 'cause Vernon, he not hurt. Little shook up's all. He cry only a little bit and I put him up in my arms. But Demetrius look *bad*. He got blood coming out of his ears and then I saw how he was all shot up by them boys. Then I just hope that Benita, don't *she* come jumping . . .

The woman stopped and looked away, back toward the window. She shifted her baby, gave the bundle a pat on the rear. Anything else? I asked. Nuh-uh. I waited a moment more, looking her in the eyes. Thank you for your time, I said. The woman just nodded. She was not shocked or distraught, at least not apparently. The events in question did not violate her view of the universe, they were just further proof thereof.

I see a lot of this, to be honest, and there was no time to stand around and be mystified by the brutalities of urban life; the story was due in the paper's computer system by 5:30 P.M.—about three hours. I had what I needed and was heading back toward the car, already composing the lead paragraph in my head—when my beeper trilled against my leg. GIVE THE CHICK A CALL, it said. Lisa, phoning from St. Vincent's Hospital, where she operates. A lot of reporters carry cellular phones, but I hate them; they tether you to other people's agendas and can interrupt you at the worst moment, ruin interviews. I walked around the corner to a little Dominican luncheonette, and when the bell on the door tinkled, a couple of the regulars turned around, and one boy of about eighteen slunk coolly out the back, just in case I was somebody he needed to worry about. They see a big white man who isn't afraid to be someplace, and so maybe I'm a cop.

There was a pay phone on the wall.

"You're due at that cocktail party tonight," Lisa reminded me. "I put your tuxedo in the trunk."

The annual party, thrown by Hobbs, the billionaire Australian who owned the newspaper. As one of its columnists, my presence was obligatory. If he was the circus, I was one of the trained monkeys wearing a tight little red collar.

"I can't go," I said.

"You said yesterday you *have* to."

"You're sure it's tonight?" I checked my watch, anxious about the time.

"You said six-thirty."

"All the management people will be there, sucking up to Hobbs."

"What can I tell you?" she said patiently. "You told me you had to go."

"Kids are fine?"

"Sally has a play-date. You're up in the Bronx?"

"Brooklyn. Fire. Guy jumped out the window with a baby." I noticed the restaurant regulars watching me. *Yo, white motherfuck, what you doin' here spittin' fuckin' whiteboy saliva on my pay phone?* "Anyway, I'll see you tonight."

"Late or early?" Lisa asked.

"Early."

"If you get home early enough, there's a chance," she said.

"Oh? A chance of what?"

"A chance you'll get to make out."

"Sounds good."

"Oh, it's *good* all right."

"How do you know?"

"I know," Lisa said.

"How?"

"Certain testimonials have been entered into the records."

"Whose was the last one?" I asked.

"Oh, some strange man."

"Was he good? Did he float your boat?"

"You lose your chance after eleven," she said. "Drive safely, okay?"

"Right." I was about to hang up.

"No! Wait! Porter?"

"What is it?"

"Did the baby live?" Lisa asked worriedly. "The baby who went out the window?"

"You really want to know?"

"You're horrible! Did the baby live?"

I told her the answer, and then I was gone.

THERE IS, in the West Village, on one of the old narrow streets (I won't specify which one) lined with three-story, Federal brick row houses, a wall. A certain wall, located in the middle of the block, about thirty feet long, connecting two houses. It's made of glazed brick and is a good fifteen feet high. The brickwork itself is topped with an ancient, black wrought-iron fence about five feet high that gracefully billows outward and is impossible to climb. Above this fence, and in many places grown through it, are the thick branches of an ailanthus tree, a weedy, fast-growing nuisance of a plant, much given to the city's empty lots, that will contort itself into any shape in order to survive. It must either die by disease or be rooted out completely. This particular ailanthus is so tenacious in its reach toward sunlight that it seems to conspire with wall and fence to keep people out.

I've spent no small amount of time standing on the other side of the street with my arms folded, looking first at the tree and its tangle of branches, then at the fence, and then at the brick wall. Until last winter, examining the wall gave me some measure of reassurance. The wall is virtually impenetrable, and this is important, because set within it is a narrow doorway secured by a gate—not the usual rectangle of vertical iron bars but a solid steel-plate door that extends down to within a quarter inch of the brick walkway. You could slip a weekday paper under that gate with a bit of effort, but you couldn't push a Sunday edition through. The gate is an exact replica of one that hung there for more than a century—iron, brittle with age, rusted here and there, repainted black fifteen times. I hired a sixty-year-old Russian welder from Brooklyn to duplicate it in steel. Then the two of us tore out the old gate, hinges and all, and set the new one in its place, repointing the brickwork. I remember how pleased I was, thinking that it would be damn tough to get through—you'd have to have a sledgehammer and a hacksaw, you'd have to back a large truck against it, attach a couple of chains, and pull forward in low gear.

But it's where the gate leads that is important. Beyond it, surprisingly, a narrow, arched tunnel doglegs seventy feet back from the sidewalk. Rising and falling, the tunnel passes along the rear foundation walls of three houses dating from the 1830s, all of which have their formal entrances on the next street. This arrangement was written into the original deed of each of these properties, and, according to my real-estate lawyer, represents quite an anomaly in New York City real-estate law. Most residential property, of course, is defined or surveyed from a bird's-eye view, the footprint of the property or building a matter of lengths and widths. Not so with the tunnel. Legally it is three dimensional, "an arched passageway, of a height of five feet and nine inches," says the original deed, "with slight variation thereof as it extends westerly." It is a quiet and mysterious conduit, and on evenings when there is little traffic, you can hear water gurgling down the soil pipes of the adjacent buildings, or a piano being played in one of the rooms upstairs. Or the indistinct sounds of conversation. Thus does the tunnel feel like a dark umbilicus, passing closely and secretly past separate lives before opening at the other end into an irregular lot, twenty-one by seventy-four feet, opening upon what my wife and I fell in love with—here, with the lighted twin towers of the World Trade Center looming not so far away, is what we were amazed to see: a small wooden farmhouse.

There it stood, despite rotted sills, termite-eaten joists, and a sagging cedar-shingle roof—a fragment from Manhattan's lost age, built in 1770 when the island was to the south a port for English merchants and to the north a landscape of streams, dirt roads, and farms owned by Dutchmen and even a few Quakers. The house's ceilings were low and the windows off-plumb, and the original bubbled glass rattled in the old frames during a storm, but for some reason the structure had never been torn down, perhaps because the walnut cabinetry was too beautiful, perhaps because of a stubborn owner, family discord, chance—the reasons had been lost to time. We didn't care. We wanted it, and the little patch of green in front, which even included a small gnarled apple tree. Anywhere else, such a house would have been mundane; in Manhattan, it was a miracle.

Lisa and I were in our early thirties then and had been married only a few years. The house was terrifyingly expensive, but Lisa, who is a hand surgeon, had come home one day with disbelief on her face and told me that the city's premier thumb man, a conceited maestro in his late fifties, had asked her to join his practice. There was a certain urgency to his offer; after marrying a third time, the good doctor had impregnated his child-less, forty-year-old wife, knowing that she had reached the age of despera-tion but not that she had been taking fertility drugs on the sly. Result: three tiny yet strong heartbeats on the ultrasound. The prospect of so much new life had nearly scared the man to death; like a lot of the grizzled heavy hitters in the city, he had suddenly reached the point where he needed a young person to carry the load. And for this he was willing to pay—big. He knew Lisa would soon want children of her own; that didn't matter; he trusted her skill and youthful stamina. "What will I do with all that money?" Lisa had blurted. And here the older surgeon gave her a fa-therly but potentially wrong lecture about the gigantism of the federal debt and the government's inevitable need to print money: "Buy as much real estate as you can," he advised.

Like a farmhouse in New York City. After stepping up on the porch and inside the front door, we examined the bedroom, trying to imagine ourselves sleeping and waking in what was then only a small vacant room, the floors dusty, the air stale. The seller had seen to it that the old plaster walls had been patched and repainted. We stood on the wide pine planks, thinking of the unknowable lives lived in that room, the voices of laughter and sexual pleasure and anger, the babies and children, the suffering and death.

It was this diminutive house, with its three cramped bedrooms, that somehow had kept me honest, or so I believed, reminding me that the city had been here a long time and would remain a long time after I was gone. My children could be growing up in an Upper West Side apartment with a uniformed doorman and the groceries and the dry cleaning and the videos delivered, and there was nothing wrong with that, but something about our little apple-tree house was memorable, and I knew that Sally and Tommy already loved the crooked brick passageway, the sloping roof, the low beams of the ceilings. (Other children had lived here, of course; my wife found hundred-year-old buttons fallen between the floorboards, tiny lead soldiers buried in the garden, and, when we redid the kitchen, the plastic head of a Barbie doll, identifiable from its hairstyle as circa 1965.) When my children became adults, I hoped, they would understand that their home was something remarkable. I wanted, more than anything, for them to know that they were loved, and for this knowledge to find its way, molecularly, into who they were. You can always tell, I think, with adults, who felt loved as a child and who did not; it's in their eyes and walk and speech. There's a certain brutal clarity. You can almost smell it.

BACK AT THE PAPER, I slipped along the wall of the long rectangular newsroom, carrying my tuxedo box past the managing editor's office, past various plotters talking in low, disaffected tones, past the sports guys eating their afternoon breakfast, past the bright cave of the gossip columnist. She was flicking through an electronic Rolodex, talking on the phone. Big hair, big attitude, today's shipment of hype—e-mail printouts, press releases, promo-videos, movie posters—piled atop her in-box. She has two assistants, both young men of postmodern sexuality who are happy to crawl through half a dozen downtown clubs every night, cellular phone in pocket, tipping doormen, scrounging for perishable scraps of celeb-gossip. And then my own office, which resembles not so much a place where a man works each day as an experiment in chaos, old papers and coffee cups ringing the desk and phone and computer.

Demetrius Smith, the dead young man in the Brownsville Houses, had been a gymnast in high school, according to his sister, whom I reached in North Carolina. All kinds of trophies, and a college scholarship that he never cashed in. This tidy little fact could be used to melodramatic advantage, and after a few more calls I reached the man's high-school gymnastics coach. No, Demetrius never had any talent, barked the coach, certainly no college scholarship—who told you that? I'm sorry he died, but he really wasn't much of a gymnast. Too afraid of heights, as I remember.

This was a twist on the twist, but hack newspaper columnists can work irony like phone wire. I slipped the coach into the piece, as well as the fact that the average income per household in the Brownsville Houses was $10,845, according to the Census Bureau; but by then the time was 5:27.

The city editor was rushing around worried about his cover story, but sooner or later he'd give me a look. I shipped the copy to the city desk, glanced through my mail, separated the bills, then closed my door and pulled on the rented tuxedo. Apparently a lot of cheap-tuxedo renters lied about their size: the waist, like the column I'd just finished, had a bit of elastic in it.

Then out and away. Good-bye and good luck—even if the president is assassinated by a movie star, don't touch my column. Other reporters were finishing up and the night editors had arrived to grind the hamburger for tomorrow's meal, and I passed them all without saying much. We get along in the usual way. Some of the older reporters sort of hate me, I know, because my stories don't get killed at the last minute, and I make a lot more money than they do. I actually negotiated a contract with the paper's executives, whereas the regular staffers are shackled by whatever meager scraps the newspaper union won in its last collective bargaining agreement.

Out on the sidewalk, buttoning my coat against the cold, I thought for a moment about skipping the party, simply going home to dinner with the kids, watch them throw macaroni on the floor. I should have done it. *Yes, you fucker*, I tell myself now, *you should have gone straight home.* Instead I found the car and crawled uptown through the rush-hour traffic. It was past dusk and I had to keep my eye on the streets; I don't know the city so well that I don't need to be attentive as I drive. As I said, I didn't grow up in the city, and for a reporter, this is a disadvantage. All of New York's great columnists came from its streets, Jimmy Breslin and Pete Hamill among them. I've had to overcome the fact that I was raised three hundred miles north of the city, almost in Canada, in a farmhouse on ten acres, under a wide sky. In the winters the icy expanse of Lake Champlain stretched before me, and I'd spend hours in the small fishing shack my father dragged out onto the ice behind our pickup truck. Other days my pals and I would tramp through the birch and pine to the tracks that ran by the water and wait for the afternoon train headed south from Montreal to New York; when it would come, huge and terrifying and whirling snow alongside, we'd suddenly stand, ten-year-olds in winter coats and boots, and fire off a good dozen snowballs each, aiming for the flashing faces in the windows, whom we imagined to be rich and important personages. It was 1969, 1970. My boyhood was indisputably small-town, suffused with a certain happy innocence that later drew me toward all that is soaring and marvelous, all that is scuttling and decadent about New York City, where, in the density of possibility, what is strange is not measured against what is normal but against what is stranger still. I've seen beggars with AIDS holding signs specifying their T-cell counts, I've seen a naked man on a bicycle thread the center lanes of Broadway against traffic, I've seen Con Ed men working in the sewers while listening to Pavarotti. I've watched detectives with French fries drooping from their mouths wiggle the toes of the dead to estimate the time of death. I've seen a fat woman kissing trees in Central Park, I've seen a billionaire adjust his toupee.

And how odd, then, that after I dropped the car in a garage and traveled the last few blocks toward the party on foot, I witnessed another thing I'd never seen before—not exactly an omen for all that followed but memorable perhaps as an emblem of the starkness of human desire. Yes, let us decide that this image is significant: It was a dark block, Seventy-ninth or Eightieth Street, I think, with some renovation going on inside one of the town houses, judging by a looming Dumpster next to the curb. In the cold I suddenly realized that there were two figures in the Dumpster, atop the debris, moving, *struggling*. A fight? I cautiously walked closer and, simultaneous with my recognition of the ragged coats and wild matted hair of the homeless, was my apprehension of the rhythm—the cadenced *stroke*—of the figure on top. They were fucking. Grandly. Two homeless people in the cold. Someone had thrown an old mattress into the Dumpster, and on a mountain of torn-out lathing and pipes and ceiling plaster, eight feet above the street, there they did it. The woman, who had hoisted her heavy layers of coats and dresses, struck the man on his bare ass with her fist, and for a moment I worried that she was being raped. But she cried aloud hoarsely in pleasure and struck him again and again, such that I understood that her heavy blows fell on the back-stroke to urge the man's rapid reentry of her, to encourage him to use a measure of force. Happy pervert that I am, I lingered a few feet away. They didn't notice. I watched for a moment, then for another, then moved on through the shadows of the street.

A minute later, I stood inside an opulent apartment building, handing my coat to an elderly hatcheck man, who was being careful with the ladies' furs. An elevator man with a green vest took me upstairs.

"Big party?" I asked.

But he didn't need to answer; I could hear the music and the murmurous roar even before the elevator doors opened. Then there I was, amid a warm mass of people, among the lipsticked lips and crinkling eyes, the teeth and the cigarettes and the expensive eyeglasses and newly cut hair and jabbering pink tongues, bright with conversation, all talking loudly, animated with great conspiratorial appetite for life's possibilities. When you enter a big Manhattan party, you know instantly whether you are of the crowd or not, whether you are one of the smiling gents holding a drink and skipping his gaze loosely about the room. I was not. But then I've never felt much at ease with any crowd—always I am outside, watching, still the kid from upstate New York who spent hours in a cold shack out in the middle of the frozen lake, staring at a hole in the ice. (The sudden brutal tug, the hand-over-hand hauling of the writhing form out of the dark, cold depth.)

It was one of the spectacular apartments owned by Hobbs. Or maybe his holding company owned it—such distinctions didn't matter; the place was a cavern of silk walls with a gilded forty-foot ceiling and about five dozen pieces of stuffed period furniture and many English paintings on the walls (selected by a consultant, bought by the truckload), with four open bars staffed by three bartenders each—and not merely unemployed actors eager to make contacts but disdainful professionals who nonetheless remembered your drink from an hour ago. A balcony overlooked the main room, and there a sextet with a piano kept the background music moving along briskly. Nearly a dozen photographers were at work, several of whom considered themselves celebrities in their own right. More rooms opened, one with tables of meats and cheeses and fruits and vegetables and mountains of little chocolates, and others where the sofas were deeper and the lights lower, places of intimate potential.

Hobbs was in town. This was the purpose of the party, to remind everyone that he was alive, that he was not just one man but a concept, an empire, a world unto himself. Every winter he swooped through Manhattan to inspect his various properties, including his tabloid newspaper, and he arrived with the predictable entourage. But this was not what people remembered after he'd gone—they remembered precisely what he wanted them to remember, which was that he threw an absolute goddamn riot of a party. He churned things up. Stuff *happened*. People made deals, they met celebrities, they sailed off into the night with someone unexpected. They got drunk and said the wrong thing to the right person. Happy insult and happier slander. Or they loudly uttered many shocking or brilliant things and hoped someone might hear them. All of this was very exciting, and if it was apparent in the next day's gossip columns that the bash had been *vulgar*, then so much the better.

Hobbs was in his sixties, but that did not mean that he decorated the setting only with well-dressed wormwood (the old but minor millionaires with their optimistic winter tans, the women with bony wrists and lifelike teeth who had ceased believing in much of anything other than the necessity of servants and daily estrogen pills); no, his Manhattan office invited a genuinely volatile selection of people—there, looking smaller through the shoulders than might be expected, was Joe Montana, and there, too, was Gregory Hines, a bit gray now, and some of the local TV news personalities, and there was the financier Felix Rohatyn of all people, in his fatly beaverish mien, talking with one of the new sorcerers of cyberspace, and Frank and Kathie Lee Gifford, and the man who had just been indicted for a $400 million securities scam, and the plastic surgeon who reinflated Dolly Parton's breasts with such flawless expertise, and not far away was the famous figure skater, whose name I couldn't remember, standing with the young black male model whose face was on all the bus stops now. Many of the women were lovely and seemed vaguely familiar, actresses on television perhaps. Then, just coming in from the elevator, was a sizable contingent from Time Warner, the newest regime of killers, looking grim and ambitious with their important neckties, and there was George Plimpton, unrecognized by a trio of very long-legged women who could only be dancers in a Broadway show, and they were being eyed appreciatively by Senator Moynihan, I noticed. It went on and on. The fat little guy from the *Times*, who carried his wit like a talking parrot. The famous Italian photojournalist, who got all those horrific pictures out of Sarajevo. He had a scar on his forehead that the women found terribly attractive. They were discussing one of the great oil sheiks, who was said to keep a carefully selected young man with him at all times to donate whatever organ—heart, lung, kidney—the sheik might suddenly require. And there, in a suit but no tie, indifferent to the long ash of his cigarette, stood the famous and formerly promising novelist, a one-book wonder who had made his name ten years earlier with his clever mastery of the Zeitgeist and who now mostly played softball in the Hamptons with other faded literary lights. He seemed to be coloring his hair, and the women ignored him. I did spot James Earl Jones, looking better than anyone in a beautiful blue suit, and he was listening to Mario Cuomo, who is shorter than you expect, who was listening to himself, and there were many other people there as well, maybe four hundred in all, not counting the publicists darting about, directing the photographers, arranging group shots, smiling, smiling, *smi-hi!-ling* till there was water in the corners of their eyes, working the buzz, surfing it, smiling and nodding and saying, *Yes, yes! Everyone is talking about it!* with the *it* itself brightly indefinable.

And there, dropped into the middle of a huge sofa, was the great man himself, Hobbs, conveying a herring with his swollen fingers through the air into his ever-spittled, never-sated lips. As the oily dead fish approached, the thick eyebrows lifted first, as if part of a complex mechanism that subsequently opened his gaping maw to reveal yellow, crowded teeth that seemed too long, like a horse's, yet stumpy and worn down from decades of chewing, and then, a further horror: his thick gray tongue—illicitly large, swollen with toxins, lying heavily upon the lower lip.

He was known as a man of immoral shrewdness, but this meant only that he bought low and sold high. Any city newspaper is dependent on its retail advertising, and it was said that Hobbs had not been planning to buy the newspaper but had been in New York on other business and noticed that its biggest tabloid was in deep trouble. Not coincidentally, he'd seen the empty hotels and dropping prices of skyscrapers. He was a man of many cities (London, Melbourne, Frankfurt) and having witnessed recurrent boom and bust in metropolises around the globe, he had developed a shorthand method for deciding when to buy a newspaper—he listened for the sound of rich people screaming. The owner of the paper at the time, a real-estate man, was getting killed as the tide of Japanese dollars receded from New York. He wanted out and had started to turn off the money; it got so bad that every night a clerk went around collecting spare pencils off reporters' desks to reuse the next day. With no warning, Hobbs had presented himself like a phantasm; the offer was very, very low, but it was in cash—not a convolution of debt instruments and stock transfers. The real-estate man huffed that he was concerned about the public good; never would he sell out a great New York institution to such a scoundrel— everyone knew what kind of shocking trash Hobbs printed in his London papers. By contrast, the real-estate man was a statue in the park, and for a time he enjoyed this new version of himself and was seen on television and at symposia at the Columbia University School of Journalism describing the size and beauty of his ethical convictions. Three weeks later he took Hobbs's deal and was gone. Hobbs came in, clashed brutally with the unions, and threatened to close the paper. This seemed impossible, considering he had just *bought* the paper, but then observers pointed out that the newspaper building was prime East Side real estate; in an up market, the building might be worth nearly the entire price of the paper. This scared the unions. The mayor made entreaties, but Hobbs seemed disinterested. He stayed in London while his deputies negotiated, and in the end, the unions caved. Hobbs cut costs, bought the drivers a new fleet of trucks, and then hit the next upturn in the economy.

Now the paper was fattening Hobbs's holding company, providing cash for him to add other properties; or maybe it *wasn't*, and he was just carrying it in order to bludgeon the politicians as necessary. Either way his genius had again been confirmed. I watched him with a kind of zoological curiosity as he muttered something wetly at a slender young thing who could not have been wearing underpants under her dress as she passed fetchingly in front of him; then the great soft wattle beneath the immense chin—a cow udder of flesh, really—shook in merriment at his own witticism, and above his bright green eyes the thick eyebrows went up and down a second time, as if connected to a string, while pieces of masticated herring frothed momentarily on the ledge of his lip before being wiped away by the same swollen tongue. The mouth then reflexively opened again, just in time to receive another shiny herring being pressed home.

A fiftyish woman with a perfect helmet of hair smiled at me. "Porter Wren, is it?" she said in a fake British accent as the piano sounded dreamily from the balcony above us.

"Yes."

She took my arm. "You must come have a word with—he's quite eager to meet—"

She conveyed me toward the clot of executives surrounding the Australian's sofa. He was so heavy that he couldn't stand for long periods. One could only imagine tailored undershirts, the twenty-eight-inch neck. Expanses of soft flesh rubbing against themselves. Ankles wide as coffee cans. I was handed off to a young man with a lemon-sucking expression, and he said, "Yes, *yes*, of course, yes . . ." and he stitched me through the people around the man and pressed me forward so that I found myself looking down at the monstrosity of silk, the immense fingers.

"Sir, Mr. Porter Wren, sir, who writes the *column . . .*"

His eyes rolled upward in my direction obligatorily, and he opened the large wetted mouth in something close to an *aah-hmm*, nodded twice vaguely, as if exhausted by his own disinterest, then flicked his view back toward some other entertainment. Here was a man rich and powerful enough that he no longer needed to speak. I beat my brains out working for him. But no matter—my labor was lint in his pocket. If I didn't want to do it, there were a thousand men and women standing in line behind me. Instantly I felt a polite pressure at my elbow, and the lemon-sucker pivoted me away from the couch. There. I was done.

Now I was ready to sit, to let the party flow past me, put in the required number of minutes. There was also the question that needed to be pondered: to drink or not to drink, and gin or vodka or rum, and to what degree, and for what purpose exactly, and why the hell not? Behind me, sitting on a huge Empire sofa that faced the other way, were two women bent close in conversation, smoking cigarettes and enjoying a bottle of wine pilfered from the bar. I was able to twist my head around and get a good look at them; they were the kind of pretty, unmarried women who, around age thirty-eight, hardened by the scarcity of prospective husbands, decide to spend the foreseeable future in offices, health clubs, department stores, cocktail parties, and the beds of married men. Such women patrol the perimeter of their careers with ceaseless energy. I suspect that they are lonely and will admit it under the right circumstances. On Sunday mornings, they generally are not seen in church (and neither am I) but out walking a big dog on a thick leash—some large and beautiful purebred that cost several thousand dollars as a puppy and who always, *invariably*, is a male, panting and nosing his way along the street, pissing, smiling a dog's smile. I was about to go talk with the Italian photojournalist when I heard one of the women say, "There's no one here, really."

"You saw Peter Jennings, though. I heard they paint his temples brown every night."

"Yes, he's a lot balder in person."

"I saw JFK Jr. last week, did I tell you?"

"No!" the woman shrieked.

"Right there in front of me."

"How'd he look?"

"Gets too much sun. Sort of like that guy I told you about, the guy I met—"

"The guy with the big wart?"

"No, the other guy, who couldn't—"

"Mr. Floppy?"

"Yeah. Only thirty-three years old." She sighed. "I guess it was the Prozac."

At that moment I noticed a blonde woman in a white evening gown. I stared liberally. (My wife is an attractive woman, a lovely woman. But I look at other women, I look at them hard and carefully and with little guilt; my lust is a cheap and ready thing, passing closely over women like a hand, pressing toward each moist possibility, and the more I squander that lust upon whomever happens to be walking by, the more, mysteriously, there is of it.) The woman in white was sipping wine and holding the fingers of a tall man in a suit who was no more than thirty; I made him out to be an executive on the way up; he had that look about him—he was handsome and trim and big-shouldered and he enjoyed the company of several other corporate men, some of them older. There were, I knew, a lot of finance people at the party whose jobs were to move the big sums around. The woman had the look of a corporate wife, and she greeted the other men with charm and deference, laughing in just the right way, the light catching the rope of pearls about her neck, the glint of something at her wrist. Her man, I noticed, seemed not to appreciate the skill with which she did this. Instead, he joked and smiled and nodded with the others. She may well have been the most beautiful woman in the room—no small feat, that—and yet I saw that she was but an addendum to his presence. Instantly I knew him, knew his soul: There is an age in men when they understand that they have crossed, irrevocably, into manhood. This is not a matter of masculinity; it has more to do with an awareness of time—that it is passing, brutally. (An interest in gardens and children often follows.) A corollary to this awareness is that one sees men who are somehow still boys, men who have not been disappointed or deeply scared yet, although their moment will come. Such was the case with the man next to the woman in the white gown.

Again, through the music and noise of a hundred conversations, came the voices behind me, and I tilted my head backward, eyes toward the ceiling, to hear more clearly: ". . . and she said she was just sitting there at the light, at the corner of Broadway and Houston, and this black squeegee man was just all *over* her windshield and it was last August, you know, he didn't have on a *shirt*—"

"No!"

"Yes!" the voice squealed. "And his chest and *nipples* were pressed against the *wet* windshield."

"I can't believe it," the other breathed excitedly. "I *just* can't!"

"And she was watching—I mean, thinking about—"

"No! Don't tell me that!"

"She just opened the *door* and told him to get in!"

"That is shocking!"

"I said, 'Alice, how could you *do* that? He could—' "

"She just took him in?"

"She's desperate. I mean, okay, she's not exactly *beautiful*, but . . ."

I tipped my head forward again, rolling my eyes back to the horizon of the room, and there, I saw, was the woman in the white gown, looking in my direction. She smiled at her date or husband and uttered a word excusing herself, and then, strangely enough, walked directly toward me, carrying her wineglass. Her face was no less beautiful as it approached, but I could see a certain determination in her features. Dark brows, blonde hair lifted off her neck. The rope of pearls. Her breasts moved heavily against the silky material of her gown, which, I now saw, was not white but, more alluringly, the color of the flesh of a peach. It seemed impossible that she was coming to talk to me, but she gave a little smile of recognition as she approached, then sat down closely, crossed her legs, and turned toward me.

"Your picture, Mr. Wren," she said in a full, throaty voice, "is lousy, you know that?"

I looked into her face. "The one that goes with my column?"

She nodded. Her eyes were blue. "It makes your neck look too skinny."

"Well, it was taken a few years ago, in the waning moments of my youth."

"They should take it again." She smiled.

I nodded a silent thanks.

"I read your column from time to time," she said.

"I see." She was sitting close enough that I thought I might know where she'd dabbed her perfume.

"But I have to tell you"—she frowned—"I don't much *like* it. I mean it's always very well written and everything"—she gave a dismissive little flourish with her fingers—"but I'd think you'd rather be *anywhere* than in one of these places where something terrible happens. You must *see* many terrible things, no?"

I've been asked this question before, and usually there is an air of frivolity to it, as if I am to enumerate urban horrors for the listener in the same way the polar bears at the Central Park Zoo have been taught to frolic with huge plastic toys. But then we live in a time in which all horror has been commodified into entertainment. Eat dinner and watch the bombs fall, the fugitive hunted down on live television, the genuine murderer cackling genuinely.

"Sure, I've seen a few things," I said for her indulgence, knocking back the rest of my drink. "But if you read my column, you have a pretty good idea."

"Yes, of course." Her voice was subtly impatient. "I wanted to ask you, though, how you find out some of the things you find out."

I gave her a shrug.

"I mean, you *do* get people to tell you things."

"I do, yes."

"How?"

I looked at her. "Usually they want to tell me. Or maybe they don't want to tell me, but they want to tell somebody."

She thought about this.

"You mind if I ask your name?" I said.

"I'm sorry. Caroline Crowley."

Her eyes seemed to search mine for something, not recognition exactly, but for an awareness that her decision to tell me her name was significant.

"What—" I stopped.

"Yes?" She was clearly amused.

"What brings you to the party?"

Another flourish of her fingers. "My fiancé's bank does some kind of business with the big company that I guess owns your paper. Something like that."

I glanced at her fiancé. Again, there was something of the youth about him; perhaps it was in the slenderness of his neck, or the way he nodded vigorously, confidently, with his executive pals. I wondered if this Caroline Crowley might be a bit older than him; on the other hand, women in their late twenties are, I think, generally wiser than men of the same age, and so it might simply have been that her manner was more mature. But there was something else. If she was not actually older, then she seemed to have been *made* older.

". . . oh, I don't mean to disparage your paper," she was saying, kicking one of her crossed legs back and forth. "It's a *marvelous* paper really. I kind of like the . . . the *feel* of a tabloid. I mean I read the *Times*, of course, for the national and international news, but I read your paper for something else—to sort of get the real city, you know? The *grit*. You don't get that in the *Times*." She glanced back at her fiancé, who appeared to be telling a story that had to do with tennis, for he was pantomiming a forehand.

"Your fiancé plays tennis."

"Charlie?" she asked. "Yes. May I ask you another question?"

"Sure."

"Don't you think what you do is sort of predictable by now?"

I looked at her carefully. We were having a dialogue, but it didn't have much to do with what was being said.

"I mean, it's the same old thing, isn't it?" she asked, lifting her dark eyebrows. "Some poor sad person has some poor sad thing happen to them and it's for all the usual reasons, *simple* reasons, and there *you* go getting the quotes right or whatever reporters worry about, and then the next day it's pretty much the same again, right?"

"I find the stories interesting." I sipped my drink.

"But I heard you used to be this big *investigative* reporter and do these stories where you actually dug into some lurid, sordid, horrid past of somebody, a politician or somebody, and found out something important, something *investigatively* important—"

"Is this supposed to be a serious conversation?"

"Well," she began, her voice coy, "if I'm being rude, it's because I think rude questions are often the most pertinent ones."

"You like rude questions?"

"Mm-hmm."

I felt the liquor trumpeting inside my brain. "*I* could well ask *you* why in the world you are going to marry such an obviously upstanding, intelligent, handsome, healthy, and soon-to-be-prosperous fellow like your fiancé, when you could pick any useless, misbegotten psychopath with mossy teeth, yellow T-shirts, no money in the bank, and a brain stuffed with pornographic impossibilities, who, nonetheless, might be more interesting to talk to and better in bed."

She drew back in surprise, her pretty mouth open.

"Yes"—I nodded—"that is a *rude* question. Maybe I'll ask another. Maybe I'll ask you how long I'm supposed to pretend that flirtatious conversation such as ours has no outcome, no *purpose*. Women who look like you don't just walk up to strange men at parties and first insult their appearance and then their livelihood under the protection of their own charming loveliness and the presence of a fiancé. Without some *good* reason, right?"

Now she gazed into her lap.

"Look," I went on, my voice softening, "I'm just saying that if you want to *play*, if you want to get *into* something here, some kind of *real* conversation, not the usual cocktail-party crap, fine. I'll do that. I deal with bullshitters all day long, with great interest, I might add, but I'm on my own time here, so do me a favor—get to it, okay? Get to whatever it is you want with me."

She looked up then, straight into my face. I hadn't scared her at all. Perhaps a hint of amusement passed through her eyes. "I was hoping I might talk to you about something important, actually," she said in quite a different voice—a calm, clear voice.

"What is it?"

"It's complicated . . . I mean, it takes a while."

"I see." But of course I didn't.

"Could we talk about it?" she asked.

"Sure."

"Tonight?"

"Are you serious?"

She nodded. "We could leave right now."

"And where would we be going?"

"My apartment, about fifteen blocks from here." She stared at me. "Charlie wouldn't be coming along."

Her eyes, I realized, were the blue of a mailbox. "I don't know, Caroline Crowley, maybe I shouldn't be left alone with you."

She touched a finger to her pearls, smiled to herself. The girlie act was gone, and she looked up at me, eyes unblinking. "Am I to understand," she said huskily, "that we're protecting *your* virtue, not mine?"

"Yes. Absolutely."

But this, I told myself, was not about sex. She had something else in mind. And maybe it could be a story. I've learned that you have to put yourself in the way of opportunity if you want to get the good stories. I told her I needed a few minutes, and then found a phone and called Lisa, knowing it was just late enough that she might have turned off the ringer so that the kids would not wake in our small house. The answering machine came on. I muttered something into the receiver about running into some people, that we were going out for a drink. Was this a lie? Yes, sort of.

I had not done anything to feel guilty about, nor did I expect to, but my lie seemed easier than explaining that I was leaving the party with some woman in a peach gown whom I'd just met. So I said I was out for a drink. My wife is used to this—it's definitely part of the job—and only expects, ultimately, that I keep my underwear on and be home by the time the kids climb into our bed in the morning—about five-thirty or six. Sally and Tommy stumble sleepily into our room and crawl into the blankets and get between us and then sometimes fall asleep again, with the sweet stink of their breathing, and more often they flop around and everybody is forced to wake up. Or I fall asleep again—a troubled, shallow sleep, always—and Sally lies there awake, thinking of something, and then rolls over and asks me directly, right in my ear, something like this: "Daddy, does LaTisha have hair on her bottom?" LaTisha is Josephine's daughter, a sullen black girl of fifteen, almost six feet tall. I quite imagine that she has hair "on her bottom," as Sally refers to it, and I have little doubt that the whole area has been thoroughly pawed over by some boyfriend or another. And then I push my eyes open and there, at 6:02 A.M., or whatever the time, is my three-and-a-half-year-old daughter, with her eyes clear and awake, watching her unshaven dad rise from the grave of sleep (maybe she sees the heaviness of my eyes, the flecks of gray in my stubble, maybe she can already intuit that I am closer to death than she), and to see her face like that, so close to mine, is the sweetest thing in the world. And then here comes her brother in his fuzzy yellow one-piece sleeper, eighteen months old, in love with his penis already, a rapist of teddy bears, chuckling fatly as he throws himself on top of me, and then I have both of them in my arms and am making growling monster noises that scare them a little and make them happy, while my wife steals the chance to go to the bathroom, and such moments I would protect with anything, even my life.

And *yet*. And yet when I hung up the phone and turned back toward the roar and music of the party, with Caroline Crowley standing to her advantage under a light, holding her coat check and ready to go, I was interested in something much different. It was not as if I was not myself—oh no, I *was* myself, I was my *other* self, the self that wishes to carry on a secret dialogue with all that is evil in human nature. Some men do not struggle with this in themselves. They seem to have a certain grace. They are happy—or rather, they are content. They swing tennis rackets in the sunlight and get the oil checked regularly and laugh when the audience laughs. They accept limits. They are not interested in what might come up from the dark, cold hole of human possibility.

THE BACKSEAT OF THE TAXI was an intimate space, warm against the night, both of us huddled in our coats. Caroline looked ahead, almost as if I were not there, and directed the driver brusquely. Then, from her purse, she removed a pouch and a small packet of rolling papers, took one paper out, and pinched a dab of tobacco onto it. This she distributed along the length of the paper, which she then rolled into an even tube. She licked the last eighth of an inch of the paper and sealed it off with a quick, sliding fingertip.

"I bet you use wooden matches," I said.

"What a smart man you are."

She pulled a box of wooden matches from her purse, took one out, and with the wooden end, poked the tobacco at one end of the cigarette. This would be the smoking end. She looked at me, the lights outside the cab passing crazily across her blue eyes. "Girls don't like tobacco in their teeth."

"Guess not."

She cracked the window on her side, then lit up. I realized that her voice was clear and measured, untainted by the whining vowels and hurried nasalness I heard all day; this and her habit of rolling cigarettes suggested she was not originally from the city or even the East. But before I could think further, we had pulled in front of an apartment house on East Sixty-sixth Street, just off Fifth Avenue, and she leaned over the seat and paid. The doorman, who with his brass buttons and epaulets looked like Napoleon Bonaparte, smiled at her familiarly and gave me a scowl. I followed Caroline across the marble hallway. She took long strides, I noticed. We entered the small space of the brass and mahogany elevator.

"I hate parties, actually," Caroline said, unbuttoning her fur, the cigarette in her mouth.

The elevator opened to a small foyer with a glossy black door. On the tiled floor stood a pair of Western boots; several umbrellas hung neatly from a brass hook.

"Here we go," Caroline said, turning the lock.

Inside, Persian rugs on the floor, white walls, a few pieces of art that did not interest me, a huge window that showed off the Manhattan skyline to the west. The place appeared to be professionally cleaned, but I was not looking at big money—not forty or fifty or a hundred million.

"Do we have polite chitchat," I asked, "or get right to it?"

"We get right to it. I want you here." She pointed to an overstuffed reading chair, and as I sat down she turned on a floor lamp, the brightness of which made her gown even more translucent.

"Before we begin whatever it is we're . . ."

"Yes?" she said.

"You came to the party and saw me and spontaneously decided to engage me in conversation, figuring that, curious idiot that I am, I'd be willing to listen to whatever it is I'm about to hear?"

"Yes." She watched me.

"I see."

"I believe in spontaneity." There she stood, the light falling on her head and shoulders and breasts.

"You better tell me what you have to tell me."

"Fine. But before the tell comes the show."

"I'm going to get a show?"

She drifted toward the fireplace, her back turned. "Don't you want one?"

"I want one very badly."

"Good. That means that despite your recent drinking you'll be attentive." She took two large manila envelopes off the mantel and held them before her. Then she looked toward the window. Before her stretched the snowy dark box of the park and, beyond, the lights of the West Side. "You know nothing about me, right?" she announced, to the night before her as much as to me.

"Nothing," I agreed. "You're about twenty-eight, you have a few million dollars, you wear nice peach gowns to parties, you don't like my picture in the newspaper, your fiancé plays tennis and knows almost nothing about suffering and grief, and Napoleon Bonaparte, your doorman, is gladdened by your existence but not by mine. Other than that, nothing."

"It must be paralyzingly fun to be as clever as you are."

"Hey," I told her, "I'm here."

She was silent, and for a moment I wondered if the whole strange interaction was now about to collapse; if that was true, I'd catch a cab downstairs, try to forget about it, and put the taxi receipt on my monthly business expenses. But then she moved away from the window and handed the envelopes to me. I chose the thinner one first and set the other aside. I unwound the red string that held the flap and shook out two dozen eight-by-ten color photographs. The first showed what seemed to be a male body in dirty clothes facedown in rubble. I flipped through a few more, variously taken from ten feet and five feet and two feet and, most unhappily, from twelve inches.

"Okay." I coughed. "So this is what we're talking about."

"Yes, this is where we start."

"This is where we *start?*"

"Yes." She stood over me and I could smell her. "Another drink?"

"Why not?" I muttered.

"Was it scotch or vodka?"

"Gin."

Back to the color photos: The damage to the body was complete; it looked as if nearly every major bone in the body had been crushed, including the skull, which resembled a pumpkin left on a front porch through the winter. One shot showed what remained of the face: a half-open eye staring into infinity, oblivious to its own seeping decay. The streaked putrefaction of the body was also evident where the shirt was pulled up. One of the photos showed an expanse of mutilated flesh impossible to identify. The picture was labeled TORSO, ANTERIOR. The next was a close-up of a gnawed wrist. I flipped through the photos quickly; I'd seen a number of after-the-fact examples of human butchery, but most of them were the result of guns and knives. This was worse, and had involved great physical forces. I slipped the pictures back into the envelope. Someone had died an ignoble death: a lot filled with rubble, a body, the attention of flies.

"To help you through the gates of hell." Caroline presented a drink on a silver tray. I took the glass, sipped it. She stood over me smoking another rolled cigarette. "Look at the next envelope."

I did. Inside was a complete copy of a police file of an unsolved death in a lot at 537 East Eleventh Street in the department's Ninth Precinct, which covers the Lower East Side. I'd seen such files a few times before, though the detectives who'd shown them to me would never have admitted to helping a reporter. I flipped through a page or two; it was the police paperwork that went with the photos: the decomposed body of a young white male had been found the morning of August 15 in the rubble of a tenement being razed, on the fifth day of demolition. It was an old case—about seventeen months had passed.

I gave my drink another sip. "A bit stingy with the tonic and ice, I see."

"I want you drunk," Caroline answered from behind me, "so that I can tell whether you are a lout or not."

"You could get in a lot of trouble for having these files."

"I know."

"Detectives don't even let other cops see stuff like this."

"Yes," she said. "I know that, too."

I read further. A bulldozer had hit the body once or possibly twice before the operator noticed; some of the flesh of the chest and stomach had been removed by the steel treads. From the dorsal lividity it was clear that the man had died faceup, not facedown, as the body had been discovered. But the detectives could not determine if the body had been inside the building prior to demolition and then tumbled to the ground during demolition, or if the man had been killed elsewhere and his body hidden in the rubble. If the body had been in the empty building, I inferred, then the man could have died accidentally—say, from a drug overdose. The other possibility—that the body had been placed in the rubble after the demolition had started—would mean that the death was probably a murder: It was impossible, after all, for a man to dig a hole, kill himself, and then bury himself with chunks of brick and concrete. Then again, I corrected myself, theoretically a man could commit suicide or be killed accidentally, and then *someone else* could bury him under the rubble, for whatever reason that crazy people in New York City do crazy things.

The corpse, continued the report, was dressed in a blue T-shirt, blue jeans stained with old paint, underwear, and red socks. The contents of the pants pockets comprised less than a dollar in change, a subway token, and a pack of Marlboro cigarettes. The breast pocket of the T-shirt contained a fragment of green stone, which an antiquities dealer consulted by the police had easily identified as jade; it appeared to have been broken off from a carved figurine. It did not match any known to have been sold or stolen in the city recently. There were no papers, wallet, or other personal effects either on or near the body.

Various technical terms described the condition of the corpse. According to the medical examiner's dictated report, the tissue was sufficiently decomposed and secondarily damaged by the bulldozer that it was impossible to determine the exact cause of death. But some causes could be ruled out: It wasn't due to an overdose. Or to gunfire; an X-ray showed no bullets within the corpse, or what was left of it. The examiner further noted that it appeared as if the neck might have suffered a knife wound, but he was "quite tentative" about this, not only because of the bulldozer damage but also because there were signs of extensive rat activity, a common occurrence on corpses found in exposed locations. The absence of the hand, for example, may have been due to rats, added the examiner. "Recent rat activity was also indicated by generalized postmortem striations and triangular dental punctures," read the report. The degree of tissue damage to the body by the bulldozer led the medical examiner to dwell extensively on the amount and stage of insect activity in the soft cavities of the corpse. The presence of diptera pupae and domestic beetles indicated that the decay had started between seven and ten days prior to the discovery of the body. Deep maggot infestation of the mouth, ear canals, and anus suggested a similar onset of decay. The report bore the examiner's stamp and signature.

I read on. I was smashed and could read anything now. The report digressed at length about the detectives' questions regarding the security of the demolition site. The wrecking company, Jack-E Demolition Co., of Queens, had erected a fourteen-foot-high sidewalk shed of plywood and heavy timber at the front and back of the building, as required by city regulations, then strung a double coil of concertina wire over that. Access to the building's double front doors could only occur via a door in the front wall of the sidewalk shed. Access to the back of the lot came through a section of the shed wall that was unchained to let heavy equipment in. There appeared to be no damage to the front or back sheds and concertina wire nor to any of the chains or locks used to secure the openings. Anyone bringing the corpse onto the site would have had to hoist the body over the concertina wire at the rear, which seemed unlikely, given how difficult and obvious such a task was.

How, then, did the body get onto the site? It was not possible that it had been thrown from a nearby rooftop, for the body lay in the *middle* of the site, a good thirty-five feet from the perimeter. To reach that distance, the body would have to have been shot out of a cannon. And even if the body had somehow been hurled from the one adjacent rooftop, that would not explain how it had come to be buried in the rubble.

Thus the evidence suggested that the body *had* been in the building prior to demolition. But this explanation created its own problems. Could the doors—first to the sidewalk shed and then the double front doors to the building itself—have been unlocked by someone? The building's Korean owner had no idea how someone had gotten into the structure. Because he had recently bought the site anticipating the building's demolition, he had never bothered to become familiar with it. But yes, he did have keys to the building—he'd had new locks put on—and he'd given them to the demolition company's site manager, who claimed he'd spent each of the previous six nights at home in Fort Lee, New Jersey, keys in pocket, in the hale company of, alternately, his bowling buddies, his poker group, and his volleyball team, claims that checked out. Did he make a copy of the keys? No. Did he give the keys to anyone? No way, pal. We got half a million bucks' worth of wrecking equipment in there.

Moreover, the building itself had been secured against local squatters a year prior, all lower windows filled in with cement blocks. There was no record that they had been broken. To get into the building had required clearance from the owner, and the only individuals let in had been from the various utility and service companies involved in turning off the water, gas, and electricity. The last person known to have been inside the building was the foreman for the demolition company, checking the structure one last time on the morning that demolition began. Had he conducted a thorough room-by-room investigation? the detectives asked. No, just glanced into the basement and first floors. But, he'd explained, it was impossible to go higher in the building, because the elevator was disabled and the fire doors to the stairwell were locked.

The roof, I thought.

The detectives had asked about the roof. Perhaps the decedent had gained access to the roof of 537 via 535, the only adjacent building, and then died there, or perhaps had been murdered there, the killer making his escape through 535. But the superintendent of 535 didn't remember anyone going in or out of his building he didn't know, and besides, the roof door was carefully locked so that kids wouldn't go up there. And only he had the key.

Even if the body had somehow found its way onto the roof of 537 prior to the building's demolition, there was the difficult problem of the rat activity, the detective had noted. The body appeared to have been ravaged by rats *since the time of death*, for at least a week, and rats do not live on the roofs of buildings in summer—too much sunlight and heat, not enough water. And pigeons don't eat carrion. It was true that crows were sometimes found in the city, but crows do not gnaw flesh, they peck at it viciously and then pull it away in strips, leaving a distinctly different pattern of mutilation. Moreover, the eyes had not been pecked out. Such information seemed to indicate that the body had *not* been on top of the demolished building, which might then mean that it *had* been buried in the lot, which, given what they had already learned, meant that the detectives were utterly stymied.

Another paragraph of the file indicated that the race of the corpse and what still could be discerned of his height and weight matched a missing-person report filed by the decedent's wife seven days prior, on August 8, two days after he'd last been seen. The report had been filed in the Nineteenth Precinct, which is on Manhattan's Upper East Side. The wife identified the clothes and the wedding ring that had been removed, with some difficulty, from the corpse's left hand. She was shown a photo of the tattoo found on the groin of the deceased. This, too, she identified. She was shown the jade fragment. She could not identify it. Then she was shown the body. There was no doubt as to the identity; it was one Simon Crowley, twenty-eight years old, of 4 East Sixty-sixth Street.

I knew this name. "You're Simon Crowley's widow?"

"Yes."

"The young guy who made movies?"

She nodded.

"Jesus." I hadn't done a column on it because I was deep into a piece about drug dealers in Harlem at the time. "You were married to Simon Crowley?"

"Yes."

The famous young filmmaker. "I had no idea."

Caroline sat down in the chair opposite me.

"How did you get this?" I asked.

"I paid a lot of money to a man who said he was a private investigator. He said he used to be a detective and could get files, that he knew what to do."

"You're a resourceful woman."

"Yes." She blinked at the thought of this. "Did you ever see any of his movies?" she asked.

"No. I never get a chance to go much."

"But you heard of him?"

"Sure. I know he was sort of an outrageous filmmaker and that he died badly."

She nodded, with irritation.

"I'm sorry," I said. "I can't keep track of all the Hollywood stars. I mean, like that guy River Phoenix, and Kurt Cobain—"

"Simon was *not* a so-called Hollywood star."

"Right."

"But you know who Simon was, you *appreciate* who he was?"

Seventeen months prior, when Simon Crowley died, I had been working my ass off at the paper and was severely sleep deprived, because Tommy had just been born and we had two babies keeping us up all night long. So, no, I didn't appreciate who Simon Crowley was, not in the way his beautiful widow wanted, and she saw this in my face.

"Wait a minute." She left the room and came back with a gigantic scrapbook, six inches thick. "These'll fill it in for you."

Someone had kept every magazine and newspaper article. Yes, here it all was. Simon Crowley, I was reminded, had been a young New York City filmmaker of note. He'd risen from obscurity on the strength of several innovative low-budget films that had become cult hits, then had been discovered by the Hollywood corporate edifice. I flipped through the articles noting certain specimens of language—gusts of breathless admiration, platforms of commentary, pearls of false insight. How stupid is the American magazine industry, really, how helplessly fawning. But I read on. Simon Crowley's first movie, *Good Service*, only forty-four minutes long, had been shot on unexposed pieces of film—called short ends—discarded or sold by other filmmakers. Using volunteer actors and technicians, Crowley had written and directed the story of a young busboy at a swank restaurant who becomes fascinated with an older woman who patronizes the restaurant. The woman, about forty, wealthy, still with a certain hard need to her face, finally notices the unnecessary attentiveness of the busboy and allows him to think he is seducing her, until the last scene when— I skipped on. Simon Crowley's work was marked, the articles generally agreed, by characters who lived their lives on the margins of the city, who inhabited the urban noir. Crowley himself had grown up in Queens, the only son of an older, working-class couple. Father repaired elevators, mother volunteered in a Catholic school, both lived small lives of habit and devotion. Mother died early. Father dutiful. Simon had been a strange and unruly boy, bright but bored with all his classes except art, hooking up with the underground party scene as a teenager, working as a busboy in various restaurants while he went to NYU film school, having his second film, *Mr. Lu*, discovered by an agent from the most powerful Hollywood talent mill at one of the film festivals, arcing his way upward through layer upon layer of fame. The black-and-white photos by Annie Leibovitz in *Vanity Fair* revealed him to be short, with a skinny, caved-in dissolution to his posture, as if he had been smoking cigarettes since the age of eight (which was the case, said the article), and beneath a mop of black hair and black eyebrows a face that appeared to dare one to describe its ugliness. It was not so much that he looked deformed; rather, his features seemed large and mismatched, as if they had been scissored out of three or four rubber Halloween masks from a costume shop. The effect was a face that was grotesque, carnal. "Several hours into the interview," an article in *GQ* read, "I came to the realization that Simon Crowley doesn't smile—or at least not like most people. His grin, when it rarely occurs, is usually in regard to the sad illusions held by some other person; his mouth—sort of a dark gash—flies open, revealing many unfortunate teeth. Next, a cynical rasp of laughter. Then the mouth snaps shut tightly and Crowley stares at you with unblinking concentration. The effect is purposeful and disconcerting. He is not a nice person, particularly, and he doesn't care if you know it. In his pursuit of great movies, woman upon woman, and cigarettes—in about that order—niceness is irrelevant and manners mask the desperate chase of existence; one may conclude that Crowley's conceitedness has not yet been adjusted by life's disappointments and suffering, but then, a humble, selfless person would not have made the brilliant movies that Crowley has."

I looked up. Caroline was watching me.

"Go on," she said.

So I did: Despite the fact that Crowley had come to dine in the company of stars and Hollywood executives, reported another piece, he still remained notorious for his late-night "investigations" into the city, and kept a small, trusted retinue of fellow debauchers with whom he traveled, one of them apparently a paroled murderer, another the dissolute son of a billionaire. After his nocturnal sojourns, Crowley was sometimes discovered passed out—in a locked limousine, naked on the Italian-marble floor of an apartment house lobby, etc. Actresses clamored to be in his movies, even those who publicly proclaimed themselves unimpressed by "asshole macho directors." Crowley's third big-budget movie went over its planned cost by thirty percent, and there were rumors of fighting on the set, of studio executives screaming at him in private lunchrooms. It was reported he'd spat back that he didn't fear any of them, and to prove his determination had picked up a steak knife and drawn a cut three inches long in his forearm, which later required twenty stitches and apparently shocked the executives into submission. His star, the very young, very ravishing Juliet Tormana, who had tantalized Hollywood's old stags (including the now-married Warren Beatty), declared that she was sleeping with Crowley and that "the sex is the best I've ever had." And so on. The usual hype, the usual drivel of celebrity culture. When *The Time of No Return* was released on nine hundred screens nationwide, it was a gigantic hit, grossing $24 million in the first week—an unheard-of sum for a "serious" film—and lauded by critics as a valuable, challenging portrait of fin de siècle America, "stark, huge, and immensely disturbing." The work was nominated for three Academy Awards, and won one for best screenplay, which Crowley had written. He was seen in every Hollywood and New York watering hole. He was arrested for picking a fight with Jack Nicholson in a Brentwood café, calling him, in front of others, "an old bag of shit with one or two cheap actor's tricks." He proclaimed that Spike Lee was "an inconsequential talent, a token black director whose work everyone knows is mediocre." Kathleen Turner, he noted, "has become fat and mean, with the fat and mean little chin of a lousy actress who can't even act the tart, so why should I want to film her?" Quentin Tarantino, he announced, made cartoons.

And so on. I set the file aside, looked up.

"They never solved it," Caroline said.

"I guess I remember that."

"They never arrested anyone, nothing."

"They probably tried pretty hard." Certainly Crowley's death had received any and all proper official attention, given the intense media speculation. The death of a celebrity in American culture is a commodity worth quite a bit of money, so long as it flickers in the nation's consciousness.

Caroline brought me another drink, and although I did not want it, I took it. We were, I assumed, now where she wanted us to be.

"So this is what you wanted me to look at?" I said.

"No, actually."

"No?"

She shook her head.

"I don't get it."

"This is what I *needed* you to look at *first*, before I show you what I *want* you to look at."

"Have I been tricked?"

She smiled. "No, not really. It will all make sense, eventually."

"Shall I look at the thing you actually want me to see?"

"I want you to see it, but not tonight. Tomorrow, or the next day?"

There was something selfish about her answer, as if I didn't have a job and a family already scheduled, or as if she was so beautiful that I would drop my duties to both to study the life of her dead husband, which, so long as she was around, might, on further reflection, be true. "What do you want?" I asked. "You want me to write a story about your dead husband? Everything's already been written about him."

Caroline sighed. "No."

"What, then? The police apparently can't solve this."

"Yes," she said quietly. "I know all this, Porter."

She seemed distracted by melancholy, and I realized that I had not asked her what it all meant to her, to have her husband killed, to have her life brutally jolted like that.

"How long did you know him?" My voice sounded thick, stupid now with drink.

"We were together only about six months."

"You got married fast?"

"Yes. Very. He was like that . . ." She carefully closed the thick album. "I was like that, too."

THE MINUTES PASSED with a strange luxury to them. We said nothing. Caroline rolled three cigarettes, laid two of them on the glass coffee table, and sat back to smoke the third. I took myself into her kitchen for a little ice and felt suddenly aware of the white starkness of the counters and cabinets and appliances. I did not necessarily expect to see a picture of her dead husband, but there was nothing there, no phone numbers of family or friends on the refrigerator, no pencils in a jar or mail in a pile or battered cookbooks or seashells from last summer. When I returned to the living room, only then did I realize that the entire apartment was sterile. Like a hotel suite, though in much better taste, it had no character, no essence of its inhabitant. When people have lived in the city a long time, their dwellings become encrusted with their personal history; this is true not only of the poor but also of the rich, maybe even particularly of the rich, who tend to be interested in documenting their own accomplishments.

I have been in many wealthy homes as a reporter; if the living rooms betray nothing but good taste and a disdain for clutter, then by compensation there is a green-trimmed den with a trophy from a club golf championship or pictures of the children on the sand in Nantucket or framed professional degrees or a photo of the occupant shaking hands with Bobby Kennedy thirty years ago. But Caroline's apartment revealed no such personality, only expensive surfaces. It occurred to me that the absence of historical detail was not because she had no history but because she had no history that she wanted to display.

"You're not from the city," I said when I returned.

She looked up at me, lost in her own thoughts. "No."

There was, in her absentminded confirmation, a revelation for me. I suppose it could be called intuition, or a lucky guess, but then again I have been banging around New York City for twenty years now, long enough to come to understand a few things, and in the case of Caroline Crowley, what I suddenly knew was that she had worked very hard for what she possessed, or rather, that what she possessed had cost her a great deal—and not just a husband. I have often thought that the most determined people in New York City are not young lawyers trying to make partner or Wall Street traders or young black men who might have the stuff to be pro basketball players or executives' wives competing viciously on the charity circuit. Nor are they the immigrants who arrive from desperate places—the Bangladeshi taxi driver working one hundred hours a week, the Chinese woman working in a sweatshop—such people are heroic in their grim endurance, but I think of them as survivalists. No, I would say that the most determined people are the young women who arrive in the city from America and around the world to sell, in one way or another, their bodies: the models and strippers and actresses and dancers who know that time is running against them, that they are temporarily credentialed by youth. I have lingered at night in the dark back rooms of the city's two or three best strip clubs—the rooms where in order to be caressed by young women, men buy bottle upon bottle of $300 champagne as if they are putting quarters into a parking meter—and I have talked with the women there and been astounded at the sums of money they intend to earn—$50,000, $100,000, $250,000 by such and such a time. They know precisely how long they will need to work, what their operating expenses are, and so on. They know what kind of physical condition they must be in and how to maintain it. (Consider, for instance, the stamina necessary to dance for one man after another, *sexily*, in heels, in a smoky club for eight hours straight, five days a week.) Like fashion models, they live in little apartments where no one remembers the name on the lease, the rooms being passed along like links in a chain as each woman makes her money and then moves back to Seattle or Montreal or Moscow. Likewise, the sufferings of fashion models, which are well known. Jazz and ballet dancers don't have it any better. (Once, visiting an orthopedist for a knee injury, I saw a lovely woman of about twenty-five hobble into the room on crutches. She was in tremendous pain and was waved into the doctor's office. The nurse accidentally left the reception-area door open, and I was just able to hear the woman's desperate request: "Please give me the shot." An indistinct male voice responded. "Please," the woman wept, "I have to dance tonight.") Caroline Crowley was not a stripper or a model or an actress, not so far as I knew, but I could only guess that she had once brought the same sense of purpose with her when she came to New York, that she had arrived in the city to have a dialogue with fate, and that she knew, as any genuinely beautiful woman knows, that the terms of the conversation would include her face and teeth and breasts and legs.

With these thoughts I drained off my drink and then indulged another. That made five or perhaps six or maybe even seven. I have been drunk many times in my life and enjoyed most of those times, but never has drunkenness revealed in me some hidden streak of self-destruction; I do not drive while drunk, I do not leap from windows or pick fights in bars. While drunk, I am incapable of the fatal gesture. This does not mean that I don't make mistakes, only that my most disastrous errors in judgment occur when I am *not* drunk, when, *presumably*, I am lucid. So, in that moment, when Caroline Crowley, the lonely, beautiful widow, stood before me, clutching her record of the violent destruction of her husband and seeming for all the world ready to be embraced and kissed and plunged into voluptuous copulation—the image of the homeless couple fucking feverishly outside in the cold returned to me—in that moment, I chose to remember my own sleeping wife, with her arm thrown across my empty pillow, and this gave me the further will to stand, quite unsteadily, and say, "I'm sorry your husband was killed or died or whatever happened to him, Caroline. I imagine it was a terrible shock, and it seems to me that you're still haunted by it. I know we've been joking around all evening, but let me say . . . let me just say that if it's possible to suddenly have a certain *affection* for someone in only one evening, only a few hours, then I feel that way toward you, Caroline, and I am saddened to think what it must have been like to lose your husband. Every week, just about, I talk to people who've just lost someone they love, and it always saddens me, Caroline, it always—it always *reminds* me that we, all of us, are—that it all—can be lost. You are beautiful and about twenty-eight years old and should have all good things come to you. If I were not married, I would—no, I will avoid—maybe better to . . . say that perhaps you sought me out tonight because you figured that, hack tabloid columnist that I am, that I've seen an unnatural amount of human destruction and might therefore offer you some useful words of solace or perspective. But I assure you"—and here I desired to touch her cheek with my fingers, just for a moment, by way of comfort, as I would comfort my own daughter—"that I'm unequal to the task. I'm as mystified and terrified by death as the next person, Caroline. I can't really say anything useful . . . in such—such a *disabled* state . . . except that I suggest that you embrace life, that you venture forth and marry your fiancé, if he's a good guy, and have faith that some losses are recoverable, that life has, finally—excuse me, please, I am *very* drunk— that life actually has . . . has some kind of meaning."

She said nothing, and instead watched me with her lips pressed in amusement, and I wish now that I had understood it to be quite an un-funny sort of amusement. She saw me struggling against myself. I stood and moved toward the door, watching my shoes to make sure they went where I expected them to go. She followed me and silently helped me with my coat, then hung my scarf about my neck. She was spectacularly beauti-ful.

"Oh, Caroline Crowley . . ." I lurched sideways accidentally.

"Yes?"

"All men are dogs, and I am one."

She smiled this away. Then she reached up with one hand, held my cheek with her warm fingers, and kissed my other cheek, slowly, with a breath. "I'm going to call you," she whispered. Then she kissed me again. "Okay?"

"Okay," I murmured, feeling that she had outsmarted me.

"Are you all right?"

"I am . . . I am *mystified*, Caroline. I'm just—" My lips had that buzzy drunken feeling about them, and I fell against the door frame. I was now suddenly so drunk that I'd have to get a cab home and retrieve my car later. I felt like a fool. "But then again," I slurred, "that may be your intention."

Twenty minutes later, my cab pulled up outside my brick wall downtown. I always get my keys out before opening the door, because once the cab pulls away, the street is dark and anybody could walk up to you. Even drunk, I had that New York paranoia. Only after I shut the gate behind me, pulling against the weight of it and turning the dead bolt, did I relax. The city, for now, remained on the other side of the wall. But gate or no, Caroline Crowley and the history of her doomed husband had now entered my life.

■ ■ ■

SIX-THIRTY A.M., and a drunken hand (my hand) under instructions from a drunken brain (my brain) crabbed over to the phone next to the bed, lunged for the receiver, which it flipped off the hook, and then felt for the last automatic-dial button, marked BOBBY D., which the drunken index finger (mine) then pressed. As the phone rang, the hand lifted the receiver from the floor, while the drunken brain thought of Caroline Crowley, the most beautiful woman I had never fucked, while the ears, not drunk, waited for Bob Dealy, the overnight guy on the city desk, a man so cadaverous that he looked like he drank gasoline and ate what the cat sicked up—which perhaps was to be expected if you spent each night for twenty years sitting in a newsroom listening to the police radio, making calls to the precincts, reading a dozen papers from around the country, eating doughnuts and, with them, no small amount of newsprint.

"Desk, Dealy."

"What you got, Bobby?"

"Aah, Porter, we have a collision between a taxi and a philosopher on lower Broadway. We got the recurrent gentleman with no name supine in an alley in the one-oh-four, and aah, in the seven-oh, we got two young pharmaceutical executives of the Nubian persuasian shot in the head. But it didn't bother them much. In Brooklyn we got somebody who robbed a bank with a jack-hammer—tore out the night-deposit box. In Midtown we got two philosophers who tried to ride a fire truck that was making a run. We also—hold on—"

Now the drunken brain discerned other voices. Lisa and the kids were downstairs. Spoon and bowl. All kids love cereal. Love her. Good with the kids. Looks good enough, swims a mile every other day, could screw me dead anytime she wants. Loves it from behind. Why? The action goes in farther, among other reasons. *Loves it.* Don't throw the eggie! Mommy, I can't eat my cereal. Sweetie, just eat it. But *Tommy* didn't eat his cereal. He's eating eggs, sweetie. She'd nursed the kids so long they ruined her tits. Sucked them *off*, basically. Wan juicee. Want some juice? Juicee! Wan juicee, Mama. Eat your cereal, Sally.

"Yeah, Porter, also we got a diving champion—"

I opened my eyes. "What bridge?"

"You sound funny. You sick?"

"Nah. What bridge?"

"Brooklyn."

"Anything?"

"Construction guy," Bobby wheezed. "Broke his leg at work, couldn't buy the groceries no more, girlfriend went shopping elsewhere. Guy died of a broken heart before he hit the water. When they pulled him out he was still wearing his hat."

"Come on."

"Hey, I'm not lying."

"Guy jumps off the Brooklyn Bridge and his hat stays on?"

"I'm telling you, the police said his hat was still on."

"Come on, Bobby."

"Hey, call them yourself."

"If it was a *hat*, it must have been a football helmet."

"No, it was a Yankees cap."

"He had duct tape keeping that hat on!"

"No."

"Then it was fucking glued on his head, Bobby!"

"No."

"All right. You saving me a good one?"

"Matter of fact, I—wait, sorry again—hold on."

I closed my eyes, listened to the chaos downstairs. You want more Cheerios on it? Juicee! Juicee! Yes, Tommy. Here. Eat the eggie. Na! Mommy cooked them for you. My wife was a fucking saint. I was lucky to be married to her. Man sees a peach-colored gown, gets an erection. Who cares if her husband got run over by a bulldozer? Fuck me. I was a cur with a hard-on. Lift up your head, I thought, see how it feels. Head just not right. Should drink more often, get used to it. I'd given some kind of cheesy speech. She'd seen right through it. Pick *up* the cereal, sweetie, please sit up, *please*, Sally, sit up this minute. I can't. Sit up, you're spilling your cereal all *over* the—I said SIT UP! All right, that's *it*, young lady, get down, now! Are we protecting your virtue or mine? Wan eggie! You just *threw* your eggie! Too coal! Too cold? Ya. I'll heat it up. Mommy, when people die, do their bodies get all rotten? Who told you that? Lucy Meyer. Lucy Meyer said that? Wan eggie! Yes, Tommy. Sweetie, when people die, they still have a spirit. What is a spirit? It's, uh—here, sweetie. Too ha! It's *not* too hot! What is a spirit, Mommy? Blow on it, sweetie. Too ha! Just blow on it. Bwow? No column was due today, I'd just make some calls, mess around in the office, pay bills. Get *up*, you fucker. *Still* drunk. A spirit is . . . it's your *heart*, sweetie, it's who you are. But Mommy, when you die, does your spirit fly home to God? Who told you that? I can't remember. Did Josephine tell you that? Fucking jig baby-sitter preaching voodoo Catholicism. Sweetie, do you have poopie? Nah. I think you have poop in your diapee. Make a few calls, get the mortgage check into the mail. No poo diapee! Forget the woman, who you may now remember as the most beautiful woman *you never fucked*. Let's get down, sweetie, you ate most of the eggie. No poo! I think you have poopie. Eyes blue as a mailbox. You're still drunk but I think you can . . . get up, do it, you can do it, I can do it, I was doing it, I was sitting up, back in the game, and Bobby was back on the line: "Porter, I do got a woman shot last night on the Upper West Side in a Chinese laundry. Maybe the boyfriend."

"What's good about it?" I asked, squinting into the sun from the window.

"Died holding her wedding dress."

I swung my feet off the side of the bed. Uglier every year, the ingrown nails permanent. "What did she do?" I said.

"Accountant, age thirty-two."

"Boyfriend?"

"Insurance guy, age fifty-six."

"She went for the older guys."

"Maybe she had a daddy thing going."

"I can hear you eating the doughnut, Bobby."

"Yeah."

"You've got to start washing the ink off your hands!"

"The coffee cancels it out."

I sighed. "They know where he is?"

"No, but they're looking."

I stood, and heard a Froot Loop crunch under my foot.

"TV do it last night?"

"Happened too late."

"The wedding dress, just standing there, boom?"

"Yeah. I got the wedding dress bit just for you."

"Could be good."

"It's good. It's the romantic angle. You always love the romantic angle."

While I was dressing I heard Josephine come in downstairs, shake snow off her boots. She had a key to the gate in the wall. Good morning, how's my little friend? I ha eggie! He just finished his egg. Josephine is an immense black woman from Haiti. We found her one day when Lisa was seven months pregnant with Sally and had called a cleaning service. Josephine arrived, huge and deferential and embarrassed by the girlish blue uniform that she was forced to wear. She cleaned for us once a week a few times and I only caught a glimpse of her before I left for work, but she struck me immediately as exhausted and too old—somewhere in her late forties—to be cleaning houses. That second Saturday I went out and bought a new vacuum cleaner and put it upstairs in the hall closet so that Josephine would not have to carry the heavy Electrolux upstairs. Then we asked what she was being paid from the cleaning service and it turned out that her bosses, a couple of clever professional white women in their thirties, were keeping almost half of her salary. We were paying the service $10 an hour and Josephine was getting $5.20 an hour, *before* taxes. So we called the service and said that we were canceling because the baby had been born. They asked whether we were dissatisfied with Josephine, and we said oh no, not at all, absolutely wonderful woman. Then we hired her for $10 an hour and paid her directly so that she got to keep all the money. After that she came in to help with the children and gradually became full-time, arriving at eight and leaving at five. There was a period of adjustment, for Josephine is, after all, from an island culture; on the way home from the playground, she would pluck plants growing in the park and cook them up in strange potions on the stove in the afternoons, mixing in a little of this or that from the local botanica. Many of these concoctions were later taken home and forced upon poor LaTisha, she of the hairy bottom, in an effort to correct certain sulky teenage behaviors. But sometimes Josephine left her potions in unlabeled jars in our refrigerator; they announced themselves by their greenish tinge and swirl of worrisome sediment, but one night that first summer I woke up in the middle of the night and, looking for something cold to drink, opened the refrigerator and tossed back a jar of what looked like iced tea; it went down blandly, but in ten minutes my mouth was full of saliva and I felt an odd desire to eat uncooked rice. Another time Lisa came home early and Tommy, then eleven months, had his head covered with bits of wet tissue paper. For a moment Lisa was shocked, but as Tommy seemed perfectly well, she only casually asked *why*, and Josephine explained that Tommy had been suffering from the hiccups and that this was the cure.

Yes, it was all very quaint and multicultural at first, with my wife and I congratulating ourselves for "saving" Josephine, but the reality was that an oppressed, uneducated black woman arrived each day wearing sweatpants and sneakers. And by now I was tired of seeing her. I was tired of her goodness, her uncomplaining suffering. I was tired of her *poverty*. I hated this in myself and felt guilty about it and would hide our pay stubs and bank statements and retirement-account statements and anything else that proved the financial discrepancy between Josephine and us. And she never let on that the condition of her family was akin to a rickety shack perched high above a river frothing away at its banks; she herself was dependable and clean-living (in sort of a starched Catholic way, such that I suspected she'd never been much fun, ever), but she'd had a couple of different husbands and occasionally made reference to a cousin or a nephew *who got hisself into all kind of trouble*, and then she shook her head as if someone was going to try to make her feel bad about *that*, too, and she just wouldn't, *she just wouldn't do it*. I'd driven her home once into the Bronx—kids on the street selling crack, big radios, the whole scene. Her husband worked for the food service in a nursing home; he was a huge man, at least six foot five, great of belly, great of blood pressure, too, and when I met him I knew he could crush me instantly, take my little white hand and break it like a handful of dry sticks. But when we shook hands he smiled deferentially and his fingers barely contracted against my own; it was not politeness—rather, I was his wife's white boss and so not to be accidentally insulted or intimidated by an overly firm handshake.

Now I was standing in the bathroom, listening to Josephine get Sally ready for school. We took turns walking Sally to school. Then I heard the little feet on the stairs.

"Daddy?" Sally burst into the bathroom, holding one of her Barbies by the leg. "Why are you peeing?" she asked.

"I need to."

"Why?"

"Why do you *think?*"

"Because you just do!"

"Right."

"Boys don't have to wipe when they pee."

"That's true."

She followed me into the bedroom. "Daddy?"

"Sweetie?"

"Daddy, do dead people all die lying down?"

"I don't know, Sally. That's kind of a strange question."

"Lucy Meyer says all dead people when they die, they have their tongues sticking out."

"I don't think so."

"Lucy Meyer told me, in school."

"Has Lucy Meyer seen a lot of dead people?"

"Lucy says they all die with their eyes shut, and if—and if they forget to shut them, then bugs eat the eyeballs."

"Don't worry about it, sweetie, okay?"

Lisa called Sally downstairs, then came up, carrying the day's newspapers, which pile up one by one outside the gate each morning and get stolen if we don't retrieve them promptly.

She was dressed for work. It's always amazed me that she puts on stockings and perfume to cut people open. "I thought you might like to know that tragedy has struck Sally's class," she said.

She handed me a notice on the school's stationery, signed by Sally's two pre-kindergarten teachers, serious young women adept at dealing not only with three- and four-year-olds, but perhaps as importantly, with their mothers and fathers.

Dear Parents:

We are writing to share some sad news with you. As you may have heard, Banana Sandwich, our class guinea pig, suffered an injury to her leg, after which her condition deteriorated. When the vet examined her, she diagnosed a neurological problem. We were informed that this damage could cause Banana to begin biting herself and others. The vet strongly suggested euthanasia, and after careful consideration, we agreed. Banana was taken to the vet's office last Thursday afternoon.

We did not share all of the details with the children. We told them that Banana had to be taken to the vet's office because she was sick, and that she died while she was there. We will share some books on the death of a pet and talk about our questions and feelings about Banana. If you have any questions, please let us know.

Patty and Ellen

"Sally brought it home yesterday," Lisa said.

"Was she bothered by it?" I asked.

"I don't think so."

"There's that creepy Lucy Meyer stuff she's worried about."

"Kids are always worried about things," Lisa said.

"Yeah, but they're just kids. It's too early to worry."

"Kids are people," Lisa said. "People worry. All people worry."

"Me included," I said.

"You *better* worry, babe."

"I do, don't worry about that."

She gave me a look, a certain look. "I liked the column this morning."

"The fact that he was a lousy gymnast was the main thing."

She smiled. "Did you see the headline?"

"How bad was it?"

She turned to page five and held up the paper: SAVED BEST FLIP FOR LAST.

"Pretty bad."

"Your head all right?" she asked as she looked into the mirror, brushing her hair.

"It will be, in an hour or two."

"You didn't drive back, did you?"

"Cab."

She kissed the air and pressed a tube of lipstick to her mouth. "Thank you," she said.

"I'm a decent guy."

She looked at me. "You still have a few indecencies about you."

"You love them."

She smiled. "True."

"Knifing anybody today?" I asked.

"Some knuckles." She stood to go. We don't often kiss each other good-bye in the mornings. Sometimes I'll say, "See you," or she'll say, "I love you," but that's it. We're in a hurry. It's easier that way.

THIS ACCOUNT IS, I think, a confession and an investigation. My wife is here and there in this story and deserves, I suppose, some sort of identification beyond the fact that she is a clever hand surgeon. She is tall and too slender, with hair the color of a penny, and she studied art history and biology at Stanford. She arranges her hours so that she operates Monday, Tuesday, and Wednesday. The rest of her week is consumed by office visits, consultations, and hospital rounds. On the days she operates she drinks thick Colombian coffee in the morning; on the other days, Earl Grey tea. Ironically, her work affects her own hands. The skin of her palms and fingers is dry and blotchy from scrubbing, not only on the days she operates but between office appointments, when she handles patients' hands as she examines them, one after another, many of them with open or recently closed wounds oozing blood and pus. The roughness of her hands is a small yet real source of sadness for her, for her children have only ever felt them as rough. When she told me this she slipped her wedding ring over her second knuckle—still keeping it on—and showed me the ring of smooth, undamaged skin beneath. Both of us see the city through our professions; her patients include secretaries with overuse syndrome more serious than mine, cops bitten by pit bulls, construction workers who have had steel beams drop on their thumbs, kids with hands blown up by firecrackers, executives in Connecticut who have cut their fingers off trying to use a chainsaw. She is smart about a lot of things, my wife, and I admire her greatly. In contrast to my work, hers actually helps people.

What else? She relaxes by reading histories—of China, the Spanish Inquisition, Mogul rulers in India. She piles her books and magazines next to her side of the bed. Bits of this or that. Jane Austen. *The Silence of the Lambs*. A biography of Tolstoy. *Vanity Fair*. Salman Rushdie. Strange accounts of sixteenth-century saints. *The World According to Garp*. Anything. She loves to read in bed after the children are asleep. She has a cunning little light that attaches to the top of her book. She has a mole next to her belly button. She has some Sephardic blood in her, and her toes are flat, sand-paddling Arab toes that have genetically trumped my Anglo-Saxon bloodlines: both our kids have Arab toes, a fact that she is proud of. She watches no television. She reads two newspapers each day and yet is largely uninterested in day-to-day politics. She's read all the major tracts of feminist ideology written in the last forty years and believes that men and women are *almost* incompatible and always will be. With the accounting nightmare of a medical practice, she prefers that I handle the family's money. She's aging like a beautiful wooden sailboat—signs of wear but all the lines intact, slightly more maintenance each season. (My own aging pattern resembles a mud slide in slow motion. In the mirror I inspect the gray hairs, pull out a few, and think myself ridiculous.) She won't yet join an HMO. She is often tired, yet usually will want to have sex, so as not to have missed the chance. Since the birth of our children, she has become progressively more voracious in bed. Every few years we seem to stumble upon a new theme in our sexual routine and of late Lisa generally wants to first suck on me while fingering herself. This can go on for some time, and eventually, as she's coming, she pushes me all the way down her throat just for a second or two. Or sometimes I push. Then we move around on the bed and go at it. She often asks me to do it as hard as I can, and I will answer that's pretty hard, but she wants it anyway. She switched back to the Pill, because although she wants another baby, she doesn't really want another baby. She has a couple of close friends—generally smart women in bad marriages—and when they come over they all sit in battered Adirondack chairs on the porch and drink bourbon and smoke cigarettes. Their laughter rises and falls and seems almost tearful at times, and then later, after her friends have gone, Lisa comes inside and seems glad to be living her life and not theirs.

We have one enduring argument. I think that society is going to hell and Lisa doesn't. The difference has been evident from the moment I met her, when she was an intern working in an emergency room. I had followed a gunshot victim into the hospital to try to get some quotes from the family. Lisa was sitting with the father in the waiting room, explaining something about lung tissue in the airway, when she noticed me and looked up. "Who are you?" she asked with some irritation. "And what do you want?"

The question is still relevant. Who I was then was a twenty-five-year-old guy working his ass off on the crime beat, in way over my head, running for my life every day. Renting a tiny apartment in Brooklyn, getting up early, into the newsroom, doing the job, going home late, then reading the early editions of all four New York newspapers. And as for what I wanted, I wanted Lisa. When I told her that, two days later, she laughed. At that time, she was almost married to a man who is now a high lord at Citibank. I stole her away from him. I out-hustled, out-talked, and out-fucked him. It was the only chance I had.

What else about my wife? She is a careful mother, and this, I think, is because she values life. Her father was one of the first heterosexual victims of AIDS. He suffered a car accident in 1979, being hit by a drunk teenaged boy who walked away from the wreck. In the emergency room, Lisa's father received a transfusion. The blood was tainted, and after he made a full recovery from a broken jaw, a perforated liver, and crushed legs, he began to decline, his body subject to one opportunistic infection after another. The accident occurred when Lisa was in college, and as her father became sicker, her course of study shifted from the humanities to the behavioral sciences, and then to the hard sciences. She was accepted by every medical school she applied to, and her interest in hands came from her desire to help people with their daily lives. She has satisfactions and she has frustrations, especially when a child has lost a finger as a result of adult negligence. She understands the way the muscles and tendons and nerves of the hand work in the way a conductor understands the complexity of a musical score. She has published some articles on nerve-sparing techniques in medical journals. Sometimes she sits up at night, thinking about other people's hands.

Beyond the foregoing, is it necessary for me to say more about my wife? I don't think so. With one major exception, I don't think I need to recount our domestic conversations during the period I'm describing. Most of what follows didn't involve her, and it would be wrong and too easy to suggest that my actions were in response to our marriage, or to her supposed character flaws. That wouldn't be true. I was happily married. My wife was smart and observant and kind, and that's all that's necessary to know, I think. I want to protect her in this. One could be clever and find ironic motivations in any word I might use to describe Lisa (thus "smart" might be read one way; "kind," another), but in fact, what happened to me derived not from my marriage with Lisa but from the actions of four people—me, Caroline Crowley, Simon Crowley, and one other. We were an odd troupe who found one another across time and space. There were minor players in our little urban drama as well, and I'll get to each one of those people, too, in time. But my wife did not drive events. She simply went to work each day and took care of the kids while I found trouble. This doesn't make her powerless or a flawless innocent, either; and this is not to say that she did not know what was going on; my wife is capable of a powerful, watching stillness. My wife, I hasten to add, is far smarter, far wiser than I.

AN HOUR LATER, I was at Eighty-third and Broadway, standing outside in the bright cold, working the wedding dress–murder story. Her name was Iris Pell, and she had spurned her boyfriend, a man named Richard Lancaster. She was dark-eyed, a bit heavy, an attractive woman who had been disappointed in love several times. She pushed paper in a large accounting firm in Rockefeller Center; he was a mid-level insurance executive remembered by coworkers for his courtly manners and fastidious bow ties. A man who got his hair cut every ten days. Iris had told Richard that she was calling off the wedding and never wanted to see him again, and yet he found her, and then stalked her, confronting her in the Chinese laundry just as it was closing. As Bobby had told me, she was in fact holding a newly dry-cleaned wedding dress when she whirled at the sound of Lancaster's voice, and the bullets, two of them, passed through the cellophane, the dress, the second sheet of cellophane, her winter coat, the blouse she was wearing, her bra, and then into her heart. Yes, as Bobby had said, Iris Pell died holding a wedding dress. There was a lot of blood, and most of it was on the floor, smeared and tracked and furred with dust, dried but then made sticky again by the snow on people's shoes. Someone had thrown some newspapers down, but it didn't help much. I watched as the detectives gave the nod to the owner of the shop, who had stayed up all night as they tramped in and out, and a Chinese boy in a T-shirt dropped a heavy wet mop onto the dark stain and wiped up what Iris Pell had left behind. There was a perceptible reverence to the boy's care with the mop; he had known Iris Pell, and it was a personal sadness to him.

Richard Lancaster—yesterday a citizen, today a criminal—had fled. But not far, as it was later discovered. He went to the movies, avoided his own apartment. Used a cash machine, ate a fancy steak dinner. Tipped the waiter well. Was seen to type madly into a laptop computer, then toast the empty chair in front of him. That same morning, even as I was riding the train uptown, he had been found by an anorexic female jogger on a park bench on the promenade in Brooklyn Heights. There the glassy skyline of lower Manhattan seems to greet the sun as it rises. Lancaster was dressed in his business suit, with full identification in his wallet, and a suicide note tucked in the other hand, which said: *I killed Iris.* He'd shot himself in the mouth and then slumped there, the blood dripping through the slats of the bench and crawling along the cant of the sidewalk toward the brightening skyline.

But he hadn't died. A second woman, looking out her apartment window, had seen Lancaster shoot himself and had called the police. The ambulance arrived and found that although he had blown away part of his cheek, skull, and left eye, he was still yet very much alive, so much so that he begged to be allowed to die in the back of the ambulance. The twist was that the police couldn't find a gun near the park bench where he'd shot himself. The woman who had called the police volunteered that she had seen a figure, perhaps a homeless man, stoop down next to the slumped form of Lancaster just after the shooting but that she had not been able to see him clearly or what he had done, only that he had stood up and scuttled away into the morning haze.

All this information took me another two hours to retrieve, and after I got back from Brooklyn, I didn't yet see how it would make for a decent column a day hence. I had facts, but except for the Chinese boy with the mop, no emotional content, no decent quotes. I couldn't reach Iris Pell's family, and the further comments of Richard Lancaster's coworkers were useless. ("Richard Lancaster was a fine employee, never a complaint," the insurance company's public-relations officer announced.) Lancaster's ex-wife had left her phone off the hook, and maybe counted herself lucky in that funny way we do when disaster brushes by us.

I was stuck on the column, and this was the moment that Caroline Crowley called me. As soon as I heard her voice, I got the nervy feeling in my fingertips that I used to get before high-school football games, when we were all on the field in our uniforms and cleats and could see the crowd in the stands, hear the public-address system booming scratchily, *Ten minutes to game time.*

"I've been trying to reach you," she said. "You're out early."

"I was running around on a story."

"You remember our conversation?" Caroline asked.

"I remember I gave a drunken, sentimental speech. The audience was weeping."

"No, what you said was very kind."

"Yeah, well."

"So," she began, "what do you usually have for lunch?"

"Whatever."

"Why don't you come up to my apartment and have some whatever?"

I said nothing.

"Well?" came Caroline's voice.

"I'm smiling," I answered. "You wanted me to smile and I'm smiling."

"Do you do other things, too?"

"Yes, I flirt with strange women on the phone."

"They flirt with you, you mean."

"Only when they want something from me."

"I just want you to come over. It's an innocent request."

"Do you have more things to show me, pictures of your dead husband in folders, neat stuff like that?"

"How about two o'clock?" she asked, ignoring the question. "I won't serve any gin and tonics."

"I'll be able to keep it all straight, then."

"Yes," she answered, "figure out the motivations and so on."

"Including yours?"

"Mine? My motivation is quite clear," she said. "I'm looking for deliverance."

"Aren't we all."

"Not like I am," she blurted.

That's what did it—I caught a tone in that remark, heard the dark spaces, Caroline's recognition of her own complicity in something. Yes, I told her, yes.

IT WAS ALMOST NOON, and in a mood of nervous time wasting, I floated outside down to the street, had my shoes shined by a man who told me he was going to be as rich as Bill Gates, and then drifted into a video store and found copies of Simon Crowley's movies. I picked up one of the bright, cellophane-wrapped boxes: "*Mr. Lu* is the second work by the brilliant young filmmaker who died a tragic, untimely death. Just twenty-six, Simon Crowley filmed *Mr. Lu* in only four weeks. The movie caused a sensation at the . . ."

The movie was sixty-two minutes long, and it seemed that if I was going to see Caroline again, it might not be a bad thing to view one of her late husband's movies. Back in the office, I slipped into an unused conference room and started the tape. The movie, set in New York, involves a black subway motorwoman, Vanessa Johnson. A world of rushing through dark corridors toward trash and rats and red signals turning green, the train's two beams of lights sweeping ahead of her as if searching interminably for something. Vanessa is about thirty-five and unmarried, the mother of three, and believes herself to be finished with the affections of men. She must deal with thieves who steal copper signal wire from the subway tunnels and lay the wire across the track so that it is cut by the passing trains, and she is confronted with a homeless man whose arm is severed when she runs over him accidentally as he lies drunkenly on one of the rails. Her face allows no expression, her eyes show no hope. Her only solace seems to be a battered cassette player, on which she plays Mozart's *Requiem* from beginning to end, starting the tape just as her shift starts. One evening she notices an older Chinese businessman. He rides her train every night, stepping onto the train at the same point in the music each time. She watches him in the side mirror of the motorman's booth as he enters and exits, always wearing a tailored suit. In time they speak. His name is Mr. Lu. He inquires about her and she tells him little, yet by her manner intimates that she would like to know more about him. Mr. Lu runs a wholesale hardware-supply store in Chinatown, rides home to Queens each night. After several dates—each of which is marked by awkwardness and tension—Vanessa gives herself over to him, insisting only that he not touch her between her legs with his hands. Something happened a long time ago and she is reminded of it when—he nods. He is gentle with her, and yet his manner remains reserved. He prefers not to tell her of himself, only that he lived in China until the 1970s. The film is suffused with a strange and potent eroticism, for while neither character is conventionally sexy, each is clearly hungry for the passion that has eluded them both until this moment. Eventually Vanessa learns that Mr. Lu has serious heart trouble—each time they have sex literally imperils him— and that he served as one of Mao Tse-tung's executioners during the Cultural Revolution. In a long and grieving monologue on the observation deck of the Empire State Building, tourists around them videotaping one another and eating ice cream, Mr. Lu explains that he has personally executed more than eight hundred men—and fourteen women, one of whom was pregnant. He goes on to tell Vanessa that he no longer understands the world, only that he has played an evil role in it. He admits that he hated black people intensely after he emigrated to America, thinking them dirty and stupid. He has never had a family, he says, and wishes fervently that he had lived a different life. He believes that Vanessa is a very good woman who "deserves honor." He wishes someone to know that he feels remorse for what he has done. He fears that he will soon die at any time, perhaps climbing a stairway or crossing the street. He asks Vanessa if she will allow him to ask her a "question very terrible." She says yes. He says that he thinks he can induce a fatal heart attack in himself and would like to try it while having sex with her, in order that he might not die alone but in the arms of a woman. She says she will think about it. Several days later she tells him no. He is respectful and quiet. When they are to meet again she is told that he has died that very day, lifting a heavy box in his store. The movie ends with an agonizingly long shot of Vanessa inside her subway car, the voices of the *Requiem* soaring and dropping, the stations and riders flashing by, mesmerizing, exhausting, Vanessa's eyes seeing them and yet not, her face sorrowful and mysterious.

It was, indeed, a quietly brilliant movie, and, remembering the photographs I had seen the night before, Simon Crowley's fate seemed continuous with the bleak vision of *Mr. Lu*. Crowley's death was now, oddly enough, a small matter of grief for me. Cultural hype aside, here had been someone with something to say.

AT TWO, sobered by the movie, I rode the elevator up to Caroline Crowley's apartment with Sam Shepard. He was going a couple of floors higher, perhaps visiting someone equally glamorous. He stared ahead, hoping not to be recognized. He was still handsome yet looked like hell, the skin loose under his chin, the eyes tired. He saw me staring at him.

"Hey, man."

The elevator opened then, and I stood in front of the black door for a moment, feeling odd that I was here again, not twelve hours after staggering out the previous night. It was both strange and deeply logical to me; our compulsions are always evident to us, I think, even if we fear them.

Caroline pulled the door open as soon as I knocked, her hair tied back in a ponytail. She was dressed in jeans and a white cashmere sweater.

"I rode up in the elevator with Sam Shepard," I said.

"He's got a friend upstairs."

The apartment was filled with pale winter light and seemed larger than it did the night before. I saw fresh vacuum-cleaner tracks on the carpet.

"I made us a little lunch," Caroline said.

I followed her into the dining room, where a spread of soup and sandwiches was laid out on a long mahogany table. In the middle of the table was a bowl of the largest oranges I had ever seen.

"Last night—" I began.

"Last night was just right," she interrupted.

I didn't know what she meant.

"You weren't expecting to meet me," she said. "I saw you across the room and just thought I'd talk to you. I know it's—it's strange, but I figured you had heard about every crazy story people can tell and this was *very*—well, you have to understand my—Charlie—is very much of a businessman, very dependable and everything, but not much interested in what happened with me and Simon . . ." She took an orange from the bowl and began to peel it. "I guess I have a little problem, and it's pretty embarrassing." She lifted her eyes. "I mean, if it was *just* embarrassing, then it wouldn't be a big deal. But it's more than that."

We did not know each other, but already a strange intimacy existed between us. She seemed to feel a great pressure to tell me certain things, some essence of a predicament, and it occurred to me that perhaps she had decided that these were things her fiancé might be better off not knowing. For if she could tell him, then why would she need to tell me? I also was beginning to wonder whether Caroline Crowley might simply be lonely. Not in the sense of unaccompanied, for a woman such as she would always be accompanied, but fundamentally solitary; I wondered, too, if she did not trust herself to keep out of trouble. She was bright and beautiful and yet appeared unmoored. That she wanted to tell me of her "little problem" was proof of the randomness of her life and, I suspected, proof that her problem was not little at all.

Caroline began to move the plate of sandwiches around. "Last night you may have noticed that the articles I showed you on Simon don't mention me. See, we didn't have a public wedding, and also I didn't meet him until just about the end of his life. The fact that we were married came out after he died, and I just flew to Mexico and stayed a few months in order to avoid the television people, people like that."

"People like me." I took a sandwich. "Ratlike journalists."

"Yes, exactly."

"How did you and Simon meet?"

"By accident." She separated each section of the orange, then laid them out in a line, eight pieces. "At the time, I was—I'd been around, if you know what I mean. I'd been here a few years . . ." She paused, and in the gesture I was given to understand that there was a story that preceded her arrival to New York, but she seemed to push it away in order to concentrate on what she was telling me. "I was living a sort of tired, pretty-girl New York life, you know? I had almost no money and I was . . . there were always *regular* guys sort of around, but I was tired, I'd been to a lot of parties and everything . . . I'd been out in California, but I'd come to New York just to see it, see something different, you know."

I nodded my vague understanding. Only later would it be clear to me that Caroline was offering an absurdly simplified, barely truthful version of why she had come to New York City; only later would I see that the reasons for her change of venue ran deep into her past and that the effects ran up to that very moment. But now, watching her fiddle with her orange peels, I knew only that she seemed distracted by anxiety.

"I guess I had been in the city long enough that I knew I had to get serious about something," she was saying. "I mean, this is a hard place. You have to know why you're here. If you don't know that—"

"You're in big trouble."

"Yes, you're in big trouble, because you'll get pushed into something or just eaten up somehow. That happened to a girlfriend of mine. She started smoking crack and I just never saw her anymore, and then she showed up and was really thin and sick, and we had to send her back to Texas on a bus." Caroline pushed an orange section between her teeth. "So at the time I didn't have work, and I went to an agency and got a job answering phones at a law firm, at the front desk, and I could sort of scrape along on that. I'd been there about three days when one of the attorneys, one of the older ones, asked me if I would join him for a drink after work. He was very important and everything, but he was just some kind of regular guy—he wouldn't have understood anything about me . . . I wasn't even looking for anybody, I had dressed very conservatively and hadn't put on too much makeup. I just didn't want to be noticed, I wanted some *stability*, and anyway, he asked me out, and there he was in his suit and gray hair and everything, maybe forty-five, and he looked sort of pleased with himself, like he had just made a million dollars or something, and for all I know he *had*, and actually he was sort of attractive, but . . . well, I had seen some people in California who were pretty unusual . . . I said that was very nice but I couldn't do it. So, he was a lawyer, after all, so he wanted a rationale, and he asked me if it was a matter of availability or a matter of preference. That was how he put it. I was sort of angry, and I said preference." Caroline bit a piece of orange. "The next day, the lady who was the head of personnel fired me when I came back from lunch. She said it just wasn't going to—"

"He'd told her to do it."

"Of course. I just got up and left, and I walked south from Midtown, just walked and walked, at least an hour—you know how that can feel good on a cold day—and I was just walking along and went into a crummy bar down on Bleecker Street. It was warm inside. I decided to sit and think and then Simon came in—he was easy to recognize, he didn't look like anybody else. I'd seen his films. In fact, I'd seen *Mr. Lu* twice. He was alone, and he saw me sitting there and came over and asked me if he could buy me another drink, and I said yes and we talked for a while. I thought that he was even uglier than what I'd seen of him in the media. Shorter, kind of meaner-looking, with cowboy boots, which look stupid on a city guy. But we had a pretty good conversation. He wanted to know about my childhood." She ate another orange section. "Specifically if there was a laundry line in the backyard, with T-shirts and underwear and jeans drying on it, and that was funny, but I said yes, in fact, we'd had a laundry line like that. Both our fathers had done physical labor . . . my stepfather was a trucker. I wondered why he was paying such attention to me."

"Hey."

"Well, all right, but Simon always had a lot of women around after his films started to make it big. I'd read about him in the magazines, and actually I'd figured he was an asshole like a lot of people in Hollywood . . . but it wasn't like that, really. In the bar we just talked. Then Simon said he had to leave—some people were waiting for him uptown. Sharon Stone or somebody. I thought that was it, end of conversation. But then he pulled up close to me. He said he was going to ask me a question, one crazy question, but that he was serious. A simple yes or no would do." Caroline stared directly at me, her blue eyes daring me not to believe her. "He said that was all he wanted as an answer. Yes or no. I said okay. So Simon said, 'I want to marry you.' I thought he was crazy and almost laughed. Then I realized he was serious and we didn't say anything. I just looked out the front window of the bar and thought about how ugly he was, but also how smart he was, and that was probably the thing that was so attractive. Then I just said it—I said yes."

"You met him in a bar, he proposed, and you said yes?" I asked. "In the space of less than an hour?"

"Yes."

"That's the most ridiculous story I ever heard."

"I agree."

"But I guess pretty romantic, too."

"No," she corrected, "it's totally crazy."

"But you did it."

She nodded. "He wrote down all his phone numbers for me and got my address and said he had to go meet some people now, he was extremely sorry, but that I would hear from him the next day. I thought maybe he would kiss me or something, but he just left. There was a car waiting for him outside. When I walked out maybe fifteen minutes later, there was a car waiting for *me*. He'd had his driver call another car."

I had finished my lunch. Caroline took another orange from the bowl and handed it to me. "These are good," she said.

"What happened after that?"

"I went home to my apartment in the car and didn't know what it all meant or whether I should take it seriously. I sort of stayed around the phone that night, but he didn't call. The next afternoon I got a package that had been sent from Los Angeles that morning, and it was from Simon. It was a tape and an engagement ring . . . and then I *really* didn't know what to think. I mean, it was weird and sort of wonderful, too. I'll show you the tape, if you want."

"This is all leading somewhere?" I asked.

"I promise."

"I mean, it's interesting, don't get me wrong—"

"No, no, you'll see."

We went into the living room, and she put a videotape labeled LOOK AT ME CAROLINE [TAPE 11] into the machine. "You have to understand that Simon wasn't a regular person," she said. "He was obsessed with these little tapes. *Obsessed*. He didn't like to write anything except scripts, and so he would make these tapes. Like diaries. He made all kinds of tapes. I mean, this was his big thing—movies were the highest art, the image had killed print, stuff like that. He had a whole philosophy . . . well, I'll just start this." She drew the shades, plunging the room into darkness, and then sat down on the big sofa next to me and rolled a cigarette while I watched.

[The static ends, an image appears: a chair and table in a kitchen in an expensive home. A window in the background is dark, and a digital clock reads 1:17 A.M. A few seconds go by, and then there is a sigh audible off camera. Then the backside of Simon Crowley appears as he walks toward the chair, carrying a cigarette and ashtray. He is a small figure, skinny, soft in the gut. He sits down and stares at the camera and then past it, his eyes calm. His dark hair flops across half his face, and from time to time he pushes it back. His face is somehow misshapen, the lips and nose too large. Yet the eyes are bright with perception, ready with thought. He sighs again, slowly.] Okay. Hey there, Caroline, I'm back in Bel Air, got in from LAX maybe an hour ago. The whole time on the plane I thought about being married to you. I kept thinking about it, and there was one thing that bugged me: I think I'm uncomfortable with the regular vows—whatever vows we decide to use. In fact, you decide and I'll go along with them. It's not the ceremony, or the language, it's that I'm—as you know—I have a copious appetite to *say* things, Caroline, and "I do" will not do. It just won't *do*. [He drags on his cigarette, his eyes squinting at the effort, almost as if he is drawing his next thought directly from the burning tip itself.] So the *reason* I'm here tonight, something like thirteen fucking hours after we just met, is that I want to make my vow to you *now*, this exact minute. It's better for me this way. I don't know exactly what I'm going to say, but when it's all said and done, it will be my wedding vow. And I'm videotaping it. Obviously. Forgive me that, if you can. I suspect that you'll have to forgive me for a lot of things. [Looks down, smiles to himself. Takes a drag.] So after I said good-bye to you I had dinner with Sharon Stone. She wants to be in my next movie. We talked about it. She still looks pretty good. It was just a regular conversation. I mean, I was there talking to Sharon Stone and I was thinking of you, some girl I just met, right? Some girl at the bar that afternoon. The beautiful Sharon Stone didn't interest me. I didn't get the click from her. I got the click from you, Caroline, I got the click in a way I have not gotten the click in a long, long time . . . And then I was thinking of you, Caroline, and I remembered when I worked as a busboy as a kid. I told you this afternoon that I was a busboy, but I've never really told anybody what happened to me, stuff I learned . . . [He pulls a pack of matches out of his breast pocket and fiddles with it.] You know, I was living in my dad's house in Queens, still in high school. I was going to so many movies, like four or five on Saturdays, and renting them, too, that I didn't have any money. My father wanted me to get my elevator electrician's license, but that wasn't for me. I helped him anyway. The union said I could be called a temporary apprentice. I went with him on his service calls sometimes. He had a lot of small accounts, old buildings downtown, wherever. But I didn't want to spend my life doing that. So I needed to get a job, and I got one as a busboy at this place called Dante's Café, which used to be down in the Village before it went out of business. I liked working in the Village, because of all the alternative movie houses. I could get off at eleven and still catch a show. Pretty soon I realized how hot the place was, how a lot of the TV people and writers in New York used to go there, even some pro athletes, Darryl Strawberry when he was still big, people like that, and models and Japanese women carrying little black purses. People were always taking pictures with instant cameras and passing around the photos, doing an instant mini-hit of fame thing . . . [He gets up and wanders away. Behind him the kitchen clock reads 1:21 A.M. He comes back with another cigarette and lights it.] Getting this job was a big thing. I could watch the people. I could understand how you acted if you were rich and famous. Of course, I was nobody, I was just some skinny busboy. It was hard work. At the end of every shift I smelled like garbage and cigarettes and every kind of stuff mixed together, sticky on my arms. After a while I got to know who the regulars were and if they needed a menu or an ashtray, whatever . . . I was invisible. I was just a kid in a white shirt with a bow tie. Sometimes the models who came in were so beautiful that I went into the restroom and jerked off. I had to. I could do it standing up in, like, twenty seconds. One time I was doing it and a rat came out of a little hole that led to the storage room. I saw the money that was being spent. A couple of people would blow a few hundred bucks on food and drinks. I was making decent tips and I bought a video camera. I used to just walk around filming things, people having arguments, the barges moving up the river, whatever. I'd been working at Dante's for maybe a year when this very beautiful model started coming in—her name was Ashley Montgomery. Everybody has forgotten about her now because she ended up marrying, like, the richest man in Kuwait. She was tall, with practically the best ass in America and long straight black hair, and she was *perfect*. For six months she was on the cover of everything. In my own private dialogues, I defied anyone to find a more beautiful woman. But it would be a mistake, a pitiful mistake, to say that I *loved* Ashley Montgomery as soon as I saw her walk into

Dante's that first night. [He shakes his head in wry disgust.] We can *assume* the oboe music in the background and the laughter and the little tables. We can *assume* that her entrance into my consciousness was constructed with the cunning of the devil. [He seems to have entered a fugue state, living within conjured memory.] Yes, we can assume that. But it'd be wrong to say that I loved her instantly. No, *that* would be insufficient terminology, which is what lawyers complain about when they are hammering out movie contracts. It would be insufficient to say that I *loved* Ashley Montgomery. She *killed* me. I mean that. In a certain sense, she killed me. Ashley Montgomery *killed* me. She did not *see* me . . . [He is no longer looking into the camera but instead, the smoke lifting and curling about him, is staring off to one side, the light from the lamp unrelentingly stark upon his strange features.] I can remember all of it—her eyes swept across the restaurant as she came in, looking for other people, the real people, not the *filler*. But she didn't see me. She just did . . . not . . . *see* me. I understood this in the same way that I understood I was fucking *breathing*. I mean, most people looking across a room, when they meet the eyes of someone looking back at them, they do one of two things—they either meet the gaze of the other person and hold it, if even for a heartbeat, or they blink as they shift their eyes away. The blink is the physiological transition. It is all. It is volumes. It says, "I am moving on, what I see does not interest my eyes." It is proof, however, that *something* has registered . . . [He closes his eyes and draws in a breath, inhaling the memory back into his head. His eyes open.] But Ashley Montgomery did not blink when she looked away from me. Why? I was not *there*. I was a spoon in a fucking coffee cup, I was a thumbprint on the fucking wallpaper, I was the dust filtering imperceptibly through the gloom of the place. I was not fucking *there*. She killed me. I used to go home and cry on the subway. Sometimes, if I was in the kitchen and she was outside at one of the tables, I would force myself not to think of her by cutting myself a little with one of the vegetable knives. Just a tiny slice . . . a stigma. It never worked. I even cut a tiny piece of skin off my penis in the men's room. Just to see how much I loved her. When she came in I would pay another busboy to switch tables with me. I saved her cigarette butts. I kept a Ziploc bag in my pocket. There was a similar pattern of lipstick to each . . . I remember this, too—the ring of lipstick was uneven, and it began about a quarter inch in from the end of the filter. Different shades. I realized that the lipstick would be coordinated with what she wore. If she came in one night in a black dress, then the lipstick would be deep red. If a lighter colored dress, then lighter . . . I think everybody is a fetishist. Ashley Montgomery wore about six shades. I was thrilled when I found a—

I leaned forward and pushed the pause button. "This guy is saying his wedding vows?"

Caroline turned to me. "This was Simon."

"Original."

She smiled. I started the tape again.

Simon:—new color. When she would come in, I'd know about the lipstick. Sometimes I'd go into the bathroom right away and sometimes I'd wait until I got home. When I got home I'd undress and lie on my bed and lay the cigarette butts all over my chest. I'd put them under my tongue and in my ears and my nose and even in my ass once. The lipstick carried the perfume, the *faintest* essence, and then . . . well, then I did the usual, the business. I didn't consider this depraved. She *was* a fetish, a beautiful fetish. After a few weeks, Ashley came to recognize me ever so little . . . a smile, a politeness. Maybe she sensed something . . . my quivering attentiveness. I tended to sweat, I tended to take away her plate too quickly, like I was hurrying her out. I realized that I had to keep my job. I became the best busboy at Dante's Café. They wanted to make me a waiter but I refused. Waiters, I saw, were too busy. They couldn't stand at the back of the room and study the people. This I could do. I could watch her talk, I could watch her listen, watch her get cigarettes out of her purse, then smoke them and put them into the ashtray. She usually came in with a crowd, maybe once a week. Actors, TV people, Broadway people. Someone else always paid. Ashley didn't even offer, not once. She would come in wearing jeans and a baseball cap, and it worked, or she would come in wearing a mink that went all the way to the floor and weighed about a hundred pounds, and that was right, too. Men didn't scare her—this, by far, is the most erotic quality a woman can have. She loved men—in their varieties. She was a little older than she looked. She was twenty-six. She could be witty and quick. It seemed that she was spending more time with movie people. Some older guys, directors. And also one man in particular. He was her new guy, and it looked pretty serious to me. God, did I watch them carefully. She listened to him. There was something about her that he understood. Sometimes they took a table in the back where they just sat there reading, sometimes he would read aloud to her. Once I saw that he was reading to her from *The Confessions of St. Augustine*. I went out and found the book and I read it. What a fucking classy thing to do together. A couple of times they stayed till closing time. They seemed to take great pleasure in each other. It was about sex but it was about a lot of other things, too. He matched her vitality. Here he was sucking in other men's cigarette smoke, *vitally*, in a pressed shirt and reading St. Augustine to one of the most beautiful girls in the city. Then one time he came in carrying an ice chest, a big one. It was early, maybe six in the evening, before it got busy. He had the ice chest up on his shoulder and took it into the kitchen. There were four yellowfin tuna in there, maybe forty pounds each. I was stupid with awe. Maybe I was at an age where I just fell in love with everybody, I don't know. Anyway, the guy said he had caught them that afternoon out in the Gulf Stream fifty miles off Montauk. He held up the fish. They were huge. Beautiful. [Simon pulls a match from the matchbook and lights it contemplatively, watching the flame burn toward his fingers.] Each fish was a grotesque amplification of his manhood. I was fascinated. [He throws down the match.] I would never have what he had, *never*. He gave one fish to the owner and another to the chef. He was going to have a bunch of people in that evening and he wanted the other two fish cooked for his table. God, he was fabulous. He was handsome and well dressed and becoming famous for something, and he was arrogant. Who wouldn't be? He was about thirty-two or thirty-three. He was very sure of how it would go—I heard the conversations, of course—I was invisible, I was a shade, I was the smoke behind the table. [Simon lights another match, blows it out. Now his face is cold, dull.] Then, a couple of hours later, when the man had just come back from the men's room, on the way to his seat he turned to me with a sort of conspiratorial whisper. I was thrilled for a moment, then he said something like, "One of the crappers isn't flushing, pal." That was what he said. I said okay and went into the men's room. The fucker had stopped up the toilet with paper. All the fixtures in the restaurant were old as hell, and I had to unclog the toilets every couple of nights. But this was too much. I collapsed in that toilet stall on my knees and looked at his shit and the shitted-up toilet paper and I fucking wept. [He looks up at the camera.] I wept because I was an ugly fucker, Caroline, I wept because I was just smart enough to understand my own misery. And I guess I wept for love, too. I wept for love. I can't really say it better than that. I was certain that I would never be loved. Never. I swore that if I ever had the chance for somebody I loved, I would take it right away. Never hesitate. I was in the stall for something like ten minutes. Finally the manager came in . . . [He rubs his eyes, breathes, looks away.] This is always who I'm going to be, Caroline. I'm always going to hate myself, I'm always going to be that fifteen-year-old kid, Caroline, always outside, always fucked-up somehow. I've made three big movies now, and each one was more successful than the last, and they gave me the Oscar, and I'm glad, I'm ecstatic. Now everyone thinks I'm a genius, but what does it really mean? Why am I saying this? I am trying to say that my whole life I have been trying to be happier. I have been trying to find my best self, and I don't think I'm getting there much. So . . . my vow to you is that I will love you as best I can, but I warn you that I am a fucked-up person in many ways, Caroline. [He sits looking at the camera, then exhales, gets up, retrieves another cigarette, and returns.] Now, if you would, please open the small box that came with this videotape. Okay? You have it there, I hope. I made some calls from the plane while I was thinking of you and had a guy meet me.

What you have, Caroline, in your hand, is a Roman antiquity. The stone is carnelian. If you hold it up to the light, you'll see that it refracts the light through it, sort of in a star . . . the gold band is highly imperfect. The figure on the stone, the goddess with a helmet on, is Athena. The dealer told me it was made by hand two thousand years ago, more or less, and was discovered in a cave in Italy in about 1947. Some Brazilian millionaire owned it for a long time. We'll never know who wore this ring, Caroline, but its first wearer was probably a young Roman girl born to a wealthy family. Perhaps it was passed on for a number of generations, perhaps it was stolen and buried in the cave with the other loot. I don't know but I don't care. I want only for you to have it . . . I hope I don't disappoint you, Caroline. We'll have to—see, when I saw you in the bar, I was the boy who worshiped Ashley Montgomery, except now it was *you* I worshiped. Today I saw a woman who had been places, who could take it, who could take *me*, who would fucking kick it *back* at me if she had to. This is my excitement and this is my terror . . . You see, my heart thrills to your heart, Caroline, my dark heart thrills to your dark heart. That is my vow, Caroline. My vow to you. [Simon gets up from the table. Static. End.]

I found the performance wildly self-indulgent yet strangely moving.

"We were secretly married three days later, back in New York." Caroline's voice betrayed no happiness at the memory. "I didn't bother inviting anybody—the whole thing was too weird. He arranged for a judge to come to his apartment. I took a taxi. We hadn't even slept together, but that night we did. He asked me not to use birth control, and I said okay. I don't know how I didn't get pregnant. We knew each other all of six months, and in that time we had, like, seven weeks together. He was working on films, flying to L.A., that kind of stuff. He bought this apartment and we started to pick out furniture . . ."

She stopped. All of what she was telling me sounded prepartory to something else, but I said nothing. "I'm sure he slept with other women in that time, but he was very caring toward me, and given the strangeness of the way we'd met, I didn't complain, although in time I *would* have. He came back to the city in August, really busy. He had an office in the Village, and he was busy there, and he had meetings with people—studio people, production people, screenwriters, whoever. At night we would spend some time together and I'd go to sleep. Then Simon would go out. He had a guy who drove around with him, Billy Munson. Billy knew the city really well. Simon would go out and just look for things, situations, whatever. I once asked him if I could go with him and he said no. Sometimes he made tapes.

"So after one of those nights he didn't come back. I wanted to call the police but I waited for an extra day, because I knew that if I was wrong, he would be angry about the publicity, people saying look, his wife doesn't even know where he is. Then I called them and the days started to go by and I started to get really, really scared. Of course as soon as he started to miss appointments, everyone started to call, freaking out, worried. And then the police found him downtown . . ." Caroline tilted her head back, eyes shut. "Somehow I wasn't really surprised. But I was mad. How could he have the nerve to die or get killed or whatever just when we'd gotten started? I'm *still* sort of angry at him. But very sad, too. We used to sit up at night watching movies, and he'd see something and stop it and go back and explain the camera angle and the light and how the dialogue worked. He knew all the dialogue."

Caroline stood up and as she began to drift along the walls of the apartment, I admired the length of her legs, the perfection of her neck. "For a long time I used to think the detectives would figure it out. They say they haven't given up, but I guess they have. The stupid *private* detectives are worthless, truly, except that one of them got me a copy of the file, the one I showed you last night."

"Has the studio helped?" I asked.

She shook her head. "It's a whole bunch of new executives from the time he was there. He's dead, so he can't make them any new money, you know? I mean the movies he did still make money, but it's all residual—" She interrupted herself. "Do people come to you with all kinds of problems? Things they know about?" she asked. "I imagine you know all sorts of important city officials and everything."

"People sometimes come to me, yes."

"Like what, who?"

The answer, I saw, was a necessary step for her. She wanted to understand herself as doing something that was not extraordinarily strange. "A couple months ago," I said, "the girlfriend of a cop came in and told me about how her boyfriend beats up dealers. That's not unusual, except that one of the dealers is his brother. Then I had one not so long ago, an old guy who reads my column tells me how his wife, who had an artificial hip, they live in Brooklyn, got run over by some kids in one of those boom cars—ran her over going forty miles an hour and didn't stop. Never caught. That kind of thing, people come in, you know."

"They want notice, some sort of—"

"They want a transaction, they want to tell about what happened, what they feel about it."

She pondered this.

"Of course, some just want attention," I added.

"I'm not exactly in that category, I don't think. I *don't* want you to mention me in your column."

"Right."

"I want it all kept between us."

"Right."

She lifted an eyebrow. "You were very drunk last night."

"Yes."

"You said—"

"I said the crazy things drunk men say."

I suppose these words challenged Caroline, for she smiled and came over and stopped an inch before me. I examined her face carefully, the smooth forehead—younger than my wife's—the eyebrows and large blue eyes—flashing with amusement as they watched my own—the high cheekbones, the nose, slightly on the strong side, the mouth, the lips pursing suggestively, then her eyes again. So blue you could just go into them. She was adding velocity to whatever it was that we were about. She drew a little breath and held it, looking straight at me. She had returned from the place that I wanted to go; she knew why people went there, she could show me my truest self, she was amused by my turmoil, she expected me to succumb to her, yet she would not judge me by it, for it was in the natural order of things. She let her breath out and glanced downward, her lashes dark, then glanced up again, then pressed her index finger against her bottom lip, pressing it ever so lightly, the fingernail the beautiful waxy white of cake icing, and then the coy pink tip of her tongue appeared, touching her finger, which then, ever so slightly wetted, the swirl of the fingerprint glistening, moved from her lips through the air to mine, and when I looked from that finger back to her eyes, she was staring into me with an appetite that went past me and whatever sexual ministrations I might be capable of and beyond, into the far reaches of her own desires.

"If I were you . . ." she whispered.

"Yes?"

She pointed at my waist. "I'd turn it off."

She kept her eyes on mine.

"Turn it off?" I said.

"Turn it off."

The beeper.

"You're fun," I said.

She nodded once. "Yes. I am fun."

HER BED WAS ENORMOUS. She pulled a barrette from her hair and tossed it onto a dresser, followed by her watch, then began to take off her clothes, pulling her T-shirt above her head and letting it fall inside-out onto a chair. Her bra was delicate and black and pressed her breasts toward each other. Then her eyes looked downward as her fingers touched the button of her jeans. Never have I felt such guilt, never such excitement. I could feel the blood filling my penis heavily as I slipped out of my shoes and shirt and pants and underwear. At my age, I'm neither embarrassed nor proud of my body—I haven't gained the weight that a lot of men do, and I still get to the club maybe once a week. She, on the other hand, was magnificent in her nakedness. She had not dieted away her essence like so many women in New York; she was fleshy and full, with muscle in her arms and back and thighs.

"Just stand there a moment," I said.

"Why?"

"You know why."

I noticed a cluster of lines and colored shapes on her shoulder blade. "What's that?"

She turned and looked over her shoulder. "That's what's left of my butterfly. That was the wing."

"Tattoo?"

"Yes. I have one more time. The doctor uses a laser."

"Hurt?"

"Not too much. The laser breaks up the ink."

"I sort of wish I'd seen it. The butterfly, I mean."

She looked at me. "It was beautiful."

Then she slipped beneath the sheets.

"You're shaking," she said.

"Yes."

We took our time. Her passions did not embarrass her. The winter light was low across the city outside the window. She held my tongue tight with her teeth; another moment, in another position, she closed her eyes and frowned, as if concentrating on an intricate piece of music. I remember her fingers splayed out on the sheets, grasping and releasing, I remember the blonde hair caught in her mouth, and the earring that came loose and fell upon the sheet that she reflexively whisked to the floor, and the width of her hips in front of me, and my sucking as much of one of her breasts into my mouth as possible, suffocating on it, and the firm tumescence of her nipple, which I could feel touch the roof of my mouth. I remember that in the last moment I pushed as hard and deep and as urgently as I could, pushed against my own inconsequence and with the meanness that most men possess. And later, I pressed my face into her warm flat belly and felt a gladness bloom in me, a gladness that life was still presenting me with possibilities— that, right or completely wrong, I had embraced, in the form of this woman, the strangeness of possibility itself. I was wrong to have fucked her, but I had not been wrong to have *wanted* to; no, that was very right.

IN MY DAUGHTER SALLY'S PRE-KINDERGARTEN CLASS, there is a boy who was born without a jaw. I see him on the mornings I take Sally to school. There, among the happy chaos of the classroom, the children peering at picture books or playing with blocks, he stands, his arms stiff at his side, eyes darting about, watching all, a boy who has not so much a mouth

as a wet, backward-slanting orifice with one or two teeth visibly protrud-
ing. Above the top lip is the face of a handsome youngster, with bright eyes
and a head of brown hair; below, a dream of fleshly horror. He is otherwise quite normal, I've heard, quite bright. He can't speak, and there is no
prospect that he will speak normally for decades, if ever. I've also often
seen the boy's parents, who are gray with exhaustion and disappointment.
I admit that my heart is tight and small, that I shy away from them and
don't wish to meet their eyes, and that nonetheless my attention is drawn
with sick fascination back toward the boy's face; if possible I steal a second
glance at it, if only to reaffirm my revulsion, to derive cheap comfort that
this has not been *my* fate. How difficult it must be for the family, how easy
my daughter's life must seem compared with their son's. I would not trade
places with the father of that boy for anything. Cut me up, I won't trade
places. What is it like, I wonder as I kiss Sally good-bye in the mornings, to
have a child like that? Could I take it? Do you blame fate or chromosomes
or God? Does the husband, I wonder, see the boy's face when he is having
sex with his wife? Is there enough love and calm and money in this family
to carry it through the inevitable operations and disappointments and
complications and frustrations? And if not? What is a family made of?
From what I can tell, the boy's family doesn't seem to be doing all that
well; the husband is overweight by a good eighty pounds, his manner joy-
less. I want to put my arm around him and say I am sorry as hell that this
happened. I want to indicate to him that I see his suffering, but instead, as
his son says good-bye in sign language, always I am a coward and slip past,
through the door, out of the momentary prison of their grief. I imagine
that the father works in an office somewhere, servicing other people's
needs. He looks like he might sell something—insurance or advertising
perhaps. He makes a salary good enough to afford the school's tuition, but
I suspect that every spare dollar the couple earns is spent on the son,
somehow, or because of him. There was a time when this man was himself
a boy, a boy on a bicycle, the wind whipping his hair, then a young man
falling in love; now he is a gray forty-year-old burdened by fat and a son
with a serious birth defect. And the wife—she is haggard and defeated, her
skin sallow with deep circles under the eyes. I imagine that she is the one

who deals with their son's special meal requirements and visits with therapists and so on, who asks the doctors about the sequence of the bonegraft operations. She is the one who manages the family's edifice of torment. Either one of those parents would give anything for their son to have a normal jaw, *anything*. And were mother and father somehow to gaze through the porch window of the Wren family, say, in the happy, noisy hour before school, either one would see what was now forever lost to them and testify that they, too, would be capable of such joy, *if only*. And either one of them, particularly the husband, himself subject to the winds of male lust, would tell me that I was insane to be gambling with the wholeness of a family. *I don't care how good the sex is, it isn't worth it,* the husband might whisper into my ear. *Look at me, look upon destruction.* And listening carefully, respectfully, I would nod my agreement.

Yet. Yet there I was, standing inside the wet black box of Caroline Crowley's shower, washing my dick. All the surfaces of the shower had been cut from an ebony marble that sparkled with starry constellations of quartz. It looked a foot deep, a thousand dollars a running yard. I smelled her soap and the shampoo and thought better of anointing myself with these odors—Lisa would notice instantly. Then, dressed, I said I had to go, and Caroline nodded, perhaps sadly. The moment was tender, but not happy, more like we'd both just been wounded. The room felt ashen and cold. We made no reference to my wife or her fiancé. We made no reference to the utter inadvisability of what we'd done—it loomed there, stupid and monstrous. She was hunched in an armchair in a white bathrobe with her legs drawn up beneath her, seeming to have passed into a mood of contemplation. There is something about the first sex with a person that invites recollection of all the other first times, near or far, that form the chain of one's memory; the step that takes us into ecstasy with a new partner is also, by the logic of time, another step toward death, and if we are not chastened by anything else, we had best be chastened by this. I left Caroline pulling a tortoiseshell comb through her yellow hair. My encounter with her had in no way diminished my love for my wife and children—no, that is plain enough; the mystery is that my love for them did not preclude the possibility that I might now love Caroline Crowley, too, in that sudden, sickening, unstable way that one craves and should rightly fear.

AND THEN, behold the adulterer. In the mirrored brass of the elevator I gazed upon myself—flushed, hair wet, lips slightly swollen. I felt less shame than I should have, I felt a dark little thrill, I felt an echoing pleasure in my balls. I tightened my tie and buttoned my wool coat. I would, of course, have to understand myself as a man who had, for the first time, cheated on his wife. Almost spontaneously. Yet I see now how much better it might have been if I'd understood myself in *another* way, too—that I had entered a labyrinth far stranger and more dangerous than I could ever imagine, far more wretched than the mere banality of adultery. The brass elevator door slid open, and I walked out of the lobby, past the front desk and Napoleon, the uniformed doorman. He was a tiny, greasy thumb of a man, and his eyes darted sideways as I went by. He gave me a slow, unctuous nod, tipped his finger to his cap, and indicated that a taxi was waiting outside. Only by the merest chance, after I had settled into the cab, after the doorman assumed I was looking elsewhere, did I see him glance at his watch, pull a pen and pad from his pocket, and make note of something— make note, I realized only later, of me.

■ ■ ■

WE THINK WE KNOW THE CITY, but we never do. For all brightness there
is corollary darkness, for all places known there are others full of unre-
membered lives and lost music. I always have been drawn to these spots;
they are damp and cold and defy hope, they sag and rust and rot, they re-
pel vanity and beckon death: a woman's shoe in a gutter, an empty bottle
left on a stone step, a door repainted a dozen times in a hundred years.
Early the next morning I stood in one such place—the north side of
Eleventh Street, just off Avenue B—for no useful reason except that I had
awoken with an odd desire to see number 537, the fenced building lot
where Simon Crowley's body had been found seventeen months earlier.
But whereas the corpse had been discovered in a rubble of bricks, the
space was now flat and divided into small garden plots, such as single families might use. I could see this even though the snow was still deep in
places, the wind having swirled violently around the lot and piled up
drifts, even building a three-foot-high ridge that began near one wall,
passed through the chain-link fence, and around in front of number 535,
the building next door. But it was the garden plots that interested me; the
corn husks, dried tomato vines, and rotted flower beds separated by

curving paths of scavenged brick and festooned with Christmas lights and chrome hubcaps. A small Puerto Rican flag flew over the garden, and despite the cold, chickens pecked around a shack at the rear of the lot. To one side was a bench seat from a car. An immense and eyeless stuffed animal, gray from the weather—a bear or a dog—hung from the wall of the adjacent building, as if blindly guarding the garden or perhaps, more particularly, the statue of Christ standing in a small grotto planted with roses and hollyhocks. All had been blasted by the winter, but come spring it would be a place of lushness and color, of life.

An obese older woman came out of the shack with a rake and started to drag it across one of the small beds. It seemed an odd activity for a winter day, even a warm one, but she seemed content, smoking a cigarette as she worked. Then she noticed me, as I'd hoped, shielding her eyes to see the figure shadowed against the fence. "*¿Qué quieres?*" she shouted. What did I want? I shrugged theatrically. She came toward me, picking her way past many of the largest pieces of rubble, and I could hear her wheeze as she approached. A remembrance of my mother, dead more than thirty years, ticked somewhere in my brain. My mother had loved me, her only child, with all her heart, but it was a heart choked with fat; she was so immense that she died lifting me out of the bathtub when I was six. I still didn't have a way to explain it to myself.

Now the woman neared; in her hand she held a small plastic canister, her finger set on a button. I saw that her face was marked by struggle and ill health and sadness; her eyebrows had the thin, hatched scars of a woman who had been beaten.

"Jes, mister, can I help you?"

"I like gardens, so I stopped to look."

"Jes?" Her eyes were wary.

"We kept a garden when I was growing up," I told her. "We grew a lot of vegetables. Corn, tomatoes. You grow that here?"

"Jes."

"We used to grow lettuce and cabbage and broccoli and all kinds of stuff. Peas early. I bet you could plant them in April here. Get some rows of marigolds in between the rows for the bugs?"

"Marigolds?" she asked. "*¿Las floras?*"

"Yes, the flowers. Marigolds. Put them in and the bugs hate the smell."
The thought intrigued her. "I show the garden to you?"

"Yes," I said, "I'd like that very much."

I followed her through the chain-link door, and she locked it carefully.

"My name is Estrella Garcia," she said.

"Porter Wren," I said.

She didn't seem to recognize the name, which was just as well.

"What is that stuff anyway?" I asked, pointing at the small canister in her hand. "Mace?"

She shook her head solemnly. "You no can use the Mace on the dogs. You have to have tear ducks." She pointed at her own eyes, which were a greenish brown, and it occurred to me that once, long ago, they must have been described as beautiful. "This is pepper, 'cause pepper go in the nose, okay? The pepper work on dogs and bad peoples, okay?"

I nodded. "I was worried you were going to give me a shot of that."

She frowned. "You no be scared now."

We followed a crude brick path around the lot. I silently located the approximate place where Crowley's body had been found; now it was a patch of dead zinnias set in planters made from sliced car tires. The soil wasn't very good, full of bits of mortar and shards of brick and window glass. The demolition company had left some large fragments of poured concrete and even some steel beams, and I wondered if the discovery of Simon Crowley's body had spooked the workers and made them finish up sloppily.

"In my country we have very many gardens everywhere," Estrella Garcia was saying. "In the little town people grow a corn, tomato, this place is just someplace for peoples to be happy and grow maybe some flowers, maybe some peppers . . ."

"It's a new garden?" I asked casually.

"Just one summer. Everybody they work very hard last spring because the peoples, they put, you know, lots of trash and broken things first, see, this was planted by my grandson—" She pointed to a scraggly row of sunflower husks. "We make it so beautiful for some peoples who live here. Everybody, you know, love this garden."

"Everybody who uses it lives on the street?"

She nodded absentmindedly, poking at an errant brick with her puffy foot. "My family, we live next door over there." She gestured at the adjacent building, 535. "Some peoples they live across the street, you know, everybody they come from right around here."

"Was the building that was here falling down?" I asked.

She shrugged. "No, not so bad, you know."

"Not boarded up and falling down?"

"Nobody they live there, but it was okay, you know?"

"How was the roof?"

"I don't know these things. Some peoples they tried to live there, but they got kicked out. Our building is better. My son-in-law is the super. He do a very good job. He always cleaning the hallway, the front steps, everything . . ."

We walked back to the high fence.

"Did they need to tear down this building?"

"No, it was pretty good, I think."

"Does your son-in-law know about the building?"

"Oh, jes."

"Would it be a bother if I asked him about it?"

Whether it was a bother or not, she didn't say. We made our way toward the back of the property, and Mrs. Garcia led me down three cement steps blocked with children's bicycles, through another door marked OFFICE, and then down a wooden staircase, where the air suddenly became quite hot, and into an immense, dark room with pipes snaking everywhere and a roaring furnace the size of a truck, a row of hissing hotwater heaters, an empty elevator cage, more bicycles, a far stairway, miscellaneous lumber, and, under a lightbulb with a long chain and a tennis ball at the end of it, a rather fine antique desk, where a graying Latino man in spattered, heavy-lensed glasses sat filing a small piece of oily equipment with an angry determination that gave me to understand that he knew exactly what he was doing and, on the whole, would rather have been elsewhere.

"Luis," said Estrella Garcia, "this man was asking about the building they tore down."

He looked up, flicked his eyes at me. "Next door?"

"Right," she said.

"Yes?" he said to me, taking off his glasses.

"I was wondering about the apartment house next door. Number five-thirty-seven. Why'd they tear it down?"

"It was no good." He shrugged, wiping his hands on a rag.

"Oh. Your mother-in-law said it was in pretty good shape."

He shook his head disgustedly. "No, no, she don't know nothing about how these buildings work. It was no good. They didn't replace nothing after, like, 1970. I was in that building a thousand times. The roof was terrible, the second floor had structure failure, it had bad cracking, no good. They didn't replace the roof, and you gotta do that. You gotta fix the roof or else that water gets down in there, see, things start freezing and cracking and rotting. Place was full of rats, too."

I identified myself, told him I was a reporter. "What about the body they found when they were knocking the building down?"

The superintendent nodded and sighed, as if all human activity was a burden to him, unsurprising in its idiocy. "Thought it was something like that."

"I suppose the cops asked a lot of questions?"

"They asked a few."

"They never solved it."

He shrugged. It was no matter to him. "People keep on getting killed, you know? We had a lady up on the fifth floor. And some kid down the street."

I nodded. "Did you ever wonder about how the body got onto the lot?"

"Not really," he said. "Not my business."

"Well, I mention it because the lot was sealed off by a sidewalk shed with concertina wire on top and the building was sealed up, too."

"Except for the front door."

"Right, but that was locked," I said. "That probably wasn't—"

"Hey, hey, wait a minute," he said, wiping his hands again forgetfully. "You know how many locksmiths there are in this city? I got tenants upstairs changing their locks all the fucking time. They don't want to pay their rent anymore and they change their locks." He shook his head. "The landlord used to change locks! Now the tenants. Always screaming about a rent strike." He threw the rag down on the desk. My inquiry did not interest him; rather, he was taking the opportunity to issue a general complaint. "I'm telling you, it gets old trying to fix everybody's sink and shit. I got only one guy helping—" He turned toward a dark corridor that ran alongside some large pipes wrapped in insulation. "Adam! Come in here."

A short, soft-looking young man in a Mets T-shirt emerged. He was chewing his lip.

"Adam," the superintendent yelled. "Get the box. Show the reporter-man how many keys you got." He turned toward me. "I got Adam keeping track of the keys." He turned back. "No, Adam, get the *big* box. Tenants supposed to notify and give me a *new* key—that's in every lease—and then they don't give me a key. I work for the landlord. Fucking shit-dick. Hairplugs on his head. Every time I see him it's more hairplugs. I work for him. I make money for him and he turns it into *hairplugs*. Looks like little bushes in a row, heh!" He smiled bitterly. "But I work for him. Everybody got to work for somebody, right? He gets me to put on these special locks, double-keyed and special hotel locks and all *kinds* of shit like that, and then I come back three days later and the tenant fucking got a locksmith to get it open so maybe she can go get her teakettle, right? *Right*, Adam? You get that box of keys, now, Adam. Hey, stop fucking around back there!" He looked back at me. "I used to know all the locksmiths, and they would check with me first on the way in, but them days is—" The phone rang, and he lifted a heavy black receiver from a set on the wall. "Yes, *yes*. No! Don't *touch* it, Mrs. . . . Tell Maria don't *touch* it. *No*, that won't work. I'm coming." He hung up and looked at me. "Lady on the second floor got a five-year-old girl. The ball thing fell off the TV antenna. The kid stuck the antenna in the light socket. That kid should be fucking toast right now, but she's okay. Don't ask me why. Maybe the socket is dead. I gotta go get it out." He picked up a toolbox, then walked over to the empty elevator cage and pushed a red button. "So anyway . . . yeah, about the whole lock thing there, that building—maybe they didn't go in the front door, but they could have, they could have done anything, they could have gone from my roof over to their roof, and then smashed in the roof-access door and had a party up there."

I was about to remind him that he had told the police that he thought no one had reached 537 from his roof because he kept his own roof door locked. But the phone rang a second time and he picked it up. "Yes, Mrs., yes, I'm coming now." He hung up and looked at the elevator cage, the side cables of which were moving. "Thing's too slow. Take forever." He turned back to me, nodded perfunctorily. "Okay, excuse me, I got to go here. Can't let that kid discover electricity." He headed up the stairs. "Adam! Forget the fucking box! We're taking the stairs. Adam, follow me, I'm going to two-oh-four. Mrs. Salcines. Adam? Adam, stop fucking around!"

And so there I stood, underground, beneath a ganglia of pipes. Estrella Garcia, her neck ringed with a sagging doughnut of flesh, looked at me. "Mrs. Garcia," I said, "may I come see your garden again?"

She nodded yes, perhaps even pleased.

HALF AN HOUR LATER, uptown, I passed through the newspaper's first-floor lobby, nodding at Constantine, the security guard. "Good morning, Mr. Wren," he said, with a generosity that confounded me. Constantine had been at the paper for almost two decades and had known hundreds of reporters, editors, deli delivery boys, photographers, advertising sales-people. Three years prior, he had been seen filling out lottery tickets, penciling in the circles behind his desk. At first he did several a day, but in time he came to fill out dozens a week. Meanwhile he smiled and contin-ued to nod hello. Soon the educated professionals passing by could not help but stop and bring up the topic of Constantine's lottery tickets. They expressed worry that he was gambling compulsively. Did he need help? A therapist? Did he realize that lottery tickets were a form of regressive tax-ation? That the odds were poor and that he could probably not afford to spend so much on this obsession? That was before Constantine won twelve million dollars. Still, he had been content to keep working as a se-curity guard, and now people in the building brought him their lottery tickets to fill out.

I rode up in the elevator with a young reporter holding a paper bag from a deli down the street. His hair was wild, as if he'd been tearing at it, and he blinked in thought to himself, tapping his foot.

"Just lay brick," I said, not remembering his name.

"What?" He looked at me worriedly.

"You having trouble with a story?"

"I—yes, I can't get it right, how'd you know?"

"No coat. No notebook. Lots of coffee. You went out and came back."

"What did you say again?"

"Lay brick."

He nodded his understanding. "Yeah."

We got off the elevator and the young reporter whisked off toward another part of the newsroom. I scuttled along the back wall. Years ago I felt a certain camaraderie with the other reporters, but that was when we were all on the way up. We used to sit around and talk about Ed Koch, how we were going to pin something on him that would stick. But we never did, and a lot of people moved on to other papers or took PR jobs for three times the money. Or blew up. You see a few people whom you got older with, and the rest of them seem ever younger. They all want to hang up a few pelts. Then there are the investigative reporters who are getting tired of the research. Too much legwork for the money, pal. They've got wives and husbands and kids and mortgages, and they're strapped in. They have to come up with the big stories and sell them to the editors and then go deliver. I did that; I was in City Hall and the police department and the DA's office and the federal courts. I sat in the chairs. I put in the time. When you get sick of being an investigative reporter, you try to become a columnist. They all think I'm paid too much. I can see it in their faces. My salary was reported in *New York* magazine. Leaked by somebody. It's embarrassing. They look at me and I know what they're thinking. They don't understand the pressure to be "Porter Wren." They can hide behind the screen of objectivity, but a columnist has to push it, has to break stories, hit page one. A newspaper column three times a week is a vulture that eats your liver away as fast as you can grow it back. You are chained to the rock, the bird approaches, eyes bright, beak stinking of its last meal, and, alighting suddenly, it pecks and tears at the wound it abandoned two days be-

fore, eats its fill, gulping the pieces, and then flies away. The other reporters think that they understand this, but they don't, and I resent their
resentment of me. So I sneak in, keeping my coat on, walking along the
back wall of the newsroom, scowling, not saying hello. Go away. Don't
bother me. I just cheated on my wife.

Richard Lancaster tore out his tubes, said Bobby Dealy's strangely precise handwriting on the piece of paper taped to my screen. *Dying pretty
fast.* This was the fifty-six-year-old insurance man who had killed Iris Pell.
The longer he lived, of course, the better the story. I stared at my notes
from the day before. The jagged scratchings disgusted me—how was it
possible to describe what had happened to Iris Pell in eight hundred
words? Did anyone care? What did a column about her amount to, really?
I'd rather be in Caroline Crowley's shower. I called the hospital, where I
knew the spokesman; he would only state that Lancaster's condition had
worsened due to infection in the brain, and would not comment on
whether Lancaster had successfully pulled out his tubes—the admission
of which might be used by Lancaster's family to allege that the hospital
staff silently overlooked his actions, which was probably the case. "The
word is he tore out the tubes," I told the spokesman. "I can't confirm,"
he answered. That meant *Yes, but get another source.* Maybe this wasn't the
way to work the story; all the TV guys would be on a Lancaster death-
watch. And the only good source would be a nurse or orderly, who by now
had probably been silenced by the hospital administrators. I flipped over
the pages of my reporter's pad. The last number belonged to Iris Pell's
mother. Maybe she would talk more easily knowing Lancaster was on the
way out.

I love deadlines, I flirt with them, I caress them and make promises to
them, I lie to them and to myself about the lie. But the deadline always ar-
rives, and so it was time to call the mother of the dead girl. You have to do
this carefully. Someone has died, for God's sake. Ten years ago I used to
blow this kind of call when I was in a hurry. Now I almost always get it
right; you have to respect the grief, not be rattled by it or embarrassed for
the person. You have to stand and take it, just unfold yourself to it, and
forget about the deadline, forget about everything else, and when you have
forgotten everything else, they know that you care and they tell you, which

is what they really want to do. I call this the point of dilation. On the phone Mrs. Pell was careful at first, as if she were biting her fist before saying anything. Then she opened up a little. Then gushed. No one had talked to her, no one had *asked*. Her daughter had walked at ten months. Her daughter had shown ability in math at age four. Her daughter had raised goldfish when she was seven. Her daughter had given blood every six weeks since she was eighteen. Her daughter had studied accounting. Her daughter had gotten a job that paid $41,000 and, after a few years, had joined a health club in Midtown, where, in the manner of the age, huffing professional people pedaled stationary bicycles stationarily or climbed mechanical stairs mechanically. In the lobby of the health club, some enterprising member—no doubt an investment banker—had placed a stack of prospectuses for an IPO, an initial public offering of stock in a company. It was a strange place to find an IPO prospectus, which of course was the idea, since people might actually look at it, and Iris Pell, the accountant, noticed. Flushed with her workout, possessed of a head of thick dark hair, she, in turn, was noticed by Richard Lancaster, the insurance executive. He made a casual comment. She gave a response. They saw in each other the appreciation for the forms and complexities of money. They discussed the prospectus. How amusing that it was sitting in the lobby of the health club, what a comment on the way we now live. Hah. Yes, hah. And so on. What they were really discussing was the prospectus for a relationship, and in that first ten minutes, in the nodding and smiling and careful observation, the deal was made. No matter that Lancaster was so much older. Soon came the wine, the bed, the plans. Iris Pell had told her mother everything. Five months later, the Pell family wedding dress, sitting in a cardboard box in a cedar closet in a suburban home in New Jersey, was solemnly taken out of mothballs. Some thirty-eight women had been married in the dress. The seams had been torn out and resewn, the bodice adjusted, either to reveal or conceal cleavage (depending on the charms thereof, the mother's concern with appearances, and the daughter's sauciness), but the dress, the basic dress, had wrapped in whiteness the dreams of thirty-eight women over a span of ninety years—almost all of the century—mothers and daughters and cousins and daughters-in-law, and although the lace had been defiled with perfume and lipstick and

cigarette ash and champagne and cake icing, and although a typical percentage of the marriages had gone bad, the dress itself remained sacred to
the Pell family; the dress suggested to a working-class New Jersey family
that they had values in a valueless world. Yes, Iris Pell's wedding dress had
made its last, late-night dance under the fluorescent lights of a Chinese
laundry on the Upper West Side, that last dance being the sudden turn
that Iris Pell took when she glimpsed her jilted lover, Richard Lancaster,
as he lunged into the shop and fired the gun he was carrying, the bullets
perforating the wedding dress before they perforated Iris Pell's heart,
and then, from afar, the heart of her mother. The daughter fell, the killer
fled, the police arrived, the mother grieved. The dress was quickly pho-
tographed by the police and returned to the mother, who, possessing a
mother's knowledge of the sacred and the profane, had the wedding
dress—*her* wedding dress, her *mother's* wedding dress—incinerated.
And then, weeping, told me about it: "I had to do it, you see, it just
wasn't right to keep it anymore. I didn't even discuss it with my husband, Mr. Wren, I just had to do it. I could never look at that dress again,
I could never . . . I—please excuse me a moment . . . I'm sorry—she was
my daughter! She was my daughter. Why is my daughter gone? Why won't
anyone tell me?"

Yes, Bobby Dealy was right, I like the romantic angle. And if the newspaper column is a vulture, then it restores me even as it tears from me. Listening to, say, the grieving confessions of a humble, decent woman in her
kitchen in New Jersey, I find that there is a moment when I am made
whole by her suffering, when I glimpse the humanity of a stranger, am
made better than I really am.

WHEN THE COLUMN WAS DONE my thoughts returned to the previous
afternoon, and I suppose that if my marital guilt were a cave, then I
meant now to feel along the dark, damp walls for the sharp places and
for the size of the cavity I had opened within myself. I wanted to mull
the thing over, to decide whether I was to make a confession of it to my
wife and, if so, when and in what form. And if there was *not* to be a confession, then how was I to think of myself? I expect that other adulterous

husbands ponder the same questions. I also expected that Caroline Crowley might appreciate my ambivalence, my hesitation, and, in this, not press me too soon for more contact. And perhaps she had her own remorse to plumb, given that she was engaged to the young executive I'd seen at Hobbs's party. But I was wrong. No sooner had I shipped the column than she called.

The talk between us was brief and full of more sexual possibility. I told myself never to see her again and I told her I'd meet her in half an hour uptown at a place off Park Avenue with a lot of abstract fish sculptures on the walls. I got there first and asked the waiter to keep the wine list, and then there was Caroline outside the restaurant window, in a fur and blue jeans, and I knew all over again why I had done it. She came inside, and all the men looked, and they kept looking as she took off her coat and handed it to the waiter. Now their day was just a little better; they were keeping a bit of Caroline for themselves, taking her in and putting her in the place where the private treasure was kept. She kissed me, and sat down with the happy sigh of a woman who has just walked twenty blocks in the Manhattan air, her eyes bright, seeming younger than when I'd first met her.

"I like this place." She looked around. "You come here a lot?"

"Never."

"Are you hiding me?"

"Yes, but in plain sight."

"What if you see someone you know?"

"I won't."

"You might."

"Yes, I might."

She giggled. "I could pretend to be your wife."

"Won't wash."

"I could be your assistant."

"Don't have one."

"I could be an important source."

"You are an important source."

"Of what?"

"Guilt."

"Well, I don't feel guilty," Caroline announced. "I know I seemed sort of contemplative before you left, but I'm not moody or glum or anything, I was just thinking about how sweet you were and how I wanted to tell you some things and how it was kind of hard to do it, and so I think what I'd like to do is just show you and then take it from there. I— I'm . . ." She played with her napkin, and I saw her fingers were trembling, ever so slightly. I'd held those fingers, against the sheet. "I'm actually sort of alone, Porter. I see Charlie, you know, but he's young. I mean he's a very good person . . ." She lifted her eyes, anxiously, and then looked down again. "He thinks we'll get married this June, probably . . ." She waved her hand in disgust. "So, this is sort of a long way of saying I want to show you the thing I've been talking about. This afternoon. Now. If you have time."

I nodded. We fell silent and I ordered a pot of tea against the cold. Caroline desired something particular from me, and what it was I couldn't say—at least not yet. She clearly wanted attention, even love, but there was no reason for her to think that I might provide her with these things, for my energies, as was obvious, were almost entirely devoted to my family and work. And if it was sex she was after, then—well, I suppose I'm as adept as the next guy, but if she wanted to pick and choose, all she would have to do was hang out in a bar for a minute or two and she could have turned up the lover of her choice. And this goes for all the lesser distractions, too; she could have turned up brilliant conversationalists, starving prophets, sweet-tempered heroin addicts, cold-knuckled businessmen with expensive hobbies, magnetic ghetto activists—whomever. I was a married newspaperman. It didn't make much sense to me. It didn't need to, not yet.

We strolled uptown along Park Avenue, passing the executives, the women in hats, the messengers and deliverymen and secretaries in sensible shoes.

"Here," Caroline said, taking my arm.

I looked up at the building facade; it was a Malaysian bank, one I'd never heard of but which no doubt catered to the ever-rising number of wealthy Malaysian middlemen who work for Japanese and South Korean manufacturing companies, arranging the production of low-technology goods at Malaysia's feudal wages. We entered a marbled lobby that featured, behind glass, an immense sitting Buddha, eight feet high, millennia old. Caroline, I noticed, looked at it with appreciation. Then she identified herself to the three uniformed guards sitting at a wide console; one of them quietly picked up a phone, spoke a second, and then nodded.

"You keep money in *this* bank?" I asked.

"No." She laughed. "I keep Simon here."

We walked through a lobby, where she nodded to a receptionist, who then pressed a button at her desk. The doors of an elevator opened behind us. We stopped on the fourteenth floor. There Caroline repeated an account number to another receptionist. Standing to one side, I could see her face appear on the color screen—it looked strangely drained of blood. Then a uniformed guard with a holstered gun met us and escorted us past glass security doors and down a labyrinth of hallways. Once past another door, this one more obviously impenetrable—polished steel perhaps two feet thick—we were led by a tiny Malaysian woman along a narrow hallway of windowless, numbered doors. A turbaned gentleman and a woman wrapped in a veil were emerging from one of the doorways, and I glimpsed behind them into the small vault to see, fleetingly, what looked to be one of those life-size clay soldiers from China. The couple looked calmly past us; clearly the protocol was that no one saw anyone else. At the end of the hallway, the attendant punched in a small code on a key-pass on a door, then turned away as Caroline put in one of her own. A pinpoint green light flashed and the attendant opened the door for Caroline. The woman nodded and then left.

I did not know what to expect, but I was struck by the spareness of the room, the contents of which were exactly five things: two plain office chairs, a small table, a videocassette player, and an immense trunk the size of the deep freezer my father had in our garage, where he kept the deer he shot each fall.

"This is something I vaguely knew about when Simon was alive but never actually saw until after he died." Caroline pushed up the clasps on the lid of the trunk; it was spring-loaded and opened to reveal a tray of videotapes. Each one was affixed with a small white label and was numbered: 1, 2, 3, 4, 5, etc. The tapes were not in numerical order; there might have been seventy-five or a hundred.

"Which tapes should I look at?" I said.

"As many as possible."

"Seriously?"

She looked at me, eyebrows lifted.

"That would take—what, are all of these two hours long?"

"No. Most are only maybe ten, twenty minutes. Some are longer. There are a couple of much longer ones."

"I'll do what I can."

"You can come back and see the rest."

She lifted the tray of tapes.

"Shall I look at them in numerical order?" I asked.

She shook her head. "It doesn't matter."

"No order or message or anything?"

"No. Absolutely not. That wasn't his vision of things. His idea was that there was no pattern. It would have been too simplistic. He thought patterns were for cowards, actually."

"Will you sit here and watch them with me?"

"No."

I looked at her.

"I'm sorry. I can't watch these anymore." Her eyes held a memory. "I've seen them all too many times. I couldn't sit through them again. It's too exhausting."

I pulled one of the chairs up next to the trunk and started poking through the tapes.

"I'll tell the people out front you might be here awhile."

"Okay."

She came up to me. "Thank you, Porter."

"This is one of the weirder moments of my life, I think."

"Just remember that Simon was very, very unhappy all his life and that he was always searching for something, for *true* life, he wanted to capture truth. Maybe that's silly, but that's what he wanted to do. These tapes are sort of a personal collection. He chose each for something he liked. He threw out many more. We talked about it once. He was trying to assemble a collection of filmed moments. Not like a movie. Not a sequence. Just a collection."

"Has Charlie seen these tapes?"

"Charlie? Of course not! He wouldn't understand."

"So—?"

"So I'm asking you to look at them."

"Why?"

"Well . . ." She gazed at me with her wide blue eyes, and they seemed full of answers that remembered not only her time with Simon Crowley but her life before that; she seemed to be intimating that one thing was connected to another and that all were connected to everything else, that the only way to understand it was to let her explain it to me in her own way, difficult as that might be. "I need to—I want you to see them because then I can talk about something *else* with you."

I know enough from my work that during an interview it is sometimes more useful to indulge the evasiveness of the speaker than to challenge it. The evasive statements carve out a kind of negative space around what is being avoided. So I just nodded. Caroline leaned forward and gave me a lingering kiss next to my ear. "Can we see each other tomorrow in my apartment again?" she whispered.

I nodded yes—stupidly.

She left and the door clicked shut. The sound of it bothered me, then scared me, and after a moment I jumped up and checked the door to be sure that I had not been locked in. Then I took one tape, labeled TAPE 26, put it into the machine, and hit play.

TAPE 26

[Dark shapes, sound of a truck engine.]

First voice: . . . Gulf Stream, man, boat was maybe fifty feet long.

Second voice: What do you got on one of those numbers—six chairs?

First voice: Yeah, two down front in the back, couple on the sides. [Engine is louder. Sunlight flashes onto the scene to reveal a huge metal lip of some sort; beyond it is a continuous stream of streetbed, potholes. The truck can be heard to shift gears, brakes screeching. Far-off traffic, sirens. The truck stops. A man dressed in a garbageman's uniform appears, dragging a large can; in go bags of garbage, shoes, loose magazines; then another man, with another can, and then the first with another; after half a dozen cans the roadway beyond the metal lip blurs for ten seconds, then the screech of brakes; the men appear, rhythmically, dumping in garbage cans, one after another: trash, clothes, wet paper bags, a few bottles, a broken radio, newspapers that should be recycled, bags, bags, bags, an old computer monitor, some children's toys, magazines, Styrofoam packaging, papers . . .] Saw a beautiful run out there, actually.

Second voice: What were they?

First voice: Yellowfins, around thirty pounds. I went up on deck, it was beautiful . . . [Truck lurches forward again; men bring more cans, dumping in one after another, breathing a bit with the effort, the sun now in their faces. Beneath their heavy green shirts are torsos thick in the shoulders and arms. When the light flashes across the men's faces, they appear to be older than one might expect, given the considerable effort of lifting the heavy cans.]

First voice: So I was up there and we saw them. Incredible. The water was blue, so blue, you know, and then the captain calls out, "Here they come," and I'm up there on deck and I see this flashing . . . these shapes, and they're going fast, flashing, like, maybe ten feet under the surface, and it's the most beautiful thing I ever saw. [Truck lurches forward again. The men work steadily, pausing only to pull the lever that activates the digestive compactor of the garbage truck. And then more societal excrement: bags, broken ceiling tiles, a bicycle, cat litter, garbage bags, ripped and spilling open to reveal eggshells and coffee rinds and pork chop bones and fashion magazines and cigarette butts and a woman's slip, dirty and translucent and beguiling as it momentarily floats atop a froth of garbage.] It was something I was never going to forget, them just coming at me like that, like a couple hundred of them.

Second voice: Yeah.

First voice: Some kind of beautiful thing, I'm telling you. [The garbage truck lurches forward again, screeches to a stop, and the men resume their work. This continues for about twenty minutes. They say nothing to each other. The tape ends.]

I put another one in.

TAPE 32

[The screen shows the backseat of a large car, a limousine. It is night. The radio is playing, faintly. The bottom half of the side window is visible. The car is moving through traffic, passing taxis, the lights of storefronts, people on the streets in winter coats. It is New York City.]

First voice: It's on already, I just hit the button.

Second voice: You're a very fucked-up guy, you know that? [The back of a head, close to the camera. Camera tries to focus automatically on dark hair. Head moves, camera refocuses.]

First voice: Give me that thing, man.

Second voice: I drink one more drop I'ma be sick, I'll just shoot it.

First voice: Just open the window 'fore you do.

Second voice: I'll be too gone do it.

First voice: Naw.

Second voice: Shit.

First voice: Ask Max or whateverz name a go overt Tenth Avenue.

Second voice: I'm not ready.

First voice: Just tell Max.

Second voice: He'll think we're bunch of fucking perverts.

First voice: He's getting paid.

Second voice: Max! Tenth Avenue, Forty-sixth Street! [A sound.]

First voice: What'd he say?

Second voice: He said sure.

First voice: He said Bush is going to get reelected.

Second voice: Fuck you.

First voice: Jesus, I feel great, I feel like my fucking head is mag-lev.

Second voice: Mag-lev?

First voice: Magnetic-levitation, man. The Japanese train is going fucking two hundred miles a hour and it's not touching anything, going above the rails.

Second voice: We can't be doing this.

First voice: Too high to die, man.

Second voice: Come on, what the fuck.

First voice: We're almost there, look! There's one. Tell Max slow down. [Sound. Car is moving more slowly.] There's one.

Second voice: God, no!

First voice: She wasn't so bad!

Second voice: She was huge!

First voice: There!

Second voice: No!

First voice: Yeah!

Second: Max, stop it here! Stop it here! [Face in the window, blonde girl with bad teeth.]

Girl: Hi, fellas.

First voice: Hi to you.

Girl: What's happening tonight? It's cold and I'm all lonely out here.

First voice: We're sorta lonely in here.

Girl: Looks like you have, like, a whole bar.

Second voice: Yeah, comes with the car.

Girl: That's great.

First voice: Billy, she for you? [Pause. Cars pass outside.]

Billy: Open the door. Let me get a look. [Door opens. Girl pretends to dance, moving her hips back and forth, clawing her short dress upward.]

First voice: Billy?

Girl: Round the world is gonna be one-fifty.

Billy: You're too ugly, spend that kind of money.

First voice: She's not ugly. Plain, perhaps. Nondescript. Generic. A certain utilitarian—

Girl: What's he saying?

Billy: You sound like you're interested, my man.

First voice: I could be int'ressed. I could be very int'ressed. But then again, you're buying. [The girl sits in the car, one leg in, one leg out.]

Billy: Closa door, it's cold.

Girl: I could do you both, if that's—

First voice: I'm not into that shit. I seen Billy naked and it's no treat.

Billy: Fuck you, Simon.

Girl [pulling up her dress]: Which of you gentlemen—

Billy: It's gonna be him, but I'm paying. So we agree—

Girl: I said one-fifty for round the world.

Billy: That's bullshit. I'm not paying that.

Girl: What does he want anyway?

Billy: What'd you want?

Simon: Plain fuck.

Girl: Most guys want blowjobs.

Simon: Hey, no rhythm in it, no power. [Takes a long drink from a bottle.]

Billy: That can't be one-fifty.

Girl: I'll go one hundred on that, but the room is twenty.

Billy: You can do it right here, the seat's big enough.

Girl: One hundred, then.

Simon: Billy?

Billy: It's too high.

Girl: Come on.

Simon: You're dealing with a very tough negotiator here, lady. This guy works for Merrill Lynch, made a million dollars last year.

Billy [with real anger]: Shit, don't tell her that.

Girl [attempting a flirtatious voice]: Don't you *want* me?

Simon: Yez, sure I do, and I'da pay a hundred, but I'm not pay-ing. He's got the money, he's the guy with the money on this deal.

Girl: Seventy-five? But that's my last—

Billy: Fuck no. No fucking *way*. There'rz girls out here who look a shit load bettern'you and they'll do it for thirty-five!

Girl: Yeah, *right*.

Billy: You don't believe me?

Girl: You want something that's better, you gotta pay for it.

Billy: All right—we're gonna go find some other—it looks like there's a girl right over there, we'll see—let's go see what she's gonna charge—

Girl: Please, please, I need some money. I have a shopping prob-lem. I shop too much.

Simon: You're a great man, Billy! Don't cry, sweetie.

Girl: Thirty-five? I'll—

Billy: Daaah! Too much.

Girl [crying]: You don't understand. I got all kinds of prob—

Billy: You gotta bring the price down.

Girl: [crying, pride gone]: Twenty? Please? I need some money tonight.

Billy: Five bucks. Thaz my . . . final offer. [Girl is weeping and cuts her eyes back and forth at the faces of the two men.]

Simon: You motherfucker, no way she's gonna—

Girl [face resolved now]: You ain't gonna pay me more?

Billy: No.

Simon: You are fucking *evil*, man. Cold-cock evil. [Takes drink.]

Girl: Twenty? That's so little. You guys are rich.

Billy: Five, you bitch, haa!

Girl: No.

Billy: That's it, then. [The girl looks out the window for other cars. None appear.]

Girl: You fucker. Gimme the money first.

Billy: No, you get in first. [She gets in. A hand appears holding a bill. The girl takes it quickly.]

Girl: You gonna watch?

Billy: No, I'm gonna jes get outa the car on this side and stand here for a few minz lookin' the other way 'n have a philosophical smoke.

Girl: All right.

Billy: Si-boy, you all right with this chick?

Simon: Yeah, I'll be fine. For someone who is totally fucking bombed, you're still a *mean* motherfucker.

Billy: Last thing to go, man, chop off my balls, I'm still mean. [Car door opens, Billy leaves. Door slams shut.]

Girl: Okay, guy. Let's make this quick.

Simon: You wanna drink?

Girl: [brightening]: Yeah.

Simon: We got all kinds of—

Girl: Just gimme that. [Girl takes bottle.] I'm gonna take a real slug.

Simon: Sweetie, I heh already drink like haff of that, so you takem the biggas fucking slug you want. Get som ta money back. [Girl tips the bottle back and it stays there for a few seconds.]

Simon: Jesus.

Girl: What is that? Whiskey?

Simon: Yeah.

Girl: I loved whiskey all my life. Take your pants off, just take them right off, it's easier. [Sound of clothing.] I just pull up my dress, see.

Simon: Hmm.

Girl: Just see what we got here.

Simon: It's clean.

Girl: I got the rubber here.

Simon: Hmmm.

Girl: Waitaminute. [Hand paws through purse.] I gotta use this one. You got a big dick.

Simon: Funny, 'cause I'm a little guy.

Girl: Biggest dick I ever saw was on this short fat guy, Hawaiian or something. [Bored now.] All right, get hard, guy. You can do it.

Simon: That feels good. Very *professional*.

Girl: Think about giving it to me, guy. About putting it in.

Simon: Right.

Girl: Who's on top?

Simon: Me.

Girl: Go easy, my back's killing me.

Simon: All right.

Girl: Go now. Gimme that thing, guy.

Simon: Yeah.

Girl: Uh.

Simon: Can't feel that rubber.

Girl: I put it on.

Simon: Sure?

Girl: I put it on, you can't feel it because you're feeling *me*.

Simon: Huuh.

Girl: I'll squeeze again.

Simon: Uh. That was. Yes, that was good.

Girl: Go, go, go, guy, I ain't billing by the minute here. [Something has jostled the camera and now the screen shows the girl's face; her eyes are open and she looks around while the figure works away on top of her; then she notices the bottle next to her on the floor of the car and grabs it and takes a long drink while he pounds her, the whiskey spilling down her chin. She tips the bottle down, adjusts her hips slightly, and then tips the bottle back again, this time draining an inch out of it. She closes her eyes and lets the bottle fall to the floor of the car. Then she presses both her hands on the figure's back.] Go now, go, come on, give it to me, guy, come on. [There's a long groan and Simon's head slumps intimately against her neck for a moment, but she is already rolling out from beneath him, pulling down her skirt.]

Simon: Fucking rubber.

Girl: It was all right.

Simon: I think it fell off, I couldn't feel it.

Girl: Naw, I could feel it. [Points to his groin.] It's right there! [She finds the bottle again.]

Simon: Take it with you.

Girl: Fuck no, just throw it on the street outside.

Simon: No, I meant the bottle.

Girl: Hey, thanks! [She opens the door and almost immediately comes the sound of another door opening.]

Billy: You still in there?

Simon: I'm all right.

Billy: She's taking our fucking whiskey!

Girl: He gave it to me. [Kicks door shut.]

Billy: You stole it!

Girl: Fuck you, you asshole.

Simon: She's mad at you still.

Billy: Max! Max! Let's get this thing rolling! [The car starts to move. Billy presses the window button and sticks his head out.] Five dollars! Hey, ev-rey-body! This fuck-ing bitch is giving it out for fi-ive dol—[He pulls his head in fast.] Uh-oh, she's catching up. [Something hits the car, the sound of glass breaking.]

Simon: She threw the bottle?

Billy: Yeah. [Looks toward the front of the car.] Max! Don't worry. The car's fine. No problem. Bill me with any problem! [Car slips along in traffic. The jiggle of city lights, the flow of traffic.] That was fucked up.

Simon: A dark episode.

Billy: *Very* dark.

Simon: And where to next?

Billy: I got Harlem, I got East Village, Central Park West . . . I got all kindz possibili-ties.

Simon: Hey, we should turn that thing off.

Billy: It's a two-hour tape, there's gonna be plenty a—

Simon: Gimme that wire. No! Just *give*—Billy, you fucker— [The image breaks. The screen is a snowy static.]

TAPE 69

[Opulent room with high ceilings and thick red drapes to the floor. Well-dressed people moving about. A woman holding a clipboard.

An older gentleman with gray hair surrounded by other, younger people. The camera is not stable, as if handheld or even concealed. A group of men enters casually, but all in the room turn. One of the men is Bill Clinton. He is younger, his hair only newly graying. He is the one, he is the power. Several come over to him. It is clear that they are used to being with him. He is obviously a tall man. The camera nears, unsteadily. A voice is heard to say, "Mr. President?" Clinton looks up, then back at his listener. They talk further; Clinton is waiting to respond, nodding, eyes cutting around the room. The woman with the clipboard approaches him and it is clear that she must speak in private for a moment. The camera is close now. It seems that the camera is concealed upon the person who is drawing closer.]

Woman with clipboard: It's just a scheduling problem.

Clinton: I can't do it.

Woman [toward camera]: Paul? Can you hold them off another hour?

Voice: I don't think so.

Clinton [face reddening, intent]: I don't have time for this.

Voice: We could split the difference and say—

Clinton: No, goddammit. When are you people going to understand that when I say no I mean it? And that your problem is not my problem? Solve it. You all are smart people, I read your résumés. Tell him we'll screw him on the bill if he tries this again. [Slashes hand through air.] Gonna kill me with chickenshit like this. [Clinton detaches himself and moves across room to greet others. Tape ends.]

TAPE 72

[Commuter train, full of men and women in business dress. The windows are dark, it is night. Before the camera are the backs of two men's heads.]

First man:—in the lowest quartile of the firm, I mean, billable hours is one of the measures. We all know that. So I ask him to come into my office and he did and we sat down and I said, "Gerry, we need to talk about how things are going for you." And he became all defensive and said he was putting in the time. I said, "Waitaminute, you billed fifteen hundred and something hours last year, that's not even in the middle." He said he works all the time but that he has a family and has to see them. He's put nine years into the firm and thinks he should get some leeway for that. I said okay, I understood that, but that there's a feeling he's not around enough. I mean, I told him that if he went on vacation with the McCabe thing not yet wrapped up, that it would fall to me and I wouldn't be able to really handle it, and when he came back from vacation, it would be a mess. And that was what had happened. Gerry says he's got a family to attend to, that his little girl was running around at a dinner party and went through a plate glass window and had nerve damage to her foot. His wife is pregnant with their third and he has to take the girl to a physical therapist or something. I say, "Can't you hire somebody to take her, a baby-sitter or something?"

Second man: That's kind of hard to do.

First man: Yeah, well, it's also kinda hard to get the McCabe filings done on time when the senior partner isn't around. I've got a couple of associates—you know, Pete what's-his-name and Linda, they're pretty good, but you know they prepared the basic contract on McCabe and there were some serious problems. These real-estate outfits who've been working in the city twenty, thirty years know all the tricks. Every one. They slip in funny little clauses that look innocuous, you know, and then you find out later that it pertains to some obscure part of the city code, and then you're fucked, because it's in the contract. Ends up costing a couple of million dollars— we've had that happen.

Second man: So what did you tell Gerry?

First man: I told him he's got to take less vacation time, he's got to be around and start making his presence known. I mean, my billable hours have gone down, but that's because I'm out there bringing in business. The guys on the compensation committee understand this. So Gerry says he doesn't see how he can bring his hours up. He's working around the clock all the time, his wife is on him to be home, he's running from one place to the next, like all of us, right? I tell him that he's got to understand that he has a problem at the firm. I can't protect him anymore. I *won't* protect him anymore. He says, "What do you mean?" We're both thinking the same thing. Two kids in private school, third coming, the whole deal. So I say, "Let's work something out where I know you're going to be billing, say, nineteen hundred hours a year and you'll take only one-week vacations."

Second man: What did he say?

First man: He didn't say anything. It's what he *did*.

Second man: What?

First man: You're not going to believe it. He freaked.

Second man: What?

First man: Yeah. He says nothing. He gets up from the desk, stands up, and turns his back to me. I think, Okay, that's weird. Then I realize what he's doing. He's taken his dick out and he's pissing—

Second man: What? Get out of here!

First man: I'm not kidding. He walks around pissing here and there, he turns around and flips the piss up and some of it hits my desk, and then he goes over to the computer and pisses a little on that, and then he's done. Zips up. He sits down again in his chair and looks at me. Like nothing happened. I'm just sitting there. I'm thinking about a million things. Can I fire this guy right now? No. That has to go through the committee. Only Carl can fire on the spot and he's in Bermuda. I'm wondering if Gerry is genuinely crazy, is he dangerous?

Second man: Gerry's just sitting there, calmly?

First man: Yeah, he's very calm, too. Not even angry looking. And one drop has even soaked into one of my Mueller depositions that I was reading. We just sat there. Then I told him I thought he'd better figure that he was going to be let go. I said this as calmly as I could. I mean, the thing is already done, he's gone way off, right? So then he says, "I will do my damn best to get my hours up to nineteen hundred a year, John, and you can be sure that I'll arrange my vacations so I don't take more than a week at a time."

Second man: That's weird.

First man: Then he leaves. So couple days later, the following Monday, Carl is back, and he and I and Gerry are in Carl's office. Not the small one but the big one down on the sixth floor. I tell him what happened. Carl turns to Gerry. Gerry says that's ridiculous, that's insane. Yes, we had a discussion about hours and I'm going to get back on the wagon, but pissed in his office? That's crazy, Carl.

Second man: Wait, wait, he's denying the whole thing? Didn't it leave a smell, or—

First man: No, the cleaning service was in there that same night; they dust and empty the trash and wipe everything down and vacuum. There was no smell left, no sign. So I had no proof. I'm sitting there looking at Carl, and I know Carl is thinking to himself, Which is crazier? One of my senior partners pissed in another's office, or one of my senior partners *claimed* that another senior partner pissed in his office? Both things are equally crazy. I can see Carl thinking like this. I've worked for him a long time—

Second man: So has Gerry.

First man: Yeah, so has Gerry. So Carl looks at both of us. Then he's looking at me with those tired old eyes. I know what he's thinking. I have no evidence. Just my accusation. Then he's looking at Gerry. Now, Gerry may not be putting in the hours, but the guy's a straight arrow, always looks right, doesn't even flirt with the secretaries.

Second man: Yeah.

First man: So Carl just sits there, thinking. Then he turns to Gerry and says, "How's your little girl doing?" And Gerry says something like "She's doing much better, matter of fact. The nerve damage in the heel isn't too bad." Then Carl says his own daughter once broke her foot horseback riding and it had to be set and then rebroken twice, and he used to hear her crying in her bedroom from the pain. And Gerry, that motherfucker, is just nodding to himself. Then Carl says to Gerry, "The doctors can do amazing things these days, I think it will be okay." And I'm thinking to myself, Waitaminute, this isn't why we're here, we're here because the guy pissed on my rug and my papers and everything, and so now we're having a sad little talk about Gerry's daughter? And so I say, "Hey, wait, Carl, we're talking about the fact that Gerry pissed in my office." [Now the second man looks out the dark window.] And as soon as I say that, I'm in trouble. Carl turns to me and he says, "That's not what I'm talking about. I'm talking about something else. I'm talking about a little girl crying in her bedroom because her foot hurts." Then I'm thinking I better watch out. I mean, this is the man who took on AT&T, right, and won. So I say nothing. Then Carl says, "My little girl used to sit in her room and cry quietly to herself because she didn't want us to hear her. We told her she had to be brave and not cry, and it was the stupidest thing we ever did with her." He's going on like this, I can't believe it. Then I realize that Gerry is going to get away with it. He's pissed all over my office and nothing is going to happen to him, I see that now. And Carl keeps going, and Gerry, that sly motherfucker, is just nodding and listening and maybe looking sort of like he's got a tear in his eye. And I'm freaking out. He's going to get away with it, he actually—

Second man [rising as train slows]: This is my stop.

First man: Oh. Yeah. Okay. See you . . . what, Friday?

Second man: Yep. [He steps past first man and into the aisle; holding his briefcase, he walks down the aisle and gets in line with other commuters. The train stops, making them all take a little step back, and then they file out. The sound of the train accelerates. The first man can be seen scratching his nose. Perhaps he sighs. Then he reaches for his briefcase, unsnaps it, and pulls out a sheaf of papers, which he begins to read. The train continues, stop after stop. The man eventually puts away his papers and stares out the window. Streaks of rain have appeared on the glass outside.]

I popped out the videocassette. Clearly Simon was interested in fragments of what might be termed "found reality," even if that reality included himself in the back of a limousine with a prostitute. I wondered if he had spent long hours studying these clips; he was a movie director—someone with an eye for the nuance of human behavior and movement and voice, someone who might feel himself instructed by these tapes in some meaningful way. Or then again, he might have just liked them for their voyeuristic satisfaction; after all, we are nothing now if not a nation of voyeurs. I stood up from the chair and opened the door and peered down the hall. Nothing, just a row of doors on either side and the expensive Persian runner down the center and a row of lights on the ceiling.

Back inside, I pulled out another tape. On the label, in clear handwriting, was the notation TAKEN BY M. FULGERI 5/94.

TAPE 67

[A Third World village. Low buildings of cheap construction, burntout cars. Camera pans across village; no one is in sight. But then it is clear that there are shapes on the ground across the way and the camera proceeds in that direction. Sound of footsteps, two people walking. The shapes are humans, flopped on the ground, motionless. Black bodies. They are piled casually, here and there, as if the whole village has been thrown violently from their beds and remained asleep. A mother with her child here, two little boys there, an old man, a small child impaled upon a thick pole—

Unidentified voice, British accent: I'd just keep it loaded, in case.

Second voice, Italian accent: Try the church. [Camera moves toward a larger building that has a peaked tin roof and low, glassless windows cut into the walls. The camera passes a woman lying in the dust, her breasts hacked off. In the entry to the church the camera is suddenly dark, and then the photoelectric eye adjusts.]

Italian voice: Yes, there, too. [Camera now enters a church full of bodies, all dead, piled on one another. It is impossible to count, but certainly there are hundreds, maybe even a thousand, all dead, mostly children, their faces slack in the repose of death, flies buzzing from one to another. There are handprints on the wall—a hicroglyphic of swipings and draggings, suggestive of frantic activity. At the far end of the church there is movement, and the camera zooms closer; it is a small dog, eating in jerky bites; it looks up, its ears moving, and then looks down again and resumes eating. Camera pans back and forth over the dead; they had clearly herded themselves into the church for refuge, far too many than could sit on the pews, and the density of corpses suggests a methodically brisk pace of killing by hand. And yet the killers have lingered here and there; several of the bodies show extensive damage to the mouth, as if teeth have been cut out.]

British voice: I thought I heard some shots.

Italian voice: No, no. I don't think so.

British voice: Maybe they're killing the dogs.

Italian voice: You know what they all are doing now in my country?

British voice: No, what?

Italian voice: They watch the NBA play-offs. You know this thing? Very big in Italy. Basketball. Patrick Ewing. Everyone knows all the names.

British voice: Have a look over there. [Camera swings around again, taking in the panorama of death, and then proceeds outside the church. Three soldiers with blue U.N. helmets approach.]

First soldier: We ask you now to leave, please.

British voice: We're documenting here. Colonel Aziz knows we're here.

First soldier: My orders say to tell you now to leave, please. Thank you very much. Thank you. I am thanking you. Thank you. [Jerky panorama of church and earth and blue sky. Tape ends.]

I turned off the machine. But for the soft rush of the ventilation system, the room was utterly quiet now, and I was surprised to hear my own exhalation. Why had Caroline not told me about what was on the tapes? I found this vaguely disturbing. She and I had now entered into some kind of manipulated dialogue. But what kind of statement was she trying to make about her dead husband and perhaps about herself, too? That Simon Crowley was a connoisseur of human suffering? That he saw nothing of the goodness of life, that by collecting examples of what was ugly and dark and eternal about man's nature he understood it better? That he was a true artist? A false one? I did not know or especially care. There is no image that is unavailable now. In terms of marvel or fantasia or

pornography, it's all been done. We carry inside ourselves an encyclope-
dia of ingested images; we can dream in slowmo and split-screen; in today's special effect and about tomorrow's atrocity. None of Simon
Crowley's images, even the tape from Rwanda, seemed less disturbing or
more real than the daily offerings on CNN. I'd only seen a small por-
tion of them, but they suggested that Simon Crowley had developed a
fascination with "authentic" images. Whether these tapes were studies
made for the purpose of improving upon his movie art or constituted
an end in themselves was a question I couldn't answer. No, the significance of the tapes for me was not that they characterized Simon but
that they might reveal something about Caroline.

I was about to slip another tape into the machine when my beeper
went off. My irritation was quickly superseded by fear. GO TO MR.
HOBBS, the message read, followed by a phone number. GO TO MR.
HOBBS. The only people with the beeper's number were my wife,
Josephine, the cops, my father upstate, Bobby Dealy, now off-duty, and
the city editor. Hobbs, or one of his representatives, had called the newsroom and gotten the number from the city editor, who, although he
knew the number was private, would not have refused Hobbs. Nor, of
course, would I.

HE MAINTAINED HIS INTERNATIONAL HEADQUARTERS in London but
kept a New York office in several floors of a building not far from Grand
Central. Outside the bank, I stood in the cold, wondering whether I should
call ahead to get an idea of what might await me or simply blunder into it.
I opted for the call, found a pay phone, and was put through to Hobb's office. "Yes, we are waiting to see you," said a secretary. "Mr. Hobbs would
like a word with you."

"We could talk on the phone right now," I suggested.

"Mr. Hobbs would like to see you in person, Mr. Wren."

It was almost five-thirty in the afternoon. "Now?"

"Now would be wonderful."

I didn't answer.

"Tomorrow Mr. Hobbs will be in Los Angeles," she said. "May we expect you in the next twenty minutes?"

The only allowable answer was yes. I hung up and put my arm out for a cab. They flew along Park Avenue as if whipped by the wind; it was the hour that men and women, hunched in coats and hats and scarves, hurried through the gloom, sensing that they were made small by the forces of nature and time, knowing that in a blink it would be all new people in the same stone grid. I wanted to be with my wife and children, warm in the kitchen, Sally drawing at the dining-room table, Tommy rearranging the magnets on the refrigerator. In my cab I pondered why a billionaire would summon a lowly columnist. I could think of no reason that comforted me. Hobbs was a man who did not waste time on people who could not provide him with something he desired.

When I arrived, a secretary was waiting for me like a sentry next to the elevator door. She smiled officially and took me back to a paneled office. Out the window, ten blocks to the south, stood the Empire State Building. I was introduced to a Walter Campbell—a polished walking stick of a man in a black suit who shook my hand vigorously, as if he were running for office.

"Always enjoy your columns," he said with a London accent. "Quite vivid, I've thought."

I blinked.

"Very good then, as to why we're here this afternoon," he said, leaning forward. "Now, this is an off-the-record conversation. You are present as an employee of the company, not, and I repeat that expressly, *not* as a journalist."

I sat.

Campbell followed my eyes. "I assume this is understood."

"Okay," I said.

Campbell nodded. "Right. You are here because we have a problem. None of us has created the problem, but there is, however, a problem." He looked at me. "My difficulty here—I—" Campbell smoothed his tie, then dropped his eyes to a piece of paper on his desk and turned it over. He gazed at it for perhaps ten seconds, then lifted his eyes to me. "You, sir, have recently been in the company of a certain woman who is not your wife. I attach no moralistic interpretation to this fact. I simply state what is known."

I sat there, confused, anxious.

"You first spent time with her two nights ago, leaving her apartment sometime after two-thirty A.M. You visited her the next day in the afternoon and spent nearly three hours with her. Today, you met her at a restaurant, and then proceeded—"

"I know where I've been."

"Right. Of course. Mr. Hobbs is going to ask you to accomplish something on his behalf. It is neither illegal nor dangerous, nor, in my opinion, unreasonable. Thus, the nature of our request is quite—" Here Campbell's face became dull and cold, so much so that I understood now that he was an expert at this sort of matter, a corporate bagman. "Quite mandatory, I should say."

"Or you'll give me the heave-ho?"

"Well, we would have a response. Let us simply say that." Campbell lifted a stapled document from his desk and handed it to me. "We've had a quick look at your contract. Look at page three, down at the bottom, please. There is a clause I should like for you to see."

"You're referring to 'professional conduct'?"

"No. Next line."

" 'Insubordination'?"

"Yes," said Campbell.

"I haven't done anything," I said.

"Yes. That's true."

"What do you want?"

Campbell stared at me, then nodded vigorously, once. "We have reached the end of this part of our conversation. If you will kindly follow me . . ." He stood and indicated another door, which he opened. I followed him down a short paneled hallway, through a door, and then into another office, also paneled.

There, sitting in peaceful immensity, drinking tea, was Hobbs himself. He looked up and lifted a giant arm. "Mr. Porter Wren, chronicler of the people's woe! Good afternoon, sir, do come in!" His fingers flicked in the direction of a chair, and his green eyes followed me as I entered the room.

To one side, set in the wall, were five digital clocks: HONG KONG, SYDNEY, LONDON, NEW YORK, LOS ANGELES. When I was seated, Campbell nodded stiffly at his boss, and then drew the door shut behind him as he left. "Quite cold out, I'm told. Now then, I'm delighted that you are here and that we may discuss a certain question." He smoothed his immense hands down the wool of his vest. He seemed like the globe itself. "I hope very much that we like each other, that we can reach a mutually agreeable understanding . . ." He lifted his eyebrows, as if acting out what my expression might be if I found out what would happen if such an agreement were not reached. "I'll get to the matter straightaway. You, sir, are having an affair with Miss Caroline Crowley, and—"

"Look," I protested, my anger returning to me, "this is of no—"

"I would ask you not to interrupt!" Hobbs dropped his hands on the top of the desk, palms down, fingers spread. "A bloody *awful* habit of Americans. Now then, why do I *claim* you are having an affair? Because you *are*, sir. I should add that it is no matter to me. Except in that it presents an opportunity. Life is full of opportunities, no?"

He was playing with me. "Of one sort or another," I answered.

"Yes, quite. This is one sort and not the other. This is an opportunity for me to get something I want and an opportunity for you not to get something you don't want." He tilted his head at me in such a way that I was to understand that he was irritated by his own cleverness. "Now then, Caroline Crowley is—"

A chime sounded and Campbell reappeared. "Excuse me. You did have an appointment with the conservator," he said.

"What was it today?" Hobbs asked, ignoring me.

"I believe it was masks."

Hobbs swirled his hand in the air. "Send him in."

A short, well-dressed man in his fifties appeared, pushing a wheeled display device the size of a high-school chalkboard, on which were hung about a dozen African masks, carved from ivory, faces elongated and fearsome.

"Mr. Hobbs, we have a very excellent selection today," he began, a butcher with his cuts. "Rather fine, I would say, these being excellent examples of sixteenth-century Nigerian—"

Hobbs thrust out a finger. "I'll take that one on the left and the two larger ones in the middle—"

"Ah!" the man said, as if genuinely delighted by the choice, "the ceremonial mourning mask, a very—"

"And the one on the bottom . . . yes—that one."

"*Yes,* the fertility—"

"How much?"

"For all of them?" the man squeaked.

"Yes, quickly."

The man looked from mask to mask. "Well, fifty . . . and eighty-two . . . it would come to about two hundred and sixty thousand, I believe . . . yes, that is—"

"One-seventy."

The man looked as if he was trying to smile while being shot in the chest. "I'm very sorry, I did not—"

"One hundred and seventy thousand for all four, take it or leave it."

The man nodded miserably. "You've been most generous."

"See Campbell on the way out."

"Why, thank you, Mr. Hobbs, I'm quite pleased that we have been able to—"

"Good day, sir." He turned back to me, green eyes bright. "Now, I was saying . . . yes, Caroline Crowley is sending me videotapes, Mr. Wren. It's the same one each time. I don't like getting these tapes. Only by the grace of my loyal personal staff do these tapes not find their way out of my office. I personally destroy each one, and then, sooner or later, she sends me another one. Here, to this office. It makes me a bit insane, Mr. Wren, it makes me"—he paused, his cavernous mouth open, eyebrows arched— "it makes me irrational, Mr. Wren. And why? For the obvious reason, Mr. Wren. I'm afraid that one of these tapes will be out and get played on television or something. It's quite a nasty little tape, very embarrassing, I must say."

"You're doing something unsavory?"

He hummed. "I am compromised by the tape, let us say that."

"You want to tell me what's on the tape?"

"Not at all."

"When did the tapes start coming?"

"The first?" Hobbs frowned. "The first was about sixteen months ago."

"Before or after Simon—"

"*After*, Mr. Wren, shortly *after* the death of her paramour or husband or whatever he was."

"Why is Caroline sending you the tape, if I may ask?"

"Ah, an impossible thing to answer."

"You know her?"

Hobbs looked at me and wheezed heavily. "I am *familiar* with her." He waited for me to understand whatever this meant, exactly. "Do I genuinely *know* the woman? No. Is it possible for any man to know a woman? I doubt it."

"Do you know that she's sending it?"

"As a matter of documented fact, no. As a matter of extreme likelihood, yes. I know that she is aware of the existence of the tape and its contents; I know, too, that she is the only *logical* person I can think of who would be in a position to have it."

"She wants money for it?"

"Apparently not. There has been no request made. Oh, it's bloody fucking psychologically clever, you know!"

He had a strange, energetic magnetism to him and for a moment I was silent.

"Why can't you hire some invisible people to invisibly go through her apartment or follow her around or do whatever invisible people do?"

"Oh, we have, we have," Hobbs said, "not that she doesn't know it. But nothing."

I wondered if he knew about the rented vault in the Malaysian bank. "And so I'm here because you want *me* to ask her to stop sending the tape?"

"Oh, better than that, sir." Hobbs smoothed his hands against each other. "A good bit better. I myself have asked her to stop doing so on a number of occasions. I even offered to buy it from her, at a sum notable for its absurdity. But she always insists to me that she is *not* sending the tape, which, frankly, I do not believe."

"So I ask her about the tape and she tells me she's not sending it."

Here he leaned forward malevolently. "Then you keep going, sir. You make do. A little pluck, a little luck. You improvise. I am told that this afternoon you entered a certain Malaysian bank with our Miss Crowley. She has been seen to go into this bank from time to time, and naturally I wonder if she may be keeping the tape there."

I looked at him. "This whole thing is crazy—"

"That's right, sir!" He stood suddenly and I realized that in addition to being a grotesquely wide man, Hobbs was quite tall, too. "Crazy is just the word for it! A crazy, bloody irritation to someone like *me* who must conduct business in thirty-odd countries. It is a point of *business*, Mr. Wren, nothing more, nothing less. I cannot have this tape just *circulating* in the universe." He waved his meaty hands about him, and the very size of them seemed to inscribe the cosmos around his gigantic bulk. "You are my employee. I can fire you and I can fire your bosses all the way up the line. I can fire everyone in your newspaper, Mr. Wren, and if I did, it would cause me no loss of sleep. I'd hire someone else. I've got a number of very good people in London this minute who would love to work in New York. Love to flit about the Manhattan candle! Talent is cheap, Mr. Wren, yours included. You think you're the only one who can tramp around some sad little scene and hack out the requisite dose of maudlin prose? Please, sir. *Please!* I can throw a *bone* in the *street* and get a newspaper staff. I've done it in Melbourne, I've done it in London, and I could do it here. Now then, you are my employee and you are fucking Caroline Crowley and that means you are *in her life.* I want you to get that tape for me, Mr. Wren. I want that tape bloody well fast, and I'm not going to listen to any protest about it. Good-bye, sir."

I didn't stand. "Hobbs, you're out of your mind."

"I said good-bye, sir."

We stared at each other. "Hey, know what? I barely know the woman. If you haven't scared it out of her, or stolen it from her, then I'm not going to get it. Seriously." I held out my hands and shrugged. "Right? Plus I could spare myself the trouble and hop to another paper."

"Won't work," Hobbs said. "We'll come up with some reason you were fired. Embezzling company gold, perhaps. Excessive drinking at social functions! Some very nasty, protracted lawsuit. Motions and countermotions, lawyers slavering away on my tab, lawyers slavering away on yours." The theatricality of the conceit amused him. "You could countersue for litigational harassment or whatever it is called over here and then we could do the same. We could draw it out for years. Years! Or as long as your money held out. Believe me, this is not hard to do. I did it in Australia just last year, as a matter of fact. Fellow called my bluff and it went very poorly for him after that." His expression went cold. "I know a bit about you, Mr. Wren, I know how difficult it would be for you to fend off my lawyers, even with your wife's income. I know what you paid for that property in downtown Manhattan. Quite a bit, yes. And you did a very smart thing, sir. You took out a mortgage, which men have been doing since the fifth century. You, sir, being an educated man, have studied the interest rate cycles. You did quite well! You re-mortgaged your house in December of 1993, and you hit the twenty-three-year low in American interest rates. You felt quite good about that, I'd bet, and judging from the size of the mortgage, you figured the more leverage, the better. Quite clever! Every last penny, I'd bet! What did you do? Mortgage your wife's shoes? Mortgage the dog?" And here he threw his head back and laughed at the vanities of a small man such as I. "You, sir, are carrying a mortgage of five hundred and twenty thousand dollars! A shocking amount! You need five thousand dollars a month to service that loan. By my calculations your salary goes toward the house and your wife's covers everything else. Do you *dare* fall out of work for three or four months? Do you think the bank will be forgiving if you fall behind?"

I shrugged. This was all bluster, so far as I was willing to let on. Lisa made a good salary; if need be we could live on it. The house could be sold.

"Or we could simply let your wife know what it is you are up to."

This scared me, but I rubbed my eyes in boredom.

"*Or* we might find that your wife had operated on someone we know and that, sadly, she did not do such a terrific job, and we could then secure an allegation of malpractice—" He saw me look up quickly. "Yes, perhaps *that* is what you will find motivating."

When two men sit in a room confronting each other, as I did then with

Hobbs, their own two fathers are also there. His father had created and then built up a chain of newspapers in Australia in the 1940s, and I knew that as a boy Hobbs had sat at the knee of some of the most powerful men on that continent, being schooled in the political and financial arts. My own father, who owned two hardware stores, was the son of a potato farmer who'd had a bag of arsenic fall on him in 1947. My grandfather had sucked up a lungful of the poison and had never been the same, weakening, then losing the farm my father grew up on. Consequently, my father had conducted himself with a cautious dignity. A good man, a kind man, devoted to his motherless son but incapable of teaching me about the worldly matters of money and power, for he had none. How he would hate to see where I was then.

"Let us understand each other, Mr. Wren," Hobbs went on. "I would not be engaging you in this way unless I thought you were capable of fulfilling my request. I have read your file. Let's be frank, you and I. You are a broken-down hack columnist. I have perhaps fifty men and women like you working at my papers in England and Australia and in the States. I know the type. Formerly ambitious, good for the legwork. Now? Well, hmm—now not so good. Jaded, making a lot of money—what are we paying you?" He looked down at the figure on his sheet of paper and shrugged; it was a pittance to him, shoeshine money, dandelion dust. "You've got some stock grammatical constructions, and some reporters' tricks, and you're careful with the good columns, and very clever with the bad ones, and you stay late to be sure the copy editors don't weaken the way you've positioned your quotes. This sounds familiar, I know. You vacillate between deep cynicism and boundless faith. You feel beaten down by the roar. You love your wife and children, but everybody is getting a little older every day. And then along comes a woman. You figure you are not getting into so much. But this was where you were wrong, Mr. Wren. This was where you didn't know enough. I came attached to Caroline Crowley. Imagine my delight, Mr. Wren, imagine how pleased I was to learn that Caroline Crowley's latest lover is a trained investigative reporter! And one of my own employees!" Hobb's face lifted into a fleshy mask of manic delight. "Here was the man who would get that tape back for me! As I said, Mr. Wren, I've read some of your work. And you know what? You *were* good . . . once. People would talk to you, tell you things they wouldn't tell anyone else. You had something. Now, who knows? What are you, almost forty? That's rather early to burn out. You need a challenge, I think. You were good once and now you're going to have to become good *again*, sir. For me."

THE ESSENCE OF A THREAT: A task is demanded of one; if the task is performed, the threat is removed. If the task is not performed, the one who has made the threat chooses whether or not to enforce the punishment, and he understands that if he does not enforce it, then soon no one will believe his threats. I know this. I know this in a thousand ways, not the least of which is as a parent. Husbands and wives also threaten each other, although usually not so overtly. An eyebrow will do. A muttered response. Lisa takes a breath and holds it and then glares. I learned long ago that her threats, though rare, are to be respected; after all, here is a woman who regularly presses a scalpel into human flesh. I take her threats as gravely as I did those of my high-school football coach, a bona fide sadist who used to promise us "whistle laps," a dreaded punishment in the August heat, if we didn't "look sharp" in practice. His was a system of interlocking, escalating threats, not just to one's immediate threshold of pain but to one's very seventeen-year-old male essence. At the Champlain Valley Athletic Conference championship game, played in Plattsburgh, New York, on December 2, 1977, with everyone in the world I knew and loved sitting in the grandstands, my coach threatened to have me "folding towels on the bench" if I didn't put the hit on the opposing team's wide receiver, a black guy named Pernell "D.J." Snyder, who was on his way to a full scholarship at USC in part because he ran the hundred-yard dash in 9.4 seconds— exactly one second faster than I did. D.J. was terrifying my coach with his blazing, high-stepping sprints down the sideline. "Do you love towels, Wren?" my coach screamed. "Do you love soft little white towels that you can fold?" D.J., getting warm with the game, was becoming *faster* and, sensing my fear, had started trash-talking me in his deep voice: "Yo, boy, I'ma catch one on you, boy." Only the ineptitude of the opposing quarter-back had thus far saved me. If D.J. actually caught the ball, he was gone— I could grow wings, I could beg God, nothing would let me catch him. Then, in the fourth quarter, with our team clinging to a three-point lead, the ball was finally thrown accurately to D.J., and as I watched it spiral across the blue sky—as I saw D.J.'s hands reach out, his black fingers wiggling—I understood that I had a choice to hit him cleanly under the knees or administer some real hurt. I went high and hard, with everything in my one hundred and seventy-eight pounds. D.J. dropped the ball and grunted as he was knocked out. I dislocated my shoulder, damaging it forever. Both of us lay still on the cold field. I was penalized, but we won the game. That night, whacked out on painkillers, I lay in the front seat of my father's pickup truck with my girlfriend. She was a sweet girl named Annie Frey, and I used to beg her to wear her seat belt because I thought she drove too fast. She couldn't see the threat of her own recklessness, however, and she rolled her car over four months later and bled to death on a dark stretch of road that I have purposefully never returned to.

Yes, I understand what a threat is and that is why I do not understand why I dallied for four or five days after Hobbs threatened me. No doubt I resented his intrusion into my affairs—my *affair*. Instead I fished around for a column. There was all manner of mishap in the city, but none of it seemed remarkable. Shoot-'em-ups, sex murders, money-laundering rings—nothing clicked. The city editor kept changing the page-one story, flipping between national and local stories. No celebrities were getting arrested, collapsing onstage, or otherwise being outrageous. The TV guys abandoned their Richard Lancaster death-watch and he promptly died. No one cared. The criminals were nickel-and-diming it. The politicians were all in the islands. The firemen were saving everybody. The city's snow-removal budget was spent. My editor looked at me once or twice, his expression meaning *Got anything good?* but he could tell I wasn't turning up the right cards. I floated a lame piece of ha-ha about an old guy who was retiring from the Coney Island freak show because kids were no longer interested in seeing him bang nails up his nose or swallow smoking cigarettes. They preferred the freak shows on the Internet. Irony, ha-ha. I was *wasting time.* I see now that those precious days could have made a difference, but I let them slide by, as if paralytically contemplating the insertion of a long needle, the injection of which would jolt me into frenetic activity. On those mornings, I retrieved the newspapers piled in front of our gate and flipped through the business sections with a sick fascination, seeking news that showed Hobbs was preoccupied with topics other than me. As his secretary had said he would, Hobbs had flown west, and I was able to track his movements from Los Angeles to Hong Kong, where he was meeting with Chinese authorities about the broadcast capabilities of his television network, and then on to Melbourne and New Delhi. In each instance he commented on whatever deal was pending or completed, or on the general direction of his company, and in reference to some South Korean officials who were slow to respond to a $900 million offer he'd made, he was quoted in the *Asian Wall Street Journal* as saying, "I don't wait for others to see it my way; I state my case and then proceed, thank you." The words weren't about me, but nonetheless I gaped anxiously at them. Isn't the measure of the man in the smallest utterances as much as in the grandest gestures?

I needed, of course, to contact Caroline about Hobbs, and the fact that she had not called me after our visit to the Malaysian bank was both a matter of relief and anxiety. I wanted to see her again (yes, I wanted to *fuck* her again, too—there was, I greedily sensed, a bounty there yet to be plundered), but at the same time I wondered if perhaps I should wisely call it quits, now, before I got in further. And hey, maybe she had beaten me to it, maybe *she* was done with *me.* She seemed quite capable of doing so without apology or explanation; there was a coldness in her warm chest, and if I was honest with myself, I would admit to being interested in *that* quality about her, too. But such a decision seemed unlikely, given her references to her mysterious problem and her effort to winch me into her life. Then again, perhaps she had deemed me no good in bed or her fiancé had floated back into the picture. I didn't know how often she saw him, or where, or under what conditions, or if he was likely to learn of me, a development I wished to avoid; on the street, it is the young men who burn brightest with jealousy. Older men presented with a woman's infidelity are furious, true, but also privately contemplative of the nuances of the situation. The younger men tend to look for a gun; the older ones, for a drink. Yes, I could work up quite a bit of anxiety about young Charlie, who was able-bodied and knew where to find me.

If I was confused about what would happen next with Caroline, I did know that I had to get back into the Malaysian bank and have a look at every last one of the videotapes stored there. I wasn't sure if I believed that Caroline would bedevil Hobbs with a video and then lie to him about it. But I couldn't simply disbelieve it either. Could I come straight out and ask her for the tape Hobbs wanted? That didn't seem wise. I didn't know her well enough yet. Better, I thought, to keep learning about what mattered to her; I made a point of seeing *Rictus* and *Minutes and Seconds*, Simon Crowley's second and third big-budget movies. Both were utterly unrelated in style and content to the grainy, jerky videotapes I'd watched, yet were preoccupied, like the tapes, with the infinite ways humans abuse one another. Was there another connection? I could only wonder.

Lisa, meanwhile, did not notice my anxiousness, for she had her own worries. She had been swimming a lot—slipping out an hour early in the mornings to a health club where she could put in forty or fifty laps—and this meant only one thing: She had a big operation coming up. One night, after the kids were asleep, I asked her about it as she washed her face.

"Toe transfer," she exhaled, her face a soapy mask.

Some unfortunate soul had lost a thumb. The patient in question, said Lisa, was a thirty-seven-year-old woman, the manager of a $500 million mutual fund, whose left thumb had been amputated by a boat propeller while she was scuba diving in Cancún the previous summer. The thumb was not retrieved. It was a risky operation and required an evaluation of the patient's psychological condition. Lisa showed me the woman's file, which, in addition to the usual write-up, included a photo of a woman's hand with the thumb sliced cleanly off and various lesser lacerations. "That was three weeks after the accident," Lisa noted. After the injuries had healed, skin from the woman's groin had been attached to the stump and web of the thumb.

"Tomorrow is the toe?" I asked.

Lisa nodded. It was an epic operation, lasting eight hours. Only two or three people in the city were capable of doing it. At six the next morning, Lisa would "harvest" the woman's toe, which would be kept cold and dry, and then spend hour upon meticulous hour connecting tendons, veins, and nerves. In effect, the operation was a transplant, and the recipient was also the donor; the patient was trading one amputation for another, and if the operation was botched—well, Lisa Wren, microvascular orthopedic surgeon, didn't botch operations, she swam laps ahead of time.

"It's all under the scope?"

"Yes." She dried her face. "First the dorsal and volar vessels—the arteries, then the neurovascular bundles."

"The toe is alive again at that point?"

"We hope. Then the bone and tendons and the joint capsules and skin."

"You'll knock it out of the park."

She shrugged. "I need some new eyepieces made."

"Microscope scratched?"

"No. My eyes are changing."

"Getting worse?"

"Just a little. But I like to have the extra resolution, the clarity."

"You're going to do a great job," I told her. "You always go through this and you always do a great job."

The next morning, with Lisa gone early, I decided that if my wife could sew a toe onto a hand, then I could pick up a phone. I called Caroline and told her I wanted to see the rest of the tapes. "Which ones did you already look at?" she asked, her voice husky with sleep. Remember how late she gets up, I told myself, that means she's awake late into the night.

"The garbagemen, the two lawyers on the train, Clinton getting mad."

"Number sixty-seven?"

"Which one was that?"

"Rwanda."

"Yes, that one."

I heard Josephine downstairs with Sally and Tommy.

"Number three?"

"Which one is that?"

"The men in the prison. It's short."

"No."

"When do you want to go back?"

"Today. This afternoon."

Caroline said she would arrange my access with the bank. "You could come over afterward," she suggested.

I wasn't ready to see her. "Tomorrow," I said.

"But tomorrow your column is due," she protested. "You're free today."

"Not actually."

"I'll be most disappointed."

"I doubt it."

"I'll run off with the first man I see."

"Charlie?"

"Maybe a policeman. I like policemen."

"Might be fun."

"I could do it—you don't know me."

"That's true." I thought of Hobbs; how did he know Caroline?

Now Sally ran into the room.

"Daddy, we have to go to school!" she shrieked.

"Yes, sweetie."

"Is that your daughter?" asked Caroline in my ear.

"Yes," I said into the receiver. Sally had jumped on my lap. "You'll call the bank for me?"

"Yes. And Mr. Wren?" Caroline added.

"What?"

"Get your column done."

Yes, I told myself. Yes. But first I needed to take Sally to school. The nine-block walk was a duty that I undertook happily, for I believed that it lay outside of whatever troubles I now glimpsed, and after saying good-bye to Josephine and Tommy, Sally and I walked there, with me holding her hand the entire way. We passed a low wall, and I hoisted her up so that she could walk atop it, her feet lifting high, as if she were marching. She became so agitated with happiness that she forgot to watch where she was going and fell into my arms. Then we were on Eighth Avenue. One of the laundries had a grimy fountain with four or five half-rotten goldfish swimming around in it disconsolately, and we looked at them, as we always did, and I explained that Chinese people came from a place called China, and then we passed by the baker's shop, where there was often a fat old cat in the window, blinking into the morning sun. Then we inspected the melting snow, and flitted past the newsstands—magazine racks of joyful disaster and approved scandal and eternal fad—and then onward, to the little private elementary school that Sally attended.

The school appeared to be a hub of enlightenment and bliss. For the children this may have been true, but for the parents the morning trip to school is a ritual of discomfort. Although in Manhattan everyone may presumably remain strangers if they wish, in practice this is not true. The parents look at one another, at one another's clothes and spouses and cars. Measuring. And just as the children take immediate likes and dislikes to one another, so, too, do their parents, but these irritations and judgments and affections are cloaked in ritual politeness. Most of the kids are dropped off by their mothers, and these women break into two camps: the hard-core professionals, dressed in business suits and pumps, who deposit their children in a ritualized spasm of guilt; and the freelancers, part-timers, and stay-at-homes, who have more time, yet who eye the professional women with a mixture of envy and maternal superiority. These two groups have their own hierarchies and channels of gossip. But the mothers are different in other ways. Some are on their first child, some are pregnant again, others are done, thank you. Some are happily married, some are not, some are divorced, and a handful are lesbian or living with two men or God knows what. The few dads who regularly drop off their kids, myself included, understand that the mothers approve of our involvement with our children or suspect that we are deadbeats—or both. And indeed, none of the dads who have the real killer corporate jobs *ever* drop off their children. They're in the office by seven, yanking on society's big levers.

I followed Sally up to the second floor and reminded her to hang up her coat. The classroom smelled like fish, and indeed, the teachers, Patty and Ellen, had a red snapper, quite dead, lying in a pan.

"We're going to paint it!" Sally said, pulling on my hand.

"Yes," said Patty, a kindly woman of about forty. "Do you want to get a smock?"

Sally put on a little yellow smock and began to dip a thick brush into some red paint. The idea was to paint the fish, then press a piece of paper on top of it. The fish would then be washed and readied for the next child.

Patty watched to see that Sally was occupied, then said to me, "Mr. Wren, I'd like to show you something that Sally drew yesterday."

She pulled out a drawing from Sally's folder. Five stick figures: Mom, Dad, Sally, Tommy, and Josephine. Each had a lurid scrawl of hair, herky-jerky limbs, big smiles. "I always ask the children what they are drawing," Patty said, "and Sally told me who each person was. I asked what this black thing was"—she pointed to a black, spiderish scribble next to the figure of Josephine—"and she told me it was the gun that Josephine keeps in her bag."

I looked directly into her face, aghast.

Patty nodded. "I asked her again. I said, 'What is that?' And she repeated it."

"Jesus." I'd seen the bag a million times; Josephine pulled out all kinds of things from it: potions, religious tracts, asthma inhalers, junk mail, just about anything. The bag was always left on a certain chair in the living room, within reach of the children.

"I thought you should know," Patty said.

"Absolutely. Yes."

"We talked about calling you, but I know you and Mrs. Wren both work late . . ."

I nodded. "Now I have to find out if it's true."

Patty looked at me. She'd taught children for a long time. She had seen a lot of parents, too, and preferred, I could tell, to trust their children.

LISA WAS NOT TO BE DISTURBED, not when she was looking at a freshly severed thirty-seven-year-old toe through a surgical microscope, trying to figure out how to connect it to the thirty-seven-year-old stump of a thumb. We would discuss Josephine and her gun, but for the moment I would have to deal with Josephine alone. I walked straight back to the house, angrily pulling the gate shut behind me. Having gone to a lot of trouble to see that nuts and idiots did not endanger my family, here I had Josephine quietly packing what I could only imagine was a loaded gun in our house five days a week. I found her in the living room pulling one of Tommy's rubber boots onto his foot. He sat in her huge lap, watching her hands.

"You forgot something?" she asked.

"No, Josephine. I just took Sally to school and the teacher showed me a picture Sally had drawn. You were in it, too, and something that Sally told the teacher was a gun. A gun you kept in your bag."

Josephine sat frozen, her eyes open. Tommy fumbled with his boot.

"Just tell it to me straight, Josephine, yes or no—is there a gun in the bag?"

"Well—"

"Just *tell* me, Josephine."

"Yes."

I said nothing.

"I only carry it to be safe." She pulled on Tommy's second boot. "Sometimes I come home very late, you know, and so many people I know been attacked and mugged, you know, so I went and got lessons on it, you know. I'm just trying to be safe—"

"Josephine! One of the kids could have pulled that thing out and shot it! Goddammit!"

"But the children never go in my bag, they *know* they not suppose to do that."

"Well, how did Sally know about the gun, then?"

Josephine didn't have an answer. She looked down in obvious shame, and I thought perhaps that Sally must have spied the gun when Josephine had the bag open and was searching for something else.

"Let me see it."

"In front of Tommy?" asked Josephine.

I got Tommy started with some Lego blocks, and then went into the kitchen with Josephine. She reached into the bag and pulled out the gun, keeping it pointed down. It was huge and ugly, like you could bang nails into a board with it. As a kid I shot a gun at crows in the woods and actually hit one once, its head turning to red mist and black feathers.

"Jesus, Josephine, that's a thirty-eight."

"I'm very careful."

"Is it loaded?"

She looked at me.

"I want the bullets."

She didn't answer.

"I want them, Josephine. I can't go to work this morning knowing there's a loaded gun in the house."

She tipped the gun up and slid out the bullets. She handed me each one. Black hand putting bullets into a white hand. Simon Crowley could have filmed the moment. I slipped them into my pocket.

"Any more in the bag?"

She shook her head.

"Sure?"

"Yes. I wouldn't lie about it."

"Did you imagine that we would be happy that you were bringing a *loaded gun* into our house every day? No, of course not, Josephine! So yes, that is *sort of* a lie, don't you think? For God's sake, Josephine, who the hell do you think you are?"

She was silent. I hated to do this. "Josephine, look, you're fantastic with the kids. They love you. We feel lucky to have you, and we've tried to show you our appreciation—"

"You and Lisa been very good to me."

"I want you to keep working for us. We need you. But you absolutely must *never* bring a gun into this house again. *Never.* I'm not fucking around, Josephine. If the gun comes back into this house, you're fired, on the spot, no questions asked. I hate to say that, but it's really that simple."

She was crying now, her hand over her eyes, lips soft and twisted, and I wanted to go comfort her.

"Josephine, I know you'd never try to endanger the kids, but I can't have this. And I'm not going to go checking your bag or your pockets or anything, so long as you give me your word."

"I won't bring the gun here no more," she sobbed. "I made a big mistake. Oh, Lisa's going be so mad at me."

This was true. I went back into the living room and hugged Tommy and kissed him for luck, looking into his happy, unknowing face, his cheeks smeared with snot and red juice, which provided an adherent for green Froot Loop crumbs from breakfast. Oh beautiful, beautiful boy. The world, and his father, were not good enough for him. I kissed him again and for a moment felt like crying myself. Then I got up, grabbed my briefcase, and went out the door, the bullets jingling in my pockets like money. Could I really have fired Josephine, there on the spot? Our children loved her with all their hearts, had never known another baby-sitter. When she got ready to go home each day they ran to her thick legs and hugged her good-bye, and Sally insisted that Josephine give her a "lickstick kiss," which entailed a huge smack on Sally's cheek that left the red lips of Josephine there until bath time. To the children she was a second mother—patient, strict, fair, untiring. As in most things, my wife had made an excellent decision in hiring her, and we knew any number of other families who had suffered disastrous relationships with baby-sitters, even one case in which the husband came home early to find the kids watching a Barney video and the sitter getting an insertion of happiness from the Con Ed man. But Josephine was another matter entirely, and other parents had tactfully inquired as to when we might be "done" with her and what we paid her. (White still owns black in America, let us admit this, if only secretly, to ourselves.) In fact, Josephine's very existence challenged my conception of myself as a parent; she had wiped more shit from my children's asses, fed them more meals, taken them for more walks than I had. She was paid for her labor and not her love, but she gave her love freely and copiously to my children, and I wondered from time to time if such a love might be equal, or even superior, to mine. Certainly she was more patient, certainly she communed more closely with the minutes of their lives than I did. She and I rarely spoke directly or deeply to each other, preferring instead to keep the conversation on a level of banality— the weather, the news—but I had a strange feeling for her. Somehow my children's love for Josephine refracted into my own grudging heart, but in a way that I could not acknowledge openly. The two of us understood that

the forces of history had created very different fates and that nothing ame-
liorated this but basic human respect. She was a proud woman, and I was
glad of it, for it meant that her life was not hopeless. Her past had largely
been concealed from me, but from time to time she and Lisa talked, perhaps both working in the kitchen together, and I imagined, perhaps unre-
alistically, that in those moments they stopped being white employer and
black employee, and became simply two women talking. Over several
years Josephine had told Lisa that she had birthed five children, three of
whom had disappointed her, one of whom had died in a fire in a crackhouse. Her first husband, whom she married young, had beaten her as
well as the boy who became the man in the crackhouse. They had divorced. Josephine's second husband, with whom she had three children,
was an older man who had died of advanced diabetes. Lisa suspected that
he had been the genuine love of Josephine's life, for he had bought her a
small home in Port-au-Prince, where Josephine hoped to retire. Josephine
had chosen her current husband less out of passion than pragmatic awareness of his basic decency and economic dependability. In fact, whether
there was any passion left in Josephine was a mystery. At times she sat quietly next to the window, reading her Bible in the natural light. Her faith
was unshakable, and made me wonder if her belief in God, which seemed
to me as humanly genuine as is possible, had been forged by her suffering
or only tested by it. I believe that grace is the most elusive of gifts, and
Josephine, slow-moving, inarticulate, superstitious, was one of the most
graceful women I had ever seen. In my heart I knew that she was a finer
human being than I. Let me say it again and know it always: Gun in her
handbag or not, Josephine Brown was a finer human being than I, and
among my other sorrows of this account, there is the miserable knowledge
that my acts forced upon Josephine yet another unnecessary dose of
suffering.

THE ONLY THING BOBBY DEALY could offer me that morning was the arrest of a demented old guy who had been attacking children with syringes,
which admittedly was a good story—especially because the man was a de-
frocked Catholic priest—but the victims were spread all over the city,

which meant a lot of legwork, and I was due to spend the afternoon in the Malaysian bank. So I passed on that one and the paper put a young Puerto Rican woman on it who was going to be as good as anybody in about three years. I didn't mind; I had the retired Coney Island nail-pounder story set for the next day, and I wanted to talk to the guys at the demolition company that handled the job at 537 East Eleventh. The firm, as I remembered from the file Caroline had shown me, was called Jack-E Demolition Co., and I found it way out in Queens, not far from Shea Stadium, on one of those avenues where the sidewalks are gone and the trees are cut off halfway up, where smashed cars and disemboweled trucks are everywhere and guys in jumpsuits with axle grease on their hands drive eighty-thousand-dollar BMWs and big dogs sleep in little sheds with a pile of chain in the dirt out front and the NO PARKING signs note that THIS ABSOLUTELY MEANS YOU. Jack-E Demolition Co. was a dirt lot filled with cranes and yellow bulldozers pocked with rust and, in the back, a trailer that served as the office. A lot of these places do some kind of illegal business—stolen cars, often—and I was wondering how pleased the management would be to answer my questions, but McGuire, the foreman, a man in his fifties with a dried trickle of tobacco juice on his chin, laughed as soon as I introduced myself.

"You're fucking shitting me! Porter Wren, right here? I read every column!" He pumped my hand, and I hoped I would get it back. "Here, here! Sit down." He rummaged through the mess on his desk and came up with a newspaper from the previous week: MOM BURNED WEDDING DRESS. "About the lady whose daughter got shot? And the wedding dress? Fucking shitting me!"

I asked if he remembered the job in which Simon Crowley's body had been found.

He nodded vigorously, as if the question was somehow an insult. "How can I forget? My son found him, head like a smashed tomato, poor kid threw up."

I asked if he could explain the demolition procedure.

McGuire nodded. "Yeah, here's what we do. Remember, we're covered by all kinds of regulations and shit. We inspect the building. Maybe there's some old blueprints on file somewhere—half the time, nobody has any plans. Maybe if there was, like, a partial rehab or something twenty years ago, but these buildings are mostly the same. We figure out how it's going to break apart. Sometimes you take it down floor by floor, especially if there's a lot of steel in the building or the space is tight. You just need room for a chute and a truck to get rid of the rubble. Or if it's not that kind of job, then we're probably knocking it down with a ball on a crane and bulldozers. If it's too big, too high, then you have to use specialized procedures like beam cutting, explosives sometimes, that kind of thing. We don't get into that—that's for the big boys. But this building you're talking about was what? Six stories? No, we'd just look it over, you know, take out the detail if there was any left. Ornamentation on the lintels, anything a little out of the ordinary. Sometimes we might take out the fixtures or doors or something, fireplace mantels, anything that can be salvaged and sold off. Sometimes people like to buy the old radiators. Myself, I hate them, make too much noise. The copper we pull out of the rubble. You got to destroy the walls to get the copper. Sometimes we'll hang on to a banister. Maybe a nice arched window, something, you know, no longer code but someone's going to want it. Then we just put the sidewalk shed up."

"Anybody else go in there?"

"Sure, all kinds of people." He fished in his breast pocket and pulled out a stump of a cigar and put it in his mouth.

"Who?"

He took the cigar out of his mouth. "The gas guys come to shut off the gas. Same thing with Con Ed. Cut the power out of the building. An insurance guy goes through there, make sure we didn't miss some kind of structural element that's fucking going to kill somebody, especially like me. Then the water has to be shut off, too—waitaminute." McGuire hollered into a squawk box. "Becky, go look up that job on East Eleventh. Maybe sixteen, seventeen months ago, just bring me the prep file." He looked at his cigar. "My son runs the jobs now." The file was handed to him. "Yeah, here it is, August two years ago. We knocked out the windows early. That's code. No flying glass. Let's see . . . turned off power, elevator company dropped the box a couple days before we wrecked—"

"Dropped the box?"

"That means—well, nobody wants a seventy-year-old elevator—so we get the elevator company to drop them back down into the bottom of the shaft, and then we fill in on top. See, most of the time the basement of the job is going to be full of rubble, because the owner doesn't want a hazard, lots of kids coming in and climbing around in a big hole, which legally you can get sued for even though you have a fence around it—you gotta love that—so we fill in the whole thing with rubble and give them a pretty good brick pack on top of that. Cap it over with concrete if they want to pay for it. Then later, if there's going to be a building erected, they gotta excavate all that shit."

"Isn't that a lot of trouble?"

"Not really, because you gotta excavate for the footings of the building anyway. Some of these new footings go fifty, sixty feet down. So fifteen, twenty feet of rubble is no big thing."

I nodded, but none of this seemed relevant to me. "So, the sequence is fence, turn off everything, inspection by insurance guy, then demolition?"

"No, you gotta get a permit first."

"Okay."

"Also a licensed exterminator has to kill the rats first."

"There were rats all over the place on that site," I said.

"Well, you pay a guy to *say* he exterminated, see." He gave me a wink.

"Then what?"

"Well, the city has an inspector, too."

"Is all this done in a rigid sequence?"

"What do you mean?"

"I mean is it always done in the same order?"

"No, the water may get turned off before the power, the power may get turned off before the water. You know, like maybe the insurance guy comes a few days early, late, whatever. See, we know all the guys down at the Department of Buildings. It's a comfortable relationship. We more or less get everything checked off before we start breaking it down."

"Must have been a shock to find the body."

"Well, I was in Vietnam, so I'd seen a few things, but my son—" He stared away. "He took a couple of days off."

"How do you think the body got in the rubble?"

McGuire laughed. "That's what the cops wanted to know."

I waited for him.

"Me? I think it wasn't in the building to start with, I think it came off the roof. There was a rope."

This fact hadn't been in Caroline Crowley's file. "You tell that to the cops?"

"Yes."

"What did they say?"

"They didn't believe me."

"Why?"

"I don't know. They just didn't." McGuire opened a drawer and found a new cigar and put the wet stump back in his breast pocket. "You know what? I wanted to see for myself if they threw the body over my sidewalk shed. So I took a stepladder and I checked every inch of that razor wire, looking for torn clothing or hair or blood or something, and I didn't find a fucking thing. I told the cops that, and they were mad at me for disturbing the crime scene. I said it was my shed. They loved me for that. I told them no way did the body go over the shed. I think it came down off the roof, and I told them that and they just looked at me like I was crazy."

"There's a guy who's a superintendent in the next building, Puerto Rican guy. You ever meet him?"

McGuire shrugged. A bulldozer rumbled by outside the window. "I might have, I can't remember."

"Okay, about the roof—wouldn't it have been really hard to throw a body that far into the lot?"

"No. That's not what I meant. They came over the roof with the body, from number, ah"—he looked at his file—"from number five-thirty-five to five-thirty-seven. This was when the building was still up, Then they reached over with crowbars or something, piece of lumber, anything, and smashed in one of the window frames on the top floor. That's, like, only four feet down from the cornice. It'd be hard, but you could do it. Then this is where the rope comes in. We found a heavy piece of rope tied on to one of the iron legs under the water tank. What I think is they tied the body with the rope, measured it, you know, got the length right, then swung the body off the side of the building and into the smashed window. Then cut the rope."

I tried to picture it. "That would mean that the other end of the rope would still be tied to the body."

He looked at his cigar. "Maybe."

"The body didn't have any rope tied to it."

"I know, I saw it, remember?" he said in irritation. "But it was missing a hand."

I thought about this. "If I was swinging a body through a window from above, I'd tie the hands together or the ankles or I guess even around the neck." If a rope had been tied around Simon Crowley's neck, the neck would have been broken, and the coroner would have noted it. On the other hand, the neck could also have been broken in the demolition, under the weight of the rubble or the bulldozer.

"I still think it was a rope."

"But your theory has a flaw."

He shook his head, stuck his new cigar in his mouth. "Come on! The body was pretty smashed up. The rope could have come off somehow."

"Did you ever measure the length of the rope that you found on the water tower?"

"Nah, this was all later."

The conversation was becoming too speculative, and I thanked him for his time.

Now McGuire lit the cigar, puffed up a bluish cloud, and squinted at me. "You going to write a story?"

"Checking it out," I told him. "Just checking it out."

THIS, I SUPPOSE, was now true. And after I worked my way back into Manhattan, creeping along behind a van with a door that flapped open and shut, the next place to check it out was the newspaper's own library, which is no longer simply a room where yellowed clippings are stuffed into file cabinets but an office containing row upon row of compact discs sold by private companies that make it their business to manipulate the electronic trail each of us leaves behind. Most people don't realize how much a newspaper can quickly learn about them, should it choose. In our library, for example, we have cross-directories on CD that we can use if we have a person's phone number but no name or if we have an address but no name or phone number. It's an extraordinary tool; give me a scrawled phone number in the city and there's an excellent chance that in a few minutes I can tell you what address it's from, who lives there, who lives in the same building or across the street, who in the building owns a car, what make and model, when they bought their apartment, their taxes on it, the purchase price, whether they are registered to vote, what party, and whether they have been involved in any recent litigation in the city. We can even get basic credit information. Is this an intrusion into people's privacy? Most definitely. Is it going to get worse? Same answer.

I found the chief librarian, Mrs. Wood, a petite black woman with killer fingernails who had helped the paper break news for almost ten years. It was said that she had a photographic memory, which may have been true, but it was my opinion that her true genius lay in her ability to be given one stray fact and to infer from it an entire structure of information.

"Mrs. Wood, can you look up something for me?"

"For you, Mr. Wren, I'll look up the moon."

"No doubt I will need to get you some coffee in a few minutes."

She nodded. "No doubt."

"Black coffee."

"Like me."

"How could I forget?"

"You couldn't."

"Because you, Mrs. Wood, are seared into my memory."

"Stop that white-boy flirting with me. What's the problem?" She pulled up a chair by her computer and I gave her the address of 537 East Eleventh Street; after about ten minutes she had determined that the lot was now owned by the Fwang-Kim Trading Import Corp., of Queens.

"A bit odd," she said.

"Why?"

"Usually vacant lots belong to the city. Seized for back taxes."

"And the Koreans buy stores, not lots." Perhaps they were just holding the land. If the area ever became gentrified, which was dubious, then maybe the value of the land would rise.

Mrs. Wood walked over to a standing microfiche file and in a minute came back. "It's never belonged to the city. But the Fwang-Kim Trading Import Corporation bought it from another Korean company, the Hwa Kim Import and Realty Corporation, and before that the lot—with a building—was owned by another company in Queens, so far back there's no microfiche record of when it was bought."

"The two Korean owners were recent?"

"In the last two years."

"Price?"

"First time seventy-six thousand, second time thirty-one thousand."

"Strange it would go down."

"I have a theory." She returned to her computers. I watched her slip discs in and out of the machine. "Here . . . all right. The two Korean companies have the same address. This means one is probably just a reincorporated successor company of the last. Small-businessmen do this all the time—lets them walk away from bad debts. The reduced second purchase price would be a way to create loss on the balance sheet of the first company. That might help an owner with his taxes. The reduced price might also be useful for the purposes of gift or estate taxes. It's pretty clear both companies were run by the same person or people." She waved her hands. "Typical financial messing around."

"But why would a Korean trading company in Queens buy an abandoned building, tear it down, and then just sit on it? It's not a prime location or anything." I thought of Mrs. Garcia moving slowly over her blasted garden. "You can't do any business there."

"Are there Korean delis in the neighborhood?"

"Yes."

"Then the Koreans have decided it's a viable neighborhood."

"Maybe. There's not a lot of money there, though."

"Could you build there?"

"Sure."

"You've seen the lot?"

"Yes."

"How big is it?"

"Maybe four, five thousand square feet."

She looked back at her screen. "You don't follow real-estate values in the city."

"Not for abandoned lots."

"Thirty-one thousand for a big lot, even on the Lower East Side, is nothing."

I shrugged. "Okay."

"Lot of people in the neighborhood?"

"Everywhere."

"See any supermarkets?"

I nodded. "There's one a couple of blocks south. But I know what you're thinking, maybe they want to put in a commercial building. But the zoning would be wrong. It's not on an avenue, it's in the middle of the street, residential. But poor."

"An apartment building."

"Maybe," I said, feeling discouraged. "I don't know what else to look up."

"I do. That valuation is way too low." Mrs. Wood peered at the microfiche reader. "Look, a comparable lot one block east—that's a worse neighborhood—sold for ninety-nine thousand."

"Why would the company that originally owned it sell it below market?" I asked.

"Now you are *finally* asking some good questions."

Mrs. Wood then did two things; she looked up in the civil litigation records the names of the former longtime owner, Segal Property Management, of Queens, and the name of the company it sold the lot to, the Hwa Kim Import and Realty Corp. "There it is," she said. "Segal Property Management was sued by Mr. Jong Kim three years ago. Now let me look up the—here it is . . ." Soon she had determined that Segal Property Management, of Queens, had filed for bankruptcy protection in the Southern District of State Superior Court two years prior. Then, using the cross-directories, she determined that the address of Segal Property Management was also the address of a Norma and Irving Segal, who apparently ran a law firm, Segal & Segal, out of the same address. Segal &

Segal had also filed for bankruptcy, on the same day as Segal Property Management.

"I've got another idea," said Mrs. Wood, punching up the New York State Department of Motor Vehicles records. From these she could determine that Norma Segal was sixty-eight years old and her husband was eighty. They drove a seven-year-old Mercury. "Old Jewish couple in Queens with a law practice and a run-down apartment building in Manhattan gets sued by a tricky Korean businessman," she mused.

I started to understand. "Maybe a slip and fall, car accident, anything."

"The old couple has no other major assets," she postulated. "They agree to give the apartment building to the Korean man as settlement. It's a legal sale but way below market. They get some cash, Korean gets maybe a great deal."

"Except that the building was demolished not long after the date of sale," I pointed out.

"Well, the price reflects that. It's so low. The Korean wanted the land, not the liability of an old apartment building." She gave me a coy little smile.

"I'd hate to know what you could find out about *me*," I said.

"You? You're *easy*."

"I won't touch that."

"That's *right* you won't."

I remembered that I needed to get uptown to the Malaysian bank, and was about to go when I had an idea. "Can you look up one more thing?" I asked.

"Haven't you given me enough trouble?"

"How can I sweeten the deal? A sandwich?"

"I want one of those ham and egg things they got downstairs and *two* coffees. And the latest issue of *The Economist*."

"You're a tough lady, Mrs. Wood. Maybe someday you'll tell me your first name."

"Ain't no reason you need to know that, now go get me my stuff!"

Before doing so I gave her Caroline's name and address on East Sixty-sixth Street, then went down to the lobby to get her food. Constantine, the security guard, saw me there and handed me an envelope.

"A guy left this for you."

"What is it?"

"I don't know."

"Sure it's not twelve million dollars?"

Constantine smiled. "All I did was keep buying tickets."

I read the hand-lettered note going back up in the elevator:

Dear Mr. Wren:

If you would like some more information about Richard Lancaster, the man who killed Iris Pell, please appear at the northwest corner of 86th and Broadway sometime in the next three hours. There you will see a rather large man named Ernesto who will be wearing a Yankees cap. Please identify yourself and tell him you are looking for Ralph.

My information about Lancaster is good.

Sincerely,
Ralph

I sincerely didn't want to go uptown and meet a rather large man named Ernesto. Who were they kidding? Besides, Lancaster was dead, old news.

"Caroline Crowley doesn't have a valid New York State driver's license," announced Mrs. Wood when I returned, "but she does have a California one, which expires in a few months. She has lived in the apartment for two years. Its purchase price was two point three million, with a mortgage of two million. Taxes on it are nineteen thousand. It's owned by a trust established in the name of one Simon Crowley, who, as I remember, is a deceased personage from the film industry." Mrs. Wood gave me a wicked little smile. "She is not a registered voter. She owns no real estate in the area. She is not currently suing or being sued. She has one outstanding violation."

"What's that?"

"She's got an old ticket for smoking in the subway."

"You've got *that* in there?" I said.

Mrs. Wood nodded, slyly. "She's one of those rich gals who rides the subway."

"What's that tell you?"

Mrs. Wood cackled. "She's worried about the money."

IT WAS TIME for me to get uptown to the Malaysian bank to look at the rest of the videotapes, but as I lingered in the newspaper's lobby, rereading the strange note from "Ralph," I began to wonder if perhaps I shouldn't squeeze in a visit to him. I was particularly tantalized by the phrase "my information is good." It could be a column—you never know. And if it was a bust, I'd go straight to the bank. I would not mention this letter from Ralph, nor what followed that afternoon, but both eventually confirmed the truth of the last words I ever heard from an old drunken reporter I knew when I was just breaking in. A tall fellow with a taste for good suits, his name was Kendal Harpe and by 1982 he was no longer good for anything except draining glass upon glass of scotch. But in his ruin I found something attractive, and he saw that before he was carried out of the newsroom for good he would have to acknowledge me. "All right, I got two things to tell you, kid," he abruptly announced one day when he had returned from lunch, swaying a bit. "One, when you get stuck, just lay brick. Got that?" He peered into my eyes to see if I was paying attention. "Two, it's not just a lot of little stories. Nope, it's all one big story. Remember that." Then he lurched out of my life forever.

Thirty minutes later I was standing at the corner of Eighty-sixth and Broadway next to the subway steps and looking for a guy in a Yankees cap. And there he was, a genuinely immense man, perhaps six foot four, at least two hundred and seventy pounds, much of it bulked in his shoulders and chest, standing with his arms at his sides, as if in a trance. I crossed the street warily, watching him, and stepped up on the curb.

"I'm looking for Ralph."

He considered me. I could not tell what race he was—his hair was loosely curled and a dirty blond, his eyes were green, his skin dark.

"I got this note," I told him, pulling it out of my pocket. "It says to come here and meet a guy named Ernesto with a Yankees cap."

He nodded and started to walk away. I was to follow, I saw. I caught up with him and we proceeded west, through Riverside Park, toward the West

Side Highway, where the traffic, mostly taxis, was racing along at seventy miles an hour. If we walked any farther, we would be killed. Ernesto hopped over a wall. I looked down; there he stood, ten feet below. He beckoned. I felt scared and stupid. He beckoned again. I jumped, and learned just how old my knees were. But then I was on my feet, and there was a certain anthropological richness to the location; here were the leavings of a stressed and mobile population: cans and bottles, umbrellas, mattresses, tires, oil cans, clothing, packaging of every form and era, junked applicances. The vegetation had penetrated and enveloped much of this detritus but as a consequence was stunted, scarred, and contorted, as if nature herself had been genetically damaged in its struggle against human personality and the rudeness of the urban habitat. Ernesto moved nimbly through this microlandscape. He seemed to be a creature without doubt, suited to stalk and scurry through darkness and filth. I followed him through a broken stone wall beneath the highway, the opening of which was choked with leggy ailanthus saplings reaching toward the sunlight. A few feet inside, the brush gave way to a beaten dirt path that led to another wall, this one not broken. Ernesto looked back to see that I was behind him, and then plunged onward. How foolhardy was I? I followed Ernesto along the wall, hurrying a bit to stay up with him, breathing a bit heavily now but still reading the graffiti.

pussy is sweet
but so is honey
so beat your meat
and save some money

you like jazz
I like swing
take it in your ass
& dont say a thing

you want brightness
I want the cave
stay down here
and be my slave

An emaciated waif of about fourteen passed us in the opposite direction, carrying garbage bags and empty plastic milk cartons. He was gray. Something in his manner—his stooped frame and somnambulant shuffle—suggested repetitive, exhausting labor. The wall continued another forty yards. Then Ernesto darted through a narrow crevice. I followed him—into darkness. As my eyes adjusted to the gloom, I could see that we were standing in an immense, vaulted space, about one hundred feet high and stretching dimly into the distance, perhaps even as far as a mile. It was an old railway tunnel, and thirty feet above the dirt floor, where tracks once ran, hung rusted transformer platforms, spaced every hundred feet or so. The iron gridwork was stuffed with lumber and sheeting and what looked to be bundles of clothing, rope, and plastic bottles of water. Individually these assemblages expressed the uniqueness of their creators, but collectively they seemed the work of an immense and clever species of bird. From there my eye moved down the walls to shanties built against them. I saw shades of movement here and there and far in the distance, and the swinging arc of a flashlight and the flickering brightness of what looked to be a fire. I hurried after Ernesto down the middle of the space; it functioned as a main street, with rubble-marked paths branching off from it. Beneath the nests were circles of rubbish, denoting, I inferred, the ground space belonging to the nest above. It was a society of sorts.

"Here," Ernesto announced thickly, and I followed him into the gloom. We passed a number of low shanties, many of them open to view. Bundled humans slept inside, men and women. In others I could see the occupant sweeping or tidying up, tying plastic bags shut, perhaps sitting on a chair and hammering something. Farther along we passed two men and a woman standing next to a fire. The woman, about fifty, tended a pot placed on the fire, lifting it with a long stick. The flames of the fire whipped upward, as if in a gale, and this baffled me until I saw that the fire was set on the iron grating of an air vent.

"Where does the smoke go?" I asked Ernesto.

"Cracks," he said, pointing to the ceiling.

We continued on until we reached a circle of rubbish that lay directly below another nest-house built atop a transformer platform.

"Ralph!" hollered Ernesto.

An aged, bearded face appeared over the edge, and almost immediately a bundle of rope appeared in the air. As it tumbled downward it resolved itself into a hand-knotted ladder, quite expertly made. Ernesto dragged a long piece of iron from the pile of junk and laid it carefully over the ends of the ladder. Then he clambered up like a monkey, as much pulling with his arms as pushing with his feet. Near the top he looked back.

"Mister, come up!"

I have stood in any number of foreboding places, including a piss-scented holding cell in Rikers Island and a pauper's grave in Potter's Field, but never had I ascended, underground, to such a dwelling. I grasped the ladder, gave it an experimental shake, then started to climb. It was not easy, and I am not particularly fond of heights, so I kept looking up, where I could see Ernesto watching me. When I reached the top, I climbed onto a makeshift platform that fronted a tepee made of lumber and heavy-duty worksite sheeting stolen, most likely, from MTA service crews. Ernesto then climbed down the ladder, leaving me.

"Welcome, Mr. Wren," came a voice from inside the tepee.

I crawled inside, past stacks of books. There, sitting in a reading chair, was a white-haired man of about fifty, perhaps older.

"My name is Ralph Benson," he said to me.

I shook his hand, which was surprisingly firm.

"Thank you for coming so far," he said, "in all senses of the word."

"Quite a journey."

He nodded thoughtfully. "Everybody who's down here arrived by— hmm, as you say—quite a journey."

I did not respond. Better, I thought, to let him speak.

"I sent the note to you because I have read your column for, hmm, several years. I read about the Pell girl. I cannot help but think about her parents . . . she died a stupid, useless death, Mr. Wren, because her lover was a coward, hmm. I had a daughter once, Mr. Wren, and I loved her—I loved her, hmm—I will not go into what happened . . . just as senseless . . . I was once a—birthday parties, and, hmm . . . she was only nineteen when they found her . . . All ruin after that, ruin and more ruin. My darling wife . . . died of heartbreak, to use Saul Bellow's phrase, and . . . and it was a spiral, Mr. Wren, I cannot . . . hmmm, a spiral . . . ruin. Society is too chaotic for me, Mr. Wren . . . I was once, no clue of it now, hmm, I was once a professor of the classics, Mr. Wren, at Columbia University, re-markable even to me now, I lived north of the city, Mr. Wren . . . New Rochelle, Cape Cod house on half an acre, pear tree in the backyard . . . so beautiful, hmm, fertilize in the spring and fall. I lived in the— lawnmowers and shopping malls, fruits of capitalism . . . not safe, nowhere is, as I know from reading the papers, and when I read of that coward, *that craven, shit-sucking, piss-drinking, pigeon-fucking coward whom I could actually cut up into a thousand pieces and eat raw like a fine delicacy, oysters perhaps, his bones cooked to paste that I might spread on crackers*—" He stopped and looked surprised, as if someone nearby had whispered into his ear. "Hmmm. Not that man, not the man who . . . our . . . but that man who killed . . . with the wedding dress, Iris Pell, hmm, funny name, rhymes with 'bell,' like wedding *bell*, hmm, or death *knell*, and then he did not have the common decency to complete his sui-cide efficiently, costing the taxpayers his hospital bill . . . anyway, I re-quested your kind presence here today to tell you that young Ernesto wanders about the city more widely than many of the people who live down here. Most of the folk down here are glad to get away from the world above us, which represents, hmmm, failure, sadness, death, vio-lence, drugs . . . and such. What communication they have outside is for the purposes of sustenance. Gathering food and water and such. Cave peo-ple, yes, hmm. History is always repeating itself, that is the great ignored fact of our civilization, yes. China will laugh at us in a hundred years. Any-way, Ernesto lives down here because he has found people who love him. My new wife—hmm, I call her my wife, we have been together five years now, my wife and I—she's out, cooking our meal, I think—my wife and I care for him. I will not recount his family history, but suffice it to say, Mr. Wren, that the only thing my wife and I can give him, love, is the only thing he requires. So long as he has some affection from one or two peo-ple, *certain* affection, he is content to live as he does. An absence of affec-tion destroys the soul. As you can see, he has a slow mind. A good heart, but a slow mind. My point is that he is happy to move about the city. He is my eyes and ears above ground, and at the end of the day he brings me all the day's papers, discarded of course. That's how I read your column. I also read Jimmy Breslin, Russell Baker, that man Safire, now Maureen Dowd, who, I have to say, really knows—" He blinked spasmatically for a few seconds and looked at me. "Where was I?" he asked.

"You were telling me about Ernesto."

"Yes." He smiled. "No!" He frowned. "I was describing my interest in the newspaper columnists. As a group, very weak, very poor, hmmm, I think. And you, too. Choppy sentences, written for a short attention span. Purposefully simple. Dull verbs. Hmmm. Not Dr. Samuel Johnson, hmmm-mmm! But I was interested to read your column from about five days ago, in which you described the scene on the Brooklyn promenade. As you remember, a woman looking out her apartment window saw a figure—you called him a 'homeless man'—possibly remove the gun from the hand of our bleeding would-be suicide, Mr. Lancaster. As it turns out, this was Ernesto. He was in Brooklyn because he, like the great American poets, loves the Brooklyn Bridge. Ernesto also picked up the man's briefcase, which he brought back to me."

"What happened to the gun?" I asked.

"He sold it."

"To?"

"To whom, exactly, I don't know." Ralph frowned. "He did not have the sense to leave the gun where it was or to bring it to me. He got scared carrying it around, and so he went into a bar and sold it. He is slow, as I said, but he knows how to do certain things. He is not a criminal, but he can find criminality. A strange trait, hmm, there he was, walking toward the murderer himself. So, yes, he sold the gun, to whom I don't know, and if I did I would not tell you. I want to keep Ernesto out of this completely, you see. He is innocent but he has a record of petty offenses. There is, in fact, a very old warrant out for him, based, I think, hmmm, on a property crime. I can't be sure. He has a memory problem, relating to the abuse he took from his father. If he committed a crime in the past, he no longer remembers it. Anyway, I want to keep him out of this. He is on the straight and narrow now, and to throw him in Rikers Island on an old car-theft charge would not be, in my mind, just. Society has taken from Ernesto far more than he has taken from it." He looked at me, glasses low on his nose, making the point. "Now then, Ernesto opened the briefcase and found a laptop computer inside it. He does not understand what a computer is, except that it should not be dropped and that it is related to literacy. My wife and I are the only genuinely literate people he knows, and so he brought the computer to us. I was once a hi-fi buff, as they used to call it, back in the seventies, when . . . hmm . . . everyone put on bell-bottoms and ate cheese fondue and pretended they had group sex—and so I was able to figure out how to use what I was looking at once I turned it on."

"The battery was still good?"

"Yes. I opened up some of the files—and it quickly became clear what I was looking at. Not one of the great texts, I'm afraid, but, rhetorically, hmmm, convincing. Here, let me show you." From within the mess of papers and books he pulled out a laptop computer and started it up. "See, here we have files that are labeled by date . . . these were Lancaster's notes. I'll open this one, which is a week before he killed Iris Pell."

I called my love three times at work today and she did not return my calls. Sent roses at noon. Flower company called back at five to say roses had been rejected. Distraught, could not concentrate in late afternoon meeting. Called my love when I got home. Perhaps we could see a movie. No answer. Went over to her building. Cold outside. Doorman would not let me in. Said it was his instructions. I offered him a hundred dollars, but he would not let me in. Most upset now. Very upset. Don't want to go home. Went to coffeeshop outside her apartment building. Perhaps Iris will come home. Maybe she went out to movies.

"You get the idea," Ralph Benson noted. "It's his record as he stalked her. We could call it *Memoirs of the Beast* and sell it for a million dollars. You can have the movie rights, hmm. It gets quite detailed. It also has the account of him shooting her."

"Can I see that?"

"Sure. You'll see that his thinking was deteriorating."

Found her. Laundry. Inside with athe blue dress that she wore had the gun knew she was there A cross the street, watching thinking and couldnt just not tell her how much I loved her forever ands that no one else could have herr. No other man, never!!! I walked in to the estyablishment and I shot at her. She saw me and I shot to tell hereverything about it. The bullets hit and everyone screamed and I ran out. Now am in a taxi, medallion #3N82, speeding over Brooklyn Bridge from Manhattan.

I nodded. It was definitely a column. "Pretty conclusive."

"Yes."

"Are you giving this to me?" I asked.

"After a certain negotiated point."

"You want me to publicize the coward's entries and thereby warn innocent young women of the murderous nature of men."

Ralph blinked. "That is an admirable motivation, but it is not mine."

"What *do* you want?"

"I want all good things, Mr. Wren, but I can't have them. I can't even have a millionth of all good things. A bottle of claret would be nice, hmm. 'Wine removes the sensation of hunger.' So said Hippocrates. But what I would like, more than anything, is a pair of decent shoes for my wife, for me, and for Ernesto. People do not discard or give away good, unworn shoes. My wife mostly wears men's shoes that are too large for her. I have nothing to give but my own ruined smile, my wit—ha!—and, last, whatever little I can pry out of the Babylon above me." He looked at me, eyes desperate. "I was thinking of a thousand dollars."

"I don't buy information."

"Five hundred—surely you're good for that."

"Look, I wish things were different for you."

He picked up the computer and held it above his head, as if to toss it like a volleyball. "I'll just throw it away like this, words into the void."

"No you won't."

"No?" This seemed to interest him, and he lowered the computer.

"You'd rather try to sell it to someone else."

"I hear *negotiation* in your voice, Mr. Wren. A tone of possibility! Five hundred. That must be close to your price."

"There is no price."

"That's quite noble of you!" Ralph Benson spat.

"Quite noble, hmmm! Your journalistic integrity is unsullied and, yes, like a well-turned-out gentleman, may strut itself on the boulevard of good intentions, admiring the cleanliness of its heels, the smoothness of its coat." He swept his arms upward, and now in his articulate anger I glimpsed who he had once been. "Very noble! Now then, Mr. Wren, let us put all this in context, shall we? I am a penniless man unable to make a living. I am so *unable* to function in the world above that I am reduced to living in the netherworld below and having a half-wit colossus scavenge for my food! The addition of five hundred dollars to my holdings would raise those holdings to five hundred dollars. You, sir, are a worldly, successful man, far more powerful than I, a holder of position and reputation and capital. I have no doubt that you are rather well compensated for your work. The subtraction of five hundred dollars from your holdings would go unnoticed by you. It is a sum that is now beneath your scrutiny. Five hundred dollars! Nothing to you. So I ask you, what is more equitable, down here in the world below? The maintenance of your priggish journalistic ethics, which are being violated every day by many of your colleagues, or the transfer of a small sum to a homeless, penniless fellow, in return for which he will hand over to you a useful trove of information?"

I looked at him and then at my watch. I wanted to see Simon's videotapes.

"How much are three pairs of boots?"

"Hmmm, the sale price per pair at Urban Outfitters is fifty-nine ninety-five per pair."

"That's about a hundred and eighty dollars." I looked in my wallet, checked my front pocket. I had one hundred and thirty-two dollars, and I held it out to him. "That's all I've got, assuming you don't take American Express."

"Sold."

I nodded, somewhat miserably.

"Ernesto!" called Ralph Benson.

In a moment, Ernesto had scampered up the rope and, seemingly using only one arm, taken the computer down for me.

"How can I contact you if I need to?" I asked. "Without coming all the way down here, I mean."

"Hmm, yes, simple," Ralph Benson said. "Every weekday, I have Ernesto stand at the corner of Eighty-sixth and Broadway at eight P.M. and midnight. He stands there for ten minutes. Anyone who wishes to contact me or send me something—and there are a few, as a matter of fact—simply hands Ernesto a note. The next day, Ernesto will bring the response. If you want an immediate response, you need to mark the note accordingly, and then wait at the corner there. Ernesto will usually be back in twenty minutes or so."

I looked him in the eye and shook his hand. He was an odd fellow, and he hadn't wanted to badger me for the money, but in the end I didn't mind giving it to him. He was a man with a philosophy, which, I'm afraid, I am not. I rather liked Ralph Benson, and I suppose he felt that I wasn't so bad. This was fortuitous for me, for later I would need his help.

I DROVE EAST ACROSS CENTRAL PARK, through the leafless trees, found the Malaysian bank, and dropped the car in a parking garage. On the street, with my breath smoking in front of me, I paused to examine the stark rise of steel and glass. Rarely had the city's physical stratification been so apparent; it is literally another city the higher you go, a world of penthouses and expensive restaurants and corporate offices. In Manhattan you are never far from the brutal verticalities of class. And then, inside, beyond the sitting Buddha, I found that Caroline had indeed called and arranged my access to her private vault. I repeated the ritual of the previous week, taking the elevator to the fourteenth floor, signing in, and being led down the long white hallway. The attendant opened the door for me and departed. The room was as I had left it.

I decided that if the tape Hobbs wanted was here, then I would take it with me in my coat, make a copy at home, and then contact him. But first I had to find it. I lifted a stack of tapes from the steel trunk, ordered them by number, and shoved each into the machine one after another, fast-forwarding with the play button depressed, so that the figures moved jerkily across the screen like psychotic crack smokers, the picture ripped with two bands of static. I was looking for Hobbs to flash into view. I wish I could say that I found him among the strange pile of sweepings from the human tragedy Simon Crowley had collected. How much easier it would have been. But there was another discovery awaiting me, and at the risk of belaboring Simon Crowley's voyeuristic sensibility, I will briefly reprise the sequence leading up to it:

1: Car accident with delirious drunk man, trapped in wreck, calling for his wife, dead of head injuries in the seat next to him. He is inebriated and in shock. Blood all over his suit. Perhaps his legs are crushed, but he seems not to know it. Gloved hand of fireman on door frame. Man discovers his wife slumped next to him. Weeps and kisses her passionately, his hands on her cheeks, touching her bloody mouth with his. Suddenly believes she is alive, seems to be insisting she is alive. More kissing, lifts up eyelid, talking to corpse. Man is cut out of his car by firemen.

2: Retarded boy of about twelve learning to tie shoelaces; fails several dozen times; is not frustrated.

3: Open prison yard, seen from atop a tower. Blue sky, haze of fences with triple coil of razor wire. Normal activities of exercise period. Then a fight on the perimeter. Guards become active, draw guns. Inmates, all black, lie down. Guards move about looking for something. Search unsuccessful. Guards move about with guns. Inmates undress, drop clothes to one side. Blue sky. Field of naked black men. Haze of fences.

4: Man of about sixty in green uniform marked FRANK on front and QUEENS ELEVATOR CO. on back. He crouches in the bottom of an elevator shaft. Toolbox and flashlight. He fixes something.

5: Asian women working in a Nike shoe factory in the Far East; piles of shoe parts around them, sewing machines and hot-glue pump-guns; a girl, perhaps exhausted, sews her finger to a shoe part and is helped by another woman; the women continue to work.

6: Southern California. Palms swaying in back. A large shed filled with lawn mowers and lawn tractors, at least a hundred, most of them painted red, parked tightly next to one another. Mexicans are fixing the lawn mowers. A blonde woman pulls up in a four-wheel-drive vehicle. Sunglasses. Thin belt. Children in back of car. A tagged lawn mower is produced and loaded in back. The woman drives off. Mexicans move slowly among the lawn mowers. None have sunglasses.

7: Sand-level shot, perhaps taken by a remote video device, of bombs dropping on Iraqi soldiers during Operation Desert Storm. Confused running, explosions, sand falling like rain. Image is not color but an odd, cool green, disturbed from time to time by adjacent, offscreen detonations. Iraqi soldiers screaming silently.

8: An old man in hospital bed, his wife sitting in a chair. Man considers her with his eyes, looks away. Plays with control of hospital bed, trying to get comfortable. Back hurts him. Minute after minute of this. Wife sighs, etc.

9: A camera follows a black woman from room to room. Cockroaches everywhere. She opens a kitchen cupboard glistening with roaches. Camera pans ceiling. Roaches. Woman and what seems to be a housing official go into a bedroom; each leg of a crib set in a coffee can filled with a lye solution. The cans are filled with dead, half-dissolved roaches. Official nods. Baby is crying; mother sees a bug in the child's ear. Can't get it out. Mother becomes hysterical.

10: Party scene, somewhere in L.A. Valley of lights in the background. Poor-quality video. Camera appears to be attached at head-level. Faces appear, speak to Simon Crowley. Nicolas Cage, David Geffen, Sharon Stone, a waiter who smiles emptily, Tom Cruise. Sharon Stone again. Conversations, etc. Trip to bathroom. In mirror, Simon Crowley looks at himself. He is checking the wire. A tiny optical cable is attached to his eyeglasses near the right hinge. Runs beneath long hair into collar, some device hidden in baggy jacket. Crowley in mirror checks face, teeth, eyes. Mouths something to himself. Grabs crotch. Returns to party. More of same, etc.

11: Countryside, shot from a distance of several hundred yards. Man in overalls driving a tractor drags an old car behind him under a tree. Jumps down from tractor. Attaches winch to tree limb. Opens hood of car, attaches chains. Winches engine out of car as tree limb dips with each ratchet of the winch. Engine clears hood. Man drives tractor around to other side of car, hooks up chain, drags car away. Engine hangs from tree.

12: Dusk, or dawn. A small, flat-bottomed boat manned by an Indian who poles the boat through a muddy river. He is skinny but vigorous. The boat moves along the bank past ancient stone temples and steps where women are washing clothes by beating them upon the stones. A water buffalo swims by. Ahead there is a fire on the bank. The man poles the boat toward it: an immense bier tended by two men with long rakes. Marigolds are strewn on the ground and two children play nearby. A small brown dog watches. The boat draws nearer. A human form is perceptible within the flames. One of its blackened arms has contracted upward in the heat. The children play contentedly; the dog snaps at a fly. Another water buffalo swims past, snorting air through his nose, eyes rolling, big as apples.

13: A suburban movieplex. On marquee: *RICTUS W/BRUCE WILLIS*. Teenagers in clots move in and out of the light. Everyone is white. High-school girls promenade self-consciously; boys slouch. Cigarettes are being smoked experimentally. A stream of people leaves the theater: couples, groups of girls, groups of boys, older married people. Looking for their car keys, eyeing the teenagers. They have all just seen the movie. They have no expression.

14: A tiny woman with white hair works in a basin, her back to the camera. She wears long yellow gloves, is hosing and washing something in basin, hosing and washing. She lifts an oily bird out of the basin, towels it off, gives the sleek little head a kiss, and takes it out into a yard. In the yard are perhaps a hundred similar birds, all clean. The woman disappears, returns with another oily bird, sets it in basin, washes and dries off. And repeat. And repeat.

15: New York City, Lower East Side, night, traffic. Shot of Tompkins Square Park. Camera pans the inside of a messy van. Camera returns to shot of park. Cops pass outside. Then more. An advancing mass of people appears. Flashlights, burning torches. Cops assume formal riot-control positions. TV lights visible in distance. A rain of bottles and cans and sticks and trash comes toward the cops. The crowd advances. Cops meet them with riot shields and batons, whacking at their legs and shoulders. More cops appear. The van is bumped. The van is being rocked, protesters climbing on top of the roof.

Suddenly this looked familiar. I slowed the tape to normal speed.

Simon [whose voice I recognized from previous tapes]: You locked the doors?

Billy [also recognizable]: Yeah. [Sounds of feet on the roof. Screams. Cops pass by van, swinging batons. Noises on van roof cease. More noises farther away, shouts. Bright flickering to one side, though the image is not in the frame.]

Simon: The tires are melting.

Billy: Destructive motherfuckers.

Simon: I think we're okay.

Billy: Fucking protesters. [The crowd has passed. Three older policemen follow, one talking into radio. A helicopter circles overhead in trees, its sharp cone of light sweeping the scene below. Men holding television cameras, reporters are interviewing policemen outside a large blue mobile-control unit. A Chinese man goes by on bicycle with a delivery box on the front of his bicycle. He is stopped and sent back.]

Simon: Over there.

Billy: That's a cop cameraman.

Simon: Why is he filming license plates?

Billy: He's coming down here.

Simon: We could drive out quick.

Billy: No, they have it barricaded.

Simon: We'll be here until, like, four in the morning.

Billy: I got some sandwiches and stuff back here.

Simon: I'll shit on a newspaper.

Billy: Thank you for sharing that.

Simon: Wait, wait.

Billy: He's coming.

Simon: Just be cool. [A minute passes. A policewoman with a small handheld camera passes by. More police walk by. Many are standing around. A firecracker goes off, and a few policemen glance toward the sound. One talks into the radio.] All right, Billy, I'm gonna shut off this—[New image: the camera has been adjusted and zoomed across the street toward the sidewalk.] Okay, now we're looking . . . [A commotion in the distance.] That's the protesters—they're unhappy with . . . [Commotion, and the crowd coming closer. Police start moving blue sawhorses into position. The streetlights above the trees cast pools of light and shadow. The crowd shouts angrily; police and crowd converge; a police van backs up and stops; TV lights are on across the park; more noise, more commotion; it seems that the surge of protesters has changed direction; the camera is now in position to show the ragged boundary between protesters and cops. People are running by. Now bottles are landing on the cops, and then another firecracker goes off; to the right, forty or so yards back, is a blinding red flash followed by red smoke; the collective attention of the crowd is jolted toward the flash. In the foreground a large white man with some kind of long bat or club leaps forward and swings at a black policeman who is looking at the red smoke, catching him in the back of the neck.] Oh, fuck! [The policeman falls limp to the ground. The assailant runs toward the camera at an angle; in four strides he is off-screen. The protesters surge forward, and the cops look confused; some have noticed their fallen comrade and have rushed to encircle him; a bright light now shines on him, and a cop is radioing; other cops run up and begin administering first aid.] You see it? That guy hit him! [The helmeted police at the protest line have already heard on their radios that one of their own has fallen, and they suddenly push against and viciously beat back the protesters; a cop on horse-back appears, rifle drawn; he aims at the heads of individuals and screams at them. The protesters fall back, and back, and back, until they are a dark mass, screaming.] They fucking whacked the cop!

Billy: I know, I know!

Simon: Wait a minute, we gotta get outa—

I leaned forward and punched the stop button. I didn't need to see the rest. I knew the rest. I knew all of it. As New Yorkers remember, beginning in the 1970s Tompkins Square Park began to devolve into a smoke-smudged encampment of homeless people, squatters (many of them the children of the executive classes and reared in such deprivation zones as Upper Saddle River, New Jersey, or Darien, Connecticut), drug addicts, hangers-on, lowlifes, part-time hookers, and street poets. I covered the story a number of times. The police would periodically roust the squatters out of their shanties and tents, only to have them return. Meanwhile the local residents living in apartments and houses wanted their park back. The representatives of the homeless made the point that these people had no place else to go that was either as safe or that offered the pleasures of a collective green. The city took the position that the taxpayers in the neighborhood and their children would benefit from having a genuine park, not a gallery of human misery defecating on what was left of the grass.

The conflict was inevitable, and I won't go into the specifics of the night of the protest or the police crowd-control strategy or the short-term political mind-set of the Dinkins administration. The important point is that one Officer Keith Fellows, standing at a curb, was clobbered from behind with a baseball bat. As reflected on Simon Crowley's videotape, the assailant jitterbugged into the surging crowd and disappeared. I was there, circling the park, talking to whomever I could, wired out of my mind on nine or ten cups of coffee, feeding uninterruptedly on the violence. Suddenly, on the cop radios, I could hear the word going out that an officer was down and gravely injured, bleeding freely from the ears and nose. In the logic of the police command, such a message translates thusly: Somebody Has Fucked with the Power. When this happens, the great logistical machinery of the NYPD moves with shocking speed; I watched as huge blue personnel transports seemed to materialize out of the shadows; suddenly there were *hundreds* of cops booting it across the dark park, and having been attacked, they now ferociously revoked any right of free assembly on the part of the protesters, arresting them by the dozens on no pretext, using disposable plastic handcuffs. Then, beneath the glare of portable searchlights that gave the scene the hyper-reality of a professional football game played at night, they conducted a careful search of the park.

At the same time, other policemen conducted a house-to-house search of the entire neighborhood, finding their way onto rooftops and into abandoned buildings (such as 537 East Eleventh Street, only a block north) and onto fire escapes and anywhere else. Dozens of people were questioned closely, and yet for the police the exercise was one of frustration; perhaps a thousand protesters had been in the park; no one came forward, and no one admitted—nor could be threatened into admitting—they they had seen the blow to Fellows's head. There was some speculation that this may have been due, in part at least, to the fact that the protesters had set off (again, as Simon Crowley's videotape indicated) a colored flare moments before; Officer Fellows himself may have turned his head in the direction of the sudden flash of light when the blow fell.

The night turned over into day, and all that was left was a trampled field of mud watched over by a detail of fifty cops. The baseball bat itself was found shoved down a sewer drain. It had been wiped clean of fingerprints. Meanwhile Officer Fellows lingered in a coma at Beth Israel Hospital, his brain swollen critically. When the rumor that his assailant was white had lasted more than two or three news cycles, the Reverend Al Sharpton appeared outside the hospital with his caravan of followers, charging that the police department was not doggedly pursuing its investigation "because they think the life of a black cop ain't worth as much as a white." And so on—the racial theater that is the city. The claim was met with the usual somber assertions. Fellows's wife was shown on TV entering the hospital, shepherding their three children. I revealed in my column that Officer Fellows had saved no fewer than four lives in the previous fifteen months, and I did not reveal that he had been accused, perhaps unjustly, perhaps not, of police brutality twice in his nine-year career. He could not respond to the charges, which by then were irrelevant anyway. I also spoke with his wife, who expressed her frustration that she could not explain to her children why the police had not caught the man who hit Daddy.

After Fellows died, I wrote about the funeral in my column. The NYPD buries its dead with pomp and solemnity; the ritual serves as a promise to the living policemen that they will be buried with honor if they, too, die. The service was held at the Brooklyn Tabernacle Church on

Flatbush Avenue, and the police cleared the streets for blocks around the church—never mind the traffic jams this caused—made the neighborhood quiet, *respectful*, then lined up thousands of cops, five thousand in all, along the avenue in dress uniforms, hats, and white gloves. Nothing moved. Traffic lights turned red, green, yellow, and no one watched. A few guys with radios worked the rooftops. At a signal, the line of cops began to stiffen into grave-faced attentiveness. Mayors came and went, mob regimes rose and fell, drug gangs flourished and died away, but never the New York City Police Department. Here on the street it was the Power, forever. Then the hard-core Irish guys with the bagpipes and the green clover tattooed on their left knees marched down the street, the drum banging slowly, then came dozens of cops on huge motorcycles, wearing blue helmets and mirror shades, looking like urban centurions, their bikes barely moving, as if the laws of physics had been temporarily rescinded by divine decree. Then the black funeral parlor car with the flowers, then more cops on motorcycles, then the casket car bearing Fellows in a mahogany casket, followed by cop brass and more cop cars, and, last, a huge police wrecker truck, in case a civilian vehicle unluckily got in the way of the procession. This police funeral, like others I'd seen, was stoic and brutal and beautiful all at once.

In time, of course, almost everyone had forgotten Officer Fellows—all but his family and a few fellow police officers and the detectives who had doggedly pursued the case. (Admittedly, his killer probably remembered him, too—the moment when the weapon sank into the officer's head, the frantic sprint under the trees, the struggling entry into the crowd, and then the flight away on one of the near streets.) And now here was this videotape, taken by Simon Crowley. It was a bit jumpy and dark, but I knew that the police would spare no expense to enhance and enlarge the image of the assailant. Upon rerunning the tape and hitting the freeze button, I myself could see that he was white, about thirty, six feet tall, bearded, perhaps two hundred and ten pounds, and wearing an old army jacket with the sleeves ripped off. He carried the baseball bat in his right hand in the middle of its length, like a relay runner clutching an oversize baton. I stopped and started the tape. There was an instant when the man ran through a column of light thrown by the streetlamp and you could see him clearly; there may even have been a tattoo visible on his meaty left arm. The police, I knew, could do a lot with this information. They might know just who that man was.

They could also do a lot with a person who had knowingly withheld such information for several years—that would be Caroline, if she had understood the significance of the tape. Such an act constituted obstruction of justice at the minimum, and in a case as charged as this one was certain to be avidly prosecuted by the Manhattan DA's office. And then, there was me. *I* could use that tape. I could *really* use that tape. It would make for a great story, it would make for helpful police contacts for years, and maybe it could be leverage against Hobbs firing me. Upon reflection I doubted that; he lived in another stratosphere; he would fire me if he had to, if only to show that his word as a despot was good. But if I had recently broken a big story, the chances were improved that I'd get rehired quickly by one of the other papers. Wren, they would see, still had the stuff. I turned off the machine and, with a sort of greedy acceleration of my breath, slipped the tape from the machine and into my own deep coat pocket. Then I put the empty box back into the steel trunk with the other boxed tapes, lest it appear that any was missing.

But what to do? Run out of the bank with the police tape or stay there, cold-bloodedly searching for the tape that Hobbs had demanded? The latter task could take *hours*—I still had dozens of tapes to see—and I was too jumpy to stay. I would only worry that Caroline or one of the bank officials might arrive, that the riot tape might somehow be taken from me. *Get out, get out*, my head told me.

But I didn't. I stayed another two hours, flitting through the rest of the tapes, looking for the image of Hobbs. It was more of the same. Finally I closed the door behind me and hurried down the carpeted hallway. I reminded myself not to walk too quickly, and I casually kept my hands in my coat pockets, in order that the shape of the Fellows tape not be perceived. It was the worst cheap acting, but guards and receptionists, being from the lower classes, are deferential to white men in good suits. When the elevator reached the ground floor, when all that lay between me and the street was the lobby and the glass doors, it occurred to me that if Caroline was not forthcoming with the other tape, I could use the new one against her. I'm not proud of this thought, but then again, measured against all that followed, this was but a small sin in the wash of great ones.

LISA WAS STANDING QUIETLY over the kitchen sink when I got home. She looked ashen. I guessed Josephine had told her about the gun.

"You know?" she asked when I came in.

"The gun."

She nodded. "I thought about firing her, right there."

"So did I."

Lisa came over and held on to me. "It's a hard decision. I was—I don't know if I ever was more upset. Not even when Daddy died."

"How did she react?"

"We both cried a lot."

"The kids love her," I said.

"She loves them."

"We're never going to find anyone better."

Lisa nodded exhaustedly, and I remembered the operation. "How did it go?"

"I think I did a pretty good job," she said. "The tissue pinked up nicely."

Later that evening, we watched the children in the bath. They shrieked in happiness and splashed water out of the tub and I barked appropriately and they kept playing with the soap and plastic toys, sweet and unknowing. Sally, as uninhibited as she will ever be, hooked her heels on the edge of the tub and thrust her hips up into the air, exactly the movement I've seen in strip bars when the women present themselves knee-first for the tip of a bill slid through the velvet garter. Now Sally put her hand on herself. "Is this my bottom?" she asked.

My wife shrugged. "Well, that's a place called your vagina, sweetie."

She looked at me in confusion. "A place called China?"

"No, sweetie, your *vagina*. Now put your legs down."

"There *is* a place called China."

"Yes, that's different, though."

And when they were out of the tub they ran around and shrieked some more, Tommy riding his fire truck naked, his little penis jiggling in a silly, rubbery way until I grabbed him and slapped a diaper on him with the speed of a short-order cook in a deli. And then the little pajamas and socks. Same with my daughter, and then the drinking of the milk, she from a cup, he from a warmed bottle. After they were asleep, Lisa called her transcription service to dictate the last of the paperwork on the operation, the first part having been dictated immediately after the operation on a wall-phone outside the operating room, Lisa still in her operating gown. Any documented advantage to avoid or win a malpractice suit. I could see her in the bathroom brushing her hair with one hand and talking into the portable phone with the other: ". . . evaluation of motion at left metatarsophalangeal joint and interphalangeal joint. Period. Monthly evaluation of extension. Period. Monthly evaluation of adduction power . . ."

She stopped when she saw me. "I had a funny new patient come into the office this afternoon after the surgery. She complained of basic rheumatoid arthritis."

"But you're a surgeon."

"I know. But she wanted an appointment with me anyway. She had called this morning, made a fuss."

"You don't do arthritis."

"I'll break a bad fusion sometimes, you know, if the fingers are terribly crooked."

"What happened?"

"Well, she came in, and I was really surprised."

"Why?"

"She was *quite* beautiful," Lisa said. "Beautiful face and eyes, sort of like Uma Thurman except with a much fuller figure. She couldn't have been more than twenty-eight, twenty-nine. I was really dumbfounded."

A silent scream in my head: Caroline—crazy, ruining my life. "What can you do for arthritis?" I said. "Aspirin, anti-inflammatories?"

"In her case, nothing."

"Why?"

"Because she doesn't have arthritis."

"What does she have?"

"Nothing. Her hands are perfectly healthy."

"Presumably her hands hurt her."

"She told me she had a lot of pain. But she doesn't."

I could see that Lisa had been evaluating it, had stacked up a set of observations into an argument. "How can you tell?"

"Twenty-eight is generally too young for the onset," Lisa began. "Ten years later, okay. And the kind of pain she was describing is more than just inflammation of the synovial membrane, it gets into destruction of the articular cartilage. She didn't have morning stiffness or redness or swelling or symmetricality of symptoms. In fact, I pulled pretty hard on her joints and she didn't flinch. Plus she wasn't *thinking* about it. Most patients want a fix, you know—an end to the pain. At least an explanation. They want to be told what the problem is, how it works, and everything, what they could *eat* that would make it better, vitamins, drugs, acupuncture, exercises, hot water, cold water, anything to relieve the pain. This woman was not in pain, not in the thumb or forefinger or the first joints of the other fingers, nowhere."

"Don't you have some kind of test?"

"We can check the sedimentation rate. It's a blood test for inflammation."

I was listening to my voice for insincerity. "Did you do that?"

"No."

"What did you do?"

"First I decided to say nothing."

"Then?"

"Then I saw her fiddle with her watchband, and if she had the pain she was describing, that would be impossible."

"You confronted her?"

"I told her it didn't seem to me that she had arthritis."

"Was she surprised?"

"No. Not a bit."

"No?"

"She knew she didn't have arthritis. She made it up," said Lisa.

This had to be Caroline. "Why?"

"Mystery."

Don't do it, I warned myself. *Don't ask her name.*

"Did she say anything else?" I asked.

"She asked me about being a surgeon. Why I did it, and so on. She asked about the children."

"Like what?" I said evenly.

"How I managed with them, school and so on."

"All right."

"She also asked me what my husband did."

"You told her he was a sex fiend."

"I said he's a reporter."

"Had she read the column?"

"I didn't ask her."

"Did she say what she did?"

"She didn't say, no."

"So—?"

"So she was letting *me* know that *she* knew that *I* knew that she was faking it. There was no shame. Usually fakers who get found out feel some shame. Not her. I think she came to my office to ask me questions about myself and my children and to tell me that she didn't have arthritis and didn't care if I knew it."

"Sounds like a nut."

"She *wasn't.*"

I shook my head at the seeming incomprehensibility of the thing. Then we sat there. A marriage has these pauses. The silence was a possibility. I could fill it up with an explanation. I could begin at the beginning and tell Lisa all about it and she would listen. She'd be furious, but she would listen, listen for the tones and words and modulations that would tell her how it would go from there on out, if this was a little problem or a catastrophic one. She would know inside the first sentence of my telling how it was all going to go. She knew me that well, she knew herself that well, and in truth I hated this. I loved it but I hated it. I saw the marital value in being known so well, but I saw, too, that it left me naked. I didn't want to be naked with my wife.

Instead, I took off my clothes. "I can't talk about hands anymore," I told her. "I need other parts."

It worked. Lisa seemed relieved. Her husband was more interested in screwing than in talking about some crazy woman. Certainly if something funny was going on, he would be unable to pretend that this wasn't so and then have sex with his wife. He wasn't that kind of a monster.

But he was. And so to bed: the darkness, the exhalation of the day, the waiting to start, the far musical hush of the city somehow inside the room, the you-first or the me-first, the decision to start, the evasions and the concentrations, the getting started. My father and both of his older brothers have all had prostate surgery, as did their father before them. It's a bloody operation, and all were rendered impotent by the surgery, so I figure that I probably have the same fate awaiting me. Perhaps I will reveal this little death to my son in the same way that my father revealed it to me. In any case, every night passed is a night closer to that possible fate, and so I take my pleasure while and as often as I can, while I am still young enough to do so easily, for time is upon us, an invisible hand upon the back of our neck, pressing down.

"Come up here now," Lisa said.

I moved toward her head, resting on my knees, and she opened her mouth for me. After a minute or so, one of her hands moved down between her legs. I have studied her as she does this, in the dark watched her closed or half-opened eyes, and understood nothing. At first, I think, she was merely being generous toward my desires. But in time, as each night Lisa urged this, I saw that she enjoyed it, the fleshy brutal possibility of it, and was teaching herself something about relaxing her throat. She liked to use her teeth and wanted to see how hard she could bite without really hurting me. She liked it to go in and out against her teeth, not only against her lips, and she was not happy unless I pushed hard into her. She would gag and I would pull back immediately, but, with an unambiguous hand on my ass from behind, she would push me back in. In this, I came to understand that as much as my wife was with me, she was also having a private dialogue with herself, one that did not need to be explained. One that needed *not* to be explained. She liked to have the dialogue, and the way that she had found to have it, at least for the time being, was to have me in her throat.

Now I moved my hands through her hair, down her forehead, her eyes, her nose, her lips, running a finger across her top lip, right at the edge where the three different pieces of flesh met, each piece feeling two others, all slipping back and forth and across in wet confusion. I could feel the stretch in the skin of her cheek, the little ridge in the corner of her lips, the warmth of her breath through her nostrils. I understood that I, the man, was a mere instrument being played by her, the woman, and there was a great, strange freedom in this. Then she uttered a deep-throated cry, her mouth full of muffled sound, and I looked down to see her closed eyes fluttering. She arced and relaxed. Her eyes opened, unseeing, then closed.

Now she got on her hands and knees, as she likes, and after I moved around her she kept one hand on the bed and one on herself. The orgasms come easily to her—five, six, eight, nine—and I feel sometimes that I am incidental, though I do not mind. Whatever flashes through our heads—children, images of others, worries, money, memories—remains mercifully unspoken; and on this night I spent myself and then sat back on my knees, then collapsed next to her. This was that moment of falling away, when all should be safe and warm and true.

BUT IT WAS NOT. In time I stood up and walked naked into my study, worrying whether Caroline had in fact been Lisa's visitor that afternoon. If she was, then she was crazy and maybe dangerous. Who else would insist on an unnecessary three-hundred-dollar office consulation, then chat about Lisa's husband and children? And who else was as beautiful as Lisa described? The idea made me sick with anxiety. I closed the door and sat down next to the phone. I might need to get Caroline off my back. I intended to tell the police about the tape but not to mention Caroline. If I did, however, she would be in a world of shit.

I called my old friend Hal Fitzgerald. As each new police commissioner is appointed, whole ranks of police department bosses suddenly advance while other ranks suddenly find themselves frozen in place. Hal had recently moved up to deputy commissioner, and at the time I had considered this a lucky thing. Now his suits were better and he had a driver and three lines into his house, one of them being the emergency line that I had dialed.

"What's up, guy?" he said.

"Hal, I got something you want, and I suppose I actually want to give it to you, but I have to lay out some conditions."

"Go," he said, his tone changed.

I described the tape in very general terms, not mentioning that it showed the murder of a police officer nor that it had anything to do with a riot at Tompkins Square Park. I wanted him interested but not too excited. If I told him the exact nature of the tape, there would be a police car in front of the house within five minutes and I would have to hand the tape over or risk being arrested.

"Tell me your conditions," Hal said, "even though I know what they're going to be."

"I'm not telling you where I got the tape."

"Well, of course that could be a problem."

"The person who had the tape didn't know what was on it."

"Pretty hard to believe that."

"I'm not going to tell you. Take it or leave it."

He was silent. He couldn't actually negotiate, I knew. If it got argumentative, soon the newspaper's lawyers and the police department's lawyers would move in, discussing subpoenas and New York State's shield laws, which are designed to protect the freedom of the press. Neither one of us wanted all that.

"My next condition is that I don't end up testifying."

"We might need to establish a chain of custody—"

"You guys can have experts testify that the tape isn't doctored."

"Maybe," said Hal.

"The last thing is that this is my story."

"Your story."

"I'm asking you not to give it to anybody else."

"Right."

"Hal, you're giving me that hedging tone."

"I'm giving you that tone, yes."

Every city official was afraid of Giuliani. Everything went up the line, maybe even this. Especially this, once they knew that a cop was the victim. "You're going to need to check on it," I said.

"I sure am."

"You'll call me?" I said.

"Soon as I can, but I got to get a few minutes with the commissioner."

"Tonight?"

"He's at a big Republican thing at the Waldorf."

"Afterward?"

"Doubt it."

"Tomorrow or so." Fitzgerald sighed. "I'll see how fast I can get back to you."

"You got my beeper number?" I asked.

"I got every number on you."

"Do me a favor, call my office or the desk."

"Not at home?"

"I'll just check my office. You can always call Bob Dealy."

"Lisa doesn't know about the tape?"

"Office."

Where does one hide a videotape in one's house? How about with all the other videotapes. Sally had a stack of Barney and Thomas the Tank Engine and a dozen of the Disney tapes, and I slipped *The Little Mermaid* out of its box and replaced it with the Fellows tape. Then I stole back to bed.

Out of the darkness came Lisa's soft, anxious voice: "Will you tell me what it is?"

That was the question. Would I tell her? And here I rip open my shirt and show my blackened heart. No, I would not, I did not tell her; instead I muttered the lies that husbands mutter and listened to Lisa fall back toward sleep. She was tired; she had woken at five, then gone to the hospital and sewn a toe onto a hand, then seen half a dozen patients in her office, including one who was her husband's lover, then confronted Josephine and made dinner and washed the kids, then called the dictation service, and then had sex with her husband; my wife was plentiful and knew it and exhausted herself every day. I loved this about her. But I also knew that if I waited, not long, with the winter wind outside brushing the apple tree against the window, soon she would be asleep.

And she was.

And I was not. I was awake with my secret. It was terrifying yet thrilling. A secret is the hoard inside the maze of lies. A secret paints your face into a mask, and makes you watch those who are fooled by your performance. To have a secret is slyly to learn anew the mannerisms of regular conversation, the shuffling chitchat that brilliantly conceals the screamer. A secret organizes your life. Mundane irritations become desirable; by bearing them silently you pay homage to the secret; eyes open, you feed it in the dark.

■ ■ ■

WHEN DOES DISASTER BECOME INEVITABLE? Only in retrospect, of course, is the moment apparent. For me the bloom of revelation began late the next afternoon, when, with the Fellows tape in my coat pocket, I turned the corner at Sixty-sixth and Madison and saw the green-and-white-striped awning outside Caroline's apartment building and, soaring above it, the sooted limestone confection of crenellations and balconies and fenestrated prewar delights. Ah, the magnificence of decadence. The city runs on decadence, if you think about it. I lingered on the green outdoor carpeting beneath the awning, taxis rushing at my back, and peered through the leaded-glass doors into the tiled lobby, where a cloud of pink lilies floated above a cut-glass vase centered on a Georgian end table. There sat Napoleon on a stool, frowning into a paperback mystery. I could not help but think of Caroline walking across those slick little squares, her heels clicking coolly, the pink lilies shuddering as she passed, the image of her torso reflected and distorted a hundredfold in the pineappled facets of the vase. Napoleon looked up and I gave him a nod. He buzzed Caroline's apartment, muttered something, gave me a hateful smile. We had the quick, silent male conversation: *Love ya, pal. Eat shit. I fucked her, you didn't.*

But I was not on an erotic mission, I told myself, I was here to do three potentially unpleasant things. The first was to ask Caroline if it was she who had visited Lisa in her office the previous day. If so, then we had a big problem; I would have to tell her that I wasn't going to tolerate any further intrusion into the rest of my life. If she continued to trespass, I might have to advise the police as to where I had found the Fellows tape. The second item involved the Fellows tape itself. If Caroline had *not* been the strange patient in Lisa's office, or had been but agreed not to intrude again, then it was only fair that I inform her that I had told Hal Fitzgerald about the tape. And that I had insisted to him that I would not reveal where I found it. Without this information, it would be difficult for the police to identify the tape's source; that same morning, before knocking out the next day's column on Richard Lancaster's insane diary, I'd made a point of reviewing the Fellows tape in its entirety; not only did nothing further of note happen—only a few lines of interaction—but, I noticed, Simon was never identified by name. Nor did his or Billy's face ever appear. Billy was addressed once by his first name, but how many Williams could there be in New York? When I wrote about the tape, it was possible the police could subpoena the newspaper, but in that instance the newspaper would protect Caroline's identity. Newspapers, even prurient tabloids owned by foreigners, still hold the line on the rights of the press. In fact, in respect to the newspaper's management, theoretically it was I who was in trouble, because I had informed the cops about the tape before I had discussed it with the managing editor. But morally, that was an easy one; a man had been murdered in cold blood—that's where I drew the line. The sooner the cops figured out what they could offer me by way of assurances, which would, I figured, be that day or the next, the sooner they could have the tape and start busting down doors all over the city. They would be looking for a blond guy in his thirties—God help you if you knew who he was. As for the newspaper, all we really wanted was exclusivity—to break the story, try to get a newsstand bounce, maybe ride it a few days. And that would be my argument with the newspaper's brass; several of them may have been newspapermen once, but for the most part they were old guys who no longer had any hair on their shins or young guys with MBAs who knew more about Monday-night football than about finding a newspaper story. I'd had my discussions with all of them over one problem or another; with the old guys, you said, *Hey, you remember what the street is like*, and then they got a soft look in their eyes, which, as a remembrance of time past, was a measurement of time remaining—pure contemplation of death. If they didn't remember what the street was like, then what were they doing in the corporate offices? They were paid to make the judgment calls, to massage problems away. So those guys were easy. It was the ones under forty-five who saw my salary and thought that they could hire three young general-assignment reporters for that sum, which was true. Usually I just listened to their rant and when they were done I'd ask them if they'd checked with the old-timers. Or I told them that they were in the entertainment business, and that to entertain they needed talent, and that it was my talent to feel along the margins of the city, finding stories. To do that I needed to stay tight with the cops, and if I showed my respect by telling them about the tape, then *hey, there're only about five guys in the city who hit the front page on a regular basis, including yours truly, and Jimmy Breslin is an old man*. I might even have done it that morning, using the Lancaster diary that Ralph Benson had sold me. I had thrown in all of Lancaster's language as he devolved from a jealous paranoid into a murderer. The thing had written itself, and I'd filed the column by three. Nobody else in the city would have this story. The editors loved it and were thinking about a page-one headline; something like DIARY OF DEATH. No, if there was going to be difficulty, then it would be with Caroline. I didn't expect her to protest the fact that I had called Fitzgerald, for, like Officer Fellows's widow, she knew what it was to suddenly lose one's husband. On the other hand, I had done so without telling her, which was inconsiderate, any way you cut it.

The third item was the disturbing matter of Hobbs. I'd resolved to ask Caroline about the tape he wanted. Did she know where it was? If she said no, then I would repeat that answer to Hobbs. If she did know, then I would ask her to give it to Hobbs and make my life less worrisome.

All of this seemed quite logical. And why not? How easy are the lies we tell ourselves! How merry and unimpeded by the friction of truth! But if I was a fool, I was a willing fool. After all, here was a woman whose husband might have been murdered, who seemed to have antagonized a powerful global businessman, and who possessed a videotape of a New York City policeman being killed. I was sure she had seen the Fellows tape, but I wanted to show it to her anyway, and in the apartment building elevator, after an older woman got off on the second floor, I removed the tape from my coat pocket, checking again to be sure I hadn't accidentally grabbed one of Sally's Disney videos. It was the right one. The label, TAPE 15, was lettered in the kind of purposeful block printing that is impossible to write quickly; however impulsive and passionate Simon Crowley may have been, he had taken the labeling of his collection seriously. I slipped the tape back into my coat pocket.

Caroline opened the door. She was holding a glass and had an ice cube in her teeth. "I'm making you a little drink," she announced. She dropped the cube into the glass. "You don't mind a little of my spit polluting your vital organs?" Her eyes watched mine, moved down to my mouth, then back up.

"Call nine-one-one," I told her. "Now."

"What? Why?"

"I'm going to have a heart attack. I'm going to die right here before I get any of your beautiful spit on—"

"Oh stop!" She grabbed my hand and dragged me into her apartment. It was the same as before: expensive, spotless, without humanity. Caroline saw me inspecting it.

"I know exactly what you're thinking." She handed me the drink and took my coat and put it in her closet.

"You do?" I called from the living room, looking out the window toward Central Park.

"Yes."

"You're wrong."

She came into the room. And right up to me. "No, I'm not."

"No, I suppose you're not."

She took my wrist and examined my watch. "Five o'clock," she said. "You're supposedly working on your column now?"

"The column is done." I looked at the mascara on her lashes. Sexy stuff, mascara.

"You told your wife when you're coming home?"

"No."

"Did you make up an excuse for being out late?"

"I haven't spoken with her since this morning."

She put her finger on my tie, running it up and down the pattern. "When do you have to be home?"

"Later."

"No certain hour?"

"No certain hour."

"But the deadline for the column is five-thirty." I nodded.

"So you're due home soon after that?"

"Not necessarily."

"Why?"

I touched her chin with my hand. "There could be a reason."

"What?"

"Developments in the story."

Her blue eyes liked this. "And your column is already done?"

"Yes."

"What's it about?"

"The guy who killed that poor girl a week ago who was holding her wedding dress."

Caroline seemed unmoved. "Got to be able to spot the psychos."

"How do you do that?" I asked.

"They're crazy." She laughed. "Believe me."

I nodded. "I see."

Her eyes played. "*Maybe* you see." She pressed my hand to her breast.

"I better tell you, I have an agenda here."

"I do, too," she said.

"Which first?"

"If you guess mine, we'll do yours first."

"And vice versa."

"Yours," she said, "goes something like this—you found a very interesting videotape at the bank and now you want to talk about it."

I looked at her, amazed, a little scared. Then: "You felt it in my pocket when you hung up the coat."

"I did. Which one is it?"

"The riot in Tompkins Square Park. The cop gets killed."

"That one."

I nodded.

"Let's talk about it later," she said.

"Later *soon*, though."

"Fine."

I couldn't stop myself. "Caroline, the cop was *murdered*."

She looked away. "I didn't know that, not exactly."

"No?"

She frowned. "We seem to be talking about this *now*, not later."

"I can't help it, Caroline."

"I saw it once. A few years ago."

"I've told the cops about it," I blurted.

"Fine." She seemed strangely calm.

"Fine?"

"Give it to them."

"I'm going to." This was easy. "I expected more of a reaction."

She shrugged. "From me? Why?"

"I—" The look in her eyes stopped me.

"You're a reporter—I *expected* you to find things."

"You did?"

"Yes. If you didn't, I would have been disappointed."

Caroline walked into the kitchen, where she pulled papers and tobacco from her purse and rolled a cigarette. I was still thinking about the Fellows tape. Caroline lit her cigarette and smiled into the smoke. Now I needed to ask her whether she had visited my wife. Maybe the question would anger her. Maybe I would ask it later.

A MAN AND WOMAN, in a room at dusk. Some kind of marvelous fast Latin music comes through the ceiling. Drums and guitars and castanets and great shouting. What's that? he asks. Afro-Peruvian, the woman says, pretty great, they play it all the time. The man whispers to her about her perfect teeth and her perfect mouth and her perfect neck, and she asks with vulnerable self-indulgence *Where is it the* most *perfect?* and so he tells

her the most perfect is in the symmetrical smoothness of the delicate inward curve of flesh at the base of her neck, centered perfectly there, a variation on a curve outward, and she smiles to herself, and then he moves her
sideways, so as to appreciate her breasts, which, unlike his wife's, have not
known children sucking upon them ruinously, or an extra ten years of
gravity. The nipples seem chaste in their smallness. What a mysterious
thing it is to touch a woman not your wife, he thinks. He has had sex with
his wife just the evening before, and remembers enjoying it, but now that
pleasure seems distant and theoretical. He moves his hands along the
woman's belly, around her back, over her breasts, then under them, cupping them, amazed at their weight, feeling that slight knotted ripple of the
glands under the skin and fat. Outside the window, the sky to the west is a
blackish blue, salmon at the far edge. He looks back down at the woman.
She is breathing deeply, her eyes closed. Their romance is all carnal, and
this is how he prefers it. "If you're going to kill me," the woman whispers,
"you might as well get started."

LATER, IN THE DARK OF THE BEDROOM, Caroline broke the silence.
"Tell me why you have sex with me." Her voice was oddly bright and
awake.

"No."

"Tell me how is it different than with your wife."

"No."

"Your wife is attractive, right?"

I grunted. "I bet you might know the answer."

"I might."

I rolled over so that I could look Caroline directly in the face. "Did
you go—"

"Yes."

"—to her office?"

"*Yes.*"

"Why?"

"I was curious."

"She knew you were lying."

"I guess, yes."

"It was an extremely fucked-up thing to do."

Caroline drew back. "I'm sorry. I didn't mean it like that."

"She's smart, Caroline. She's very, very smart."

"Smarter than me?"

"Yes."

She didn't like my answer. "How do you know?"

"Nobody is smarter than my wife, believe me."

"Smarter than you?"

"Double or triple."

Caroline was quiet. I felt the difference in our ages.

"My wife is a good person, Caroline," I said, "and I really don't want her to be hurt by this."

"I shouldn't have done it."

"No."

"I'm sort of interested in her, though. I mean, I'm supposedly going to be a married woman sometime."

"You *were* a married woman."

"Not really. It didn't feel like that. It was always just a strange arrangement. Simon never knew me, I think."

"He never knew you?"

"Well, he knew me really well in some ways, but in other ways he had no idea. He *wanted* to. He kept trying to turn me inside out."

"It was never something where time just went by," I interpreted.

"I wasn't really a wife to him."

"What were you?"

"A—I was—a *specimen*."

"A specimen of what?"

"That's a good question."

"I think you're actually a fine specimen."

"You know what I mean," she said.

"*Are* you a specimen of something?"

"Maybe—probably. But it was never of a married woman. That's why I'm asking questions about your wife."

"I don't mind telling you things, but no more contact with her."

"All right."

I didn't reply.

"I said all right."

"Okay."

"I'll ask a question now."

"Sure."

"Is she good in bed?"

"Absolutely."

"You love her and she loves you?"

"Very much, yes."

"Then how is it different?"

"If you don't have children, it's hard to understand, I think."

"Try me."

Her question seemed naive, but I attempted an answer. "After you have kids, death gets into it. You understand, now, like you never did earlier, that you are going to die. I didn't get that before I had kids. Now I worry all the time about them getting sick or dying, and I know that my wife is worrying, too. I think, What happens if I die? What happens if she dies? And who will die first? Who will be left alone? What happens if one of the kids dies? All this sort of gets into the sex. I mean, I watched both kids be born."

Caroline rolled back toward me. "What did it look like?"

"The head looks like a little wet tennis ball. With Sally, Lisa had back labor."

"What's that?"

"The baby is pushing against the spine, hitting the spinal nerve. Lisa was delirious with pain. I told the doctor to give her an epidural."

"That's a shot for pain?"

"They stick a long needle into the spinal cord. They have to time it between contractions."

"Did you see the umbilical cord and everything?"

"I cut it."

"What's *that* like?"

"It's sort of like a thick bluish rope."

"Is the afterbirth disgusting?"

"None of it's disgusting."

"They pull out the placenta?"

"They put it in a stainless steel tray and you can have a look at it. Looks like a piece of liver the size of a phone book."

"Both kids were okay and everything?"

"Sally had jaundice, which is not so bad, though she had to go back into the hospital, but Tommy came out blue."

"Why?"

"The cord was around his neck." I took a breath, perhaps sympathetically. "We got through that and then he caught pneumonia nine days later. That wasn't fun. An oxygen tent and so on."

"He's okay?"

"He's very okay."

She was quiet a moment. "All this is in the sex with your wife?"

"Somewhere."

"Do you think about other women with her?"

"Yes."

"Who?"

"Temptresses of my own devising."

"Have you had sex with her since having it with me last time?"

"Yes."

"Once?"

"Yes."

"When?"

"Last night."

"So maybe eighteen hours ago."

"Yes."

"Did you take a shower?"

"Yes."

"Good. Did you think of me when you were with her?"

"Absolutely."

"I mean thinking of me not just because you feel guilty about me."

"Yes."

"I mean you were fucking her but actually thinking about fucking me."

"Yes." I looked at her. "I can sort of switch back and forth with no interruption."

"You're making fun of me."

"No, actually I'm not."

"Did you think of her just now when you were with me?"

"Yes."

"And not just because you feel guilty?"

"Yes."

Her voice rose. "You thought of her just a few minutes ago?"

"Yes."

"How about the other temptresses of your own devising?"

"Yes."

"Do you think of men?"

"Sometimes."

She thought. "Are you having sex with them?"

"No."

"Who are they?"

"They are men and they are not me exactly but I am them. I am watching them have sex with the temptresses of my own devising."

Caroline seemed dissatisfied. "What are some of the *other* differences between us?"

"You don't want to get into that," I said.

"No, *you* don't want to get into that."

I shrugged.

"There's a physical difference?" she asked. "I mean does it feel different, inside?"

"Yes."

"How?"

"She's had two kids. You've had none, as far as I know."

"It makes that much difference?"

The question hung in the dark room, the music rapid and faint above us somewhere. Outside it had started to snow.

"It makes a difference."

"Do you look at your wife when you're having sex and think 'I am going to be with her until we die'?"

"Yes."

"And what do you think about that?"

"It's both a comfort and a horror."

"Why?"

"Because it's comforting to think that we will be together, and also I am horrified to think what time will do to us, to all of us. I am terrified by that. So to answer your original question, the difference between you and my wife, aside from all the obvious differences, is that with you I am not responsible for our future. I am not beholden to you, or you to me. It's all here, now. It's new snow on the windowsill. Very lovely now, then gone. You'll go off and do God knows what, marry Charlie, and I'll go back to Lisa, and I think we both know this. You are *now*. You will not age before my eyes for the next forty years. You will be here and that will be it. I can be with you and also not care whether you love me."

"*Do* you love me?"

"From the moment I saw you."

She smiled, pleased. "Maybe it was just cheap lust."

"I guess you're right."

"Really?" She gave me a little punch. "Well, maybe I was just a temptress of *my* own devising, catching you in my little web."

"I don't care."

"It doesn't bother you?"

"No."

"But I could have all kinds of schemes—"

"I don't care."

She retrieved a cigarette and match from the bedside table. "Why?"

"I'm smart enough to get out."

The match flared. "You sure?"

"Yes."

"Maybe I'm very, *very* smart and you *won't* get out of my web."

"I'll get out."

"Why are you sure?"

"I'm smart."

"Smarter than me?"

I thought of various answers. "We don't know yet, do we?"

I turned over to see her reaction, but she had closed her eyes, the lashes so thick and long they seemed to rest upon her cheek. I cursed myself for being fascinated by her. What an asshole I was. There was Sally, perhaps that very minute, cutting a piece of red construction paper with a pair of rounded scissors, or there was Tommy dragging one of his soiled stuffed animals through the apple juice he had just spilled, and there was Lisa, running the warm bathwater; all this while I, father, husband, protector, lay on a king-size bed uptown, my dick wet and limp against my leg, with another woman. Yes, I cursed my fascination with Caroline, but so, too, did I feel uncommonly happy for it.

"Tell me something else, about the difference," she said.

I thought. "Well, there's the *ugly* difference."

"Oh?" she said with interest.

"When my wife and I have sex, it's at the end of the day. We're tired. She's tired. She's worked hard, the kids have worn us out with dinner and the bath and the pajamas and the stories and so on, and we're tired. Usually she reads a little while—"

"What does she read?"

"The most terrifying stuff she can find. Right now, something called *Poison*. Anyway, when we get into bed, we're going to sleep the night through, we're finding something together and then that goes into sleep, into unconsciousness, into death in the future. With you, you're not tired, your life doesn't have much going on. Maybe you worked out. Maybe the mail arrived. A few bills, some catalogs. Maybe you dusted your coffee table or called Charlie or told the maid to clean the shower—"

"Oh, fuck you."

"Let me finish. The point is that I'm a diversion, a game. A trifle. A bonbon in the afternoon. I know this. I'm not taking you anywhere you want to go. I'm taking you *away* from the place you don't want to be. I don't suspect that you think much of me when I'm not here. You go to the gym and talk to your friends and go to Bloomingdale's or the movies or whatever, but I'm not part of your life, not in any way that's important. We're screwing each other. That's what this is, Caroline. Nothing more, nothing less. You know this. It's at the surface, nothing deep. There are no stakes, no mortality to be found in the relationship."

"That's pretty harsh."

"I'm taking you to the next level."

"Oh, of course."

"It's the only advantage older guys have."

She smiled and rolled over and kissed me. "So since you've got this death-is-life thing, tell me a story about death, sweetie."

Now, I understood, she was bothering to know me. I glanced outside, again saw the snow. "Get me another drink."

She did, and one for herself, too, and we pulled ourselves up in the bed under the blue blanket, and I found myself remembering for her one winter in my little town in upstate New York, when I was twelve. It had snowed heavily for three days and my friends and I had heard that the freight cars were frozen to the tracks. To the twelve-year-old mind this is a fascinating idea, for we had spent hour upon hour watching trains go back and forth, throwing sticks and rocks at them, putting pennies on the rail, even a dead raccoon, the decapitation of which we studied with great seriousness. On that day we tramped through the deep snow down to the far end of the passenger station, which had a number of side tracks. Two freights were frozen in place next to each other fifty yards south of the station, and we hiked down there, examining the engines for signs of activity. There were none. We knew that we should not be near the train, but we had not climbed past any fences or gates to get there, and anyway, we enjoyed that boyish certainty that the town was ours, made for our inspection. We clambered over the engine for a few minutes, kicking off great pillows of snow and looking into the narrow, streamlined windows at the gauges and controls and what seemed to be a small, uncomfortable seat. Then we climbed down, having discovered that the wind had piled the snow between the adjacent boxcars of the two trains, almost to the actual tops of the cars themselves—perhaps sixteen feet. A tunnel. That is what boys think of, and we set about digging one between the two boxcars, postulating snowy caverns lit by flashlight. That is what boys think of, not that they will find, while digging, a boot—"

"Oh," Caroline said aloud.

"—which, in but a moment, turned into a boot with a frozen leg attached, and the tip of a hand. The two other boys jolted backward, screaming. I was a few feet away and had not seen it. The others took off hollering across the train yard, running awkwardly through the deep snow, exercising their terror, invoking an official adult response. I was left there. I began to run but was not compelled to do it. I turned back to the anonymous leg, and then stepped between the boxcars of one of the trains and in the woods stripped a leafless branch from a young maple. Then with the stick I swept the snow away from the body. The boot and leg became two legs. Then the hand became an arm and shoulder. I gingerly brushed the snow from one side of the face. The head was sunken into the chest. A chin. A cheek. A frozen, glassy eye. It was an old man, and the snow stayed piled on his hatless bald head and on his ears. The other eye was almost shut. His ears had snow in them. There was a cigarette butt frozen to his collar. I was terrified now, but also strangely thrilled, and I kept brushing at the body, even using my hands a bit. We seemed to be in intimate relation to each other. I took off my glove, looked over my shoulder, then touched my finger to his cheek. It was hard as ice. I could see that he had built a small, useless fire next to himself. The little bottle in the paper bag, the week-old newspaper—no doubt gathered from one of the trash cans in the train station—the hat on the ground. It was a tableau of the last despair, and I stared at it for a long time, begging to hear the secrets contained within, desperate to know what was happening to me as I looked. Then behind me came the excited shouts from my friends as they raced ahead of the stationmaster, a fat man of maybe fifty who huffed up and yelled at me with nervous anger to step back. Not long after that, the town sheriff ordered us to leave and go home, and I held myself a few steps away from my friends, feeling myself made different and strange by what had happened, by what I had chosen to do while they were gone.

I stopped, looked at Caroline.

"That was a good one." She moved close to me in the darkness, as a siren raced down the avenue below. "Tell me another."

"Is this what we do for entertainment? Lie around at night and tell dead-people stories?"

"Yes." She flicked an ash off her breast. "It's fun and you know it. Anyway, I'm just accommodating your perversions."

The cigarette smoke was poisoning me deliciously. "You don't know me well enough to know what my perversions are."

"Yes I do," she laughed.

"Tell me."

"You don't want to know."

"Tell me."

Silence. Then: "You look for death. I think that's a kind of perversion."

"You were right," I said after a moment.

"What?"

"I didn't want to know that."

"Tell me another one," she said.

"There's the first body I saw as a newspaper reporter."

"Okay."

"I was nineteen."

"Did you know anything yet?"

"No," I said. "Did you know anything when you were nineteen?"

"I knew how to get in trouble. Tell me your story first."

"I was in Jacksonville, Florida. I was a summer reporter at the *Florida Times-Union*, a big regional paper. My girlfriend at the time and I drove down in her 'sixty-nine MG convertible, full of rust, you could see the highway going by between your feet. We rented a cockroach apartment. She got a job as a cocktail waitress, I worked at the newspaper. I started out on the news desk but they moved me to features, because there wasn't much local news, really, just corrupt real-estate deals and navy pilots dumping their planes, and they could see that I could do the feature stuff. So one of my features was a day in the life of an ambulance crew. Pretty clichéd story, but I was a kid, I didn't know anything. So I rode around in the ambulance. There was a lot of boring stuff, heart attacks, stuff like—"

I looked over at where her hand was on herself.

"You're doing what I think you're doing?"

"Yes. Your voice is sexy."

"Would you like—?"

"Keep telling the story."

I looked at the ceiling.

"Just tell the story, sweetie."

I took a breath. "A call came in and we drove into a trailer park. Depressing place. Everything was sand and scrub pines and old cars and busted-down trailers. We pulled up to the one we were looking for—does that really feel good?"

"Yes. I'm listening and I'm doing this—and it's just right."

"When we got there I saw that a neighbor was leading a little boy away from the trailer. This tall, skinny guy comes out in bell-bottoms. He was a sailor. There was a big navy base in the area. The tall guy doesn't have a shirt. He waves us closer. He was skinny and blond and he's just about my age. I mean, he's exactly my age but we're living very different lives. So we get out quickly, and he's worried and upset and says, 'It's my baby, it's my baby girl'—I can't tell this—Jesus, you're lying there masturbating."

"Tell it."

"It's a fucking sacrilege."

"Tell it."

"We go up the steps of the trailer and inside there's a pretty Puerto Rican girl, and she is weeping and taking her fists way above her head and slamming them down on her legs, really punching herself hard, really hurting herself. And the sailor takes us through this cramped trailer into a tiny nursery with no pictures on the wall, no Mickey Mouse or anything, and there in the crib is this six-month-old baby girl lying faceup, and the EMTs get to work on the baby and they try for a while, while the woman is wailing outside in the other room. I'm just standing there like the most freaked-out person in the world."

Caroline's hand touched my penis.

"They worked on the baby with their oxygen and tried to get a heartbeat going, and then they gave up and called the code and one of them went out to talk to the mother and father. And so it was just me and this older guy, the EMT, and he started looking at the baby very carefully, even opened up the diaper. And I asked him what he was doing—I mean I was still freaked out, but I had to ask him. He said he was checking the baby for signs of abuse, bruises, whatever. And I said, What do you see? He said that the linen on the crib was clean, the baby was well nourished, there were no bruises, cuts, or marks on the baby, the baby's hair was clean, her fingernails were trimmed, the diaper was clean, the little—do you *have* to do that?"

Her mouth was on me now. She lifted her head. "Talk. I'm listening."

I took a breath. "The baby was clean, there was no diaper rash, not even a tiny spot. The EMT looked at me and said that the baby had received perfect care. Perfect. Then he turned the baby onto her stomach and pointed out two purplish stripes on either side of the spinal column. That was the lividity, the blood settling in the corpse. Then he turned the baby over and brought down her eyes and cleaned up the little bits of wrappers and tubes and stuff in the crib and then told the other EMT to call in the mother and father. I was there when they came in and the woman's face . . . she saw her daughter . . . ah . . . she saw her daughter, and it was like wires yanking her face back across her skull . . . I looked at the boy, the father, and he was military, he'd been trained not to show emotion and he was biting his bottom lip so hard that there was blood on his teeth. I saw—ahh . . . I saw that and—never—never forgot it."

My words seemed to echo in the darkness. It might reflect better on me if I could say that my tale finally short-circuited our lust, but that would not be true, and a reporter is supposed to tell the truth. Caroline, straddling me, presenting her hips forward, pulling back, presenting forward, seemed to be arguing a point—that her appetite could not be dulled by stories of wives and frozen drunks and dead babies. In this, I felt her to be my teacher. I have no doubt that we could have had graphic footage of the Holocaust projected on every wall, truckloads of gray, emaciated bodies being emptied into mass graves, and that I could still have effortlessly pushed myself into her, my face a mask of satiation and triumph. Perhaps that makes me godless, awful. But I do not think so. For I think that when we have sex, those corpses are always projected there on the walls of the imagination, dropping limply and heartbreakingly into the mass grave of time. Yes, I am sure of this. Those bodies are always there; they are the people outside the room and the people past, the people future, our parents and our children; they are our lost selves of youth, our selves of the moment and selves of tomorrow, all doomed.

WE FELL BACK TO THE SHEETS. "I'm finished," I told her. "That's it."

"Out of gas?"

"Out of juice."

She got up, brushed her hair at the dresser, and collected our glasses. "You hungry?"

"Yes."

"I'm going to make something." She left the room.

It was close to eight now. Lisa would be putting the kids to bed, waiting for a call from me. I wasn't ready to make it. I couldn't be sure of my voice. Maybe the drinking helped, maybe not. But there was something else, too. As a reporter you have conversations with strangers by the thousands. Some of them go quickly, some are agonizing. But in a successful interview, there is an identifiable moment, which, as I have mentioned, might be called the point of dilation, when the speaker opens up. Did I intend to interview Caroline? In a sense, yes. The dilation was coming, I could feel it. I knew that now that I had talked she would, too. This is why people exchange stories. They want to be known. The story is a kind of currency. If you give one, you usually will get one back. I didn't want to call Lisa, because I didn't want to break the moment with Caroline; either she would overhear the call or I would hang up the phone possessed by guilt. The chance would go, maybe forever.

But there were some other calls I could make. I picked up the phone next to the bed and dialed Bobby Dealy, who had just started his overnight shift.

"What's going on?" I said.

"Burning building in Harlem, one alarm, lady says her grilled-cheese sandwich caught on fire." His voice was flat. "Man left a snake on a bus outside St. Patrick's Cathedral. Cop shot in the leg in the Bronx. Several Nubians arrested on suspicion of being suspicious. Let's see—two guys from New Jersey jumped two gay guys in the Village, called them fags, the gay guys beat the shit out of them. Also, we got a girl in a nursing home who has been in a coma for twenty years who is pregnant."

"Raped."

"Right. Thing is, her eyes move. Follow people around the room."

"The guy raped a woman in a coma and she could still watch him?"

"TV people are all over it."

I sighed. "What else?"

"Philosopher with a knife arrested in the U.S. Passport Office in Rockefeller Center."

"What was that one?"

"It was the line for emergency passports," Bobby said. "The guy wanted to get out of the United States. Country going to hell, couldn't stand in line with everybody else."

"What else?"

"Body found on the Whitestone Expressway."

"On or next to?"

"On."

"Drug hit, in the car."

"Right."

Caroline came back in with two bottles of red wine and two glasses.

"What else?" I said to Bobby.

"You made page one for tomorrow."

"The Lancaster diary thing."

"Yes. How'd you get that?"

"A guy took it off Lancaster." I picked up one of the wine bottles. The price tag was still on it. Fifty-nine ninety-five.

"Nice piece," Bobby said.

"That it?"

"No, you got a call from Fitzgerald."

"He's at home?"

"Yes."

I called Hal.

"We're cool on your conditions," he said.

"I have your word on that?"

"Yes."

"No testifying, no identification of source, no giving the story away in the first twenty-four hours."

"Yes."

"I'll drop off the tape at your office tomorrow morning."

"Fine," Hal said. "Now what's the story?"

I told him. He was excited. "This is major, you realize."

"Yes, Hal."

"You're *sure* it's Fellows?"

"Tompkins Square Park. Rioters fighting the cops. Officer Fellows standing near curb. Tall black guy, about thirty years old. Firecrackers go off somewhere across the park. Fellows gets it from behind, perp runs away, crowd surges past body, cops see it, push crowd back. You know the rest."

"I'll send a car over to get the tape now."

"No."

"It's no problem."

"I'm not home."

"Where are you?"

"Not anywhere in particular."

"We can send a car there, too."

There was a pause while he realized I wasn't going to tell him.

"Tomorrow morning, I promise."

"Has to be the first thing."

"You got it."

"Thanks, Porter."

Sewn in. I hung up as Caroline returned with a tray of hot soup and bread. A naked woman carrying a silver tray. "Developments in the story?" she asked.

"Big."

She put the tray down. "Big is good."

"Sometimes."

"Oh, usually, I think."

"A small problem is better than a big problem."

"Well, I suppose." She gave me a bowl. "Were you calling somebody?"

"Yes, the police."

"Why?"

"Chitchat."

"About me?"

"No."

"Honestly?"

"No."

"You won't turn me in for anything?"

"Nah."

"For crimes, I mean."

"Like what?"

"Making pornographic statements, maybe."

"I didn't hear any."

"You weren't listening."

"I listen to everything you say to me. I remember every word."

"Sure."

I took a sip of soup. "Try me."

"What were the very first words I said to you tonight?"

"You said, 'I'm making you a little drink.' "

"How about the last words I said yesterday on the phone?"

" 'Get your column done.' "

She shook her head. "That's kind of scary."

"Not really."

"Can you remember what my very first words to you were?"

That was a little harder. I recalled Hobbs's party, and how Caroline came across the room toward me, how she sat down. " 'Your picture, Mr. Wren, is lousy.' That's what you said."

"I did?"

"Yes."

We ate the meal silently then put the dishes on the floor.

"This is the longest time we've been together," she said.

"Yes."

"It's nice."

"When I was that young reporter looking at the baby in the trailer," I said, "where were you?"

"I was probably about nine," Caroline answered, finishing her glass of wine. "We lived in South Dakota. I guess that's where I'm from. My mother got pregnant when she was seventeen. With me. She was from Florida, and one winter she had sex with a boy from a rich family in Connecticut who was vacationing down there. He didn't want to get married, so she lived with her parents, and then a couple of years later she met this guy Ron Gelbspan, who drove long-distance trucks. They moved to South Dakota and then they had my brother. I was born with my mother's maiden name, but then she changed it to my father's, which is Kelly, but she changed it again after she got married to Gelbspan, which I hated. I always thought of myself as Kelly. I never minded changing my name to

Crowley. Sometimes I think if I get married to Charlie and take his name, then that will be five names, which is kind of fucking ridiculous. I guess after a while the last name doesn't really matter. Anyway, my mother worked for Visa. She was on the phone all day, talking to people about their charge accounts. We lived in a little house maybe ten miles outside of town. I got two letters from my real dad, the last one when I was about ten—that was it. Ron was totally crazy, he wanted to own a long-distance trucking company. He was trying to build up a business, you know. He was really crazy. He had a shrine to Jackie Onassis in the house, this little corner where he had a lot of books and pictures of her. He had a lot of guns, too, especially shotguns. He used to hit us; one time we were riding in a motorboat and he threw my brother right out of the boat." She refilled her glass and then mine. "Anyway, by the time I was maybe eight, I wanted a horse, badly. Some of the other girls were riding by then and I wanted a horse. That was a big thing with Ron—I used to bug him for a horse, and—" She paused. Her blue eyes blinked. "It didn't work out. In high school I had boyfriends and everything, but I started to ask my mother about my real father—who he was, where he was, and all that—and at first she wouldn't tell me, but I kept asking and she told me she thought he was living in Santa Monica, California. That sounded so beautiful to me. Santa Monica, California. I had let my hair grow really long, maybe halfway down my back, and Mom and my brother and sister and Ron all had brown hair, so I asked Mom what my daddy looked like, and she said that he had blond hair and blue eyes like me and had missed Vietnam because he had scoliosis of the spine, just enough, but maybe the doctor was paid to say that. His daddy was an Atlantic Richfield Oil Company executive here in New York—you know, the name before ARCO. When I was eighteen, that would have made him about thirty-seven. Mom hadn't seen him in almost fifteen years. I asked her if she missed him, and she said she wondered what happened to him, and she told me how his mother was very, very beautiful, with the same forehead I had. My mother was so beaten down. She listened to credit problems all day long. I told her I wanted to go see my dad and did she have his phone number in Santa Monica. She said no, but his sister in New York might. So the summer after twelfth grade, I took the bus to Los Angeles."

Two days later, Caroline said, after seeing and smelling the ocean for the first time, she was standing in a large parking lot in Venice Beach looking at a skinny man with long graying blond hair washing an ancient rust-eaten VW camper that appeared to be parked permanently. He did not recognize her as he saw her walk up and stand in front of the camper. Clearly he was watching her breasts move inside her shirt, her long legs. "Hey, what can I do for you?" He squared up his shoulders to present a more compelling version of himself, which was unlikely, given that his body was both soft and malnourished-looking, his legs and arms and chest skinny. She stopped fifteen feet away from him and asked what his name was. "All depends on who's asking," he said.

"Suppose it's your daughter?" she said.

The man stiffened. "The fuck you talking about?"

She saw how the sun had damaged his face, burning and reburning the skin across his thinning hairline, his nose, and shoulders.

"I said, suppose it's your daughter?"

He winced. "I'd ask her what she wanted."

"Maybe she wants to know you."

"Then I'd say forget it."

"Why?"

" 'Cause I don't want to know her."

They stood there under a brilliant, perfect sky. Nearby a stray dog nosed through garbage around a trash can. She looked back at her father. "You're my daddy. My name is Caroline Kelly Gelbspan and your name is John J. Kelly III, and you grew up in Greenwich, Connecticut, and your father worked for the Atlantic Richfield Oil Company, and you met my mom when you were in college on vacation and she got pregnant with me—from you. She remembers everything about you. She told me the whole story fifty times."

He stood there, wiped his hands on his shorts.

"Get out of here."

"You were supposed to be my daddy."

"I mean it." He waved his hand, pushed air. "I don't know you or what kinda thing you're telling me here."

The dog had found something in the garbage and looked up, chewing.

"I came here from South Dakota. I wanted to see you."

"I don't care if you came from fucking Mars, I don't know who you are or any of that shit you just told me. You just get on along outa here. I don't have any business with this whole line of bullshit."

"I don't have very much money."

"That's not my problem and neither do I."

She stared at him. "You once told Mom how you were going to—"

"Hey, I told *lot* a chicks *lot* a things back then, and most of it was so I could fuck them."

This was the closest he came to acknowledging her.

"But I'm gonna say it again, I don't know who the fuck you think you are coming up here and telling me you got some kinda claim on me that I'm your father because that don't mean shit to me. I got all kinds of other things I gotta worry about besides some girl coming up to me with this kinda shit."

She didn't move.

"Go on, get the fuck out my sight."

She lingered a moment.

"Unless you want to give me a blowjob."

For the next week, Caroline said, she slept in the sand with the other kids who hung out along Venice Beach around the T-shirt shops and bike-rental places, trying to keep her long hair clean and washing in the public bathrooms. The novelty of the ocean wore off quickly. They kept telling her she could be a model, she had beautiful hair. There was another girl who looked like Caroline did and she had gotten a modeling job and had never been heard from again. All the talk was about either music, tattoos, the police, what the best drugs were, opening a business on the beach, or being an artist. It was high-school talk, not so different from what she had left in South Dakota. She called home, but her mother was out. Ron said, You got to take care of yourself, Mom got put on shorter hours. Perched over the beach was an immense new hotel, a multilevel pink confection, the Loews Santa Monica, and she found herself watching the people who sauntered down from it; usually they rented bicycles or spent money in the shops. She told herself that she would be like that. She went into the hotel's restaurant and asked if there was work. An officious woman in a suit told her they only hired through a union. On her way out she noticed that there were a lot of young white men in excellent physical condition sitting around the Jacuzzi. The Montreal Canadiens, whispered a towel-boy; they always stay here when they're in town. One of the players beckoned to Caroline, but she kept moving.

An hour later she had put her hair in a very tight braid and was in a coffee shop two miles down the boulevard asking an old woman for a job. I worked in a truck stop back in South Dakota, lied Caroline. Girl pretty as you never worked, the woman answered. Hair like that. Let me wait tables for a week, and if I'm no good, then you don't have to pay me. Just give me some food. She could keep herself clean for a week, she figured, and she was right.

In this way she successfully rented a room for a hundred dollars a week and could just get by, but it was never going to get her anywhere. One of the patrons of the restaurant, a trim man in his thirties, already going a bit gray, gave her his number at the hotel; he would be there a week, he said, please come see me if you wish. She did, lying around the room while he conducted business on the phone. He bought her some clothes and was kind to her. She watched him do push-ups and sit-ups in the mornings. There was something about him that was safe. He was clean. He had an American Express Platinum card. At the end of the week, he said that he knew he would never see her again but that he wanted to give her a little unsolicited advice. You need a plan, he said. You're beautiful, but there are a lot of beautiful girls out here and most go in the wrong direction. I know, she said. You don't, he said, not really. If you don't have a plan, you start to go hard. Little by little, and it takes you places you don't want to go. How do you know all this? she asked. I know, believe me, I'm old enough to know. You're going hard already. How do you know? Tell me how many men you've slept with. She paused to think. Including him, maybe about ten. That's a lot already, he said. You need to go to school, get on that track, you're plenty smart enough. Where did you go to school? she asked. I went to a place called Yale, he said. And the law school there. Am I smart enough to go to Yale? she asked. Yes, he said, but you don't have the preparation. I could get the preparation. He looked at her sadly, and all of a sudden she despised him. I hate rich people, she declared. They think they are better. They *are* better, in some respects, said the man. And you want to be rich, right? Yes, of course, she said. All right, one last piece of advice, he said. What? She found the conversation exasperating. Men will always want to take from you, he said, remember that. I already know that, she told him. Maybe you do, he shrugged. Did *you* want to take from me? she asked. Of course, he said. And did you? Yes, absolutely. Yeah? Yes, and I'm trying to give a little back, too.

She decided that he was a self-important jerk, and she regretted the time with him—but what he had said also made her anxious. A few weeks later she heard of the bars and clubs in other areas of the city, and she was as intrigued by the action there as by the possibility of making money. One of the waitresses knew of a place near the airport called Club Comanche; by day it was little more than a door in a wall with a guy standing outside, but by eleven P.M. the night crawled in—bikers, Iranians, off-duty cops, local businessmen who didn't wear a tie to work, washed-up screenwriters, and black guys in good suits. Girls were there for three reasons; either they were somebody's girlfriend, or, by the benevolent permission of the club, they were looking to be somebody's girlfriend, if only for a night, or they sported short little red dresses and black fishnet stockings and carried full glasses on trays one way and cash and empties the other. On Saturday night, as many as fifty women worked the men and thirty worked the alcohol. Within a year, the place would become a real strip club, Caroline said, and too bad for her, because they tended to be better run, but for now the essence of the place lay somewhere between hell and breakfast. She called ahead and was told to come in when Merk was there, Merk being the guy who interviewed all the new girls. She spent the morning trying to decide what to wear, and finally showed up on a rainy Saturday afternoon in a sweater and jeans, her long hair pinned up. A man and a woman were arguing in the alleyway, and that didn't inspire her confidence, but she knocked at the door, a curtain moved, and she was let in. Merk wasn't there, she was told, but she could wait for him in the back where the waitresses kept their things. There were some uniforms hanging in a closet, and she might as well try one on, since Merk would ask to see how she looked in one. So she set her things down in the room, which was nothing more than some lockers, a torn-up couch, three sinks, three toilets, and an exit door. A wastebasket was filled with cigarette cartons, Tampax boxes, and beer bottles. She picked out a size-six uniform that didn't look too dirty and was down to her panties and bra when Merk came in, his penis already in his hand, and told her to get on the couch. He was not tall, but he had that sort of fattened bulk that suggests violence. Oh, you are just about the sweetest thing I ever saw, he said, big tits like that, oh shit, and when she resisted he took her arm and pulled her onto the couch. Put up your legs, he commanded, and she didn't think it was worth a fight. He had known all along, he must have been watching, the others had set her up. Take off your bra, too. She did, and again he said, Oh shit. It won't hurt too much, he added, I got Vaseline here. And indeed he did, and he slowly pushed himself into her with far more skill than she had actually yet experienced with the boys in South Dakota and the boys on the Santa Monica pier, there being two already since she had arrived, but that didn't mean that she liked it, and because he was above her she stared at him defiantly. What're you looking at? he demanded between breaths. Hello, she said, my name is Caroline Kelly, and I'm applying for a job here. Merk smiled, and his teeth had been everywhere he had. Hold on there, little girl, just let me—and he went at it pretty hard then, so that it hurt her back, and she knew enough already about the refill capacities of men's reproductive systems to know that he had fucked someone else recently enough that he was going to have to labor a bit to get his shot out, and that was exactly what he did, labor at it, banging at her with a sort of wheezing determination to finish what he had started, club life not being the healthiest of living, and when the bicycle was just about at the top of the hill, the confidence flowed back into his face, and he started to tell her that he was going to have to fuck her every day she worked there because she was just about the most beautiful thing he had *ever*—and that was when the screams in the alley behind the club began. It was a woman crying out as a knife entered and exited her just about that quick, and she was begging, Please don't do it, please, I'm begging, but whoever he was he did it again three times and Merk yelled shit and immediately lost his erection, there being some tattered morality still hidden in his loose gut, and with his pants unbuckled and a gun now in his hand he slammed open the fire door, and that was when the woman whom Caroline had seen arguing outside slumped into the doorway, her neck bubbling blood from the side, her face white, her eyes falling in frantic sisterhood upon Caroline's.

The police asked her what she saw, and, standing next to Merk, she told them, never mentioning the rape. When they left she turned to him and said, "Now you have to give me the job." He nodded, and he did. Thus was the first part of Caroline's Los Angeles education completed.

SHE SAT WITH HER KNEES DRAWN UP, remembering it to herself. It was a very bad story, and I appreciated that, but I needed to ask her about the Hobbs tape, I needed to force our conversation back to that question. Yet my instinct was to wait a little longer; perhaps her story might find its way there. But first I had to clear away the other problem. I excused myself and went into the kitchen and finally made a short tortured phone call to my house, intent on leaving a message that Lisa would hear in the morning. Josephine picked up on the third ring.

"Wren residence," she said sleepily.

"It's Porter," I said, surprised.

"Lisa called me in," Josephine responded softly. "Somebody's little girl got her finger cut off."

Somebody important enough to get a specialist in the middle of the night. This happens—if the victim is rich or important enough, he or she can get a top Manhattan surgeon on demand. The distraught party will call someone who will know a hospital board chairman through social circles, who will then call the hospital's president of staff and explain that they have a VIP situation. In the case of a hand injury, the president of the staff will phone the chief of the orthopedics department, who will then figure out which microvascular surgeon to call, one who's got a good hand at night, who is not drunk, who will present well to the parents. Hence a call to Lisa. The process can happen so fast that the surgeon may arrive at the hospital before the helicopter. I know Lisa had nodded yes when the call came, cursed me for not being there, and dialed Josephine.

"I'll be home very late," I said. "Please tell Lisa. Tell her I'm fine, just working on a story." Josephine, I have always feared, knows every thought that runs through my mind.

"Yes, Porter."

"Well, good night, then."

"Good night." As I hung up I passed my eyes around Caroline's kitchen and found myself looking at the refrigerator; again there was nothing on the door, not a magnet or a photo or a calendar or a postcard, nothing. Like the rest of the kitchen, it was spotless. I felt an urge to pull open the drawers and fling open the cabinets, to see what all this stark cleanliness might be concealing.

But then Caroline's voice came from the dark hallway that led to her bedroom, and when I returned she asked, "You called home?"

"Yes."

"What did you say?"

"Lies."

She nodded. She had opened the second bottle of wine.

"You were describing your descent into the L.A. pretty-girl life. I assume you then got the job at the club, and that for a couple of years you screwed a lot of people, including maybe a few other girls—as a relief from the men—and did a lot of drugs and saw a lot of pools in Bel Air or Malibu. Maybe a few movie stars or producers or pro athletes."

"Oh, fuck you."

"Am I wrong?"

"You're not right, not exactly."

"No?"

"Well, there *was* Magic Johnson." She sighed, as if trying to remember a movie she once saw. "With me and this other girl named Shari. He told us to call him Earvin. He was very nice, actually. We all rolled around in a big bed. I don't really remember much about it, except that I was really, really sick from Mexican Quaaludes. I went into the bathroom, and there was a pair of bedroom slippers, and I put my feet in them and laughed they were so big. I think I got sick then, right on his slippers."

"Very beautiful." I pulled on my socks. It was after one A.M. I had to get this around to Hobbs. "Why did you come to New York?"

"It was sort of from knowing Merk." They had fallen into something like a friendship, strangely enough. Caroline said, "I really liked him. Actually, he gave me my tattoo. Paid for it. It took a long time to get it done;

the wings had lots of different colors. It was beautiful." She laughed. "I miss it."

"Why're you having it taken off?" I said.

"Oh, Charlie. That whole world, you know."

"Merk was saying he was sorry."

"I guess. It got a little complicated, actually."

Merk provided her with the one drug she really liked, crystal methedrine, she went on, and soon they could even laugh about his rape of her. "I was really into the crystal, you know, doing it and then cleaning out my purse for five hours, stuff like that," Caroline remembered. "He was into smoking crack, too. We went for the double master blaster a couple of times, where, you know, I did him with my mouth, and when he was about to come, he took a huge hit off the pipe. He got it once. We tried it with me, he went down on me, but it didn't work. He wasn't really concentrating on me. Besides, what I wanted to try was heroin, but I told him I wouldn't shoot it. He got some of the stuff you could smoke. You can do it once or twice, maybe three times, you know, without getting hooked."

"How many times did you do it?"

She giggled. "Three."

It was while doing drugs one April afternoon before the club opened, Caroline said, that a biker Merk knew, known as Chains, arrived and suggested they take a ride down to South Central. Chains had heard that some riots were starting at the intersection of Florence and Normandie Avenues and he wanted to have a look. The niggers were burning down the city, Chains said. You never knew when you might see a riot again, might as well take advantage of the opportunity. And to see a riot while you snorted crystal—chance of a lifetime, bro. They loaded up in Merk's car, with a friend of Chains's, and rolled through one gang territory after another: the East-Coasts, the Brims, the Hoovers, the Underground Crips, the Raymond Avenue Crips, the Watergates, the Rollin' Sixties, the Eight Treys. Except for the red of the Bloods and the blue of the Crips, no one who wasn't a gang member or a cop could keep them all straight. The sky was full of smoke and helicopters, sirens near and far. Anybody else beside me got a gun, man? Merk asked. The others shook their heads. They rode past burning cars and looters, and then a black kid with a blue bandanna taunted them from the curb. Gotta stop here and deal with this, announced Merk. No, man, said Chains, it's not— But Merk rolled to a stop and that was when a can of beer hit the hood. Then another black kid came up with a shotgun, butted Merk with it through the open window, yanked open the door, pulled Merk from the car, and began kicking him, keeping the gun trained on everyone else. Chains jumped out of the passenger side with a knife, came around the front of the car, and, with a smile on his face, the kid fired: Chains's hand was blown off. Now Caroline was screaming and trying to hide in the backseat. Another blast of the shotgun blew out the side window. She knew it was double-barreled from Ron's gun collection and popped her head up to see if the boy was reloading. He wasn't, so she jumped out of the car while the boy stood calmly lecturing Chains about respect for the black man. Caroline dragged Merk into the backseat, his face dripping. His gun fell out of his shirt and she picked it up. Yo bitch, laughed the boy with the shotgun, what's up with that? Caroline fired, without aiming. The shot missed the boy, but across the street another man grabbed his ankle and screamed. Chains, meanwhile, had the presence of mind to jump back into the front of the car, clutching the bloody stump of his hand, already looking for a tourniquet. People were running across the avenue. The gunman was now patting his pockets for more shells. With Merk in the backseat, Caroline put the car in reverse and ducked her head down. She did a U-turn in the middle of Normandie Avenue and drove directly to the hospital. That night she watched the riots on television with the other girls in her house, smoking pot. Merk had a blood clot in his eye, and they wanted him to stay in the hospital for a couple of weeks. She called her mother to tell her that she was okay and listened to the weeping on the other end. There was no particular reason for this; her mother did it almost every time they talked. Ron came on and said he had watched the riots on television, then checked a map to see that she wasn't close by. No, she said dreamily. I'm fine.

Two days later, as Los Angeles counted its dead and put out the last fires in South Central, Caroline arrived in New York.

I HAVE FOUND in my years as a reporter that people don't seem disturbed by genuine surprises as much as by events that they themselves have created.

The occurrence that is unforseeable cannot really be regretted, whereas the occurrence that one has helped to author can cause remorse or anger indefinitely. So, too, with Caroline. Her rape by Merk in the club was a cruel surprise but not in any way her fault; subsequent incidents, however, derived from a sequence of conscious actions. Yet the two events are related; the two *types* of events are related. The first was brutalizing, and yet it demonstrated to Caroline that she could be brutalized and survive—if not utterly intact, then at least functionally intact. The spectrum of experienced abuse was thus widened. If she still feared being raped, she did not fear it in exactly the same way. If she had seen herself understood by another human as just a thing, then, if she wanted, she could understand herself as just a thing; in the words of feminist theory, she could "internalize her objectification," which is concise and correct. If she had been brutalized, then at least she could now measure the distance between the experience of being brutalized and the imagining of it. There are people who enjoy degradation, or who seek it thinking they will enjoy it, or who seek it because it is the way they know how to have pleasure. After all, the experience is theirs. Perhaps they lived through the degradation and found pleasure in that realization. Or perhaps they found that in degradation there is a releasing of oneself; one is powerless; responsibility is taken away. I am not describing what occurs during the actual event but the subsequent thought about the event that accumulates in a person's mind. A fellow reporter once told me that as a seventeen-year-old boy he had been raped in a park by three men. They did everything that three men could do to him, and he was hospitalized for two weeks. The man was now grown, had four children and a content wife. He had in no way elicited the attack; he was on his bicycle on the way to the grocery at the request of his mother; the men dragged him off his bike and into the park. The odd thing is this: he didn't regret the incident. He admitted that if he had the chance to erase the event from the blackboard of his memory, he would keep it there. He still thought about the event; it was important to him and had allowed him to contemplate other expressions of sexuality. He had, in fact, become a true voyeur, a fact that he traced, not unhappily, to the incident.

In the case of Caroline, the interplay between accidents and self-authored events was too complicated for me to understand, but nevertheless it had occurred. This, I think, is what the man who went to Yale intuitively foresaw when he warned Caroline that she would get hard. He knew that if she had slept with him so easily, then she would sleep with others the same way and that such randomness contained the certainty that others would not be so kind as he had been. As parents we are quickly sobered by seeing just how impressionable a child is and how that soft, new impression quickly becomes the groove of habit, even the final dent of personality. Listening to Caroline describe her odyssey from Los Angeles to New York City, I could not help but experience a strange fusion of the dispassionate journalist, the lover, and the father. No doubt my musings were self-important and shot through with flawed reasoning, yet they began to coalesce around one powerful question. Lost in a trance of contemplation, I understood that long before she arrived in Los Angeles, Caroline must have suffered some primary period or episode of brutalization, some moment that jolted her away from the normal arc lived by most little girls and into the odd zigzag of violence and sexuality that she had described. The experience would have to have been survivable—for she *had* survived—yet unusual, even for a girl in a rural, lower-middle-class family with a depressed mother and a stepfather of questionable intent and sanity. It came to me that this event may have been as typical—though horrible—as incest or some similar abuse. Yet I sensed that it was something else, something that did not correspond to sociological trends but that had a poetic unity and intensity recognizable by a little girl. Children are capable of a kind of concentrated attention that we adults more or less have lost. Their minds are not cluttered with the debris of existence. The world is new, language powerful, images as yet unseen. Who was the girl, I wondered, that became the woman? If one thing had happened, what was it?

But then, looking out the window of Caroline's apartment, I cursed myself for entertaining such foolish, half-drunken speculations. There was no sentimental education here; I was simply an asshole with a promiscuous woman in a room. In the city, there are always people in other rooms, doing other things. Now I was one of them. And with that I returned to the bed to hear more of what Caroline had to tell me. Unknown to me then was that my question about Caroline's childhood, which I had formulated

with such tedious rumination, was uncannily similar to one that Simon
Crowley had instinctively seized upon before his death. That I wondered
about the answer and he *demanded* it was one of our great differences. And
yet, oddly enough, it was Hobbs who had heard it—from Caroline herself.
Thus were the three of us bound together in ways unknown to each of us;
thus was the complexity of our relationship mysteriously centered on an
event none of us had experienced.

Later—much later—all this would become clear to me, but for now I
listened to Caroline describe her early days in New York. It was April and
at first she stayed in a cheap hotel right off Washington Square Park,
watching the leaves appear, the faces, the buildings, the motion, the shadows moving down avenues and across streets—particularly Midtown,
where money walked the streets incarnated as humans. Women, she could
tell, were taken more seriously in New York; they didn't look as good as
the women in L.A., but they had more power, they were in the game.
Everywhere she went she understood that the America she had heretofore
known was strangely lacking in density, in straight-ahead power. Even
L.A. seemed dissolute, distracted by its highways, flung outward, small beneath the sun. In New York, all contexts were intimate. Even the wretched
and impoverished seemed magnified in their suffering; monstrous men
dressed in rags shouldered like giants through the crowds, pushing past,
say, a hawkish woman in her forties who could recite from memory all the
apartments selling for a million dollars or more in a given block on Park
Avenue, who was herself talking on her portable phone with a man who
each night composed the look of the country's biggest late-night talk
show, choosing from eleven camera monitors the flowing sequence of
long and close shots—the crowd pan, the tight shot of the guest smiling,
the cut to the host's mocking eyebrow action—in this, fortunes were
made, and Caroline understood, sensed, that the ongoing dissolution and
fragmentation of America may have been replicated in L.A. but in New
York it was anticipated; in the cultural crevices and breakpoints and dis-
junctions here were people who knew how to rush in with their software
and images and words and analysis. She could see the people haggling in
restaurants, the photo shoots on the avenues, the attitude, the *fucking fuck
you I'm talking to you* attitude that said it knew that the world was not

giving away any of the good stuff, the good stuff would have to be bought or seduced or stolen outright. And where she would fit in in this place she did not know, but for now this did not worry her; for the first time she felt herself to be free of all she had come from, free even of herself, and whereas in L.A. she had been eager to please, to laugh and fuck with the others, now she gathered and preserved herself. It had been years since she'd lived in cool weather, and she liked it, liked being forced inside coats, inside cafés and museums and her first Manhattan apartment on West Ninety-seventh Street, where she could gaze down on the crowds moving along the wet ribbon of Broadway, the booksellers miserable in the drizzle, look down on the clots of taxis stopping and moving, stopping and moving, the heavy centeredness of it, the old buildings, the grime, and know that for the first time she could remember she might describe herself as happy.

Her first affair in the city, she told me, was with a young doctor she met one night outside a Korean grocery, and for the few weeks that she saw him he was distracted and exhausted. He possessed a slender body that she thrilled at, but again and again he had difficulty with his erection; he was a resident in an oncology ward and spent his days gazing into the eyes of the wretched and dying, breathing the exhalations of the living dead, learning of the floridity of tumors, the liquefaction of bones, the godlike beauty of morphine. Each day he expended his spirit in the hospital, and although she had a new, pale love for him, she was not surprised when he slipped away from her, no longer called her back.

For a time, she stayed to herself, running her savings down, not working.

"Did you work?" I asked.

"Not really."

"How did you exist?"

"I gave up my apartment," she answered.

"Where did you live?"

The answer was to be found in the advantages of what was now Caroline's more conservative appearance and in the functional inefficiencies of wealth. Rich people may only occupy one space at a time. Yet they may own two, three, or more residences, and once she had apartment-sat for one such person, she found that people were always going off to Italy for six months or being transferred to Hong Kong. These were people who belonged not to a particular nation but to the country of wealth; they needed someone in New York who would pass on messages, or forward the mail, or water the weeping cherry trees atop the penthouse. The arrangements were always casual, and made easier by the notion that Caroline was "between apartments," "not settled into the city yet." Of course, the owners of the apartments knew or sensed the truth—that Caroline's only agency was her beauty—but they also knew that her loveliness suggested that the owner of the apartment was a person of largesse and refinement. Caroline's presence was a form of self-flattery.

So she drifted from one apartment to the next, living a hand-to-mouth life of luxury, always short of cash, yet somehow skating by. In each place she inspected the rugs and the books and the china. She also always read what letters and diaries she found and was struck by how unhappy the rich were, or how unhappy they imagined themselves to be. She knew that she needed to be discreet about whom she brought back to the apartment, lest word leak back to the owners that she was defiling their good name and rugs with men tramping through. And the apartment buildings always had older men who found her intriguing and were unable not to offer her "advice on her investments" or small gifts of significant cash value, so long as she remembered not to say hello to the men in front of their wives.

I will interrupt my summation of Caroline's long account to note that even as I listened to her describe her early days in New York City, I was seized by the strange realization that there would come a time when the older Caroline would describe *these* days to someone. If she did not mention me, then at least she would describe the few years before she had turned thirty, when she was living just off Central Park and was engaged to Charlie. I suspected that I was not going to see her in her future self, and there was a far toll of sadness in this for me, for I find, now that I near forty, that women, all women, are beautiful to me. No, that is a lie—not all women. But many of them. Of course, little girls and teenagers and girls in their twenties. But equally compelling are the older women in their sixties, seventies, or even eighties. They seem to know so much about their worlds. They gaze upon younger people, men and women, with a gentle clarity. They have lived the cycle, or most of it, and in seeing others' struggles—for love, for identity, for security—they remember their own. And then there are the women in their fifties; they have arrived at the age of wisdom, and they are exhausted and sometimes bitter and frequently tough from the long climb. They seem more certain of their power, finally, as the men their age begin to collapse, and as their own bodies settle into whatever form of ruin will carry them the rest of the way—fleshy heaviness, a slow, shrinking boniness, stoop and gnarl and bad toes. And then there are the women in their forties, fired by the intensity of their desires. There may be nothing sexier than a woman in her forties. She has arrived at new freedoms, yet she knows that time is taking from her even as it presents more bounty. When I was a young man of twenty-five, I could not see the sexuality—often hard-won—of a woman, say, of forty-three. But I see it now. It is a kind of glory.

Looking at Caroline, I could imagine what she would look like in fifteen years—the teeth and mouth still marvelous and the sunglasses and lipstick and the lines at the corners of the eyes and the ankles still slim and ever more money to keep her hair blonde—but I did not know her well enough to guess whether the next two decades might be largely good or offer some new occasion of suffering. I wondered if in some inexplicable way she had arrived at a moment of reckoning with herself. It was not only me she was telling her story to—no. Her own future self was also listening.

It had been about a year after she arrived in New York, Caroline said, that a letter from her mother arrived, saying that her father had died out in California. The cause was unknown, except that he had been lingering in the old VW camper for several months. Caroline stared at the letter for almost an hour, trying to understand why the news hurt her so much. She had never known her father, never seen him but for that one day in Venice Beach, and yet his death was shocking to her; the universe seemed diminished. The unhappiness of their brief relation was now eternal. If she had hoped that one day they might meet again, and somehow redeem each other, then such a possibility was now foreclosed. She would die having never known her father; she would die not knowing if he had loved her or missed her or even ever thought of her.

After that came an Israeli businessman who was all curly black hair and gold. He seemed powered by hate, hate for those whom he bested in commerce, for Arabs, for chickenhearted American men, for blacks, for Russians, who were cheats, for anyone who did not live with the toughness that he did. She did not know why she even put up with him—perhaps it was because inwardly his tirades broke her heart. He confessed to her one night after they had made love that as a boy he had heard an explosion up the street, and when he ran to the bus that the Palestinians had bombed, the first thing he saw was the top half of his mother's body, tossed like a rag doll into a leafless tree. After this, Caroline felt that she would forgive him his brutality. But one night he slapped her in his anger, and she saw that the damage would never heal, that the bomb twenty years prior exploded again day after day, and that he was doomed by his anger.

She understood by now that she was attracted to men who were in some way excessive. The bars and health clubs and office buildings were filled with fine and boring men, and their reasonableness and good humor held no attraction for her. They were interested in mutual funds and pro football and they were too witty on the first date and too polite in bed. They described themselves as political but didn't understand the streets. They seemed mass-produced, they exhibited the impotent irony of their generation, they were television. She found that men on the margin were more interesting, had more at risk, were forced to live with greater consciousness.

And then came Simon. He was on the West Coast half the time. He didn't want her along. When he was in Manhattan he disappeared with Billy. Or he blew into town with a schedule of appointments, people to see, parties, nightclub acts, plays, one-man shows. She went with him, and at times he seemed to forget that she was there in the room, so vociferously did he argue with the others. And she watched admiringly. He was one long riff. He was about conversation and nuance and observation, and all the better if it was at a restaurant with twelve other people and the tab was running into the thousands of dollars. Then at one or two or three they would stumble into a cab and shoot back to the apartment.

"We would get home and get into bed and maybe we had sex," Caroline remembered. "But usually Simon wanted to watch movies. He would watch the lighting of the scene or the way a sequence had been edited, with long takes or short ones." She understood that he did his best thinking at night, that only by filling his head with the conversation and images of the day was he able later to concentrate, to let it all back out again. "And then he would go to L.A., not bothering to pack anything. He just took the limo to the airport and then was gone. He liked airplanes—"

"All right," I interrupted.

"What's that mean?"

"It means all right."

"You're bored, you want me to shut up?"

"No, I want to know—"

"What, what do you *want* to know? That I—"

She didn't finish her sentence, and for a minute, perhaps more, neither of us spoke. The night was at its fullest, snow still falling. I have thought often of those long hours—in the room in the million-dollar apartment (where someone else lives now), Manhattan twinkling out the window, the rush of traffic below—examined its moments and stages and levels; it was, in its own way, a spectacular night that I do not yet think I completely understand. And, as it turned out, we were not done with each other, not at all. Finally Caroline got up to pee, and I stood naked at the window, my head full of expensive wine, somehow seeing the beauty of the dark skyline in a way that I never had before, feeling the bulk and heaviness of each building before me, apparitions of shadow notched with the odd lighted window, the lives there transpiring with the same predictability and mystery as my own.

"There's another part of your story I want to hear," I said, when Caroline returned.

"Is it bad?" she asked.

"Probably."

"We finished the wine."

"I could retreat back to gin, continue with wine, or make a leap to whiskey," I said.

"You might regret it."

"I might regret a lot of things."

She disappeared into the kitchen and returned with a bottle and two shot glasses. She poured them out.

"Let me have it."

"I want to hear the part in which you meet Hobbs and it ends up that he's being sent a videotape of himself."

"Sebastian Hobbs?" she asked.

"You know him?" I said.

"*You* know him?"

"Yes, unfortunately." I told her about our conversation in his office—the threats, the African masks, everything.

Caroline sank down on the bed. "Come on!"

"No, I mean it. You don't believe me?"

Caroline began to laugh, madly, and then lay down, making sounds that were no longer laughter exactly but a sort of wretched coughing. "I can't believe it," she cried, "I can't *fucking* believe it!"

"What? What?" I said.

She looked up at me with large, streaked eyes. "*I* want you to find that tape for me."

"What?"

"For *me*."

I held her face with my hands. But it was no good. Her top teeth pressed horribly into her bottom lip, eyes brimming. She stared at me with terror. "I really need to find that tape," she said between heaves. "He keeps threatening me, says he's going to sue me for harassment, says he's going to buy the rights to Simon's movies and take them out of the stores. He says he'll tell Charlie. He has people who watch me, I think. People went through my apartment. That sounds crazy, but it's true."

"What's on the tape?"

"I don't know!" she cried. "I mean, I know, sort of—it's not very nice—" She looked at me plaintively. "It's not good, it was something that Simon . . ." She turned away and threw herself back onto the sheets. "That's why I wanted you to *see* all of Simon's tapes. I thought you needed to see just what kind of stuff he liked, how he *collected* weird tapes of things—the people in Rwanda and everything—how he had a sick curiosity about things."

"I got that, yes."

"This is very hard to explain, this makes me seem like some kind of *slut* or something. We were at the Waldorf for something, some party upstairs that the studio was throwing, and Simon and I slipped out. He kept telling me that he was going places and he didn't know if I was, if I could keep up with him. So naturally I would get pissed off about that, and we would have these fights, and so we were at the bar, back in one of the private rooms, and he challenged me. He said he would do anything I asked him to do, as long as it didn't hurt somebody, and he could ask me to do anything, too. I mean, it was ridiculous, but it had a certain kind of effect. I mean, I liked it, I thought, okay, this guy, this person, is interested in how strong I am, and if we do this, then we'll have done something together, there'll be this *bond*, I guess, and so I said, okay, fine, fuck you, Simon, all right. And he said, okay, we're gonna have to have *proof*. I said, fine. Then he said, when are we going to do this? And I said, tonight, we'll both do it tonight, lots of possibilities out there—clubs, bars, the streets. It was still early, maybe eleven. And so I started to wonder what the thing was that he *really didn't* want to do. So I said something like you sure you want to do this? I mean, I knew that what he wanted was for me to go have sex with somebody, something like that. Pretty predictable. So he said, you know what I'm going to ask you to do? And I said, yes, you want me to go fuck somebody. And he said, yeah. All I want is it to be someone I never would have guessed. You got to surprise me, you got to really surprise me. He said it couldn't be, you know, the bellhop at the hotel or one of the producers or studio people upstairs. And then he said it couldn't be a woman, that wouldn't count. Had to be a guy. I mean, the psychology of all this is pretty obvious, I know, but the thing is that if you are *really* going to play this kind of game, then it gets pretty interesting, it gets exciting, sort of. Maybe I can't explain it. Anyway, so I said yes. Fuck yes. But then he had to do something for me. I wasn't going to ask him to go out and have sex with some woman, that was too easy, that was nothing. Then I thought maybe I'd ask him to go have sex with a *man*, but then I worried about AIDS. I'd had AIDS tests—all negative, thank you. Besides, Simon would probably just get totally drunk and then screw somebody down on the East Side or something. Or go to some gay bar and just . . . you know, whatever. He might be disgusted by it, but it wouldn't *rock* him. I wanted to think of something that would rock him, maybe even be edifying in some kind of way so that we could stop playing these fucking *games* with each other. So I was sort of thinking this was an opportunity, and so it came to me, and I said, I want you to be with somebody tonight when he or she dies. I want you to be right *there*, even touching the person, if possible. And I said I didn't want him going off and running over somebody with a car or something but actually getting into some place or situation, like an emergency ward maybe, something like that, and just being with somebody when they died. I mean, Simon could talk himself into all kinds of places. And when I told him that, that sort of shocked him, it sort of made him realize that if he thought he could ask me to prostitute myself for him, his whim, his amusement, then I was going to push back at him, I was going to play even harder. And I guess that was the only way that I knew I could earn his respect. There was no way that the relationship was going to work if he didn't have respect for me. So I told him that, and he was quiet for a moment, and then he looked at me and I could see that he got it. He saw what I was doing, he accepted the challenge. So, fine. He got one of the studio people to go to his office and get two microvideo recorders with wires and little batteries, the really expensive ones, and he rigged one up my purse; he cut a hole in it and showed me how to start the tape when I was ready. Then we said we would meet here at nine o'clock the next morning. He would show me his and I would show him mine. I mean, we were both drunk and pissed and excited. He called up Billy from the bar phone and told him to pick him up. Billy—I guess you figured this out from the videos—Billy was sort of his sidekick, they did stuff together. They'd hide the camera in Billy's coat or something. Anyway, Billy came in and was parked outside, and then they left together. So there I was. For a while I thought the whole thing was stupid and demeaning and ridiculous. And it *was*. But if I didn't go through with it, he'd be furious. And I sort of felt that I would be letting him down. Letting *me* down, too. What happened if I didn't go through with it and he did? Then that would be bad, I would have tricked him. Of course, I thought that the opposite could happen, too. I'd go out and have sex with some guy and then find out that Simon didn't do *anything*, went to a club or something. But I had to take him at his word. I had to do it. So I began to think about it. The hotel was full of tourists and businessmen and all the usual kind of guys. I could go out into the world and find a guy, but which one? I mean, finding any old guy would be easy. I was thinking that I could go over to one of the bars where I knew that some of the Yankees go after their games, but even that was sort of predictable. A lot of those guys are into partying. I saw all that in L.A. I actually got into a cab and had him drive me around the city, trying to think something up. I even had him go by the mayor's mansion, but the lights were off. Finally, I just came back to the hotel. I decided to sit in the lobby and see who came in. I sat there for maybe half an hour. A couple of men came up to me and I sort of talked to them, found out who they were, but they were just regular businessmen from Philadelphia or officials from Washington or something. Then I was sitting there and a group of people came in, energetic and nervous and sort of clearing the way, and I watched the guy behind the desk put down the phone and wave over a couple of other hotel people—I mean, they were nervous, it was obvious—and then came in this huge fat man—"

"Hobbs."

"Yes. But I didn't know that yet. All I could see was that he was huge, tall, too, and that his suit must have cost something like ten thousand dollars. He was wearing this great bowler hat. He didn't even look at the hotel desk or anybody, he just walked straight toward the elevator. Then he disappeared. His people checked in at the desk, and then they went up on another elevator. Everything calmed down. The whole thing lasted maybe a minute. He couldn't walk very fast but he wasn't in the lobby more than fifteen seconds. So I asked one of the bellhops who it was. He said it was Hobbs, the Australian who owns newspapers all over the world. A billionaire, he said. I remember that. I said, billionaire? And he looked at me like I was an idiot. He stays here when he's in the city, he said. So then I said, I want to know something. And the bellhop just says, no lady, no way, can't do it. Shakes his head. You don't even know the room number? I say. Oh, I know it, lady, but I can't give it out. I tell him I'll pay him to know. Come on, he says, I could lose my job. Five hundred bucks, I say. He sort of says, oh shit, lady. Then I say, a thousand. He says, you don't have a thousand. But I did. I mean, Simon's making so much money that we're just carrying around a ton of it, for no real reason. So I show him the money. He was dark, sort of skinny, maybe Pakistani or something. He tells me the number. That's the main suite, he says, which bedroom it is I don't know. I ask him how I'll know if he's telling the truth, and he says, because if I'm not, then you'll come down here and tell the manager and I'll lose my job. This seemed pretty good, so I gave him the money. Then I figured I should get up there before Hobbs went to sleep. If he's coming from England or someplace, then he's going to be really tired, and if he's coming from the West Coast, then he'll stay up a little while more. I'm thinking like this and also wondering what the hell Simon is doing. So I go up there and knock on the door. It opens and there's a guy on the telephone. I smile and say, I'm here for Mr. Hobbs. The guy looks at me and just waves me in. It's a big, big suite, maybe six rooms. The guy motions me into the next room and there is Hobbs, sitting, reading a paper, and then he says, well, what do we have here, something like that, you know, and you can pretty much imagine the rest of it yourself, or some of it at least. He was different, and sweet, too."

"You taped it."

"It was easy. I put the purse on a dresser and started the camera. It was a silent drive, with a fish-eye. It took in the whole room."

I said nothing, only nodded.

"I came back to the apartment the next morning and Simon was quick to tear into my purse. He took the tape away and never let me see it. It turns out he never did his part of the bargain, either." She sighed in bitterness. "I hated him for what had become of me, how I was willing to do something like that. I took a shower that must have lasted three hours—I told myself never again. We had a big fight about the tape, but he wouldn't give it back, and then after he saw it we *really* had a big fight. What did he expect? Then later, after Simon died, I figured that the tape would be in his collection, but it wasn't."

"Why me?" I said, trying not to feel angry.

"Oh, I don't know," Caroline exhaled, her voice tired and confessional. "I thought maybe you might be able to help me. Maybe just give me advice or something. I've hired private investigators or whatever they call themselves, and they can't help me. I don't know where the tape is. I don't know what's on it that's *so* bad, really."

I stared at her. "This whole thing with us is about getting me to help you find the tape?"

"Well—"

"Just tell me."

"Yes."

I found myself looking toward the window.

"Do you forgive me?" she asked.

"No. Or myself."

"I like you, Porter, I like being with you. But I was hoping that I could get you to help . . . I mean, if I *don't* find that tape . . . I thought I could ignore it, just not think about Hobbs. I get these—"

And here she flicked on a table light and fumbled nervously through a drawer, pulling out a sheaf of letters on heavy bond. The law firm was London-based, with a sizable office in New York.

"I got this last week," she said. "And this one was before it, and—"

Dear Mrs. Crowley,

Pursuant to our last communication with you, dated January 12, we still seek to impress upon you the serious nature of this matter. Your purposeful reluctance to call this office or to respond to Mr. Hobbs's direct inquiries is most troubling. We continue to maintain that you are in possession—

And so on. "Why don't you hire a lawyer to deal with this?" I asked. "Certainly Simon had an attorney who handled the disposition of the estate?"

"Yes."

"So there was a complete accounting of the estate, no?"

"Yes."

"Why not ask that lawyer to respond to Hobbs? Write him a letter saying that no such tape was in Simon's possession at the time of death, something like that. I mean, this is pretty simple stuff."

"I haven't wanted to deal with the lawyers. The estate was so complicated . . ." She looked at me with hope in her eyes and took my hand. "Please help me, Porter."

But I felt only a smoldering fury, and I got up, saying nothing, and went into the bathroom; there I washed my face and looked in the mirror. I'd heard a lie in Caroline's voice somewhere, maybe more than one, and I wanted to think carefully about what she'd told me. But I was tired and my head swam with the drink. And now home seemed a better place to be.

NAPOLEON WAS OFF-DUTY AND, without his impressive buttons and collar, was only some guy in a T-shirt, sleeping in a cheap apartment, dreaming the gray dreams of depression. In his place in the apartment house's lobby was an old man whose lower eyelids sagged so far down that the lips of them hung outward from the curved surface of his eyeballs, as if he had not slept in twenty or thirty years. One of those New York night characters who seems to have stepped out of an Edward Hopper painting. He watched me walk down the hallway, past the lilies again, a few pink petals of which had now fallen to the table, time passing wretchedly as always, and then he croaked, "Cab there, fella?"

I nodded, and while his eyes seemed too tired to move from my face, his hand crept over the worn mahogany desk to a round brass switch, which he flicked back and forth with irritating energy, like a man urgently signaling the end of the world. By the time I was outside, a cab was sitting there, roof light haloed by the swirling snow, the driver sipping coffee.

"Cold night, pal," he said when I got inside. "I mean cold."

"Yeah."

"Starting to get some real accumulation here."

I moved my head in the affirmative. He had a little jazz coming out of the radio, soft, lulling even, and I pulled my coat tight and slumped sleepily back in my seat. I was exhausted and vaguely anxious. It was nearly five A.M. The cabbie nosed the car into the light traffic, then glanced back in his mirror.

"You all right back there?"

"Aaah, yes and no."

"Yes and no? Ain't going to crap out on me here or something? I had a guy with a heart attack once. Not a bowl of cherries, I'll say that."

The cab flew down the avenue past the snow-flickering lights, past the few shades hunching along the white sidewalks, the city a fantasy of dreams, in which the morning world would never come. I watched the driver change lanes without signaling. The interior of the cab was suffused with bluish light, some kind of saxophone coming faintly from the radio. The entire night seemed impossible to me, impossible and true. We sailed past a white, double-length limo. The boys in it—sailors or high-school football players—had taken off their shirts and were hanging out of the windows and sitting on the roof. "Look at those fuckers," the cabbie muttered.

We pulled up next to my brick wall. The street was quiet. I paid the driver and walked heavily toward the gate. Ten feet away, I looked up to see a car jerk to a stop. Two men jumped out. They wore good wool coats, and one was hatless, I remember that. I didn't like their interest in me, and I got out my key.

"Wren."

I had the gate unlocked when they reached me. The bigger man put his foot inside the gate. They looked like businessmen. They weren't cops. No one could see me inside the tunnel.

"What can I do for you guys on this lovely evening?"

"Give us the tape."

The snow was making me blink. "I don't have it yet."

"You have a tape in your coat."

I was astounded. "That's not the right one."

"Give us the tape now and there's no problem."

The closer man pulled something from his coat and swung at me. I jumped back but was off balance. The other man kicked me between the legs like the guy who knocks them into the end zone for the Giants, and I defecated instantly, a shocked shit right there in my pants. Then I was down, down hard. A gloved hand was at the back of my neck, pressing my right cheek against the cold brick walk while my coat was searched. They took the tape.

A voice close to my ear: "Hey, Wren, you're an asshole, you know that?"

I heard the sound of aerosol, and then my left eye and nose and throat ignited in pain, my mouth became a great hyperventilating orifice, and as I writhed I heard myself howling, as if from a far distance. And they kicked me a few more times, once in the head and twice in the stomach and once more in the balls, and, rolled tightly inside myself, clenched and blind and brain aflame, I yelled for mercy, the sound loud in the tunnel. No answer came, and I tightened, waiting to be hit again, covering my head, drawing my legs up. And then I realized that nothing was happening. My right eye, the one pressed to the cold brick, had taken only an incidental shot of the Mace, and I opened it to a watery blinking slit and began dragging myself toward the open gate. It was maybe six feet away. I wanted to cry. I crawled some more but made no progress. There were many parts of my body I needed to think about. I collapsed to my belly. Finally I was able to cup my balls tenderly, determine that they were still more or less there. I rolled over onto my back, feeling the shit move in my pants. The burning in my nose eased. I forced that same right eye open again to look with watery clearness beyond the open gate into the January sky, where one late star winked against the fading darkness, cold and beautiful. It was that moment when night gives way to day. Snow was still falling. I could see it drifting into the tunnel doorway, landing on my coat sleeve. I could feel it against my cheek, on my lashes. I remembered that I had told Caroline about finding the dead man in the snow. It was snowing, but I was not a dead man. I would be fine. In general I was drinking too much and fucking around and getting beaten up, but I was fine. Yes, I would be fine in a few minutes. But minutes are a strange thing. You do nothing and they pass. You do nothing but lie on a brick path with the gate still open, reasonably warm in your wool coat, your face cold, waiting for something, an answer, perhaps. I hoped that my balls would still work. I saw now that I was no longer in control. Events were running past and over me. I was in a kind of trouble that suggested that all that was bad would soon be worse.

Then a car stopped outside the gate. I could hear the motor running. A door opened, footsteps on snow, footsteps closer, the sounds clear in the still, cold air. The gate remained open. Were the men coming back? I tried to push myself up. Nothing. Arms were dead. The steps were coming closer. Get up, you drunk fucker, save your own life. Be a hero. Steps. One person. I staggered to my knees.

"Please," I cried.

No answer came. Something flew in through the open gate, hitting me in the chest. Flopping to the ground.

The newspaper. Page one. PORTER WREN: DIARY OF A MADMAN.

GOOD MORNING! You have a furious wife, you have blood in your piss, you have a great story in the paper. But—after Lisa had given me a cold look on her way out the door with Sally—I couldn't think about these things. No, what really needed to happen was that Hobbs had to call off his two businessmen. I could only assume that once they saw that they had the wrong videotape they would practice some other beautiful tricks. Did they know that I was alone in the house right now, Lisa gone and Josephine out with Tommy? And how had they learned that I was carrying a videotape? Except for being hidden while at home, the tape had stayed in my coat pocket from the moment I'd left the Malaysian bank. I had never taken it out in public, never showed it to anyone. It occurred to me that Caroline had been lying about Hobbs and almost everything else and had called Hobbs or Campbell or the two executives and told them I was going down in the elevator with a videotape. She was, after all, the only one who knew that I had it in my pocket. But following our long conversation the previous night I wasn't ready to believe this about her; it made no sense. Maybe Hobbs had her apartment bugged. That was a little far-fetched, though not impossible. You could bribe the building's management, get inside. Obviously the doormen were already paid off and kept track of the comings and goings of people—obviously this had not been obvious to me. Then I remembered that I had taken the tape out of my pocket on the way up in the elevator to check that it wasn't one of Sally's. In a premier building like Caroline's, the elevator would have a closed-circuit video camera hidden in it, available for review if necessary. They had seen me go up, perhaps observed on a monitor as I had smiled stupidly at the old woman, watched her get off on the second floor, and then reached in my coat pocket for the tape. Then it was just a matter of a phone call. Had they waited for me to go home, thinking they would grab it when I got out of the cab? That didn't make sense—I could easily have left the tape with Caroline.

This last thought left me sick. How would they have known to follow me? *They had to have visited Caroline first.* I called her and let the phone ring. I let the god-awful phone ring five, ten, fifteen times. It was eleven-thirty in the morning. Caroline hadn't left the answering machine on. I let it ring fifteen more times. Then, just as I was about to hang up, the phone picked up.

"Yeah."

"Caroline?"

"What?" This was a voice I'd never heard—dead, full of hatred, tougher than I'd ever be.

"It's Porter."

"Yeah?"

"Did I wake you up?"

"Yeah. And I wish some people wouldn't let the phone ring eight hundred fucking times when I'm in bed."

"Hey, I'm—"

"Call me later."

She hung up. I hit the redial button. She picked up the phone but said nothing.

"Did some guys come looking—"

"Yeah. I told them I didn't have it."

"They left?"

"Well, at first they didn't believe me."

"Then?"

"Then they believed me. It only took them two minutes but they believed me. They could have fucking killed me." She gave an anxious sob. "Now you know why I'm so scared of Hobbs. After they left I almost called you."

"But you don't have my home number," I said.

"Fancy that." Her voice was bitter. "But I was worried. I checked information."

"Unlisted."

"Yes. Totally unreachable."

I needed to change the temperature of the conversation or she would hang up again. I couldn't think of anything clever. "Okay, why are you so pissed at me?"

"Why? *Why?*" she screamed. "Because it took you until *eleven-thirty in the morning* to figure out that I might have had a *problem*. You were probably pouring goddamned Sugar Pops and milk into your kids' cereal bowls and kissing your pretty wife good-bye on the way to work while I could have been lying dead in the kitchen with a knife in my neck!"

"That could, in fact, be true."

"Well?"

"But, in fact, it is not true."

"Then what took you so goddamned long?"

"I had to explain to my wife why I didn't want breakfast."

"What?" she screamed. "That's all?"

"I also had to explain why there was blood in our bed, blood in the snow outside our house, in the broken capillaries of my left eye, in my hair, on my shirt, on my tie, and in the toilet bowl."

"Oh, shit."

"Maybe in there, too."

"Stop."

"I think I will indeed have to stop for a few days, let my testicles knit themselves back together."

She was laughing. "You're okay?"

There was a picture of Lisa on my dresser. I picked it up. "I'm running on three wheels, but I'm all right."

"Good." She sighed. I heard her light a cigarette. "What did you tell your wife?"

"I told her three guys jumped me and took my money."

"Did she believe you?"

"I don't know."

I heard her exhale smoke. "I could never get married again."

"What about Charlie? What's that gig?"

"That gig? Well—"

"Wait, let's talk about the tape Hobbs wants."

"Let's."

"Tell me the truth now—you don't know where it is or who has it?"

"No," she breathed. "Not at all."

"You can tell me a million other lies, but please tell me the truth on this."

"I am."

"Okay. What did Simon do with his tapes?"

"He ran around with them, he left them in his car, he had them in L.A., in his office here. I don't know."

"So someone might have made a copy?"

"It's possible, I guess. But he didn't lose things. He was messy but he didn't lose things. Also he was pretty jealous of me, so he wouldn't have just let that particular tape drift around among people."

"What's on the tape?"

"Oh . . ."

"I mean, I'm assuming it's you and Hobbs screwing, something like that."

"Well, I've never actually *seen* the tape. But we don't—well, mostly we just talk."

"What's the most compromising thing about it? For Hobbs, I mean."

"I don't know. Honestly, we mostly just talked. Chitchat between a girl and a billionaire Australian—the typical, you know."

This was no good. "Who controls all of Simon's business stuff?"

"Lawyers."

"It's complicated?"

"Very."

"Here in the city?"

"Yes."

"He has an estate, right?"

"Well—"

She was stalling, unsure about telling me the financial structure of her existence.

"Caroline, I already know that your apartment is owned by a trust in Simon's name and that it cost two point three million dollars. The annual taxes on it are nineteen thousand, incidentally."

"How do you know all that?"

"Reporters know everything. Now, I want to go over Simon's arrangements at the law firm. This afternoon at, say, one. Please call them, line it up."

She told me the name of the firm.

"One of the best."

"I don't see why the law firm will be useful," she said. "It's just a lot of bills and papers."

"Well, look at it this way: You made the tape, then Simon took it. If he destroyed it, we would not have this problem. If he gave it away, that would be contrary to his character, according to you. There was no reason to sell it; he had plenty of money. To me this would suggest that he kept the tape, valued the tape. Maybe in his financial plan he made—"

Caroline laughed. "Simon? He couldn't keep anything straight. He was terrible with money. He didn't understand it, really."

"Do *you* understand money?"

"No, but I can tell when someone does."

"Like who?"

"Charlie understands money," she answered quickly.

"I see. Another reason to marry him, no doubt." It was an insane conversation; I was in my bedroom looking at a photo of my wife while listening to a woman I was sleeping with compare her late husband with her fiancé.

"Maybe the firm is paying for a safe-deposit box or something that you don't know about."

"Maybe."

There was a hesitancy in her answer, a reluctance to deal with the law firm.

"Why aren't you handling the money?" I pushed. "I mean, they could be robbing you blind, you know."

"They could?"

"Sure, that's what law firms *do*."

That worked. One o'clock. Fifth Avenue and Forty-ninth Street.

"How will I recognize you?" Caroline asked.

Jokes. We were still making them.

I STOOD ON THE FRONT PORCH watching my breath steam in the cold and listing some bad things that could soon happen. Hal Fitzgerald and I would definitely have a bad conversation. Hobbs and I might soon have a bad conversation. Lisa and I would not yet, I hoped, have a bad conversation. Perhaps men like to stand on porches thinking about bad news; perhaps once upon a time a Tory farmer had stood on this same porch, or a previous version of it, worrying about the revolution, and looked down at a dirt road or a field and seen General George Washington ride by, adjusting his wooden teeth or scratching his syphilitic crotch. History—chews up the best of them. My groin and ribs and head ached, but it was like after a football game; you hurt like hell afterward, but you were secretly pleased. The pain reminded you that you were three-dimensional, occupying space in the universe, someone the world had to deal with. On the other hand, I didn't really want to deal with the world from my front porch. The two business executives could come back, and, behind my wall, no one would see or hear what they were doing. They knew where I lived.

So I decided to do a little business before going uptown to Caroline's law firm. I hobbled down the path, through the tunnel and gate, and around the corner to Eighth Avenue. Was anyone following me? Maybe there was a way to find out. I ducked into one of those alternative video-comic book stores that specialize in animated Japanese pornography. I stayed in the shop a few minutes, bought a cheap video, tore away the cover and peeled off the label, junked the trash, and walked out, the video in my hand. Then I walked into a deli, asked for a paper bag, and could be seen stepping out of the deli into the winter sun while slipping the video into the paper bag. This I kept tucked under my arm as I strolled south for fifteen minutes, away from my neighborhood.

The restaurant was a small place with a tile floor wet from the snow and little tables too close together. The clientele was mostly people from the big galleries nearby or tourists who wanted to see people from the big galleries nearby. At the bar was a guy in a suit with a ponytail, maybe forty-five. I'd talked to him exactly twice; he had one story that he told to the tourists, and the first few lines went like this: *This city, let me tell you, heh, this city calls your bet, boy. It calls your fucking bet. Heh. You're not looking, that's when the big finger taps you on the shoulder. Heh, heh. Happened to me, back in 'eighty-seven. I was a major guy at Morgan Stanley—* The place had liquor licenses up on the wall that went back to 1883. There was a lot of talk about art, and all of it was about money. I dialed Hobbs's New York office from a pay phone. Three transfers, through successive layers of secretaries. He was in Brazil, I was told. But I've talked with mayors and senators and mobsters; big men can always be reached; it's just a matter of who has today's phone numbers. I hung up, called back, and asked for Campbell. "I'm his neighbor. It's not a matter of great importance," I said, "it's just that our apartment building is on fire and I thought he might want to know."

That worked. "Campbell," I said when he came on, "the tape your guys took off me last night isn't the one Hobbs wants. You probably know this by now. It's a tape of a policeman getting whacked. Now, the cops know about this tape. And they want it. I'm going to have to tell them that you have it and that you took it from me."

There was no pause to consider. "Mr. Wren, I do not follow your rather strange story. In the meantime, I've quite a schedule today and—"

"Listen, you fucking British prick! You don't understand the New York City Police Department. All I have to do is tell them that you guys have the tape of a cop getting whacked and they get this little smile on their faces. They love taking down guys in suits. It's a class-warfare thing. The deputy commissioner of police knows about the tape. He's just one phone call away from knowing that *you* have it. And after that, anyone could know about the story. Especially the other papers in New York."

"Then we would have a very interesting situation, Mr. Wren," Campbell said with the smooth violence of a man who was paid big dollars to slap problems back into the face of the people who presented them. "We would have the owner of your newspaper suing one of his *former* columnists for defamation. And he would win. He would also sue any other newspaper that hired this columnist to tell his libelous story. But then again, this is all, as they say, idle speculation, because I am confident that things will not come to such an unhappy climax. My guess is that you will exercise prudent discretion."

"Give me the tape back, Campbell. And tell Hobbs that you fucked up."

"We have nothing more to discuss here, so far as I can see, Mr. Wren." And then he hung up.

I put another quarter in the phone and called Hal Fitzgerald. "I need to talk, Hal. I've got a problem."

"Problems are a problem. You still have a tape for me?"

"No."

"Where are you?"

I told him, then asked the waitress for a window seat. I went back outside the restaurant and casually tossed my paper bag with the video in it into a trash can on the corner. Not looking back, I returned to the restaurant, glancing at the way the sunlight worked against the window. I would be able to see out, but from across the street no one could see in. In my seat I watched the early lunch birds arrive. One of them sat next to the guy with the ponytail, who was contemplating his cigarette smoke.

Twenty minutes later an unmarked police car pulled up at the restaurant, Hal in the back. I watched him get out; he closed the door and smoothed his tie, which was a mannerism he'd adopted on his way up. He was getting vain as the years went by; soon it would be Italian loafers and monogrammed shirts. We shook hands without enthusiasm.

"I got to be uptown in, like"—he shot his wrist out of his sleeve, looked at a big gold watch—"in like forty-nine minutes."

"Get the chili."

"Yeah. All right, listen, this tape thing. We need the tape, Porter."

"*I* need the tape."

"What, somebody took it off you?"

I nodded. "Last night. They thought it was something else. They thought it was another tape."

"They took it right off you?"

I glanced outside. If someone was following me, he would have to see what I'd put in the trash. "Yes."

"What'd they do, show you a gun?"

"They showed me that and they showed me their shoes."

"Kick you around?"

I nodded. "I'm all right."

"What's on the other tape?"

"It wouldn't interest you. Not professionally, I mean."

"People fucking?"

"Maybe, I'm not sure."

"I'm always interested in people fucking."

We ordered the chili.

"You know who they are?"

"More or less."

"Who?"

"I can't get into that."

"You can't."

"No, Hal, I can't."

"I still need the tape."

"When I get back this other thing, this other tape, I can trade it for the Fellows tape. They'll give it back to me, they don't want it."

"You've seen the Fellows tape."

"Yeah."

"Maybe you could tell me exactly what's on it."

"Big white guy hits Fellows with a bat, runs away."

"What else?"

"He runs right at the camera."

"What else?"

"Blond, maybe twenty-eight, thirty. Big guy. It's very fast. I've seen it only once. Your guys would have to—"

"They'd blow it up and everything. They'd get it. Could you ID someone in a lineup?"

"No. It's too fast."

"We need the tape."

A man in a suit was standing next to the trash can. He might have been one of the entrepreneurs from the night before. "See how I'm doing in a week," I said.

"Porter, you don't understand. I got to go back there with something."

"Five days."

"Three."

The executive had the arm of his nice suit in the trash can. A quick dip at the knees, he had the paper bag, he was gone. "I'm doing the best I can, Hal," I mumbled. "I'm under a lot of pressure here."

"Hey, Porter, I don't want to start talking about pressure." Hal leaned over his chili. He could have detectives looking up my rainspouts in fifteen minutes if he wanted to. "You fucking call us up and say you got the tape that solves the Fellows murder and you can give it to us, and then you tell me you *can't* give me the tape? It's getting very complicated. I mean, I vouched for you, said this guy, you know, he likes cops, is fair and everything, but now the story is getting complicated. It starts to make me look bad, starts to make me look compromised, which I'm *not*. All *I* did was pick up the phone when you called and then, afterward, naturally, I went to my boss, my guy, who has got don't let me tell you how many fucking problems of his own, and I give him a little good news, cheer him up, we're going to collar the guy who killed Officer Fellows a couple of years ago, looks good for the cops, detectives still on the case, Patrolmen's Benevolent Association feels the allocation of resources was sufficient, because it's one of about fifty-eight little things that's bugging them. I mean, we had that young kid killed on the beat a week ago partly because of a radio malfunction problem, okay?"

I gave him an obligatory nod.

"You got to understand after you tell me all this stuff I naturally go in there to my boss and give him the good news, and then I gotta go back in there now and give him the *bad* news? That's complicated. He looks at me like he wants to scramble my fucking eyeballs and maybe eat them, all right? You don't understand the budget pressures. Giuliani doesn't have any fucking money; Dinkins gave it away to the teachers' union. So then I go tell him, Sorry, there's been a delay, my guy has some kinda little problem, there's some *other* tape with a bunch of people fucking on it, and the tapes got mixed up, and so maybe we don't have the Fellows thing after all? You think that goes over good? It doesn't. You know what my boss's favorite expression is? It's this, he says this all the time, he says, 'Sorry doesn't feed the cat.' That's it. 'Sorry doesn't feed the cat.' I go in there with nothing, he's gonna say that to me."

"Hal—"

"No, no. You listen to me. Don't think of me as a friend, Porter." He waved his hands in front of me, like someone ordering a plane not to land. "That's where the problem starts. Think of me as an asshole. That will help you. I'm on the other side of the line. I mean, you know what happens when a ten-thirteen is called? When a cop is shot? The radio goes quiet, the chatter stops. Becomes fucking *solemn*. Then cops start to check in— do they got anything, did they get the guy?"

"I know all this, Hal."

"You know it but you don't feel it. You're not a cop, Porter. You don't know the life." He had to say all this, I knew; it was part of the negotiation process. "You don't understand the loyalty thing, Porter."

I swabbed around in my bowl with a piece of bread. "Tell me more about what I don't understand."

"You know that a cop can retire, put his badge in a special vault, and then have his kid or grandkid wear that badge? There are actually a few guys walking around with three-digit badges, badges maybe a hundred years old. That's something, okay? That's in the life. Cop signs on, he knows stuff like that. Cops hate each other, the whites hate the blacks, the blacks hate the whites, the men hate the women, guys hate the gays. There's all this fucking hatred in the system. Desk guys hate guys on the beat and vice versa. We got hierarchy stress, we got corruption all over the place, we got tension between the union and the command structure, we got every fucking kind of pressure and hatred, but goddammit, Porter, there's this fucking loyalty. Every cop out there knows that something like eight hundred cops have been murdered on the job over the years and every one gets solved! We only got two outstanding now, the Fellows one included. And we'll solve those. Every one, sooner or later. Never missed.

That's like gravity, Porter. It's pulling on me, it's pulling on you. There's only so much I can actually do in a situation. The game already started, you know? Now you want to slow it down, reset the clock? You can't. You have to play the tough ball. You have a forty-foot shot with three seconds to go. It's not my fault if it is almost impossible. Get that? Some of these captains have been around, they don't give a shit about a guy like you. For them it's a war and it always will be. I can't control them necessarily, these guys. I mean, you tell me you don't have the tape, and then tomorrow cops find you got drugs in your briefcase, I can't do anything about that. And God help you if my guy tells Giuliani. Let's hope that doesn't happen. If you want to pray, pray for that." Hal ate a bite of chili. "This is too big, Porter, it moves too fast. I mean, I got this theory that society is really about velocity."

"Is it?"

"If you can't control your velocity, you're in trouble."

"That sounds very clever."

"Think about it."

"I will."

He got up, threw his napkin on the table brusquely, and checked the time. "Velocity management."

"Five days."

"Three."

"I need five, four at least."

"Three."

He was staring at me. "Okay," I said. "Three."

AN EXECUTIVE'S WIFE stood in the lobby of the law firm. Pumps, pearls, wool suit, Caroline. The makeup had been taken down a few notches. The look was cool, hyperrational. I think she had even changed her watch. Here, no doubt, was the apparition that Charlie wanted to marry, not a woman who had passed out while being screwed by Magic Johnson.

We were taken into an office not big enough to be a partner's and met Jane Chung, the lawyer overseeing the management of Simon Crowley's estate.

Caroline introduced me and I watched the wariness pass into Jane Chung's face.

"He's here in what capacity? As a reporter?"

"Just as a friend," Caroline said.

"And he has no financial interest in the estate?"

"None."

"None whatsoever," I repeated.

Jane Chung sat down at her desk, and I could see that she had already recaptured her composure. She dealt with all sorts of strange family arrangements in estate matters, and no doubt the wisebeards of the law firm had chosen her for her tact and judgment.

"As I mentioned on the phone," Caroline began, "we're here because I would like to see the accounting of the estate's expenses, each of the little costs and so on."

"I have a printout." Jane Chung handed each of us a half-inch-thick document. "As you can see, there are a substantial number of payments."

And indeed there were. I glanced at the first few:

Sally Giroux, Inc., New York [public relations]	$15,000.00
Sally Giroux, Lim., London [public relations]	$15,000.00
Greenpark Nursing Care facility, Queens, N.Y. [personal]	$6,698.19
Bloomingdale's, New York [personal]	$3,227.03
Rego Park Hearing Aids, Inc., Queens, N.Y. [personal]	$1,267.08
Photoduplicators, New York [business expense]	$174.23
New York City Unincorporated Business Tax [taxes]	$23,917.00
FK Laundry Services [personal]	$892.02
FederalExpress, New York [business expense]	$189.45
Citibank Mortgage Services [personal]	$17,650.90
Harvey's Meats, New York [personal]	$217.87

The entries went on throughout the entire document.

"The estate collects revenue and royalties from the continuing licensing and replaying of Mr. Crowley's films." Jane Chung blinked, as if listening to her own dictation. "That's the income. The outgo includes disbursements for the maintenance of business activities, for his father's nursing home costs, for the monthly payments to you, Caroline, for the apartment fees, and so on."

Caroline was flipping through the long printout. She seemed distracted, even dazed. I wondered if she was even seeing the figures and words. "This is complicated," she finally said.

"What about the physical contents of the estate?" I asked. "Is there mention of anything in Simon's will?"

"No," said Jane Chung. "His will only established an estate. No specific objects were mentioned."

I nodded. "We're back to the accounting printout, then."

Caroline sighed. "I guess."

Jane Chung watched Caroline impatiently. "Indeed. Now then, do you have any particular questions?"

Caroline was staring at the printout.

"Caroline?" I asked.

"Well, it seems to be all here," she said, with some resignation.

I turned to Jane Chung. "We're looking for something, Jane, that's why we're here. We're looking for some indication of certain of Simon's activities while he was alive."

"Perhaps we can—may I ask what they might have been, or whom they might have been with?"

"Uh, no," I said.

She looked at Caroline.

"I don't understand."

Caroline sat up. "I'm just going to let Porter talk for me here. This whole thing is pretty exhausting, frankly."

Jane turned back to me. "Mr. Wren, I really can't say that I understand *what*—"

"Jane, just listen to me. I'm going to explain it as best I can. We—Caroline and I—are looking for some information relating to Simon. We need this information pretty badly. We're not going to tell you why. That's personal business. Be assured that our inquiry in no way reflects poorly upon or creates a liability for your law firm, although it occurs to me that if we are not successful, it *could* create a liability for the estate. Now then, our method is somewhat scattershot here. We don't even know if looking further into these records would be useful or not. But we have nowhere else to start. What we would like to do, today, *now*, is have a look at the individual invoices received by your firm for each of these zillion expenses, just flip through each one of them and try to think—"

She was already shaking her head. "I'm sorry, that is *highly* unusual. Those records are probably in storage, and it could take quite a bit of time to assemble them. This summary accounting of the expenses would certainly seem sufficient to determine—"

"Why not just let us look at the actual paper?"

"Because it's not—"

"Not what?"

She blinked in suppressed irritation. "This is most unusual."

"So?"

"So, Mr. Wren, we have certain *procedures* here that we have developed over time for maximum efficiency. I'm sure you understand that."

"It's all billable time to the estate, so what's the problem?"

"Well, frankly, I have appointments throughout the day, and I would be unable to supervise—"

"There's no reason to supervise. We're all grown adults. Just stick us in a room with the boxes and we'll have a look."

"I'm sorry, but a request of this unusual nature really needs to proceed through the Estate Division Oversight Committee, which meets only monthly." She shrugged and smiled. "It's a matter of firm procedure."

"Is it because I'm a reporter?"

"No."

I looked at Caroline. "I'm going to speak plainly now, on your behalf, Caroline. Is that okay?"

She nodded. I turned back to Jane Chung.

"Jane, let us agree that the estate of Simon Crowley is not a typical estate. It is 'most unusual,' to use your words. *It makes money.* It makes money for itself and for its creditors and for Caroline here, and, particular to my point, it makes it for your firm, for *you*. When you buy your toothpaste, Jane, some of that money has come from the estate of Simon Crowley. I find it *unfathomable* that you would not accommodate Simon Crowley's widow."

"Mr. Wren, these kinds of threats are useless."

I bent close to whisper into Caroline's ear. "Remember that incredibly tough bitch you told me about last night?"

"Who?" she answered, eyes large.

"You," I said. "I need her to show up here."

Her blue eyes blinked in amusement. Then her face went cold as she turned toward the attorney.

"Jane, help us, or I'll move the estate to another firm."

Jane gave a dry little laugh. "I don't think you appreciate how complicated that is. It takes years, you have to petition the—"

"No I don't," Caroline interrupted in a voice of great bitchy irritation. "All I do is call up the people I know at the studio and tell them that there's an irregularity at the *fucking* law firm and would they please send the *fucking* check to me directly so I can pay my *fucking* bills."

A FEW MINUTES LATER I was in a small book-lined conference room on another floor. Caroline had begged off after her outburst, and I said I would meet her in a coffee shop outside in an hour. The door opened and a pimply kid with red hair pushed in an office cart stacked with boxes.

"Howdy, esteemed client of our venerable firm," he said, bowing with his hands pressed together. "My name is Bob Dole. Oh, I guess it's not. Actually it's Raoul McCarthy."

"What's a guy with red hair doing with a name like Raoul?" I asked.

"Well, my mother lived on the Upper West Side in the seventies, if you really want to know."

"Right."

"Anyway, here they are. The last year's worth."

"Where were they?" I asked.

"Oh God, they were way back in the—" He rolled his eyes. "We call it the hell room. Way back there."

"You're a paralegal?"

"Para*slave*, you mean. Jane has *three* paraslaves." He started to stack the boxes on the table. "I just move around paper. Lots of paper in a place like this. I mean, the hell room, they could shoot a Freddy Krueger movie in there. We had some boxes fall on a guy last week, almost killed him practically. The lawyers never go in there."

"Never?" I asked.

"What are you, kidding me? It's the *hell* room."

"What about computers and document scanners and stuff like that?" I asked. "It's practically the millennium."

He looked at me. "Surely you jest."

I shrugged.

"You got to realize that all those computer files, all the important ones, get backed up on paper. And all the letters and motions and depositions and discovery documents and all that stuff is still on paper. And a lot of these files go *back*. We've got active files that are forty years old in there. But the problem is that stuff gets lost. We had a little problem last month where the cleaning guy accidentally took something like nine boxes of an active file and threw them out." Raoul permitted himself a sly grin. "They had to find the truck and the landfill and then a bunch of paraslaves went out to Staten Island to look for the paper. We had to have dysentery shots. They had a guy with a front loader and everything—"

"Did you find them?"

Raoul hitched up his pants. "Yeah, under about ten million used diapers."

"Jane Chung seemed pretty nervous about these papers."

"Like I said, we've been having a lot of problems lately. The stuff doesn't usually get *really* lost, it just gets *sort of* lost. See, we have a filing room and a *refiling* room, and things can get stuck in there for a few weeks—"

I waved him off the topic. "Okay, let me know what's here."

"Well, speaking as your basic para-enslaved employee, I would say what you got here is a bunch of bills. They're in chronological order, but that's it."

"Who actually pays the bills?" I asked.

"I do."

"You write the check?"

"I write the requisition order for the check."

"Jane looks over everything?"

He glanced at the door, lowered his voice a bit. "Nah, not really."

"Would rather be elsewhere in the firm?"

"I think she'd rather be *anywhere*, actually."

"So you're the guy handling the payments made by the estate of Simon Crowley."

Raoul shrugged. "Yeah."

"You."

"You got it. As a paraslave I bill at fifty-five dollars an hour, but the firm can write that up as an associate's time at three hundred and ten an hour."

"Very beautiful."

He nodded, then opened the first box. "You're going to go through all of these?"

"I guess so."

"Why don't you just ask me what you're looking for?"

"Well—"

"I mean, I can tell you everything in these boxes."

"You can?"

"Sure."

"Tell me about Sally Giroux."

"Movie public-relations firm," he recited. "There's a domestic company and a European one, based in London. She—or it, whatever—handles any kind of media inquiries, handles re-release PR, like getting video clips to the TV tabloid shows, stuff like that. She once worked for the studio, but she became a consultant a couple of years ago. She bills on a quarterly cycle, and every year she adds to her fee. My guess is it's a waste of money. I mean, nobody ever checks on these people or anything."

"You just pay the bills."

"Every one. Shoot them through."

I opened my briefcase. "I'm going to take some notes on this."

From there we went into which bills were personal and which were business. "We pay for Mrs. Crowley's apartment," explained Raoul. The mortgage on it, plus the maintenance and all the related expenses. Actually I know what's going on in her life, sort of. If she gets a new sink put in, then I see the bill. In fact, I remember she had a new shower put in last year. Nine thousand dollars, for *a shower*." He shook his head while I remembered just how wonderful that shower was. "We pay everything. Her telephone bills, her electricity, her credit cards, everything."

There was an odd helplessness in this, which I didn't understand. "Seems like a crazy way to run your life. You can't really keep track of anything."

"I guess."

"Does she even have a checking account?"

"Maybe technically."

"But—"

"But the bank statements come here, and I have to reconcile them, so I see what she's doing."

"Which is?"

"Just taking cash out at the cash machine."

"How much a month?"

"Maybe a couple of thousand a month."

"What's the trend line on the income?"

"Going down."

"Gross income last year?"

"Maybe eight hundred thousand."

"This year?"

"Six hundred and twenty, more or less. It's because of payout schedules ending, royalties dropping off. The big money with movies is in the first few years, and it's been a while since Crowley's last movie—"

I nodded that I understood. "Next year? You have an income number for that?"

He pulled out a pen and made a column of numbers, then added it up.

"Maybe four hundred and ten thousand."

"It'll keep going down?"

"Yes."

"What about the net worth of the estate?"

"Going down."

"The estate is running out of money."

"It would seem so."

"Does Mrs. Crowley know this?"

"You really ask the questions."

"Hey."

"Yes, she knows. She calls me sometimes."

"Why is the net worth dropping?"

"Well, her living costs, including the apartment and the maintenance charge and everything, are around four hundred thousand. Then taxes on the income of the estate are going to be a couple of hundred thousand. It's a very poorly structured arrangement, not well positioned in respect to taxes. All the investments are in income instruments, which get taxed at a higher rate than vehicles with capital gains. Then there are some payments that are going to Mrs. Crowley's mother out—"

"How much?"

"Two thousand a month."

"What else? The law firm's fee, what's that?"

Here his voice stiffened. "It's calculated in respect to a percentage of the estate's gross value, a percentage of the gross annual income, and itemized legal costs to administer same."

"Come on, a number."

"Maybe sixty thousand."

"What else?"

"Well, the nursing home for Mr. Crowley, the father. That's like six thousand a month. They've got a lot of Medicaid patients, for which they don't receive the same rate of compensation from the federal government. So they bill private-pay patients like crazy. I mean, they bill us for everything—extra socks, special doctor's visits, stuff like that. A new cane. All the paperwork and medical reports come here. At first I worried about this, but Jane asked Mrs. Crowley if she wanted it sent to her and she said no. There are other bills for the father, too. Stuff like special therapy nurses, hearing aids, caretaker visits, special boxes of fruit at Christmas, gum surgery—"

"Who is the caretaker?" I asked. "Some neighborhood woman picking up a little extra money?"

"It's a law firm, actually."

"I don't get it."

"Well, let me show you it." He dumped out one of the boxes and spread its contents across the table. In a few seconds he had fished out a document that had SEGAL & SEGAL at the top, with a location in Queens. This stopped me cold. Segal & Segal had filed for bankruptcy on the same day that Segal Property Management, former owner of 537 East Eleventh Street, had filed for bankruptcy. "See, here, it lists the visits to Mr. Crowley."

I checked the paper. It detailed visits twice a week by a Mrs. Norma Segal for the monthly billing period. Each visit cost the estate fifty-five dollars. This had to be the same elderly Norma Segal whom Mrs. Wood had found on her databases.

"Fifty-five dollars a visit—I don't feel bad about paying that," Raoul was saying. "Some kind of neighborhood law office. If you look at the nursing home bill, you can tell it's nearby. Same zip code."

"Seems like money well spent," I noted.

"Probably," said Raoul. "Sometimes they bill for other things. Usually five thousand dollars, but that's irregular."

"What's it for?"

"I don't know. I just pay it."

"How about any safe-deposit-box fees, storage facilities, private mailboxes, that kind of thing?"

"None."

"Getting back to other personal expenses, are there any payments in here to other parties—you know, people who aren't billing for a service or a good, just a payment?"

"Yeah, a lot of them. They come through Mrs. Crowley. We just get a note from her that says, Please pay so-and-so this much."

"I suppose she could just pay them out of her own checking account."

"Yeah, but her income from the estate is taxable. Expenses incurred by the estate are tax-deductible. It's like, if she fixes a broken sink and pays for it out of her checking account, then that expenditure is, at the end of the year, an out-of-pocket expense she pays for with aftertax dollars. If she forwards the bill to the estate and the estate pays it, the expense is deducted from the total income of the estate, thereby reducing the estate's total annual federal and state tax liability, if only by a little bit."

"You should be a lawyer," I said.

He smiled. "I'm working on that."

We went on from there, and by the end I had looked through all of the boxes, hunting for something, anything, that might tell me why somebody was sending a tape to Hobbs. But after a while, I felt myself deflate; the boxes of paper, in sum, seemed only that: boxes of paper, the dead skins of small financial transactions, notable for the cost of maintaining the luxury of Caroline's lifestyle but little else.

I FOUND CAROLINE in the coffee shop downstairs. She was reading *Vogue*.

"I don't see how you can find it," she said, putting down the magazine. "This whole thing is crazy. Why don't you call Hobbs and tell him it's impossible?"

"Why don't *you?*"

"I have. I've tried to call him."

I found this comment interesting. "When you did, how did you do it?"

"I just called him."

"Where?"

"At his office, wherever."

"Where is wherever?"

"I don't know, his office, basically."

Her mind ran to precision. She was lying.

"Do you want me to find the tape?"

"Of course."

"Then stop fucking around, Caroline."

"I'm not."

"Yes you are. If you didn't call Hobbs at his office, then where did you call him? At his home? Oh, Porter Wren's mind begins to ask, why is that, why would she call Hobbs somewhere other than his office? Well, the answer might be because she has his home number. How could that be, I wonder. How could she have his home number? Presumably these people are adversaries. Or maybe they are adversaries now but weren't always. Perhaps they knew each other a bit. Perhaps they saw each other more than one night in a hotel."

She had a beautiful face, but she could make it ugly, and now she did. "Screw you."

"No, Caroline, no. You brought me into this. You thought you could just be the sweet fuck bunny and lead me around. But you didn't study me very carefully, Caroline, you didn't figure out how a small-town boy like me with not one connection in New York City elbowed and hustled and hassled his way to be a newspaper columnist. You didn't think about this, Caroline. You need to understand something else, too. The police are going to tear me apart looking for the Fellows tape, and they will tear you apart, too. So we have to get the Hobbs tape back, and you have to tell me what happened with him."

We had quite a long conversation after that. After the first meeting with Hobbs, she had seen him a few more times. Only to talk, she said; when Simon was out of town she would go to Hobbs's hotel and spend a couple of hours. Did Simon know? I asked. Yes, she admitted. Simon knew about it. Hobbs had sent her a little gift and, finding it, Simon had confronted her. Caroline admitted to him that she was seeing Hobbs. So Simon had a reason to hate Hobbs. Yes, she said. But the tape didn't get sent to Hobbs until after Simon died. Did she know any of the businesspeople Simon worked with? I asked. Some. There were dozens, of course. Maybe Simon gave them the tape. No—it would have gotten back to her, she said, Hollywood being what it is. Someone would have sold a copy to one of the television shows. And besides, what was the motive? Hobbs was apparently not being blackmailed; moreover, he could pay just about any sum if he was. What about Billy? I asked. Who is he? Caroline shook her head. They ran around, but Billy has gone straight, he's a big-deal businessman now. A banker or something. Did Simon have any other confidant? She shook her head. You mentioned the studio, I said, how does that work? She sighed. Well, the studio makes its payment to the production company. The production company makes payments on the first two big films to Simon's agency, and they take their cut, then forward a check to the law firm. Now, for the third movie, Simon owned the production company, but it's basically defunct now, so the check from the studio goes directly to the agency, and then the check comes here, to the law firm.

"Any reason to think that he could have set someone up out there to do this, send the tapes to Hobbs?" I asked.

Caroline shrugged. "I don't think so. Why would they do it? It's stupid. It could cause them a lot of trouble. Everybody in Hollywood tries to be nice to one another because someday they might work together. Plus you have to understand, Simon's time out there was pretty short. Everybody keeps shifting around. His little nucleus, you know, all over the place. Some of them are working for Quentin Tarantino now, John Singleton, all kinds of people."

"Tell me about the physical spaces Simon controlled or owned or rented when he died."

"We had the apartment. I know everything in the apartment—the tape wasn't there. He had an office downtown and I cleaned that out. There wasn't much there, anyway. Old scripts, a lot of trash. He also had an office at the studio, but that was cleaned out after he died. They sent me all the stuff in it. He had a room he used at the Beverly Palms a lot, but that probably doesn't count. He had an apartment out in Brentwood that he bought right before we were married, but he sold it later, because he started worrying about earthquakes. That's all I can think of."

"How about his father's house?"

"His father has lived in the nursing home for maybe six or seven years. The house was sold a long time ago."

"Tell me about Mr. Crowley," I said. "How sick is he?"

Caroline put some sugar into her coffee. "I don't know."

"You haven't talked to his doctors?"

"No."

"Do you know him?"

She shook her head. "No."

"You've met him, though."

"Actually I haven't."

"Why not?"

"Simon never took me out there to see him."

This struck me as strange.

"Simon never took me back to his old neighborhood," she protested. "He said he was going to take me back to the house where he grew up to see the neighbors and everything, but he never had any time. So I don't really have a connection to those people."

"But didn't the father come to the funeral?"

"No."

"Why not?"

"Well, it was small, Porter, and, you know, very private, and he just didn't come."

"Was he invited?"

"I assume so."

"You didn't send word to the nursing home and tell him that his son was dead and that he should come to the service?"

She looked down at the table, pressed her fingers to her forehead. "The studio handled the funeral, Porter. I was in no shape to do it."

"You're telling me that Simon Crowley's father was never told that his son was dead and that there was a funeral?"

She looked at me. "I think that's what happened. Maybe they told him later."

I watched the people passing outside the coffee shop.

Caroline spun my briefcase around and fiddled with the contents. "You should have a picture of me in here. Every time you open it up, you would see my smiling face."

I turned back. "My wife would make this a topic of discussion."

"She wouldn't know," said Caroline.

"She'd know," I said.

"Why?"

"She knows everything, my wife." She would certainly know to invite my father to my funeral.

"You say it with pride."

"I *am* proud of her."

"But you're here with me."

"I'm there with her, too."

She snapped my briefcase shut. "I'm going. You're fucking bugging me."

THE GREENPARK NURSING HOME in Queens was a hulking institutional structure whose very architecture suggested that all hope was an illusion. I signed in at the desk. The reception area was populated by ancients in wheelchairs, ancients shuffling across the waxed floor, ancients staring fixedly at the bright slogans of happiness stapled to the bulletin boards. The uniformed staff was, uniformly, black. I asked where I might find Mr. Crowley and was directed to the sixth floor. Usually the floors in such places are organized by the functioning level of the patients, and I wondered about the condition of patients on the sixth floor. I rode up with a whiskery ancient who performed a sequence of knee bends while standing in a puddle of urine, not necessarily his own. I signed in on the floor and was asked which patient I was visiting, and the nurse pulled down a binder notebook marked CROWLEY, and I signed in there, too, marking the date as well. The last visitor had been Mrs. Norma Segal. In fact, no one else had visited Mr. Crowley recently. Mrs. Segal, it appeared, arrived every Monday and Thursday without fail. Her signature was tight, careful script, the style of which I associate with third-grade teachers. I flipped the page left to right, which took the visits back a few months. Mrs. Norma Segal, without fail.

The nurse directed me to the dayroom, and I passed several Chinese ancients, all women, sunken into their wheelchairs. Another woman in a red robe shuffled by, spied me, and shrieked, "Hey! I'm so tired!"

In the dayroom I encountered a dozen ancients in wheelchairs. A television was on and being watched, but without irony—or perhaps with the greatest of irony. Each ancient had a small paper container of some nutritional drink, and a straw. No one was drinking it. A woman gobbled wetly at me.

An attendant, a young black woman slumped in a chair, looked up. "Yas?"

"I'm looking for Mr. Crowley."

She pointed casually.

He was sitting with a large urine bag fixed beneath him in his wheelchair, and although his eyes were open, awake, his mouth hung slack and wet. His teeth, I saw, were exactly like his son's, crooked and large. His face had not been shaved in days; his neck, much longer than that.

"Mr. Crowley?"

He only stared at me. The lip of skin beneath each of his eyes had fallen inward, as if the eyeballs had receded.

"Hello, Mr. Crowley."

"Ain't going be much use there, mister," called the aide.

Mr. Crowley smelled, I'm afraid to say, like an old animal. But I tried again and he lifted a papery hand in the air. I shook it gently, noticing that the hand of a retired elevator repairman still had quite a bit of strength in it.

"If you want to take him to his room, you can do that," the attendant said.

As I wheeled Mr. Crowley out of the dayroom, I noticed he still had a good head of hair, though it was flat with grease and flecked with innumerable stars of dandruff. The floor of the hallway was spotless, but beneath the pervasive smell of disinfectant, the air seemed stale, recycled, forced through someone's kidneys. An atmosphere of compressed exhalations. We passed room after room, each a variation on the same theme: ancient asleep in bed, chin up, mouth drawn back, as if rehearsing for death; ancient in wheelchair, his aide making a bed; ancient standing naked from the waist down, her aide dressing her; ancient in wheelchair looking at cereal on wheelchair tray; ancient asleep in bed. Mr. Crowley's room—a private one, I noticed—was small and sparsely furnished. There was a sink on one wall, a built-in closet of drawers, a shower. A heating vent whistled in the corner. On a night table next to the hospital bed stood a small framed Kodachrome photograph, and I bent down to inspect it: a small dark-haired man, Mr. Crowley, and his wife and their son, Simon, about age three, standing between them. The background: Queens, New York, circa 1967.

"That's a nice picture," I said, somewhat idiotically.

He gave me no answer, though his eyes watched me. I walked to the window and looked down on the nursing home's parking lot. Three aides in blue uniforms were throwing tied-off garbage bags into a Dumpster. Another aide was washing a car from a hose that ran from the building.

Outside the door, the old woman in the red robe shuffled by. "Hey! I'm so tired," she exclaimed. She looked into the doorway, and, appearing to hope that another patient's visitor might pay attention to her, she addressed me: "I'm so tired."

"I'm very sorry."

"My name is Pat," she said thickly. "He can't talk."

I noticed food stains on her robe.

"I know everybody here. I'm so tired."

"Perhaps you should sit down."

"I can't." She looked at me, munched her mouth. "I had three children."

"I'm very sorry, Pat."

"I had three children and now I can't find them."

"I'm sorry, Pat."

"Thank you," came her thick voice. "Thank you." She looked back down the hallway, as if contemplating her endless, appointed rounds. "Here comes James." She shuffled on.

A footstep outside the door, and then a portly middle-aged man in a Hawaiian shirt and green pants strode in. He was holding a clipboard and seemed surprised to see me. "Well, well, Mr. Crowley, you have a visitor!" He turned to me. "Hello, I'm James, the barber. I have to find out when this fine gentleman would like to have his hair cut! We *must* have a look at the fingernails, too, Mr. Crowley. We must do *that!* Are you a relative of Mr. Crowley's, sir, if I may be so bold as to inquire?"

I told him I was just a friend of the family's.

"Well, that is fine! Mr. Crowley does not get many visitors! Except for Mrs. Segal, bless her heart, this fine gentleman is left alone!" He leaned forward and pressed a hand affectionately on Mr. Crowley's emaciated shoulder. "And except for me, of course, isn't that *right*, Mr. Crowley? We have a fine time. He comes down to my barbershop and I give him a good wash and a cut and have a look at the nails and just try to tidy him up! He has rather thick nails. Tidy up the ears and nose. Maybe a good shave if he is feeling up to it. Some of the girls want me to do their old hairstyles from forty years ago, and I try to be accommodating. Isn't that right, sweetheart?" He turned to me conspiratorially. "I know he understands. He can't talk back, but I know he understands. It's in his eyes, it's in all their eyes. You have to look in the eyes to see anything. But let me tell you, when Mr. Crowley came in here he was sharp as a *tack*, just a little problem with his—maybe it was diabetes, I can't remember *what* it was. And up to maybe two or three years ago, he could still talk. They do go downhill, I'm afraid, just like children on sleds. But we try to be brave about it, we try to think good things—don't we, Mr. Crowley? The staff "—he gave a sad little wave of his hand—"well, they're overburdened, so it does no good to be a *critic*, but I *do* think he still can—" He glanced at his clipboard. "We'll just put him down for ten A.M. tomorrow, I think."

Mr. Crowley lifted his arm feebly. A sound came from him.

"What *is* it, sweetheart?" James said, his face alert. "Hmm? Yes? The drawer? You—why, *yes!* He wants to show you, do you know about this? It's the most fantastic thing I have *ever* seen, and I've been working in this very lovely land of hope for twenty-seven years!" James went to the drawer. "He made this, you see, didn't you, Mr. Crowley? Yes!" And then in a quiet aside to me: "It was some time ago, when the old sweetheart was more—still himself, if you know what I mean." Then from the drawer he pulled a strange arrangement of string and old cereal boxes. "Let me just—it's a bit tangled, yes, Mr. Crowley, *yes*, we'll hang it up. You see, he made this thing, he made this thing by himself. What an achievement! We have some of the sweethearts painting a little bit downstairs in the crafts center, marvelous colors, but no one has ever—there!"

The contraption hung by a stick off the headboard of the hospital bed: a vertical sequence of six little Frosted Flakes boxes held together by string. Hanging beneath them was another box, heavily altered, scissored such that the box had an arched roof.

"Now watch. No! Would you like to do it, Mr. Crowley?"

He said "Oooh," and we wheeled him over to the bed. He extended his spidery old fingers and delicately pinched one of the various strings. His eyes were now bright with determination; in the ashes of his mind a coal still burned. His fingers pulled downward on the string and the small, arched box at the bottom slowly rose upward, inside of the boxes. He stopped the arched box as it went inside the top cereal box.

"See?" James said, leaning forward. "It has little doors!" And, indeed, he pressed his fingers through a Lilliputian set of doors that swung on tape hinges. Opened, the door revealed another door in the interior box, one that corresponded perfectly, and which also opened.

"Isn't that the most spectacular thing you ever saw?" James said. He glanced at his watch. "Ah! I'm due in Mrs. Chu's room. Appointments, appointments. Good-bye, sweetie!" He patted Mr. Crowley's hand, and then disappeared.

We were left in the room with the contraption hanging in front of us. "Mr. Crowley?" I asked. "Do you know that your son, Simon, is dead?"

He contemplated me in the way a horse contemplates a man who knows nothing about horses, then closed his eyes. For a moment I feared that he might collapse in his chair, but he opened his eyes again, looking sideways, and a sound escaped his chest, an exhalation that may have carried an involuntary whimper of grief. We sat there. I moved closer to the toy elevator and inspected it. Mr. Crowley had attempted to make various markings on the inside and outside of each box, such as might correspond to buttons, panels, windows, and whatever other details of elevators I didn't understand. There was a certain obsessiveness to it. When I looked up, Mr. Crowley was asleep, his head slumped back in the wheelchair and his mouth agape. I watched. His throat rattled as he breathed. After a minute his eyes opened just a little, and I could not tell if he saw me or was gone. I leaned forward and lifted my palm to the old man's brow, silently urging him, as I have urged my children, to close his eyes and release his fears. The comfort of another's warm hand. Mr. Crowley eased into the chair then, and his breathing deepened. After a few minutes I stood quietly and left.

The next stop would be Mrs. Norma Segal's residence, which was only about ten blocks away. The fact that Mrs. Segal was Mr. Crowley's caretaker and also, with her husband, the former owner of the building in which Simon's body had been found meant something, if only that the universe still coughed up coincidences now and then. I was eager to speak with her, and thus I do not know why I again checked Mr. Crowley's visitor log on my way out, except that it had been a strangely compelling record when I'd looked at it on the way in, and now, having met Mr. Crowley, I viewed it as a document of great poignance. A man is born and grows up, learns to field a grounder, brushes his hair in the mirror, is married, has a son, works and eats and buys a bicycle for his son and screws his wife and goes to Yankee games and fixes his car and votes for Nixon and picks up a loaf of bread at the corner grocery and writes out his bills each month and brushes his teeth carefully, and then bang he is living in a nursing home and there is a three-ringed binder that proves that except for the bill collectors and a Mrs. Norma Segal, he is alone. The world has forgotten that he is alive. Even the well-meant affections of James the barber were generic. It also fascinated me, as I flipped the pages backward in time, and saw only Mrs. Segal's signature, that Caroline had not visited Mr. Crowley after Simon's death. Assuming that she loved Simon, her inability to visit his father *even once* seemed an act of remarkable callousness. She knew that he was here; she knew that the old should not be left to rot in warehouses. I kept flipping pages, and then I was back more than a year and a half, to the time before Simon died. Mrs. Segal had visited then, too. Her signature was occasionally interrupted by Simon's, his being more of a dashing scrawl, as if he was hurried or irritated by formality. It appeared more frequently as time went backward, and I could see that his visits occurred in clusters, three visits in five days, or two in six, and then a long run in between. Mrs. Segal's signature continued twice a week. As I went back further, Simon's signature appeared every other day, and I assumed that this frequency had only been possible before his career accelerated. Back a few months further, and the visits were daily. Simon had been an extraordinarily devoted son. I flipped forward in the book and found his last visit and, surprisingly, this, too: a small parenthetical remark next to Simon's name, in his own hand—(*and Billy*). The date was August 6, seventeen months prior. This, I remembered, was the last time Caroline had seen Simon alive. Billy Munson had been with Simon on that day. Who would have known?

THE VOICE WAS FEMININE, professional, efficient, and in no way interested in my problem. So was the next one. And the next. Billy Munson had left three banks in two years, and then the business altogether. Finally I located him in a small but potent venture capital firm, and his secretary allowed as to how he might be available that evening after a 5:30 P.M. business meeting at the Harvard Club. I needed to talk with both Munson and Mrs. Segal, but Mrs. Segal was an old woman with an old husband, hardly a moving target, and what sense I had told me that Munson was the more dynamic figure of the two. If he was around, I wanted to see him as soon as possible.

Inside the club, I nodded at the desk man gravely. "Mr. Munson's group?" I asked.

"Third floor, sir."

I was greeted by a woman who looked like one of the second-string models in the Victoria's Secret catalog. "How nice to see you," she said, holding the smile too long—to show she didn't mean it. "You can hang up your coat over there." I followed a paneled hallway into a small room. A little man came forward as if propelled on wheels and grasped my hand.

Golf clubs floated across his necktie. "We're glad you could make it!" he said, conspiratorially. "With the weather like this tonight—" He shook his head as if contemplating a great sorrow, and then indicated that I should step forward to the bar. I waited for a gin and tonic. The bar adjoined a conference room; drink in hand, I wandered in. The women were all about fifty and wanted it extremely clear that they spent a lot of time in the gym. Their makeup and hair appeared to be variations on the themes of waxed fruit and injection-molded plastic. One of them looked about six months pregnant, and as I drifted past her, I heard her describing her Svengali, the fertility specialist. The men were older and moved about with a certain goatish pleasure; that they were here, in this room, for whatever purpose, seemed a matter of private congratulation. I looked about for Billy Munson. He would be easy enough to recognize, I figured, from the Simon Crowley videos: flamboyant, heavy brushlike hair.

A large, tanned man came up to me. "Jim Krudop," he announced. "Glad you could make it." He had a grip like a plumber's, and unlike the other men, he unapologetically sported a pillowed gut that pushed at the buttons of his shirt. I was about to ease out of the door when everyone began to sit down, with an air of expectation, children at the circus. The short man who had greeted me by the elevator sailed into the room. "We're going to try and keep this brisk," he announced. "All of you know *me*, so I'll just introduce Bill Munson, who's working out the legal aspects of the partnership and is overseeing the financing and budgeting. Bill has worked with Jim Krudop for quite some time and feels—can I put words in your mouth, Bill?" The little man smiled as if being electrocuted. "Bill feels great confidence about this project. He'll introduce Jim, and then we'll hand it over to Jim and his slide show."

Another man stood—in his late thirties, slender, going reassuringly gray, his face solid and deliberate, his hairline looking wiser as it disappeared. This was Billy Munson, soldier of capital. "I'll just say a few words," he began. "As you know, we're trying to raise ten million. Each investment unit is set at one hundred thousand. That is to say, the minimum investment is one hundred thousand. We've raised four million so far. We'll be in Hong Kong tomorrow, then Tokyo, then Rio after that, and I expect by this time two weeks from today we'll be oversubscribed. I'm trying to keep the costs down by having the legal work done in exchange for several units of partnership—Beppy Martin's husband's firm will be handling this, as a matter of fact." He waved at the pregnant fifty-year-old. "Hi, Beppy, glad to see you here. The corporation will be either Swiss or Bermudan, for tax purposes. Now then, the ten million being raised will constitute seventy percent of the company, which monies will be returned, before the other thirty percent ownership receives anything, with interest at a reasonable percent, which would be accrued. The balance of the ownership includes Jim's share, which is thirteen percent, and he would quickly tell you that out of that share he has to pay his divers and technicians, as well as certain government officials in the Azores. Ten percent is a good-faith payment to Bluegreen Exploration Limited, Jim's previous limited partnership, which funded a great deal of his exploration of the Azores over the years as well as the recent technical survey of Graciosa Island, where the wrecks that Jim is interested in are located. Four percent of the ten million goes to the people who develop the financing, and the remaining three percent goes to Gripp Investments, for administrative support, ongoing assistance, supervision, and so on. The ten-million budget covers activity forward for four years. Some of that outlay Jim will describe further, but I can tell you that it includes a Phantom ROV with sonar, video, and still cameras for objects up to two thousand feet deep. There's also a side-scan sonar unit, a magnetometer, a recompression chamber, four Zodiac boats, things like that—money well spent, I assure you. We also are paying an annual licensing fee to the Portuguese government of one hundred and fifty-five thousand for the six-month working period, as well as about one hundred and fifty thousand a year to GeoSub, the deep-water search group we'll be subcontracting. I could go on with the financing, but I'll let Jim tell the fun part."

Munson sat down in front; I couldn't reach him. I'd have to wait.

Krudop stood up. "Thanks to everyone who came here this evening," he said. "As most of you know, I've been diving for wrecks for almost my whole life, ever since I got out of the marines. Now, I'll just—can you get the lights?—thank you. I got interested in the Azores a long time ago, but the Portuguese government has had the place locked up for thirty years. There . . . ha-ha, I was a lot skinnier in this photo; that's me working my first wreck, 1957. Now, the Azores were an important way station in transatlantic shipping from the late fifteenth century until the middle of the nineteenth century. That's a typical galleon, one hundred feet long. They would stop on their way back from the New World, going back to Spain, or from Brazil to Portugal. Also, the Portuguese East Indian ships coming around the Cape would land there. That's the map of Graciosa Island. They dropped into the harbor for water, supplies, food. Often they picked up an armada escort if they were bearing gold or silver, as a lot of them were. That's a shot of some gold ingots we found off Florida in 1962, just the kind that many of these ships had. Without the smelter's marks, they're worthless, and sell at the market's spot price of gold. With the marks, and you can see that this one has several, and the date is 1547, they sell at about forty times spot. Not bad. The big silver ones like these, which we found in 1977 off St. Croix, we call doorstops. From 1500 to about 1825, the nine islands of the Azores were visited by maybe six hundred, eight hundred ships a year. We know that from the records in South America, in Lisbon, all the places where the governments have the old documents. This is one. I've spent thirty years learning to read these—usually they're a mix of Portuguese, Castilian Spanish, Latin, sometimes even Dutch. They have the manifests of the ships. This one is for a Dutch trader, around 1550. It lists about thirty-six thousand gold coins. It was a deep-water wreck, and we found those gold coins inside a forty-square-meter area in 1969. Unfortunately, most of them were confiscated by the Panamanian government. Each of those would be worth about twenty-five thousand now. Anyway, in the Azores, you had all these ships going through. There are thousands of wrecks in the broader vicinity. That sounds like a lot, I know. But, for instance, in 1591, one hundred and twenty Spanish ships returning from South America were hit by a hurricane. Eighty-eight of them sunk. Here's a cannon. We get a lot of these long-barreled ones in terrific condition, if they were cast in bronze. The fishermen sometimes bring them up. They're about twenty thousand apiece these—"

Sunken treasure. I sat in a room full of very rich people who wanted to find sunken treasure. I was looking for a videotape of a fat man, they were seeking sunken cannons. Everybody wants something. I glanced at Billy Munson, wondering how I could get him to talk to me.

But now the show was getting good, better than anything on the shopping channels. "—in anaerobic zones," Krudop was saying, "which means they are oxygen free, and that prevents the worms from chewing up the wood, which is good because the wood holds the treasure together better. The stuff is—that's one of our divers operating the old sand vacuum we used to use. It would take three days to dig out the sand, say, in a room this size, but now we have this—it's just like a big elbow, and we place it over the ship's propeller and we blow the sand away. We can blow away the sand filling this room in maybe ten seconds and get down to what we call hardbase, where the ship will actually be. That's a shot of some of the pearls we pulled up in Jamaica. We got seventeen thousand of them; four boats went down. Now, a lot of these boats were from the Far East, carrying porcelain. There, that's Ming Dynasty porcelain we brought up in 1983. Every piece was broken. Every single piece. We brought up over two million shards, not one saucer. It was a shallow-water wreck; the stuff got knocked around, smashed up. Often the wrecks on reefs are not worth the effort, the stuff is too spread out. There, that's a gold chain; we get a lot of those. The ship's manifest always lists the contents, but often the ships have much more than that in contraband. The legality was that a sailor was not taxed on anything he had on his body if he was carried off a boat by two slaves. Very tricky wording. So the sailors would have gold chains made up that they wrapped their body in. Very fine links. Longest one we found was one hundred and twenty feet. Here's a Portuguese astrolabe. We've found seventeen of the known sixty-nine ancient astrolabes in the world. Sotheby's sold the last one for eight hundred and eighty-two thousand. Very rare. But we expect to find several. We're estimating that if we make some hits we could average fifty million a boat. Of course, it takes years to get the money out, I want to stress that. This one shows a silver coin before cleaning, almost black, and after, with all the markings showing. We pulled up about eight thousand of those in Florida in 1969. There, that's an entire rickshaw carriage made of jade that we brought up in 1978. It took a curator five years to—"

I stopped listening and watched the flickering succession of doubloons, pieces of eight, pearls, ingots, ivory, bottles, vases, knife handles, bronze gun handles, snuff-boxes, cannon, gold spice chests, porcelain shaving bowls, silver horse stirrups, chests, silver combs, gems, crucifixes, and so on, a fabulous enumeration of ancient wealth. A woman came by with a platter every few minutes, and soon I had eaten about a hundred dollars' worth of caviar. Eventually the lights came back on and Billy Munson took some questions. A wizened man who looked about eighty asked some sharp ones. He, of course, needed his investment back sooner rather than later. Then the gathering started breaking up. Munson didn't look like he scared very easily. I eased over to him and, when I had the chance, whispered, "I was wondering if we might have a moment to have a slightly more private conversation."

Munson flicked his gaze past me to the little smiling man, who flashed *yes* with his eyebrows.

"We'll step into another room."

There I identified myself and explained that I had some unsubstantiated rumors about his activities with Simon. I did not believe them, I said, because they were too outlandish, but I was wondering if we could discuss this shortly.

Munson's voice was calm: "What part of your story is full of shit?"

"The part about not believing the rumors."

He had to get on a plane to Hong Kong, he said, but I was welcome to ride with him to JFK. "Hey, I knew Simon better than anybody. We spent a lot of time together. Lots of time."

"Must've been bad when he died."

"Bad. Very bad."

We walked outside and caught a cab. Munson rolled down his window, took out a joint, and began to smoke it. He relaxed visibly, which was good because I was about to attack.

"Caroline says you two were close."

"We did some stuff."

"I heard something about you guys making some tapes together."

He laughed. "Yeah, the word got around about that."

"Wild times and so on."

"Pretty wild."

"You ever show them to people?"

"The tapes?"

"Right."

"I don't have them."

"Where are they?"

He loosened his tie. "Gone."

"Really?"

"Gone." He shook his head at the tragedy of it. "Lots of people would give their left nut to see those tapes, man. Some wild stuff, with Simon Crowley doing it. Believe me, the studio came looking for those tapes. Simon was supposed to be working on a new project and the studio was thinking maybe he did some kind of handheld thing, which is crazy, but they put their people on it. If the studio couldn't find those tapes, nobody can."

"What happened to them?"

"I don't know. Simon never used to talk to me about them. Maybe he mentioned them once or twice. I never saw them, and I wish I did because I'm on them, I know that much."

"Weren't they in his estate?"

"You mean did he leave them to somebody? No way. Who would he leave them to?"

"I don't know. His wife?"

"Caroline? No way."

"She was his wife, though."

Billy shook his head. "Hey, you got to understand, I was around Si in a lot of places. He was fucking a lot of girls. He married Caroline because it was an interesting thing to do. *She* was an interesting thing to do, if you know what I mean. She was like a riddle that he played with. But he was never into the husband thing. Besides, they knew each other only, like, six months or something."

"You and Simon went out a lot?"

"A lot of times, yeah."

"What were you doing with him the day he disappeared?"

"I wasn't with him."

"Where were you?"

"I was on a flight to Hong Kong. Just like tonight. I do a lot of moving around."

"Why didn't you tell the police that you saw Simon on the day he dis-appeared?"

"Because I didn't."

"I would disagree."

"Hey, you know what?" he said amicably.

"What?"

"I did not see him on the day he disappeared."

We drove on. The cabbie looked into his mirror from time to time. "I could tell you my problem," I said, "but it's not going to make you feel bet-ter."

"Tell me your problem."

"My problem is that I've seen all the tapes, Billy. All of Simon's tapes."

He looked at me. "I'm listening. I'm waiting for the hook."

"The hook is in the proof that I've seen the tapes."

"Yeah?"

"On the tape it's the West Side, maybe Tenth Avenue and Forty-sixth Street. You and Simon are cruising in a limousine. You stop and pick up a hooker and you bargain down her fee to five dollars. Then you get out of the car while Simon screws her. You get back in the car after they're done, and then you drive on."

"Okay."

"Okay."

"So?"

"So that's *one* of the tapes."

"Well, fuck me!" He smiled hatefully. "Hey! You saw one of Simon's tapes! Where does this give you the idea that you can show up out of the blue at one of my—"

"The other tape," I interrupted, "the pertinent one, is set inside of a van. The van is parked in Tompkins Square Park prior to and during a riot by a mob of squatters and street people. The van is situated such that the important action of the riot is filmed through the back window. You were in the van with Simon. The camera catches both of you, and your voice is plainly recorded. You know the tape I'm talking about, Billy. Even if you never saw it, you know the one I'm talking about. I know you remember it, because anyone would remember what it was like to see a policeman struck in the head with a baseball bat. One blow, down he goes. You saw it, Billy, you saw it with your own two eyes and, in fact, you commented on it. But there it was. A black cop was murdered by a white guy with a baseball bat and you saw him do it. You watched. You read the papers the next day. Maybe you even read my column. You saw the news. You and Simon both."

"He said he was going to use it in a film. He said it was so good he might just have to use it."

"Okay."

"Okay?"

"Okay."

"What do you mean, okay?"

"I mean you can tell that to the cops."

"Why?"

"Because they're very interested right now. They know about the tape, Billy. I've told them about the tape. I haven't yet handed it over to them. We're negotiating under what terms they're to get the tape from me. See, the tape confirms who the killer is. Now they can arrest him and put him on trial. The assistant district attorney will need to present, or will contemplate presenting, a chain of custody. Then they'll want to haul me up there in court and identify me as the guy who gave them the tape. They'll ask me who I got the tape from and so on. Now, I don't want to go up as a witness. It's not in my interest as a journalist. Somewhere in there they'll ask me about you. Did I talk to you, did you know about the tape, that kind of thing. I mean, the cops know that it would be natural for me to ask you why you didn't tell them about the tape. And I would be forced to tell them that yes, I did talk to you about the tape, and that you told me exactly what you just told me, Billy, which was this: 'He said he was going to use it in a film. He said it was so good he might just have to use it.' You said that. You said that about a minute ago. I didn't write it down and I didn't tape it, Billy, but I remember it. I can remember quotes for years, as a matter of fact. So where were we? Okay. So if I tell the cops what you said, they'll say, 'Holy shit, that's an admission of cognizance. This William Munson figure was holding back on evidence about the murder of a cop.' Do you know what they'll do to you, Billy? Have you ever looked Rudy Giuliani in the eyes? You're going to be up in Attica State Prison pitching your sunken treasure thing, maybe getting some other guy's treasure sunken in you, you know? Maybe. Maybe you'll beat the rap. But the papers would eat your face off, Billy. I'll write the headline: 'Investment Banker Held Out on Cop Murder.' That's page one, Billy. That's Tom Brokaw, *CBS Evening News*, CNN. *Vanity Fair* will do a piece on you, interview all your old girlfriends. Use your imagination, okay?"

"Wait, wait—"

"No, you wait," I said, poking my finger at him. "Keep listening. There's a way out. If I don't tell the cops what you said, then you can go to your lawyer, tonight perhaps, and start figuring out what you're going to say when they ask you. It'll be much better to have an answer. A severe drug problem would be useful. I suggest that you develop or enhance a record of drug addiction, Billy, or a drinking problem, anything so that you can tell the cops that you passed out later that night and couldn't remember a thing. A long record of headaches, treatments, dizzy spells, passing out, CAT scans, stuff like that. There are lawyers who specialize in this kind of defense—"

"Who? Do you know one?"

"No. Get your secretary on it. Now, as we were saying, what happened on the day Simon disappeared?"

Munson gazed out of the cab window. He was defeated now. "We just drove around, man."

"What did you drive in?"

"His dad's van."

"His dad's?"

"The one that his father used to use for work. It was his."

"The one the two of you had in the park?"

He fingered his shirt cuff. "Yes."

"Was there video equipment in it?"

"His dad had all kinds of old tools in there, and Simon had cameras, drugs, booze, he had books, a mattress, a bicycle, a lot of hand tools, things like that. He had everything in there."

"Where did you go?"

"We went to the nursing home, and Simon and his father talked about some shit. I didn't listen. I just hung out in the hallway. I didn't want to see

Simon with his dad. I figured he might cry, and I didn't want to see that. I just shook the old man's hand."

"How lucid was the old man then?"

"He was okay on some things but—it wasn't Alzheimer's but something else. He'd lost the ability to read and write. He could still talk a little, I guess. I couldn't understand him. Simon could."

"You guys left and then what?"

"I don't know. We drove around. I can't remember the order. We got something to eat, we stopped at some kind of an office."

"A lawyer's office?"

"I don't know. An office in a house, something like that."

"People named Segal?"

"I don't remember."

"Why did you stop?"

"Fuck, man, I don't remember," Munson protested. "I stayed in the van. It was a very quick stop."

"Was it in Queens?"

"Yes, near the nursing home."

"Did Simon ever talk to you about Sebastian Hobbs?"

"The guy who owns your paper?"

I nodded. "Yeah."

"Why would he do that?"

"I'm asking if he ever mentioned him."

"No."

"Did he ever show you his collection of tapes?"

"No, absolutely not."

"Why not?"

"Simon wasn't like that. The tapes were a private thing, like an internal dialogue, okay? He made them for his own purposes. People gave him tapes, too, when they thought they had a good one. I went with him sometimes, yes, we did stuff, but I was never allowed to see them. He never offered and I never asked. It was sort of a compliment to be taped with him, and I didn't want him to feel self-conscious about it with me. He made a lot of tapes without me, too. I never saw them. And you know, toward the end we both got busy in our lives and didn't see each other so much."

"Where were you the day after you two drove around?"

"Hey, I got the ticket stub, the records from the airline. I was on my way to Hong Kong. I always stay at the Conrad. I have phone records from the plane. I even have phone records from the hotel car. They've got a red stretch Rolls-Royce that picks you up at the airport. I didn't know that he was dead till, like, a week later. I saw it on CNN."

"You never told the police that you spent some of the day with Simon?"

"No."

"You were his friend?"

Munson frowned. "Hey, fuck you. Si and I parted ways at, like, maybe three in the afternoon. He dropped me off at the airport. Where he went after that I have no idea. I spent a few hours with him. We drove out from Manhattan, saw his dad, boom, stopped at the office, boom, and then to the airport. That's it. From what I understand, the police never even figured out exactly when Simon was killed, okay? Why should I get involved with that? I wasn't part of the story. Simon could have had a hundred interactions with people after that. And you know what? I thought long and hard about it. I thought about it and I thought what should I do? I got a wife and two kids. I'm making money for them, too, and this stuff would just have screwed things up for me. For no reason. Simon would have agreed with me, matter of fact. He would have said, 'Don't do it.' "

The cab was racketing over some bad road. "But there was also the matter of the Tompkins Square Park tape. The less connection between you, the better."

"I suppose."

"Weren't you afraid the tape was going to appear somehow?"

"I knew that depended on Caroline."

"What do you mean?"

He gave me a little smile, acknowledging his earlier lie about not knowing where the tapes were. "She called me one day and said she'd seen the tape and thought it would look bad for Simon's memory if we told the police."

"She did?"

"Yeah. But she was lying."

"I don't get it."

"I mean, it wasn't for some high holy purpose. If the thing about the cop tape came out, it would damage Simon's marketability. You got all those videos being rented, all the royalties and so on. You could have the people pissed off that his estate was still making money."

"Did she know you spent time with Simon that day?"

"I don't know. I didn't tell her."

"He could have seen her between the time he left you and the time he disappeared," I said, remembering Caroline had made no mention of Munson in the police report. "He could have told her he'd seen you."

"That's possible, I guess."

The cab was pulling into the airport.

"So you're going to Hong Kong anyway?" I asked.

"Sure. Out of the country. Hard to reach." He pulled out his wallet, pushed four twenties through the glass. "Cabbie, I want you to take this fellow back to the city."

I could throw in a couple of junk questions now. "Did Simon ever talk to you about Caroline?"

"Yeah."

"What?"

"He said she could just about fuck his dick off." He looked at me. "That's a quote. I can remember quotes for years."

I was going to smile, but my beeper went off.

TOMMY SHOT. GO ST. VINCENT'S HOSP.

Little bright letters, big events.

A BOY. a boy of only eighteen months, asleep in a hospital crib, a bubble rising and falling on his lips, dreaming whatever a child dreams—mother, milk, cookies, sister, animals, red, yellow, green. That a bullet has passed through the tiny biceps of his left arm is not understood by him, only that a bad man was in the room, that Josephine screamed and there was some noise and something hot cut his arm and he was crying, Sally was crying, Josephine was screaming. He cannot know that the bullet, meant to splinter and mushroom at the touch of flesh, has passed through his arm as if it were ethereal, too young yet to present the warm, wet smack of resistance to a projectile. That same bullet, he does not know, has, after passing through his arm, entered the same knee he was hugging in fear, and the bullet has bloomed in accordance with the diabolical specifications of its manufacturer into a many-toothed brass-jacketed blur of fleshly destruction, taking with it the kneecap of a fifty-two-year-old black woman.

I stood at the edge of Tommy's crib in a fugue of fear and anger and guilt. I wished that I could weep. Lisa came up.

"I examined the wound myself," she said, her voice dead.

"How serious is it?"

"Bottom line? Scar tissue in the muscle but not through its entire depth." She rubbed Tommy's back gently. "He's going to need some rehab, especially stretching to keep the tissue pliant. The arm will not be weak, but he'll never have the absolute contraction in that muscle that he would have."

"Scar?"

She gazed at Tommy, blinked. "He's going to grow so much that it won't be too disfiguring. Maybe a dimple. Very little keloid—he's too young."

"Josephine?"

Lisa sighed. "It hit the left patella. That's unsalvageable. She'll need some operations, rehab. It will take a year, certainly."

Lisa went to check on Sally, who was sleeping on a sofa in an office. By now I knew that they had all ridden in the ambulance together—Josephine and Tommy and Sally—Josephine insisting with hysterical strength through her pain that she not be separated from the children. Lisa had arrived within an hour of the shooting from her office and found, she had told me when I first appeared at the hospital, that the children were strangely calm. Upon seeing her, they erupted into sobs of terror and clutched at her, Sally especially, who, unwounded, was yet traumatized by the blood of Tommy and Josephine.

"I've arranged everything for Josephine," Lisa said.

"Paying for everything?"

"Yes."

"Private room?"

"I got her the best room in the hospital. And doctors."

"Can I see her?"

"She's sedated, but I think so." My wife's voice was cold, abstracted. She looked alone to me.

"Sedated?"

"She's been through trauma, and also antianxiety medication is one of the ways they treat pain now. Anxiety amplifies pain."

"Whose gun was it?"

"The man's."

"But Josephine fired her gun?"

"The police think so. She was incoherent. She'll be better now." Lisa sighed. "I didn't get to talk to her. They were working on her knee."

"She kept her gun after all."

"Yes," said Lisa. "I feel like I don't understand much anymore."

We stood there, my wife and I. There was something she wasn't saying to me.

"They're going to want this bed."

"Tommy's?"

"Yes." Lisa turned her eyes to me.

"But Jesus, he was just shot in the arm."

"It's a comparatively insubstantial flesh wound, disinfected, sutured, bandaged. He'll take a little antibiotic and be okay." Her voice was tight, disinterested in my anxiousness over Tommy.

"I don't understand your point. Your tone, to be more precise."

"You know who the man was, I presume."

"I have a good idea."

She considered me. She was purely the mother of her children, not, for the moment, my wife. "This is not finished, whatever this is?"

"No."

"I can't have the children be part of this, Porter."

"No."

Tommy stirred, and she readjusted his blanket. "You've been acting like you're in a lot of trouble."

"I am."

"I mean staying out all hours, getting beaten up, and making up a story that you were mugged. You must think I'm a fool."

"No."

"You must really have some misconceptions about me."

"No."

"Then about yourself."

"Perhaps."

She set her dark eyes upon me. " 'Perhaps' is the answer of a coward."

I said nothing.

"Can you guarantee that these men won't come back again?"

"No."

"You seem to have *really* pissed somebody off, Porter."

"It's not exactly like that."

Her face was clenched with bitterness. "Well, I hope it's for a *good* reason."

"It's not exactly like that, either."

We stood there, my wife and I, she in her pretty dress and sensible heels.

"I'm going to take the kids to Mom's," she announced. "Tonight. I'll get tickets at the airport. I have a car that'll be here in maybe ten minutes."

Her mother lived in the hills outside San Francisco and made birdhouses from pine boards and old California license plates.

"What about your practice?" I asked.

"I feel pretty damn shitty about that, Porter—a lot of patients are waiting for surgery. Luckily it's elective for the next week or so." She was disheartened that she might be failing them. "As for on-call coverage, I've worked that out, but I don't like to do it. It doesn't make me look very good to suddenly run off. Everybody at the hospital will hear about this, too. But these are my *children*."

"Yes."

"I have a lot to say to you, but I'm too furious and upset about Tommy." She glared at me, then let out a breath. "Damn it, Porter, this really sucks, it's really shitty."

"Yes."

She left then, holding Tommy, with a nurse carrying Sally for her. I kissed both children good-bye and was glad they were asleep, that I didn't have to say why I wasn't going with them. I could follow Lisa and try to explain all of it. I didn't.

UPSTAIRS, IN JOSEPHINE'S ROOM, I poked my head inside, expecting her family to be there. "Josephine?"

She was lying on her side watching a screen set into a large entertainment console. On it was a menu of hospital services. Next to the screen were some complimentary movies if she wanted to watch them.

"Oh, Porter!" She turned to me and I could see the tears in her eyes. "I was with Tommy and Sally, you know, I was starting to cook some noodles, and then I heard the buzzer from the gate, and you know I thought maybe Porter is coming home early, something like that, and then I look up and saw this man at the window—"

No doubt Hobbs's man knew how to slip a lock. "What did he look like?"

"He was a white man, maybe, oh, I would say maybe fifty years old, in a heavy coat, and I was thinking, Oh, no, that's not right, that's not good, nobody say nothing to *me* about some man coming over to the house, you know, and then he smile and knocked on the door, and I called through the glass, 'Who are you?' And he didn't say nothing, so I said, 'Go away, I'm calling the police.' And then he kicked in the door, just like that. The kids saw that. Sally, she was very scared by that. Then the man was inside the kitchen and I was thinking, Oh, no, *that's* not right, *that's* not a good man, you know, and he said, 'Where is Porter's office?' and I said that wasn't his business, and then he say, 'Show me the office or I'll hurt somebody,' you know. So I show him the office, you know, because I think that—"

"No, no, you did the right thing," I said. "Absolutely."

"So then he starts messing around in the office, just pulling out stuff, and then I start to pick up the kids to get away, and then he says, 'No, you all come in here.' I was trying to pick up Tommy, you know, so I could run. But he came out of the office, and he had a gun and said, 'All you get in the office,' and so I took my bag and the kids and went in there, and he was pulling your papers and opening drawers and throwing your papers everywhere and saying, 'Where is it, where is it?' Then I said, 'Mister, I don't know what you mean,' and then he said he was going to have to take one of the kids away with him, and then—oh *my*—" Josephine pressed her hands to her neck and looked down, blinking. "I just—I *know* you tell me don't bring the gun to work no more, but—"

"We're past that now, Josephine," I said.

"I just said, 'No, you can't do that, mister, you can't take these kids,' and I pulled my gun out and I pointed it and just pulled. He yelled and called me some names—you know how they do when they're mad like that— and then he fired and that was the one that hit Tommy and me, and then we both screamed, you know, and I fell down with Tommy and I shot it again, and I think I hit him, maybe, and I fired again and that one missed him, that one hit the wall, and then he started to run outside. He went out the kitchen door right across the yard, and then he fall down, once, you know, and then he kept on going. I didn't follow him. I just held on to the kids. They was so upset that I just held them and kissed them, you know, like that."

From the hospital I traveled directly to the newspaper's offices and bought a couple of liter bottles of Coke. I'd drink them and be able to stay up all night, which was the idea. Hal Fitzgerald had left two messages on my machine and sounded worried on his own behalf. But I couldn't think about him now. I had the guard open up the newspaper's information services office. Mrs. Wood was gone, but I knew my way around. Campbell. I needed to know where Campbell was. What was his first name? I couldn't remember. You could line up ten thousand men and I could identify him that moment, but for the life of me I could not remember his first name. I could look up "Campbell" on the CD phone directory, a very accurate one provided by a private company and updated every three months, but that would give me too many names. Instead I did a Nexis search with Campbell and Hobbs. A recent story in *The New York Times* on the paper might give Campbell's first name. Nothing. Perhaps Campbell had been promoted while stationed in New York; the newspaper's PR office would have cranked out a release. How about "Campbell" and "London"? "Campbell" and "England"? Here it was, a tiny item: *Walter Campbell promoted to the position of executive vice-president . . . A native of London, Campbell will head up the . . .*

With "Walter Campbell" I could begin. Where did he live? New York? New Jersey? Connecticut? An expensive neighborhood. Upper Saddle River, New Jersey? Very nice place. Darien, Connecticut? Also a nice spot. A tough call. Maybe not. Presumably he flew to London on business pretty frequently. He would be flying out of JFK. Not as many international flights used LaGuardia. A man who uses JFK frequently, who needs to take early-morning flights and so on, will not live in New Jersey or Connecticut. Even with a limo driver, it was simply too far in the morning, too much wasted time. He'd be in New York, either in Long Island or in the city proper. I looked up Walter Campbell in area codes 212, 718, and 516. Eight of them. I threw out the six that were in middle-class or poor neighborhoods. Two remained, both in Bridgehampton. Three hours on the Long Island Expressway every morning—forget it. Campbell had an unlisted number. I remembered that he did not have a wedding ring. He was either gay or divorced; that could put him in Manhattan, which for a wealthy middle-aged man was where the action was. Was he a registered voter? Only if he was a naturalized citizen. Not likely. Retirement benefits are better in the U.K. I had nothing. He was Walter Campbell. I didn't have a birthdate or a Social Security number. How do you find a British citizen in Manhattan without a phone number, an address, or a Social Security number? The man drives a car. I popped in the New York State Department of Motor Vehicles disc. Eighty-four people named Walter Campbell. No address listed. Real estate. I entered a search for Manhattan only. There was a W. Campbell at East 148th Street. Spanish Harlem. No chance. The man did not own property in the city. If he did, then I would have all kinds of ways of finding him. But it made sense that he had not bought property, Hobbs probably moved his key people around every few years. I flipped through the list of possible ways to search for people: Bankruptcy; Mechanics Liens; Sidewalk Violations; Environmental Control Board Judgments; HPD Emergency Repair Liens; Uniform Commercial Code Filings; Inactive Hazardous Waste Sites. Here was one: Parking Violation Judgments.

The computer took a few seconds and then informed me:

PVD JUDGMENTS—Walter K. Campbell
ADDRESS: 107A EAST 35th #2
JDMTS—14
AMOUNT—$1,090
INT—$102.16
PLATE—JD0876

Here was a British executive scofflaw who rented an apartment within
walking distance of his office. Now I could learn something about him; I
flipped one CD after another into the machine. He was fifty-one years old.
He drove a '95 Lexus. He did not have a gun registration. He was not currently being sued. He had never been given a summons for smoking in the
subway. His apartment was owned by a Lucy Delano, purchased in 1967,
no amount given. Campbell's neighbor in #3 was Mr. Tim Westerbeck, age
thirty-six, who had paid $345,000 for his apartment in 1994. Campbell's
neighbor in #1 was Mrs. Lucy Delano, age eighty-two, who bought her
apartment in 1964, no amount listed. I needed Campbell's phone number.
I looked up Westerbeck's number: The message said that he was on his
honeymoon in Baja and "whatever is left of me" would be back later.
Screw him. I looked up Mrs. Delano's number and called her.

A tentative, old voice: "Hello?"

"Mrs. Lucy Delano?"

"Yes?"

I told her my name and that I was a reporter at the paper.

"What do you want?"

"We're terribly eager to reach your neighbor, Mr. Campbell."

"How do you know he's my neighbor?"

"It's a matter of public record, ma'am. Would you happen to have his
number?"

"Yes, but I can't give it to you."

"I see."

"I'm sorry."

I made a sound of discouragement. "I very much need to speak with
him, you see."

"I'll go knock on his door, if you like."

This was risky. "Okay," I said.

I heard the phone being put down. Coughing. Indistinct noises. Nothing. Nothing and nothing. Nothing and then nothing. Perhaps she had died in the hallway. Nothing. Indistinct noises and coughing. Then: "I'm afraid he is not there."

"Mrs. Delano?"

"Yes?"

"I really need that number."

"I'm sorry. I've lived in this city a very long time."

"Mrs. Del—"

"The first time they mugged me was in nineteen sixty-five."

I said nothing.

"So you *see*."

Yes.

THIRTY-FIFTH STREET, eleven P.M., a January night. The apartment was part of a four-story brownstone, which was good; there was no doorman. The building was about twenty-five feet wide, a standard Manhattan brownstone width, with bay windows on the first and second floors. The stoop had been removed, and the main entrance was now three steps down from the street into the ground floor. The buzzer had three bells, which meant that there were three apartments in the four floors: One of them was a duplex—probably the ground and first floors. Mrs. Delano, thinking ahead the way old women do, would have taken the ground floor to avoid the stairs; that meant that Campbell lived on top of her and that the goofball Westerbeck lived above him. I buzzed Campbell's apartment; no answer; he was not yet home. Or perhaps he would not be coming home; he could have a lover somewhere in the city. Some chick in red boots who kept a poodle.

The lights were out in #1; Mrs. Delano was asleep. I looked for a way to break into the building. I saw nothing but alarm-service stickers and iron bars on the windows. I stood across the street, found a shadow, folded my arms into my coat. While waiting, I noticed that the lid of the garbage can next to me was attached to a fence with a short, cheap wire.

AN HOUR LATER Campbell arrived, walking alone, carrying a bag of groceries. I watched him stop in front of the brownstone, get his key out. And then, light as blowing trash, I was across the street in ten steps. "Hey!" he said, but I already had the wire around his neck. He dropped the groceries and I kicked them through the open door and shoved him in, taking the key out of the door.

"I'll give you money," he barked. "My wallet—"

"Up the stairs."

"My wallet—"

"Shut up." I yanked on the wire and he coughed.

"Pick up the groceries."

He did. This would keep his hands occupied. At the door of #2, I had him identify the right key.

"Don't kill me. Please."

"Turn on the light."

He did. A nice apartment, rugs, lamps, Victorian decor—all in all, perhaps a bit sad for its neatness. The loneliness of an aging bachelor.

"Sex?" he coughed.

"What?"

"You want sex?"

"What?"

"I'll do you. I'm good. It'll be good."

I laughed and yanked on the wire. I was a lot stronger; it wasn't even close. I dragged him into the kitchen.

"Point to the drawer that has the biggest, sharpest knife."

He froze.

"Do it!"

"No. You'll kill me."

"Do it, Campbell." I yanked brutally on the wire and he went weak in the knees. When he went down I could see that he dyed his hair.

"Get up, you fucker."

"Uh. I'm. Dying."

"No you're not, not just yet."

"Uh." He stumbled to his feet.

"Show me the drawer."

He didn't. I dragged him backward toward the drawers, pulled open a few, grabbed a huge carving knife, and then a little one, which I slipped into my back pocket. Then I pushed Campbell toward the phone.

"Do you know who I am?"

"No," he coughed. "I can't see you."

"Wren. Porter Wren. I work for you."

"Uh."

"Your goons shot my little boy this afternoon. Did you know that?" But I pulled on the wire before he could answer. His hands fumbled on the edge of the phone table. "I should kill you, Campbell."

"No, please."

"Call Hobbs."

"I can't."

"Why?"

"He's. In Brazil."

"That's not good enough."

"I swear!"

I took the little knife out of my pocket and I stabbed Campbell in the ass with it, once, maybe an inch deep. He screamed. It hurt but it wasn't serious.

"Start thinking, Campbell."

Now I broke him at the knees and made him lie down on the carpet. I sat on his back. I weigh about two hundred and ten pounds. I pulled the phone down, as well as what looked like a rather well-organized international personal phone directory.

"Put your hands behind you."

"No."

I stabbed him again.

He put his hands back. I tied them tight with the wire. Then I put the directory on the carpet next to his face and pushed the speakerphone button so that I could hear the conversation.

"Who do we call?"

"It's impossible," he moaned.

I moved my lips close to his ear. "Campbell, pal. My son is eighteen months old, he is a perfect angel, he is innocent. You have damaged his body and perhaps his soul. I am not a violent man by nature, Campbell. But I swear I will torture you until you get Hobbs on the phone."

"I'll lose my job!" he screamed, kicking.

I stabbed him in the ass again. Pretty deep. But it didn't bleed much. I did it again, twisting the knife. It was a weird yet familiar sensation, sort of like testing the readiness of a Christmas ham. I did it again. Campbell was starting to hyperventilate.

"Call him," I said.

"You don't understand," Campbell said. "I can't just—"

Politely stabbing him in the rear wasn't working, I realized. Maybe he had a pain thing. I grabbed a lamp from the table, knocked off the shade, and waved the hot bulb in front of Campbell's mouth.

"Open wide," I said. "This will be a new feeling."

"No!"

"What do you want next, the knife or the bulb?"

"All right, all right! Call London!" he breathed. "Wake up Mrs. Fox!"

We did this. It took a few minutes. Mrs. Fox was Hobbs's housekeeper. Campbell explained to Mrs. Fox that he needed Mrs. Donnelly's home number. Mrs. Donnelly was Hobbs's personal secretary, went with him everywhere. Mr. Donnelly answered. It was early morning in London. A sleepy fellow talking to a hysterical countryman in Manhattan. I need your wife's number in Brazil, said Campbell. Why? Just give it to me! Bloody rude, aren't you? And so on. A call to Brazil, with the correct country and city code. No answer. Ten rings. Then a voice in Portuguese. Mrs. Donnelly was summoned. She had been asleep. Yes, she remembered Mr. Campbell, what could she do for him? I need to talk with Mr. Hobbs. I'm very sorry, he's out right now. And so on. Campbell was sweating heavily, wetting his lips. Please, he said, please, Mrs. Donnelly, I'm in a very difficult situation, an emergency situation. Give me the cellular number. He always has a cellular phone. I'm sorry, Mr. Campbell, he's asked that there be no disturbances— Campbell groaned. I'm thinking! he breathed aloud. Is there a cellular, Mrs. Donnelly? Not that I know of. No cellular; that means the cellular service is bad. Mrs. Donnelly! Yes? The driver will have a satellite phone! What's that? Direct phone to a satellite; it fits in the limousine trunk! I'm not familiar with this— Yes you are, it's the car number, call the car number. Oh, the car number. Well, then. She gave it to him. I dialed. Five rings. Yes? came a British voice. Is this the driver? Yes. This is Campbell in New York. Give me Hobbs. I'm afraid— This is an emergency. He's attending a dinner inside. There're a lot of people inside. Get him out to the car. I can't do that, sir. This is Campbell in New York. I don't know who you are. Campbell in New York. I run the U.S. operations! I'm sorry, sir. Listen, go to the door and get the number of the house inside. You can do that. We'll call them. There was a long pause. I'm fucking trying, can't you see that? spat Campbell. My ass hurts. You stabbed me in the ass. Then the voice came back with the house number, which we dialed. A maid answered, speaking Portuguese. Much miscommunication. Then the teenaged daughter, who spoke perfect English. Yes? They are in the dining room. I will ask my father. English, Daddy. Yes? A deep voice. This is Arturo Montegre. This is Walter Campbell in New York. I must speak with one of your dinner guests, Mr. Sebastian Hobbs. This is irregular, no? Yes, sir, it very much is, but I'm in a very bad spot. A long pause.

Yes? Hobbs. Who is calling?

I let Campbell go on a minute, explain the basics. How he had fucked up. But he was apologizing too much, nearly weeping in exhaustion, and my message wasn't getting through. I took over: "Hobbs, listen to me, you motherfucker. If you do not call off your fucking goons, I will make a thousand copies of the videotape." This was the easiest lie of my life. "I will make a thousand copies and I will send one to every fucking newspaper and television station in the country and I will provide a transcript of the conversation for the idiots who can't do it for themselves, I will go down in a glorious fireball, you fat cocksucker, and I will take you along. Your fucking goons beat me up, stole the wrong tape from me, and shot my boy, Hobbs, and you are smart enough to know how stupid that is. You can sue me into the next century, I don't care. I'll be a fucking wild man, Hobbs, if anything more happens to my wife or children. I will hunt you down and cut out your heart, you fucking fat monstrosity, do you understand that?

And before I do that I will also tell the New York City Department of Police that your man here, your *executive*, has possession of the tape that your goons took off of me, a tape that happens to show a policeman being killed. The cops want this tape. They're gonna throw Campbell into fucking Rikers Island. You ever hear of Rikers Island? Largest penal colony in the world, right here in New York! Seventeen thousand inmates! Campbell goes there, he'll—wait! Your man is crying, Hobbs. Here he is."

I put the phone next to Campbell's lips.

"Beg him," I ordered.

His breathing was panicked but he said nothing. I poked the tip of the knife into his ear.

"Mr. Hobbs! Mr. Hobbs!" Campbell screamed hoarsely. "It's my fault! I'm very sorry! I went too far with the men! I need—please give me authorization to withdraw them!"

A pause. His head dropped to the carpet.

"Okay," he said.

I took the phone. "I want to hear it, Hobbs."

"You have my word, Mr. Wren. I will be in New York soon. We will exchange the tapes then. And now, may I go back to my dinner?"

IT WAS NEARLY THREE A.M. when I returned to the gate in the wall, watching carefully behind me. Inside the tunnel I saw a few drops of blood on the brick and then a long oblong streak flung on the porch and then inside it was everywhere, on the floor, smeared on the phone, soaked into two large towels, and thrown in a dark splatter on the wall. The EMTs had left their litter of torn gauze packaging and syringe wrappers. All this bleeding was my fault, and I was glad that Lisa and the kids were far away from me. I wasn't worthy of them now. Somehow this was not a surprise to me; always I have known that I am selfish and small-hearted, an asshole among assholes. I am not good. I am selectively bad. I am capable of what should be rightfully condemned. My father, in fact, a gentle and patient man, always worried about my nature when he was raising me without my mother. Standing in my kitchen, gazing at the red spots flung about the room, I was reminded of a day many years past, a July afternoon when I was fifteen. My father had asked me to paint the kitchen of a Miss Whitten, an old woman who lived in town. My father was one of the church's elders, and I suppose that it had come to his attention that Miss Whitten lived in reduced circumstances. I told him I didn't want to do the job, but my protest was halfhearted, because I knew that my father would not have asked of me such an onerous task were it not somehow important to him. He explained that he had volunteered to paint the kitchen himself but that his back had been bad for a few days. Indeed, I saw the pain in his face as he lifted a gallon of house paint into his truck. We drove over to Miss Whitten's house after breakfast, and along the way my father explained to me how one paints a room, using drop cloths, masking tape around the molding, and long, easy strokes. "The important thing is not to hurry," he told me. Miss Whitten met us at the door of her modest clapboard house, standing with the help of a cane. "So, yes, here you are," she said. As soon as we were inside, she sat heavily into a wheelchair, sliding the cane into a loop that hung from one of the steel armrests. My father was unusually solicitous of her. She led us back to a large, old-style kitchen with appliances from the 1950s, cracked linoleum flooring and counters, and paint falling like leaves from the ceiling. My father helped me with the cans and drop cloths and told me he would be back at six that evening.

I worked diligently, first scraping all the loose paint off, then masking the parts not to be painted, then setting up the drop cloths. Miss Whitten inspected my progress from time to time, wheeling her chair over the ancient red carpeting of the dining room up to the doorway leading into the kitchen. She didn't say a word. It was a hot day, and by one P.M. I had taken off my T-shirt and was drinking water from the tap. Miss Whitten appeared. "Young man, put on your shirt," she commanded from her wheelchair. I looked at her, shrugged, and put it back on. Her peevishness could not quite reach me; I had settled into the not unpleasant rhythm of the work and, more to the point, was thinking about the cotton panties that Annie Frey wore, the soft flimsiness of the material, the puckered border of elastic at the waist, that, once breached by my fingers, gave way to a musky mound of pubic hair. Annie always sighed resignedly as I moved my hands about her—what she wanted, of course, was *emotion*—and in those sighs were entire markets of sexual transaction. Each good was

purchased at the price of a certain number of tolerant exhalations, and once I had learned to ignore Annie's eye-rolling displays of patience, I blundered on. Such were my preoccupations as I painted Miss Whitten's kitchen and thus was my surprise absolute when she shrieked from the doorway to the dining room, "You've ruined it! You've ruined it." With that she jabbed her cane at a dime-sized spot of errant paint that had violated the airspace of the kitchen proper and landed on the faded red carpeting in the dining room. I hurried anxiously over to the offending spot. "I can fix it," I assured her, bending down close to it. "I'll just get a cloth and—"
"No! No!" she cried out above me. "It's ruined! Oh, you stupid boy." And with that, incongruously, she lifted her cane and brought it down sharply on my shoulder. "You stupid, *stupid* boy! Paint all over the rug!" She was set for another swing and I jumped backward. I was about to protest how sorry I was, but I chanced to look directly into her eyes; I saw a lantern of hatred, still lit brightly by the fires of a lifetime of bitterness. She scared me, but only for a moment, and I was cocksure enough of myself that I could not suppress a bit of my own cruelty. As Miss Whitten continued to glare at me, her cane poised, I gave her a mean smile of disgust, which, translated from the body language, went something like this: *I'm not scared of you, you fucking old hag in a wheelchair.* But Miss Whitten wasn't scared and she wasn't done. She lowered her cane and narrowed her eyes dramatically. "You are a bad, bad boy," she proclaimed. "Don't think *I* don't see *just* who you are, young man. I see you. I can see it right there in your face. You think you're so clever. But you will disappoint your father, you will disappoint everybody." And with that she wheeled backward and remained unseen for the rest of the afternoon. I finished the job hurriedly, pissed in her kitchen sink, and then took the drop cloths and the cans outside to the front porch, there to wait for my father, to whom I did not report the incident.

You will disappoint.

■ ■ ■

THE COLD NIGHT came around again, and I didn't want to see it. In the kitchen, I was too disheartened to eat—the cereal boxes just killed me, the little plastic bowls that Tommy and Sally used. I hunched out into the cold and looked again at the bloody snow. Then I heard someone at the end of the brick tunnel.

"Yeah, what the fuck do you want?" I yelled.

"Mr. Wren?"

"Yeah," I said, walking toward the gate.

It was a young policeman. "Got a message here from Deputy Commissioner Fitzgerald."

I took the envelope.

"Thanks."

I waited until he returned to his car and drove away. One sheet of paper. *Hurry*, it said.

So I did, skipping breakfast to drive out to Queens again, noting the different traffic pattern, it being early still. The Segal residence was overgrown with unpruned azalea bushes. The sidewalk was cracked; the porch looked like it would fall off anytime. A small sign in the window read

SEGAL & SEGAL, ATTORNEYS' OFFICE, but no one could possibly believe that much legal work went on inside. I rang the buzzer. There was no answer. I pushed the buzzer again, this time pressing harder. The intercom made a scratchy noise.

"—a minute."

A wizened man of about eighty answered the door. He peeked out, his thick glasses fuzzed with dust and what looked like jam from breakfast.

"Yes?"

"I'm here to see Norma Segal."

"She's shopping."

"Are you Mr. Irving Segal?"

He extended his lower denture far out from his mouth, like the drawer of a cash register shooting open. Then he sucked it back in. "Yes."

"Yes. My name is Porter Wren—" I mentioned the law firm where Caroline had her account.

"I am well acquainted with the firm," the old man croaked. "Well acquainted, young man."

I told him that I was here on Caroline Crowley's behalf. Mr. Segal gave me a limply tentative shake, as if wary of having the bones of his hand broken, and then led me to a paneled hallway where the carpeting was at least forty years old. A worn path led to a closed door; inside was a large paneled office with stacks of paper everywhere. The shutters were closed, and except for one desk lamp, the room was dark.

"What'd you say your name was again?"

"Porter Wren."

"You got some kind of identification?"

I spread out a few cards from my wallet on the table and the old man took each, one at a time, and examined them under the lamp. "Nobody is who they say anymore," he grumbled. "You just never know. Everybody's identity—nothing is private anymore. Nowadays it's all sex this and sex that. I see some of those novels you get in the drugstore, I can tell by the covers, let me tell you, but the point is sexual intercourse between a man and a woman used to be a private act. Nowadays these kids are doing all kinds of things that are unnatural, if you ask me." He shook his head, grimly agreeing with his own assessment. "Now, of course, it's the schools, too. Teach them how to do it, teach them the whole gadblamed alphabet. What we have in this country is a—you could call it, why, a disgrace would be generous, yes. I think the word *generous* would be rather—I mean the word *disgrace* would be generous, when in fact the situation with these *filthy, filthy* sex books are—I looked at a few of them once, and some of those filthy magazines, in the store right there where little girls can see them, those little, little girls—ah—and I said to the clerk at the drugstore that in my day such things were unacceptable."

He was looking straight at me and not seeing a thing.

"Patently unacceptable. I remember when that drugstore was run by the Ezzingers, a fine family. Bert Ezzinger was a good father, had three daughters as I remember. One of them was a few years younger than me, and she had—she was a real . . . well, back then we had words that were respectful when a girl was . . . not this filthy, filthy sex sex sex like these kids are always talking about on the television."

The old man stopped for a breath and I took the opportunity to get my identification back. "Mr. Segal, I'm here to inquire about the special arrangement you have with the estate of Simon Crowley—"

"What did you say the name was again?"

"Crowley."

The old man slid me a paper and pencil.

"Please just write it there."

This I did and he picked up the paper, then laboriously stood and shuffled over to an immense green filing cabinet. He pulled out a drawer and some papers fell out, which he ignored. "Hmm, no, C. First we will find the B, here . . ." Another drawer and more papers. "It will be here— she's filed it . . . I asked that she do the paperwork, how can I remember? I run a busy office, how can I spend all my time filing when I—" He turned around. "The name again?"

"Crowley. You had the paper in your hand."

"Yes, of course." He looked in his hands, but a moment earlier he had put the paper down and already it was lost in the puddle of files on the floor. My beeper trilled. I glanced at it. PORTER CALL ME. HAL. Now Mr. Segal was cleaning his glasses.

"Did you know Simon Crowley?" I asked, thinking that I had to drive the conversation.

"Why yes, he came to see us quite some time ago."

"What did he want?"

"I can't tell you. It's a privileged client relationship. Of course you understand that."

"He's dead."

"He is?"

"Yes."

The old man frowned suspiciously. "Do you have a copy of the death certificate?"

"No."

I was ready to give up. But Irving Segal was starting to remember something. "There were . . . certain instructions . . ." he mused. "I remember we had it all written down—we were to—and then the arrangement was to bill, to send a—you see, we had things nicely filed down in the basement, but then that pipe, we had an awful mess and some bats, too, terrible problems at the time, I didn't put on the brake in time and we were sued by a Korean man, so—" The old lawyer pulled out a drawer, looking for a pad. "We're going to have to clean up this office sooner rather than later," he announced. "Generally our system is very . . ." He pulled a stack of pornographic magazines from the drawer and they fell to the floor in a lurid heap. "I was looking for—" He stopped, then cocked his head. "Normie? Normie, is that you?"

There was the sound of a door closing and groceries landing on a table, and then a woman in her late sixties walked in. She was surprised to see me.

"Normie, this man is here to ask about the, uh—"

"Crowley, Simon Crowley."

"Yes," she said without hesitation. Then she turned to me. "I'm familiar with my husband's business affairs, and I'm afraid that we once did some work for a client named Crowley, but that was years ago, perhaps two or three years ago, and I don't think we've done any more since then."

"Yes, yes," Mr. Segal said. "That's it. A bit of work some years back, but nothing lately, sir, nothing at all that I can help you with now, so I'm afraid I must direct my attention to other . . . very busy, sir, nice to speak with you." And with that he began to pick through his papers and junk mail with interest, turning them over as a child might examine colored cards with animals on them. He selected a *Reader's Digest* printed during the first Reagan administration and settled into a chair.

"Let me show you out," Mrs. Segal said. When we were beyond her husband's earshot, she turned to me. "I didn't want to hurt his feelings, you see. Now then, what about Simon?"

I explained who I was and why I was there.

"You write for the newspaper?"

"Yes. But I'm not going to put this in the newspaper."

She eyed me warily. "I can't be sure of that."

"I should also tell you that yesterday I visited Mr. Crowley in the rest home—"

"You saw Frank?"

"Yes."

"How was he?"

"Well, of course, I don't know how he usually is, but he didn't seem too well to me, Mrs. Segal." I looked at her, decided to gamble. "Was he a good father to Simon?"

"No."

I waited.

"You see, we're all from the old neighborhood, Mr. Wren. We used to live six houses down. Mrs. Crowley died when Simon was very young, two years old, I think. Breast cancer. Died just like that. After that Simon started to spend some time with us. I wanted a child, you see, and it took me seven years to get pregnant. I thought something was the matter with me, but finally, when I was thirty-six if you can believe it, I did. I had a little boy, Michael—"

My beeper went off again. "Excuse me."

CALL ME ASAP—HAL (YOUR PAL).

I put the beeper away.

"Anyway, I had a son named Michael, and the two of them, Simon and Michael, used to play together. All the time. I picked them up from school. They were like brothers. Mr. Crowley—Frank—worked long hours. He was a good man, but I think—well, he was never very imaginative. That all came from the mother, and I felt it was my duty to do what she might have done if she had lived, you see. The boys played together, and sometimes Frank would give me money to pick out Simon's clothes. He didn't re-marry. I don't think he knew how. I don't know if it occurred to him. It was just elevators. All over the city. But Simon and Michael had a great time—"

She stopped and pulled off her glasses. Then she put them on and looked up at me. "Michael was killed when he was five. He drowned in a motel swimming pool. It was my fault. I ran into the room for another towel and he hit his head, and to this day, Mr. Wren, I curse myself for my stupidity. That was twenty-five years ago last July."

"I'm very sorry."

"It was . . . we were making money, thinking maybe we'd just move to Florida for the good life. Irving was making good money, we drove a Cadillac in those days. I was past forty, Irving was older, in his fifties. He was on his second marriage, see, and with Michael we used to just drive up and down Route 1, there on the eastern coast of Florida. This was back when Florida was safe, before everybody—well, that's the story all over. We had a house down in St. Petersburg and were thinking about moving. Irving incorporated his business down there. He owned some properties. This was all before Michael died. When Michael died, that was—that was the end of it, Mr. Wren, we just couldn't hold on to anything anymore. My drinking started to get very bad. I—part of the reason Michael drowned was because I wanted to go get another drink, and I spent too long mixing it, that's the god-awful truth, Mr. Wren—"

She looked at me, her eyes wet.

"Go on."

"I suppose that then I really started to drink after that, and Irving, he just couldn't remember anything. We had some properties, some good ones, but—"

"This was in St. Petersburg?"

"Yes, beautiful, the sky and air—"

"Did you own any properties in New York City?"

"Yes."

"What were they?"

"Oh, we had four, I think. We had a couple of little houses in the neighborhood, around here, rentals. We had a store. And we had a building in downtown Manhattan."

"Number 537 on East Eleventh Street?"

"Yes, terrible building. Frank—I mean Irving—never should have bought it."

She had made an odd mistake. "That was where Simon died."

"Yes."

"What's the connection?"

"Oh, Simon had keys to our buildings. He sometimes looked in on them for me."

"Why? I don't get it."

Her eyes searched my face, deciding what to tell me. I was pushing too hard.

"I'm sorry," I said. "Go back to what you were saying."

"I got ahead of myself, I think. See, after Michael died, Simon was over here a lot. I didn't have a little boy anymore. These things, you can't always come back from them, you know? By then I was too old. It was no good. But as I was saying, Michael—I mean Simon—used to come over and spend time with me, and I would read to him and show him stories and everything. I had a little easel in the kitchen, and he used to paint pictures. A very talented boy. We had one rule and that was no television over here. He was a very bright little boy, the brightest little boy this neighborhood ever produced, if you ask me. But he was short, you know, and he was starting—he had a kind of funny look about him, he took after his mother—the kids would sometimes tease, and he used to come over here and I would comfort him, I guess you'd say. We'd draw and look at books and sometimes cook together. I think Frank was—it made me mad to think of it—Frank had no idea how bright Simon was. Not one idea. Here he had a boy who was—well, I better hold my tongue. Anyway, those were good years for me. I had Simon, and I didn't mind so much that Irving's business wasn't so good. Sometimes he used to take Simon around to all the buildings, and that way he met people or looked at people at least, because he was a quiet child. Somewhere in there Irving bought me a home movie camera, because we were still going to Florida, and I showed it to Simon and he wanted to use it. He used it a lot. He was about ten, I think.

This was before these fancy new—I can't remember the name. I don't think I ever used it, but we have some—" She stood up. "I know I'm going on and on, but you see there's nobody I can talk to about these things. Nobody is interested in what an old woman remembers, but what I was going to say is that I have one of Simon's old movies that he made on our camera, somewhere upstairs—"

"Is it a lot of trouble?"

"Oh no, no, I'll just be a minute."

And she was, for evidently she knew right where to look. She returned with an old Kodak projector and a box of faded yellow eight-millimeter film boxes. "My fingers . . ." she said, and I did it for her, carefully threading the film and aiming the white box of light against her kitchen wall.

"Okay," I said.

Mrs. Segal turned off the kitchen light, and after the obligatory flickering frames there was the Segals' house, the bushes pruned. The camera panned jerkily up and back. Then there was a cut of a dog playing in a modest backyard.

"That was his dog. Can't remember the name."

Then came a shot of Mr. Crowley sitting at a workbench.

"That was in their basement."

Mr. Crowley looked up at the camera, then tipped his hat. He had the same flashing black eyes as Simon. The next shot was an interior, with Simon, age about ten, standing before the camera. He is small, smooth-cheeked, exuberant. He holds up a finger. Wait. Then he dashes out of the frame.

"Irving or I took this, I think," noted Mrs. Segal.

Simon is gone from the frame for a moment, and I thought I recognized the scene as the Segals' living room. Then Simon dashes back. He has on a New York Yankees uniform, a cap, a mitt, and a baseball bat. He struts around importantly, and then the reel ends.

"That's the only one I have of him," she said.

"Mrs. Segal, I need to ask you a question now. You've told me about your relationship with Simon when he was a boy. But what about as a man? There are a cluster of facts that I can't explain. You used to own a building in Manhattan, and Simon looked in on your buildings, and had access to the keys, I think you said. And he died in a building you used to own." I took a breath. "You are seeing his father twice a week and have been for a long time. You are receiving regular compensation for that service from Simon's trust, and you are receiving larger, irregular payments from the trust. I don't know what all this adds up to, Mrs. Segal. I can't connect everything. Can you?"

The moment of dilation. Mrs. Segal stared at me fearfully and I reminded myself that I didn't know what it was like to be a sixty-eight-year-old woman with a senile husband dottering around and no children to take care of me. Mrs. Segal fingered the porcelain salt and pepper shakers on the table, little Dutch boys that somebody probably collected now.

"Mr. Wren, I—oh, I suppose I'm just an old woman with my silly secrets. You see, I loved Frank Crowley," she cried. "I loved him—like a wife, I guess you could say. He was, he was gentle to me. We—for years—if you understand." Her eyes were wide at the magnitude of her confession. "My husband—after Michael drowned, he didn't want another child—he couldn't, or wouldn't—and Simon was here a lot, and it's hard to explain. My husband knew, of course, but he didn't mind, he didn't—" She shook her head sadly, as if she wished her husband had cared enough to be jealous. "Frank was . . . he was a lovely man, very compact, very fine. After his wife died, was the most gentle—" Mrs. Segal looked away. "Oh, all of this is silly, of course, no one cares."

"I care."

She lifted her eyes. "You do?"

"Yes," I told her softly.

"Well, I don't know what question you want me to answer first. I can tell you that Simon asked me if he could take care of us, once he started making some money, and I told him no, that it was his money, he made it. But he insisted. His law firm started sending me money, a thousand a month. Well, I felt terrible about that, and I thought I should show them something for their money, even though it was Simon's money. I was seeing Frank twice a week or so, and so I just started to write down my visits with a thank-you note. They called me and said, 'Please formalize your bill on business stationery,' and so I did. We have some old legal stationery here, and so I did that. Simon found out about it and was very pleased. He didn't like these lawyers and accountants and people. It was our little joke, you see."

"What about the big payments?"

"That was something different. Simon knew we were having money troubles. Irving hit a Korean man with his car and the man had a very bad broken hip. Couldn't walk anymore. Then he sued us. So we had some money troubles. I didn't really tell Simon how bad it was, but he offered to buy us a new house, anything. But I said no, I was happy where I was. I mean, everybody I know lives in my neighborhood—the butcher, the people at the supermarket. Finally Simon said he wanted us to do something for him, and we could bill the firm. I was to send something to a third party, and then I was to bill the firm on the old stationery—"

"For five thousand dollars?"

"Yes."

"Was it a videotape, Mrs. Segal?"

She looked at me with great brimming fear. No one spoke, and I could hear the radiators hissing softly, the sound of her husband shuffling papers in his office. The house was full of time gone, death approaching.

"Yes," Mrs. Segal said, "it was a videotape. I was to send it and bill for special services or something like that. Vague, you know. Simon seemed very pleased by this arrangement."

"Were you supposed to send out the tape at a particular time?"

She shook her head. "Whenever I wanted, Simon said."

"Keep going."

"I found Irving holding the tape one time and I took it from him so he wouldn't lose it. Then I had the tape copied down at the camera store where they know me, just in case Irving lost the first copy. I've had a terrible time, you see. We've lost all our old clients, we've had a terrible—well, you can see—"

"The tape, Mrs. Segal."

"Yes, well, I sent the tape to the address—I mean the copy of the tape. I didn't dare look at it, of course, but I sent it, and then I sent the bill to Simon's law firm. I hope I haven't caused people too much trouble with this.

I just put the tape in a brown envelope and mailed it, and then three weeks later I got a check for five thousand dollars. It was the most remarkable thing I ever saw."

"This was after Simon died?"

"Yes. We had just gone through this terrible lawsuit, see—"

"So did you send it again?"

"Well, it didn't start out that way," explained Mrs. Segal. "Not really. But then one month we were behind on something, one thing or the other, you know how it is, and so I just thought maybe I'll try it again, and so I made another copy of the tape and sent that one to the same address, and then I typed up another bill. I just billed it to Simon's estate as per instructions prior to decease, special services, something like that—I've picked up a lot of this language over the years—and again, I was so surprised, I got another check for five thousand dollars!"

"You kept doing this?"

She nodded. "We do not have very much money, Mr. Wren. And I, well, yes, to answer your question, yes, I kept doing it. I figured, Who is going to throw a poor eighty-year-old man and his wife into jail? So yes, I did it a few more times."

"I was told that it's been four or five times over the last sixteen months or so."

"Well, again, I hope I have not caused anyone any trouble," she insisted, "because certainly I thought that if the law firm decided not to pay, then they would have a good reason . . ."

"I want the tape now, Mrs. Segal."

"Mr. Wren—"

"You can give it to me now or deal with some very unpleasant people, Mrs. Segal. I daresay I'm saving you some unhappiness by taking it off your hands."

"I'm perfectly willing to comply, but you have to understand that we have very little—"

I nodded, knowing what she was going to say. In the great scheme of things, hers was a small transgression. "Keep billing the firm, Mrs. Segal. In fact, you can raise the bill to seventy-five hundred."

"I can?"

"Yes. Just give me the tape now."

She stood up and went to the kitchen counter. My beeper trilled again: NO JOKE, PORTER. I slipped it back into my pocket, trying to remember what question I had forgotten.

Mrs. Segal was opening a wooden recipe box. "I always kept it here, see, because that way I would know where it was. Irving is very forgetful. Can't remember a thing." She handed me the tape, and I looked at it intently. Simon's hand-lettered label was still on it: TAPE 63.

"I need to use your phone." I called Campbell, skipping any inquiries about his health, and told him to tell Hobbs to get on a plane north from South America.

"He's already in the city," Campbell said.

Amazing. "He flew last night?"

"He likes to sleep on planes, prefers it."

"If he wants his little tape, tell him to meet me at the Noho Star, corner of Broadway and Lafayette, two o'clock."

"Mr. Hobbs usually lunchs at the Royalton."

A ridiculous place full of trendologists who talked only with one another; the urinal was a chrome wall you pissed against. "Why inconvenience him?" I said. "Let's make it there."

And then I was out the door, tape in my pocket. I knew there was some question, or maybe two, I had forgotten to ask Mrs. Segal, but for now I was too excited about the tape to try to remember them. And, anyway, I needed to call Hal.

"Porter, we have a velocity problem," he said after I found a corner phone.

"What are you talking about?"

"My guy got a little excited about the Fellows thing—I told him we had a delay but he didn't listen—and well, he told Giuliani."

"Oh, fuck you, Hal." I hung up. Inside the five boroughs a police trace on a call takes under ten seconds. The notion that a newspaper reporter might be delaying the identification and arrest of a murderer of a cop would send Giuliani into an insane rage. Here, after all, was a man who loves Italian opera. I dialed back.

"Hello?" said Fitzgerald. "Porter?"

"Where are we?" I asked frantically. "Your guys torn apart my house yet?"

"Well, they've been through it."

I hung up. Then called back.

"Porter. We're not trying to—"

"Yes, you are."

"You need to come in."

"That won't help. I'm working on it, I'm almost there."

"Listen, now, Porter, let's think this thing—"

Ten seconds. I hung up. Dialed back.

"Jesus, Porter."

"Tell the mayor I'm working on it."

"You fucking tell him, Porter!"

"I will."

A pause. That made ten seconds.

"Porter Wren?"

A stern voice. A voice that ran a city. Giuliani.

"Mr. Mayor, with all due respect, I'm working on it, I promise." I hung up and walked briskly away from my car. The cops would find it within ten minutes. They probably already knew the phone booth location and were sending a car over. I went down the subway steps and took the train away from Manhattan. Then I grabbed a cab and hopped on the Brooklyn-Queens Expressway, ran into lower Manhattan, right along Canal Street, thinking, worrying, keeping my head low. The city is full of police cars if you don't want to see one. Before I met Hobbs, I needed to view the tape to be absolutely sure it was the right one. But where? The police would be watching my home—a car outside my gate, engine running. My office? Too many people around. Maybe a detective sitting in my chair right now. I needed a videotape player and privacy. I wondered if the location of my beeper could be traced—I clicked it off. On Seventh Avenue I hopped out and bought a red knit cap and some sunglasses. Then I called Caroline. Ten rings, no answer. Maybe she was out. Maybe fucking Charlie. Protecting her investment. Maybe I could go to the Malaysian bank and talk my way in and use the machine in her walk-in vault. But maybe not—they would have to call her for approval to let me in. And she wasn't there and might not be for hours. I could walk into an electronics shop, buy a videotape player and a small television, then rent a room in a hotel. But it could take a good hour to find a hotel that actually had a room. I needed something much quicker, a place where— I had it, and not far away, either.

WE LIVE IN STRANGE TIMES. A fifty-two-year-old black woman with a shot-up knee lies in her bed in her private hospital room, the one with all the amenities available in the land of the dollar bill, her mind a biblical dream of morphine, and when she opens her eyes, as she seems to do slowly every ten minutes or so, she thinks that she is seeing a white man sitting in a chair next to her bed, not paying attention to her but staring intently at her television, which she likes very much. The white man is familiar. He is her employer, in fact. She prefers the wife, actually. She would like to ask how are the children, how is Tommy, but somehow the formulation of the question removes the necessity to ask it, and besides, now there are funny pictures of a fat man on the television and so she watches it, or dreams it—she will never remember.

> [Jerky view of an opulent hotel room. Camera stabilizes. One corner of the frame is blurred by an unidentifiable object, perhaps the strap of a purse. On the far side of the room is a large bed, a plush chair, and a window. It is night.]
>
> Caroline: . . . would be interesting, that's all. [Into view comes the immense figure of Hobbs, wearing an expensive suit. His back is to the camera. He picks up the phone.]
>
> Hobbs: Operator, this is room 1412. I want no interruptions, no calls. With one exception. If a man named Murdoch calls, that call gets put through. Murdoch, Rupert Murdoch. M-U-R-D-O-C-H. Yes, quite right, thank you, nobody but him. [He replaces phone.] Unlikely he'll call, but there is a chance that my office gave him this number. [Hobbs turns his head at the sound of a knock. He checks his watch.] Yes?
>
> Voice: It's Springfield, sir.

Hobbs: Come in, Springfield.

[A figure appears in the room, back to camera.]

Hobbs: Yes.

Springfield: We've finalized the London schedule, sir. Mr. Campbell said that I should inform you.

Hobbs: Very good, Springfield, give me the schedule.

Springfield: Well, sir, we have Mr. Trump at eight A.M., then Mr. Ridgeway from the bank at ten; then lunch with Mr. Lok's group—

Hobbs: Do we have the figures put together for that meeting?

Springfield: I'll have to ask Mr. Campbell, sir. But I would assume so.

Hobbs: Tell Mr. Campbell that if he doesn't have the figures prepared, he can buy himself fish and chips.

Springfield: Yes, sir. Will that be all for tonight?

Hobbs [turning toward Caroline]: Miss, is there anything you want, anything Springfield can get you? Cigarettes, flowers, anything you'd like?

Caroline: No, I'm fine, thanks.

Hobbs: [lifting a hand]: Okay, Springfield.

Springfield: Good night, sir. Miss. [Springfield leaves.]

Hobbs: Let's be very clear about this.

Caroline: Okay.

Hobbs: [takes off his suit jacket awkwardly]: I want you to tell me what you want, exactly.

Caroline: Okay.

Hobbs: You were looking for some sort of payment?

Caroline: No.

Hobbs: Odd. You're not expecting some kind of job or regular money or anything?

Caroline: No. Just a little time with you. I'm curious about you.

Hobbs: You see, I must ask because a man in my position, people are bloody always asking me for money or a job or something. It was Carol, right?

Caroline: Caroline.

Hobbs: Of course. I'm terribly sorry. [She shakes her head and then pulls something out of her hair, making it fall.] Do you want the lights on or off?

Caroline: Off. There's a lot of light from the city.

Hobbs: [He moves to the wall, and the lights go out. They settle on the bed.] Now . . . [She takes his hand into hers.] Let me tell you something, my Miss Caroline. We gaze at each other across a far gulf. Of course, we know what these things are. [His voice is deep and slow and full of affection.] You are a beautiful young woman, you are an American, you have your whole life ahead of you. And we know all too well what I am . . . yes. I am a—

Caroline: Shhhh. [She begins to undress.]

Hobbs: That's quite kind. But let me just say this, my Miss Caroline, I want you to know that I know who I am. I know what I look like, to you. This is very important to me. Because it allows me to express my gratitude to you. I am a fat old man. I am a horror, an obscenity. It's been thirty years since I could touch my toes. I also am incapable of normal sexual function, my Miss Caroline.

Caroline: Are you sure?

Hobbs: Quite sure. [He kicks off his shoes.]

Caroline: Can't have sex?

Hobbs: No. But please—

Caroline: [She resumes her undressing.] Do you mind me asking why? I mean, is it—

Hobbs: Not you, not at all, of course not. [He drops his pants, unbuttons his shirt.] It's something that happened—quite a long time ago, I'm afraid.

Caroline: I want to hear about it.

Hobbs: [sighing]: It's an old man's tale.

Caroline: I can hear it. I've seen a few things.

Hobbs: Let me get a cigarette. [Disappears into bathroom, his fleshy bulk suddenly illuminated, like a moon, by a light that flicks on, then just as abruptly off.] Now then. Well. If you insist. I haven't spoken of this for many years, actually. Once upon a time, my dear Caroline, I was twenty years old and my father was the ninth richest man in Australia. My father and I did not get along then, not at all.

He wanted me in the newspaper business and I had other ideas. I was rather interested in sailing and the girls, you know. I had quite a bit of money to spend for a boy my age, and I used to go to the brothels in Melbourne, which, I shall say, were marvelous. My father had failed in his attempt to get me off to Oxford or Cambridge and had been forced to settle for the University of Sydney. Quite a disappointment, that. He was worried for my future, he was. I don't blame him. We had terrible rows. The summer before my last year of university I did the unmentionable—I signed on to work on a freighter.

Caroline: A boat.

Hobbs: [lies on bed]: Yes, a freighter is, or was, the ship that hauled everything around the world. Coal, steel, grain, whatever. Now, except for the big container ships and the oil tankers, it's all jumbo cargo jets. But back in 1956, the freighter was the thing. I loved working on the ship. There was quite a bit of painting. Scraping and painting. We worked our way up the west coast of Africa, then around Gibraltar toward France. I mailed very short letters to my mother and father from each port, knowing that they would arrive in Australia weeks later. In Marseilles, we put in to drop some automobile tires that we had picked up. Marseilles was a tough town, quite a tough town. Our captain had even warned us, but I wasn't scared. No, not at all. We had a boiler problem, so we were in port for five days, and for much of that time I was free.

Caroline: There's a woman in this story, I can feel it.

Hobbs: There most certainly is.

Caroline: Was she beautiful?

Hobbs: As beautiful as you, except that she was dark, like mahogany. She was the most expensive prostitute in Marseilles, that is, if she wanted you. I had quite a bit of money with me that I had kept hidden, and I did the most stupendously stupid thing I could have done.

Caroline: What?

Hobbs: I fell in love with her. I kept giving her money to spend time with me, and she obliged.

Caroline: She was taking advantage of you.

Hobbs: Which I knew. But I did not care. We spent half the time in the French countryside, drunk. I'd rented a car. She called herself Monique. She was half-Indian, a quarter Zulu, some Chinese, and the rest Boer. Born in Cape Town. Quite a life she had had. Her French was rudimentary. Very tough little cat—just like you, I'd bet. She had been kidnapped and taken to Marseilles by a captain after the war ended. Kidnapped by him, then fell in love with him. You can imagine how thrilling all this was to a twenty-year-old lad lying in the grass in the French countryside, half-drunk. I was quite smitten. The affair was doomed, of course. I knew I was back on the freighter in a few days. These days are as real to me as this morning's break-fast. I can look out of that window, Caroline, and I know that I am in Manhattan at the Plaza Hotel and that it is June eighteenth or whatever—I never know the date anymore—but I am simultane-ously back there, looking into the dark, dark eyes of my Monique. I do not have a photograph of her. I do not have a letter. I have noth-ing but the memory of her, the last day we saw each other, which was May the twenty-third, 1956, at eleven-fifty-seven P.M. I was due back on the ship at midnight. We were shipping out at two A.M. to catch the tide. [Caroline lights a cigarette.] Her flat was two floors up, four blocks from the docks. I had given her every last franc and pound and dollar I had, willingly and happily. We had been together for almost five straight days. I was broken to pieces at the thought of leaving her, for I knew I would never see her again. But also I was strangely happy, because I knew I had just had quite a little adven-ture of the heart, you might call it, and soon I would be back on the ship safely steaming across the ocean.

Caroline: You said good-bye to her?

Hobbs: Indeed. I said good-bye to her and kissed her and told her I loved her and would never forget her and all the other things one says when one's heart is full, and then she told me I had to go, it took three minutes to get down to the docks, and I told her I could run it in half that time, and she said, "Well, maybe two minutes," and I believe we kissed one more time. Then I looked at her, that very last look, that look that you know will have to do you until you are dead, and then I flew down the steps and into the dark streets, and it was maybe a block away that some of the regular Marseilles sailors caught me, even though I was a pretty big lad and put up my best fight, and they beat me badly, and one of them stuck me with a knife about a dozen times around the groin, and they left me there for dead.

Caroline: God.

Hobbs: They hated me for having taken Monique, you understand. They knew that I must not really be a sailor if I had paid her for five days and had rented a car and bought a lot of wine. They had been waiting for me. They knew when my ship was off. I was in a very bad way. My boat left without me. They had dragged me off the main street, behind some rubbish. An old woman found me in the morning. I was very bad. The doctor said that he thought I had lost half my blood, that I was saved only by my youth. But the sailors, they had cut up my nerves, they had cut everything down there that you could cut. Lucky I still have my balls actually, but after that it was no good. Couldn't get hard. Wanted to. I've wanted to for almost forty years. Nothing. Seen the best doctors in the world. The best. Kept hoping some kind of technique would come along . . . some drug, but nothing. The nerves are all dead in there. I can feel when I am pissing, sort of, but that's all. Otherwise, almost nothing. Hot and cold a bit. Erection impossible.

Caroline: What happened to you after that?

Hobbs: I stayed in hospital. I was in a bad way. I had no money, I didn't know much French. Finally I asked a nurse to contact the editor of the newspaper. Instead she came back with a man who used to work for the BBC. Retired. We could talk in English. I gave him my father's name and address. He contacted him. Three days later my father arrived. Then a private hospital in Paris. He stayed with me for a month there. Read me the papers. We were very much changed, he and I. He started to explain some of the problems he was having with his newspapers. He was wise enough to make it seem interesting. Every day, hour after hour. Sometimes he would read to me. Had a special phone put in the room so that he could do a bit of business while sitting right there. When I was well we flew back to Australia. He brought me right into the paper. I never would have done it if I hadn't been attacked, but I needed to have something. He was quite wise, my father. I miss him. [Hobbs is silent.] Three years later he was dead of a coronary and there I was with the whole bloody business. [In the darkened room, she is curled against Hobbs's great bulk. Minutes pass. His breathing is pressed and often; hers, unstrained, is inaudible. It seems that his hand is moving slowly back and forth on her shoulder and neck. She takes the large hand and lays it on her face, kisses it.] You are not repulsed by me?

Caroline: I think you're sweet. [She is taking one finger at a time and putting each one in her mouth, withdrawing it and then doing the next one.]

Hobbs: There is something else I would like to do, here.

Caroline: What?

Hobbs: I think it will be something . . . it's quite meaningful to me in its own way.

Caroline: I don't—

Hobbs: Let me just . . . [The immense bulk of Hobbs moves off the bed and passes by the camera.] Here, if you just, just move down here a bit—[Hobbs is at the end of the bed, kneeling, with some difficulty. She is lying with her legs open. Hobbs lowers his bulk between them.] You see, my Miss Caroline . . . [Hobbs has put his head between her legs; his words are somewhat muffled.] I have a— perhaps you've seen it, my tongue is—I have a rather—why, here, if I may, I'll just . . .

Caroline: Hey, oh.

Hobbs: [lifting his head]: Yes? I think that's probably quite— [Lowers his head, drops one meaty palm on each of her thighs.]

Caroline: Oh. That's your tongue? I can't *believe*—oh! It's . . . [Indecipherable sounds. Several minutes pass, Caroline breathing deeply.] Don't—slow down—a little bit slower . . . a little—no, now go in with it and side to side . . . I . . . [Twisting her head back and forth.] Now come out, now go—*uh*, in, now, that's *too* . . . I said don't do it but please do it again—*oh*, yes, that's— [The room is silent for a time, but for the wheezed breathing of Hobbs, and the sounds of Caroline as she twists on the bed. A siren passes on the street below. The air has a far buzz and hum. Then she rolls onto her side.] That was—I feel so relaxed.

Hobbs: [standing slowly]: I'm cheating now, you see, cheating time. [Lies on bed.] When I am here, like this, in the dark, with the feeling of you here next to me, I actually recall the past, Miss Caroline, I go back there, I'm not destroyed by time . . . I used to spend quite a few hours with the prostitutes in Cairo. I cannot possibly describe to you how pleasurable this was. I cannot possibly tell you how happy I am at this moment; this is all that a man such as I can enjoy anymore. I used to smoke quite a bit back then, sitting on the balconies of the brothels and watching the crowds. After my accident I found that I took very little pleasure in such things. I felt myself to be disfigured and so I set about to disfigure myself more—or, at least, that is how I understand it myself. It confounds me that I am alive, Miss Caroline, and yet I am now quite glad to be alive. Oh, I know what they think of me, and I understand that, but they are sort of a family now to me. I feel a certain pride that I have created jobs for these people, almost nine thousand people around the world, Miss Caroline, and there is something in that, I would hope people might agree . . . [He is suddenly quiet, perhaps melancholy.] I was flying over what used to be Yugoslavia the other night, and the sky was clear. I could see the rocket fire below, flashes . . . and here I was on my way to Frankfurt. They were mortaring Sarajevo. It's . . . terribly odd, really, I don't live anywhere, my Caroline. I move about the world, but . . . I would have to admit . . . I never had anyone, Caroline, perhaps I should have married, but I never understood the human need for it, I was a fool. It's too late now. I can't live anywhere. I don't live anywhere. I don't know anybody . . . All I do is fly and fly and fly. [She takes his arm and rubs it.] I do find solace in interludes such as this. You are young and willing to listen to me . . . your very strangeness allows me to be intimate with you. I see that you are from somewhere, you have stories, you would not be here . . . We are beauty and the beast, perhaps. [Laughs.] No, let me amend that thought: beauty and capital. How odd that these two things always seek out each other. I look upon your face and I forget myself, I forget the . . . the flying, the— [He buries his massive head in her breasts and she strokes it. Half a minute passes. Finally Caroline leans her head down over Hobbs, her hair curtaining the two of them. Perhaps she whispers to him, kisses the back of his head, whispers something more.] Have you always done this to men, turned them into wrecks?

Caroline: I love men. That's sort of my problem.

Hobbs: Men will always wreck themselves for you.

Caroline: That scares me.

Hobbs: It should. I will think of you.

Caroline: You will?

Hobbs: Yes. I will remember the beautiful young woman who was so patient with the fat old man, who let him ramble on, deluding himself that there was meaning in what he had to say.

Caroline: You're too hard on yourself.

Hobbs: I have nothing, Caroline. I wish you to understand that. I have perhaps a moment like this once every year or so, but that is all I have. Everything else is nothing to me . . . nothing. [The two figures slowly dress, saying nothing. She is slipping on her dress and he intimates that he will help button the back of it, a task that he concentrates on, his breathing labored as his thick fingers pinch each button through its hole.] Very good. [She turns.] I would like to see you again.

Caroline: I'm not sure.

Hobbs: Fair enough. If you do want to, call my office here, ask for Mr. Campbell. [Puts on his jacket.] Do you need anything? A car?

Caroline: I'm fine.

Hobbs: Let me at least get a car. [Picks up the phone.] Springfield, a car downstairs, please. Yes. All right. [Hangs up.] All set, then?

Caroline: Yes.

Hobbs: It'll just be a quick good-bye.

Caroline: Where will you be next week?

Hobbs: Next week? Perhaps Berlin. No, London first and then Berlin. [He picks up the phone again.] I'll be in the lobby in five minutes. Hmm? Yes. Fax him that. Yes. Tell the pilot we'll leave at three-thirty. Yes, five minutes or so. [Hangs up.] I'm going to give you my farewell.

Caroline: Are you flying tonight?

Hobbs: London, yes.

Caroline: Have a safe trip.

Hobbs: Thank you.

Caroline: Good-bye.

Hobbs: Call Mr. Campbell if you wish.

Caroline: I'm not sure.

Hobbs: Good-bye, then. [A door opens and shuts; his bulk can be seen going through a square of light. Caroline Crowley sits in bed, not moving. A minute or two passes. She looks out of the window and then turns back toward the camera. She walks directly toward it, quickly, her face passing out of view, reaching an arm toward it. The image goes black.]

AT THE ROYALTON, Hobbs was sitting in an immense booth. I noted a black valise at his feet. An assistant sat at another table.

"Mr. Wren—" Hobbs swept his hand toward my chair. "Please. I hope that this time we may be gentlemen with one another."

I felt differently about him now; I understood him to be vulnerable and anxious just like anyone else.

"I trust you will allow me to buy you a spectacular lunch," Hobbs said.

I wasn't interested in being charmed. "I want the name of the man who shot my son and baby-sitter," I said.

Hobbs stared at me. "No."

"Deal's off." I stood up.

"Just a minute." He beckoned his assistant, who brought with him a portable phone.

"Phone number and address, too."

Hobbs and the assistant talked in a low voice for a minute. When he was done, he slid a piece of paper over to me. Phil Biancaniello, Bay Ridge, a Brooklyn phone number.

"You understand that I have a personal problem with him still."

Hobbs opened his hands. "Of course."

We ordered, and then I drew the tape out of my coat pocket and handed it across the table.

Hobbs looked at it. "Appears quite innocuous, wouldn't you say?"

Then he signaled to the assistant, who reached into a briefcase and pulled out a piece of equipment about the size of a laptop computer. It had a tiny monitor on top, and Hobbs pushed the videotape into a slot on one side.

"Where's the battery?" I said.

Hobbs was slipping on some half-frame glasses. "Oh, it's somewhere in there, the size of a pill, no doubt." He looked at the screen, frowned angrily. "Nothing but fuzz here, sir."

Cold fear. But then: "Rewind it."

Which he did. The machine hummed companionably, clicked, and then began to play the tape. Hobbs plugged in an earphone, then hunched over the machine intently, so close that no one else could see what he was looking at. Our food came, several steaming vessels of it, and Hobbs did not look up. His expression relaxed, and I saw now a face that I had not seen before, one that seemed weary and contemplative. I ate my food. Hobbs had been right; it was quite good. Around us was the clatter and clink of silverware; it was a room in which almost everyone was rich or well known in some way, and yet the dense celebrity of the room fostered a strange privacy. I noticed Larry King, William Buckley, and Dan Quayle. Hobbs was oblivious to them. Finally he unplugged his ear set and reached into his bag. He brought out a similar-sized piece of equipment and slipped the tape out of the first machine and into the other. Then he consulted a small readout. He nodded, then looked up at me. He turned the small piece of equipment around so that I could read the display. It said: ORIGINAL, NOT A COPY.

"Well done, sir."

"I was highly motivated."

"Indeed you were, and so was I. Now I must ask you three questions."

"Shoot."

"Do you know of any copies of this tape?"

"No."

"Was Caroline Crowley sending me the tape?"

"No."

"Who was?"

I explained who Mrs. Segal was, her innocence in the whole thing.

"Did she see the tape?"

"That's the fourth question."

"Indeed, I think I have a few more. I think you might indulge them, as I will later indulge you at this lunch."

"Fair enough. No, Mrs. Segal hasn't seen the tape. Who knows if her husband has, but he seems pretty scrambled."

"He's how old?"

"He appears to be at least eighty."

"I won't worry about him, then."

"I wouldn't."

"Did you show the tape to Caroline Crowley?"

"No."

"Why not?"

"I figured the sooner I got it out of my hands, the sooner I could get my life back."

Hobbs nodded.

"Your man shot my son, Hobbs."

He picked up his fork. "I'm going to try my shrimp. Now then, last question. Did you look at this tape?"

"Yes."

We stared at each other.

"I'm quite a lovely sight, aren't I?"

I said nothing.

"You can see why I wanted it back. A matter of privacy, I guess. A certain pride, nothing more."

I nodded.

"Being the gentleman that I am, I have something for you," Hobbs said. "Two things, actually."

He reached into his bag and pulled out a videotape. Simon's writing: TAPE 15. The Fellows tape.

I took it from him.

"May I?"

I slipped the tape into his portable player. There it was: Tompkins Square Park, the protesters, the police. I hit the fast-forward button, wanting to be sure that the key segment was still there. It was. Fellows toppled like a tree, the assailant fled. I stopped the tape, rewound and ejected it, and put it in my briefcase.

We ate heartily then, Hobbs and I, and then followed dessert with coffee.

"And now the last thing, sir."

"Yes."

This time he drew an envelope from his breast pocket.

"We've had this for quite some time, but in the spirit of all's well that ends well, I thought that I should give it back." He handed me the envelope. There was something small and hard in it; I laid it on the table without opening it.

"As you might imagine, we gained access to Caroline Crowley's apartment. Looking for the tape, of course. I don't know whether or not she suspects this."

"She does."

"That doesn't surprise me. Women usually know things like that. We had a look at all her keys, searching for a safe-deposit box, another apartment, car, whatever, and we identified all of them but this one. I no longer need it and thought it should go back to her."

I opened the envelope. One tiny key, nondescript, flat and old. Three little holes instead of one. It was toothed on both edges. I knew enough from messing around in my father's barn as a boy that this was a key to a small padlock. I had been in every room in Caroline's apartment and had seen nothing that might match it. The key was intriguing enough— unidentifiable enough—that Hobbs's spooks had confiscated it. Perhaps they were amateur lock experts in their own right, if they so easily broke into apartments.

"Not a house key, I should think," Hobbs said.

We left then, he and I, some of the other patrons watching him walk slowly, and when we stepped outside, a limo was waiting. Hobbs handed his bag to the driver and turned to me.

"Every loose end tied up, I believe, no?"

"Believe so."

He stepped into the car and the driver shut the door. My curvilinear reflection became his face as the window went down.

"Incidentally, Miss Caroline kept the key above the refrigerator, in a cupboard." His thick face looked up at me, green eyes bright, lips still wet from lunch. "Quite an odd place for a tiny key, I would think."

Then he was gone.

I CALLED HAL FITZGERALD from the corner. "I have the tape."

"Porter?"

"I have it."

"Good, that's very good."

"Just tell me where I can take it."

"Well, let's see, uh—you're in Midtown?"

The cops' technology was getting good.

"Yes, I—"

"Corner of Sixth Avenue and Forty-fourth?"

"Yes."

"Hold on. We'll have a car come around."

"I can bring it to you if you want."

"No," Hal said. "We're, uh—hold on, Porter." He was covering the line. "No, if you'll just wait a minute there. It'll be an unmarked car. About four or five minutes."

I waited. The sky looked like snow. There wasn't much traffic. The light changed twice, and then far down Sixth, I saw a black sedan traveling at high speed, a flashing red light behind the windshield. The car pulled slightly past me and the door opened. I bent down and looked in—looked into the roiling dark eyes of Rudolph Giuliani, mayor of New York City, avenging archangel.

"Mr. Mayor."

Eyes burning, mouth an inverted smile, he put his hand out. I put the tape in it. He nodded, glanced at his driver.

"Go," he commanded.

And they surged forward into traffic.

But I wasn't done with Hal. I stepped onto the curb and called him back.

"Hal, one more thing I have to talk about with you."

"What?"

"I'm coming downtown. Meet me outside."

I got a cab on my first try.

"You ain't Porter Wren?" the cabbie said. "The guy who writes for the paper?"

"You got it."

"I think the column is sagging a bit," he told me. "You got to hit one pretty soon, you know what I'm saying?"

"I do."

"I mean, that thing about the guy who killed his girlfriend, diary of a crazy man, something like that, with the wedding dress and everything, that was okay, you know."

"Not my best work."

"Well, I'd have to agree there."

"Give me another shot—maybe I'll surprise you."

"Sure, no problem."

Then I was standing outside police headquarters, with Hal coming down the granite steps without his overcoat on, wind blowing his hair, looking excited. He had delivered as promised, if a little late, and now his scorecard would look very attractive indeed.

He shook my hand. "The mayor is pleased."

And so, evidently, was Hal. The mayor's pleasure was a form of currency, convertible into at least one promotion and therefore into a marginally higher salary; Hal had delivered not just a videotape but a little extra cash for his kids' tuitions, a few trips to Atlantic City with the wife, maybe a couple of monogrammed shirts for himself. Now was the time to press my claim.

"I've still got a couple of conditions, Hal."

"Now, wait"

"No, you wait, goddammit."

We stood there staring at each other, two guys in the cold.

"I'm the guy who got kicked in the balls to get this tape, the guy who had his house torn up by your cops and had his boy shot and his wife leave the city, Hal. I'm in a bad mood. I have a few conditions, Hal, and you're not going to mind any of them. One, I get to break the story—tomorrow. Two, I'm not mentioned when you get asked about how you got the tape. Not now, not ever. It was mailed in anonymously. Three, you send some detectives to get this guy and do something very bad to him." I held up the slip of paper, which had Phil Biancaniello's name on it.

"One and two are no problem, three I don't get."

"This guy shot my little boy."

Hal smoothed his tie in the wind. People walked past.

"This is my little boy, Hal."

"We can't kill the guy—it's not like that."

"Just even it out. Have him pay the bill."

We just stood there for a while, then he nodded, looking me right in the eye, which men generally do only very carefully, and I knew that it would be taken care of. Maybe not that day, or not even very soon, but eventually. You have to have faith in the police department, and I do.

I COULD HAVE LEFT IT THERE. I could have walked away from anything else. Sent the key to Caroline, taken a vacation, flown to California, driven a rental car to Lisa's mother's house, arrived as a great surprise, and started to cut my losses. But I didn't. There were too many questions piling up in my head, like the light but persistent snowfall that had started. I called Caroline and said I had some good news for her.

"Why don't you come up to the apartment?" she asked brightly. "We've just come back from a reception."

"You and Charlie?"

"Yes. At Charlie's bank."

This talk was for him.

"I can come another time."

"No," she protested, "I'd like for you to meet him."

Here was an opportunity to understand Caroline better; perhaps that was what she was offering. Perhaps not.

NAPOLEON WAS THERE, reading a different crime novel. He looked up.

"Are the good guys winning or losing?"

"Losing."

Upstairs, Caroline had opened the shiny black door for me to enter, and, not knowing what she had told Charlie about our involvement, I remembered to walk in as if I had not spent many voluptuous hours there already.

And there he was, in a suit that made him look like a senator, putting a log on the fire in the living room. He stood up, and I suddenly saw the future—forty years of big money.

"Hey, you must be Porter." He smiled easily as we shook hands. "Charlie Forster."

"I understand you were just at a reception," I said politely, making a point to remember Charlie's last name.

"Yes, we—our bank—was announcing a new—"

"I'll be out in a minute," called Caroline from the kitchen. "Porter, what do you like to drink?"

"Oh, can you make a good gin and tonic?"

I sat on the big white couch next to a silk purse. "I'll try," she called back.

"You follow the Knicks?" I asked Charlie.

He was poking the fire now. "Sure. Absolutely. I just went the other night with a couple of Japanese clients. We—the bank—has a pretty good box."

"Does Caroline like the games?"

He gave a wince of thought. "Not really. I took her to one or two, but she didn't seem interested, really."

"Not interested in what?" She walked into the living room with the same silver tray I'd seen before, but this time, instead of nothing, she was dressed: long-sleeved black velvet dress, diamond bracelet, Cartier watch. Her earrings were diamond, her shoes high-heeled pumps, her hose the color of champagne. Her hair was up in what I think is called a chignon. "What am I not interested in?"

"Just the basketball games, the players and teams, all that," said Charlie. "I was telling Porter I went the other night."

"He's right." She sat down and turned to me. "Charlie knows everything about me."

"A very good way to begin a marriage." I didn't dare look at her, so I sipped my drink.

Charlie was checking his watch.

"Now, Porter, you don't know it," Caroline said, "but this happens to be a bit of a celebration. Charlie was made vice-president today."

"Congratulations."

He gave a nod. "Thanks—it's really not such a big deal."

"You're pretty young to be a vice-president."

"Well, they throw the titles around, you know."

"We've been looking at houses," Caroline announced. "Mostly up in Connecticut."

"Some beautiful places up there," I agreed.

"I grew up in Litchfield," Charlie said. "So—well—I guess I don't want my kids to grow up in the city."

"Mmm."

She lit a regular cigarette. "Porter has two children."

"Yes?"

"Girl and a boy." I looked at Caroline. "I can't remember if you told me where you grew up."

"Oh, I grew up in a little town out west."

Charlie checked his watch again.

"Well, it's late," I said, "so I should probably—"

"Oh no, no," Charlie laughed. "That's not—I'm waiting for a call from our Beijing office. I may have to go back to the office. We're structuring the debt on a new truck factory."

"You can stay and talk a little while?" Caroline asked me.

"Maybe half an hour."

Charlie frowned, still thinking about his international phone call. "He might have tried my office."

He got up and went into the kitchen.

"Nice guy, your fiancé."

"The nicest." She smiled. "How's your drink?"

"Tastes professionally made."

I looked at her blue eyes, then her dark eyebrows, then down her nose, and then her lips. Then her eyes. "So—"

"You have some good news?" she said.

"For you, only the best."

"You keep charming me, I'll leave a wet spot on the couch."

But here came Charlie. "Well, their deputy minister of heavy industry met with our guy last night, last night in Beijing, I mean, and it's all done. I have to get the numbers to them right now, sweetie."

I actually liked him.

"You really have to go?" said Caroline.

He was already pulling his coat out of the closet. I stood and shook his hand. "I was hoping to ask you all sorts of questions about your work," he said.

"I'll come down with you." Caroline turned to me. "Don't go anywhere."

There were two meanings to this statement: Don't snoop around, and don't leave, and I planned to do both, in that order. As soon as I heard the elevator outside in the foyer, I went directly into the kitchen. I stood on a stool and opened the cupboard over the refrigerator, which for a refrigerator had a surprisingly clean top, no doubt a testimony to the quality of the cleaning service. It was a tough reach to the cupboard, and finally I just sat on top of the refrigerator and opened the cupboard door. Crockery was piled on the two shelves, and I gently extended my hand toward the back, as if I were reaching into the mouth of a lion. I felt along the left side of the cupboard under the top shelf. There I felt three tiny nails in a tight little triangle. Did the key fit them? I pulled back my hand, found the key in my pocket, then reached in again. Yes, the key fit. I could do it by feel.

I returned to the living room and stood at the window. Caroline came in, her hair veiled with melting snow.

"He seems like a nice guy."

"He is," she said sadly.

"Do you love him?"

"That's a hell of a question." She picked up her drink, knocked it back. "I love his goodness. But no, I don't love him."

"Does it matter?"

"No."

There was, I understood, something about Caroline that allowed her to invent herself out of one situation and into another. Maybe she was just getting older and worried that only a certain number of trains would pull into the station. Maybe I had no idea what the truth of the situation was—yes, that was it.

Why does a woman keep a key on three nails in the back of a cupboard above the refrigerator? There were easier places to hide such a thing.

"You have a column for tomorrow?" she said.

"I'm having some problems."

"Am I one of them?"

"You are all of them, in one way or another."

This pleased her.

"Well," I began, "it's time for the big news."

"Tell me."

"You're free to marry your vice-president without interference from the fearsome billionaire."

She studied my face. "What do you—"

"I found the tape."

"How?"

I told her the whole story, leaving out my conversation with Billy Munson and the fact that Hobbs had slid a key across our table that happened to correspond with the three nails in her kitchen cabinet.

"I can't believe it," Caroline said. "Little old Mrs. Segal was sending the tape?"

"She needed money after being sued by the Korean guy."

"You told Hobbs this—the whole thing—how it wasn't my fault?"

"Certainly."

"And he believed you."

"Pretty sure."

She pressed her hands together as if praying, and her face brightened.

"Oh, yes! Yes! That is *so* good. I was *so* worried he was going to do something to me or get Charlie fired, something like that."

"No, he was very civilized."

"Do you have to go home?"

"My wife took our kids to California."

"Why?"

I told her about Hobbs's men breaking in, what they did.

"I want you to think about something else for a little while," Caroline said.

WE FORGET, I THINK, how quickly we come to know another human being—if not his or her history or secrets, then at least the basic physical nature, the habits of his eyes, the way she walks, the pauses of speech. I was reminded of this as I lay in bed waiting for Caroline to emerge from her bathroom; we had spent no more than about twenty-five hours together, but already listening to her on the other side of the door, I could swear that I knew exactly when her diaphragm went in—heard the slight grunt she made, a cough almost, followed by a deep breath—knew a few minutes later when she had traveled far away from me and when she was close, riding my breath. That evening was the last time we were to have sex, and I don't think I am fooling myself to say that I knew it and that I paid what extra measure of attention was possible. Here in front of me in the shadowed gray of the bedroom were Caroline's neck, her breasts, her cunt, her belly, her eyes—shut, open, shut—and her hair, gray against her gray skin. We were comfortable enough that much of it took place at a great distance from each other; I don't recall what was said or if anything was said at all. We moved slowly, perhaps even with a sad reverence for the things that lay just beyond our perception. We were almost done, and I think she knew it, too.

"Look," she said, a few minutes later. She flicked on a light on the side table and lay on her stomach next to it, showing me her shoulder. "All gone."

Indeed, all that remained of her tattoo was a slight blue blurring beneath the skin.

"That last little cloud of color will disappear in a week or two."

I rubbed my finger over the spot. "Incredible."

She was pleased. "Yes."

"All marks gone."

"Just about."

"Just about?"

"I have one that won't go away."

I was at a loss. I'd been all over her body. "Between your toes?"

"No."

She sat up Indian style on the bed and put her hands between her legs, brushing her pubic hair back. "I used to have a little clit ring."

"You never told me."

"You never asked."

I moved the light closer.

"See?" she said, touching her finger to the musky folds of her labia, just above her clitoris. "There's a little, *little* scar."

As indeed there was, more like a bump. I touched it. "You had the ring removed when you met Charlie."

"Yes."

I put the light back on the table. "You miss it?"

"A lot." She got up and pulled on her panties. "Charlie wants to take a trip soon," she said. "China and Japan."

"A business trip?"

"Yes. But he wants me to see all the sights."

"You should go."

"I am."

She got a cigarette from the kitchen and held it in front of her. "I must be crazy."

"Why?"

"I told Charlie I'd quit."

"Will you?"

"I hope not." She blew a long plume of smoke. "What did you see when you saw the tape with Hobbs?"

"Literally?"

"No, I mean what did you understand—about me, I mean."

I thought of the way she had curled into the man's corpulent bulk, her obvious pleasure as he spoke to her. "I think I understood why you enjoyed being with him. He understood something about you that you hadn't found in other men, or much of it, and you surrendered yourself to him. It was partly about him being a lot older."

She pulled on a T-shirt over her breasts. "It's sort of why I like you, too."

"Why not marry an older guy?"

"They're too smart. They figure out who I am."

"Did Hobbs?"

"In about three seconds."

"But you saw him again."

"Yes."

"It must have driven Simon crazy."

She let out a breath. "Oh yeah." She recalled again that Hobbs had sent her a little gift, and Simon had inquired as to where it had come from.

"What did you tell him?"

"I said it was just a gift from a friend. But Simon had seen that video-tape, and I guess he saw whatever you saw. That's why it makes sense that he set this thing up with Mrs. Segal. I mean, I sort of suspected it might be something like that, but I had no idea of the mechanism, you know? I didn't understand how it could be happening." She found a pair of jeans in her closet. "Anyway, the thing about Charlie is that he's never going to hurt me. He's always going to be nice to me."

She uttered these words without appreciable affection for Charlie, and the matter seemed to present some unspoken difficulty for her, as if it was the better of two questionable choices that she would be required to gut out. In my experience, men and women who have a kind of brutal fortitude have been made that way by a sequence of events, until the person passes beyond a point of no return. They learn that life requires the ability to coldly stand pain of one kind or another. I am not this kind of person, nor is my wife, and would that I could be sure that my children do not become such people. But the world is full of them. You can see it in some of the lit-tle black boys on the street, not even yet eight; you can see it in the Chinese women selling pig heads downtown; you can certainly see it in the faces of many policemen. They will do what is necessary to survive; they will con-ceal and protect their vulnerabilities, except from those who cannot hurt them. Above all, they will press their advantage when it presents itself.

The phone rang. Caroline picked it up. "Hi, sweetie." She listened for a moment. "Yes. Yes. Wow. Sure. I can be—I have it in my drawer. Sure. Good. Yes. Bye." She hung up and looked at me. "I'm going to China tomorrow."

We managed a good-bye then, and if it was going to be the last time we ever saw each other, you never would have known it, so casual was Caroline. I could see that her thoughts had already moved on to the trip—to Charlie, the clothes, her passport, the rest of the world.

BUT NOW I KNEW SOMETHING. I knew that the key had indeed been in Caroline's apartment, just as Hobbs had said. And I remembered that the police had talked to the Korean owner of 537 East Eleventh but not to the Segals. I also knew that Simon Crowley had stopped off at Mrs. Segal's home the day he disappeared. I called Mrs. Segal from a pay phone outside Caroline's building.

"I have to ask you a couple more questions," I said.

"Let me turn the television down."

When she came back, I asked her if she remembered the day that Simon last visited her.

"Yes, of course."

"Did he get anything that day from you?"

"I can't remember—"

"A key, did he get a key?"

"He might have, yes."

"A key to the building at 537 East Eleventh Street?"

"We had many keys."

I tried to remember the sale date of the building. "Mrs. Segal, you had, I think, already closed the sale of that building to the new buyer, the Korean man. You would have had to give him the keys to the building. In fact, I happen to know that he was given the keys to the building."

"Yes."

"So why did you still have copies?"

"Oh, I don't remember, I—he—they were going to tear the building down, that was it."

There was something I didn't understand. Simon had a key to 537, but the new owners had new locks put on. Perhaps the locks hadn't been changed yet when he entered, but afterward, in the few days after he died but before his body was found.

"You told me you knew that was where they found Simon, Mrs. Segal. You knew that."

"I—yes—"

"Why didn't you tell the police that you knew Simon had gotten a key to that building?"

"Mr. Wren—I—this was a time of difficulty, we had terrible problems with money—"

She stopped talking and I could hear her breathing anxiously into the phone. Now I understood. "Was it because you and the new owner of the building had cut some kind of deal, Mrs. Segal? You had sold it to him at a very low price and taken a cash kickback?"

"These things are complicated. We—yes, terms were negotiated . . ."

I hung up. She had been scared, nothing more. The police had been unable to explain how Simon Crowley's body had appeared on the demolition lot if they assumed that he had not been in the building prior to his death. But the presence of Mrs. Segal's key blew that assumption apart. Supposing Simon had walked into the building using a key? But had the Hobbs's key been found on Simon's person by the police and then returned to Caroline? No. That would have been important. I would have read about it in the detectives' report. The police would have quickly figured out that the key fit a lock and had an explanation for the presence of the body. No, if the key left the building, it did so some other way, and it ended up in the possession of Caroline, then Hobbs's men, then Hobbs. Now me.

But then I realized that the key would *not* have gotten Simon in—not through the front door of 537 at least, for as the detectives' report had said, Jack-E Demolition had built a sidewalk shed in front and in back of the building prior to demolition. To reach the front door of 537, Simon would have needed a key to the lock chaining the shed door closed, and that Mrs. Segal did *not* have.

It was confusing. I was holding a key that may have gone to a building that no longer existed and that should not have been usable when the building last stood. The thing was driving me mad. There was something I wasn't seeing.

MY CAR WAS STILL ABANDONED in Queens, so I sat in a cab now, on my way toward Alphabet City. Off the avenue, the snowy streets were almost deserted. On Eleventh Street, I rang the bell to 535, and after a minute Mrs. Garcia answered. She let me in, through a hallway, and down the short staircase again, past the children's bicycles, through the door marked OFFICE, and there was Luis, her son-in-law, sitting at his small desk.

"Yeah?" He looked up, as from a trance.

"You know this key?" said Estrella Garcia in Spanish. She handed Luis the key, and he looked at me and then at the key, and then he tipped his thick glasses forward.

"It goes to the sidewalk doors."

"The sidewalk?"

"The sidewalk doors that open up outside the building. Where did you get it?"

I said it had belonged to Mrs. Segal. He nodded wearily. Everyone was stupid, except for him. "Why would the Segals have a key to your building?"

"Come on. I could explain it, but you can take a look."

He stood up and got his coat and a pair of gloves and a hat and scarf, and we went out the door and past the bicycles and back upstairs, then out to the front of the building. He pointed at the metal sidewalk delivery doors. They had been covered with heavily drifted snow the last time I'd been there. "The guy who built these two buildings made, like, a bunch of mistakes. He built them too fast, probably. They were supposed to be just like each other. Maybe he was running out of money, I don't know. He only built one coal chute. Look." The doors fronted the far right-hand side of 535. "This is the coal chute. Coal man only had to deliver once to both buildings. It's in front of 535, but it was for 537, too. I don't know why. This is a copy of the key that opens it up." He bent down and slipped the key into the padlock securing the two metal doors. It popped open. He handed the lock and key to me, then pulled up on one of the doors. It creaked but opened readily. He shined his light down the steps.

"So then at some time they sold off the other building and built these doors." And indeed, the stairs went down and there were two doors, one leading left to 535 and the other leading right to 537. I stood staring.

"What happens if we open 537's door?"

"Then you're the strongest man in the whole world."

"It's locked?"

"The lock on that door's been broken maybe, like, twenty years."

"I don't get it."

"That door opens *inward*."

I understood. "And the basement is full of rubble from the demolished building."

"Yeah."

"So you must have given this key to the owner of 537."

"The guy before me did, long time back, yeah."

I examined the metal sidewalk doors. The inside edge of each had a welded mount with a hole through it; a padlock could slip through each, locking the doors from the inside.

"You're telling me that when 537 was standing, this key, which the owner of 537 had, unlocked this padlock on the outside of the sidewalk doors, and that once inside them, then 537 was completely open? You could walk right in?"

"Yeah."

"The police ask about this?"

"No."

"Because it looks like the sidewalk doors serviced your building, not both buildings."

Luis shrugged. "Probably."

"Why didn't you tell that to the police when they were trying to figure out how the guy got killed in the building?"

Here he was indignant. "Because I didn't see nobody unlocking this door, you know? I didn't know this guy Simon. The lock was always here. Nobody cut it off or anything. It was right there for anybody to see. I don't tell the cops how to do their job."

It was cold and we were done. "You mind if I use your phone, make a local call?"

We tramped back down to the basement, into the dark, oil-fumed heat. The only question was how the key got from Simon's hand into the cabinet over Caroline's refrigerator. I dialed her phone. She was probably packing for China. The phone was ringing when I heard a noise. The elevator was coming down to the basement, dropping into its bay. I studied it, feeling odd. It was a relatively narrow elevator with an ornate, arched ceiling like a birdcage and a door that accordioned back.

It was the elevator that Mr. Crowley had created out of cereal boxes.

Exactly. I saw this and remembered that McGuire at Jack-E Demolition had said the elevator company had "dropped the box" before he started tearing down 537. That elevator was sitting in its bay in the floor of the basement of what used to be 537. Simon Crowley had seen his father on the day he had disappeared. Simon Crowley's father had been an elevator repairman. Simon Crowley's father had, since his son's death, been constructing a scale model of the elevator in the building in which Simon Crowley had probably died. Elevator, elevator, elevator. Now it was sitting under tons of broken concrete about twelve feet or fifteen feet below the surface of Mrs. Garcia's winter-blasted garden.

I turned to Luis. "Was 537 an exact copy of 535? Or a mirrored copy?" I said.

"I don't get it."

"Did the two buildings have the exact same floor plan?"

"Same, to the inch," he said. "Same everything."

"Hello?" came Caroline's voice now into the phone. "Hello."

I was thinking now. I hung up. Softly.

CAPITAL, LABOR, AND TECHNOLOGY. Capital was easy. I stopped at a cash machine, took out a couple of thousand dollars, which you can do now. From there I took a cab down to Chinatown. My driver was a short, balding man, and the name on the license was Abdul Jabbar.

"Abdul Jabbar?"

The man nodded wearily. "I know, I know."

On Canal Street, all the shops were locked up. But I talked my way into a wholesale hardware store where a light was still on. A Chinese boy came to help me, and I handed him a list made out on my bank slip. The boy stepped back.

"I must ask my father," he said. "You please wait."

The father, a bowlegged man in his fifties, returned frowning at the list. "This is very long list."

"I'm paying cash."

The man nodded and called over several of his assistants and they began to fill my order. Then I asked him where I could rent a small truck or van until the next morning. The men conferred in Chinese.

"You do not mind very dirty van?" the older man asked. "Very bad dent, very bad graffiti."

"As long as it works fine."

"It will cost two hundred dollar."

"Fine. I need it right now," I answered.

Then my order was carried to the front of the store: four pairs of cold-weather work gloves, four heavy worker's sweatshirts, four wool hats, four pairs of size-twelve work shoes, four pairs of wool work socks, a five-foot steel crowbar, three hundred feet of heavy-duty extension cord with a multiple outlet box at the end, four high-powered work lamps with tripods, a one-hundred-foot measuring tape, an acetylene torch with one tank of gas, a regular crowbar, an assortment of screwdrivers, heavy-duty double-jointed wire cutters, two sledgehammers, three large flashlights, and one folding aluminum ladder, eighteen feet long.

"I need some guys to do some heavy work for me."

The men looked at one another. They were too old. The lot was full of big chunks of cement and pieces of steel.

"Never mind."

TWENTY MINUTES LATER I was headed uptown. The van pulled to one side badly and the brakes were spongy, but it would do. The snow had stopped. I drove up Tenth Avenue, past the all-night garages and flat-tire places that the taxis use, then turned east around to the back of the Port Authority bus terminal. A homeless man watched me, munching his mouth.

"Hey."

"Hey what?"

"I need three men who can work hard for about four or five hours."

"Three men what?" He stood up and walked over. He had sore feet.

"I need a couple of men who can work. I'm paying."

"When, tomorrow?"

"No. Tonight. Now."

"You're crazy."

"Each man will receive two hundred dollars cash."

"Hey, you killing people or something?"

"No. Moving broken cement and bricks. It's heavy work."

He looked at me. "Everybody's asleep in there."

"I'll get coffee, food, whatever."

He shook his head. "Shit."

"I'm talking about some money."

"Show me."

And I did.

"You need two guys?"

"Yeah." I was parked illegally, but it didn't matter.

He hobbled into the doorway and I looked at my watch. Seven minutes and one passing ambulance later, he came out with two men, both young, wisecracking. One was thick and the other was wiry. They came over to the van.

"You guys want some work?"

"What is it?"

"Moving bricks. Concrete."

"It's pretty fucking cold out here."

"I'll buy some coffee, food."

"Shit."

"I need guys who are strong."

"We're strong."

"Show me twenty push-ups."

The two young guys each knocked off a cheap twenty. The older man with the sore feet did three, then collapsed.

"When we getting paid? That the main question of my agenda."

"As soon as I get what I'm looking for."

"What?"

"That's my business."

"If we looking for it, too, then it's part of our business."

I said nothing.

"What happen if you don't find it?"

"You'll get paid anyway."

"Why can't you do this in the regular day? Police grab your ass?"

"They don't want it."

"They want everybody's, way I look at the situation."

"Then you still got—" I didn't like the smile on the man's face, the sudden eagerness. "Wait, how many times you been in Rikers?"

"Me? Never."

The other man started to laugh. "Yo, they fucking got the permanent reservation!"

"Least I didn't jump a cop."

"You jumped a cop?" I said.

"I was messed up."

The other man cackled. "You was *transmogrified*, man."

They moved off, insulting each other.

The old man looked at me.

"They no good. But I can go. Name's Richard."

"You got pretty sore feet, I think, Richard."

"I can do it."

I doubted that. "All right."

He climbed into the cab and I nosed the van into traffic. In the rearview I could see the men fighting. I had capital and technology but not enough labor. Where does one find grunt labor on a night late in January? It was past eleven-thirty.

"You know anybody else?" I asked the man.

"Man, I know all kinds of people, but you gotta understand not too many men in that place ready to go out and lift rocks. People be weak from drugs and shit."

I had an idea, checked the time, then headed toward Broadway and Eighty-sixth. Ralph, the philosophy professor, stationed Ernesto at midnight to get messages. I had a few minutes and pulled up the van. Richard played with the radio, could only get AM stations. At three minutes past midnight Ernesto appeared. Richard leaned forward, wiped the windshield. "That there is one *big* fellow."

I called across the street to Ernesto and he skulked warily over to my window. I reintroduced myself, then handed him a message to take to Ralph:

> *I need to employ Ernesto for a period of about six hours. Can you spare him? I'll feed him and get him hat, coat, gloves, etc. Labor involves moving pieces of concrete. Not illegal. Five hundred dollars, half up front.*

"I hope he says yes," Richard said.

Fifteen minutes later, Ernesto reappeared holding a piece of notebook paper:

> 1. *Ernesto is not a slave whose labor can be bought or sold.*
> 2. *However, for $1,000 I will forgo the entire moral instruction of my life and tell him to work for you for not more than six hours.*
> 3. *If these terms are agreeable, send $500 down now.*

Ernesto nodded in comprehension when I gave him the money and then disappeared in the same direction a second time. This time he returned within ten minutes and climbed into the van. I could smell him now, and the odor was both original and familiar. I rolled down my window and headed south.

I FOUND LUIS AGAIN and talked him into letting me run the power off a dedicated line in the basement of his building. Then I drove the van across the rubble of the lot, probably ruining the tires, and closed the gate behind me. We began to dig; it was slow going, but Richard and Ernesto warmed to the work. Using the tape measure and making trips into 535, I was able to estimate the location of the elevator shaft. Great slabs of brick wall were left from the demolition, and needed to be broken apart with a sledge-hammer before being moved aside. After nearly an hour, we had a pile of rubble but not much of a hole.

We kept going. Richard got tired. Ernesto did not. He and I lifted some large chunks of concrete. He lifted some by himself—pieces very few men could have moved. Another hour. He worked in tight spaces, with Richard giving him directions. The long crowbar came in handy. I think Ernesto's hands were bleeding but he said nothing. He was not working for me; he was working for Ralph, his labor an act of loyalty. Down five feet, six feet, more. We passed strata of brick, plaster, wood lathing, brick again. I was breathing in cement dust. Past pipes and trash and shards of porcelain fixtures and bathroom tile that poured like coins into the hole. Now we had the ladder in and were throwing the little pieces out of the hole and dragging the big ones up the ladder. Ernesto's chest rose and fell as he evaluated which piece of rubble to lift next. I climbed out for a rest; he kept working. At twelve feet there was nothing, and I began to worry that I'd missed it.

I had. Sideways. By three feet. Then I saw the elevator cable, a loop of it, lying in the rubble like a dead snake. We dug sideways, then down another foot. A piece of rubble shifted, fell on Ernesto's boot. He said nothing, and I helped him move it. I pulled off my gloves and looked at my hands. They didn't look good. I put the gloves back on. Then we found the roof of the elevator. It had been heavily damaged by the rubble that had fallen on top of it, but instead of being split open, it had merely crumpled like the top of a can attacked with a hammer.

"I see it but I don't believe it," croaked Richard.

I had used an acetylene torch once when I was a teenager. I hooked up the hose to the tank, and twisted the knob to start the gas. I lit a match and touched the edge of the nozzle. A flame leapt forth, almost two feet.

"Holy cannoli." Ernesto smiled.

It took me a while and I made a lot of sparks and nearly burned off my toes, but eventually I etched a ragged square, off-center, in the top of the elevator between two thicker beams of steel. The squarish piece fell suddenly into the black hole. I motioned toward Ernesto to bring the rope over and we dropped it down. I lay on the top and shined the flashlight inside.

. *Empty.* The floor of the elevator was a black-and-white tile mosaic patched with linoleum and blown over by the roseate dust of pulverized brick. The bars of the elevator's cage were gracefully curved in the style of the 1930s, exactly like 535's, and in different circumstances I might have admired their artistry. But now I lowered myself into the cage past the jagged edge of the hole, so close that I could smell the burned steel, and dropped heavily the last few feet. I shined the light around—outside the four sides of the elevator, piled like lost history, was more brick and lathing and plaster. Then I noticed something in the corner, a fragment of green stone, and picked it up. It was a piece of carved jade, about an inch and a half long. The head of a horse with the ears broken off. I remembered, of course, that the detectives' report had mentioned that Simon had a broken piece of jade in his breast pocket. Perhaps the two pieces were from the same statue or figurine. I slipped the fragment into my own pocket and looked around. I felt like a fool. There was nothing else in the elevator.

Nothing except the panel. So why not open it, now that you're here? A screwdriver was useless; the screws set into the brass cover plate were specially made so that idiots with common screwdrivers could not open the panel. You needed a custom tool. So I went at the panel with the sledgehammer, buckling it enough so that I could slip the crowbar in and tear out the cover plate with three quick jerks. Although I don't know the first thing about a tangle of spliced electrical wiring, especially that of a seventy-year-old elevator, I am perfectly able to recognize the jury-rigging of a miniature video camera with an optic cable aimed to shoot through the missing button for the tenth floor and wired into the elevator's power. My hands were so cold that I didn't trust myself to disengage the tape cartridge from the magnetic recording head and the gearing that advanced the tape. I put my hands in my pants to warm them and noticed that the mechanism engaged the tape with a spring-loaded arm, and once I knew this, it was easy to jam the screwdriver in and depress the arm. The tape fell right out, into my gloved hand. I turned it over; the label had Simon Crowley's neat block letters: TAPE 78 (REUSED).

"Ernesto and Richard!" I hollered through the black hole above me into the night.

"Yeah!"

"Start throwing everything into the truck."

THE NEWSPAPER NEVER CLOSES. Never. (It may *die*, if the owner goes bankrupt and there is no new buyer, but it never closes.) There might be some news. Armies moving in the night, earthquakes in Turkey, celebrity murders, anything. If the Brooklyn Bridge began to collapse at four in the morning, the paper would have a photographer there in ten minutes. After I dropped off Ernesto and the old man uptown, I parked my dented van in the paper's garage, right in the spot reserved for the vice-president of finance—a fat little fellow who, it was known, decorated his house on Long Island with eight thousand Christmas lights. The garage attendant woke with a wide-eyed jerk, then sat warily in the booth wondering if it was killers. I waved.

He edged out of the booth. "Kinda late tonight, Mr. Wren."

"It's always kind of late."

"I'm with you on that one."

Upstairs in the newsroom, Bobby Dealy sat at the city desk in a haze of cigarette smoke, hunched over a model airplane with a doughnut in his mouth, gluing a tiny wheel onto the landing gear. Maybe some of the glue was going on the doughnut, too. A phone was cradled against his head, yet he seemed more interested in the crackling, overlapping voices on his police scanner. In front of him, AP summaries from around the world scrolled up one screen, and a soundless CNN report played on another. Next to the half-completed model airplane lay the doughnut box and a pile of tomorrow morning's newspapers. He put down the phone when he saw me.

"You have mud on you."

"I know."

"Want to talk about it?"

"Can't now."

"I got a good one. The cops have a guy who—"

"Can't."

"On a story?"

I shrugged.

"Need anything?"

"Yeah, I need one of your doughnuts."

I closed the door to my office, pushed the mail off my chair, pushed the tape into my machine, and rewound it.

Then I hit play.

[Four men in business suits standing outside a huge warehouse under a cloudy sky. The season is summer. Three men are older and one is younger. He is animated; the others are mute, cautious.]

Younger man: The building is still large enough for expansion. Fifty-eight thousand feet, well over one square acre. Let's go inside. [He opens a door and the men step in one by one. When the camera adjusts to the change in light, a huge, brightly lit interior space becomes apparent, housing a series of immense water tanks. Pipes of all widths lead into and out of them. In the middle distance are two men in orange aprons, moving long poles in one of the tanks.] Please put your feet in that blue pan.

Voice: Why?

Young man: Disinfectant. Keeps the bacteria down. Two lines, guys. As I said before, the line of world fish consumption keeps going up and the line for available supply in the oceans keeps going down. Here's the first tank. [Shot of a tank with thousands of darting black shapes.] The fingerlings come in at two months. It's a hybrid of saltwater bass and freshwater white bass. We control their growth, incidentally. [Points at a digital temperature readout.] If we want to speed them up, we just bump the water temp up about nine degrees. We give them a current to swim against. The bigger they get, the stronger the current. We keep them moving through these tanks. That's the quarantine tank, where we vaccinate them, then the nursery tank, then the grow-out tank, where they start to get some real size to them, then, way down there, the harvest tanks, where we sort them, and then we either sell them alive to restaurants or stun and process them here. We've got one point three million fish in here. That's not as large as the outdoor fish farms. But this is state of the art. Our mortality rate is twelve point seven percent, and that's a lot lower than the outdoor farms, and we reuse the water. [Pause while he watches their reaction.] A closed system. Most farms use maybe a thousand gallons of water per pound of fish. You're going to run out of water using that much. We're down to a hundred and twenty-eight gallons per pound here. And we get the feces back into the natural cycle. We sell it to local farmers at transportation cost. That plus the dead fish. Did I say we count the dead fish? We count the dead fish. We know how many fish are dead, so that way we don't—

I stopped the tape. I didn't get it. It was impossible that the camera in the elevator had taken this, assuming the camera had worked. Maybe I had gotten it all wrong. I started up the tape again.

—waste feed. A lot of farms just dump the stuff in. They use transient labor, teenagers, whatever. We use people skilled in the natural sciences. Lot of farms are going two, three pounds of feed per fish-pound. We're way below that, down to one point five. That's unheard of, way out on the curve. Here—[The men follow him past a sequence of tanks. The workers look up, then back to their tasks. The men stop at a huge tank.] Roy, get me one of the mature—fourteen inches, if you got any. [A worker climbs a ladder, pulls a small net out of a ring, looks in the tank like a bird, and in a second has a fish flopping in the net. He picks it out with a rubber-gloved hand, puts away the net, climbs down the ladder.]

Worker [hands fish]: Here.

Young man: Thanks, Roy. [Holds up fish. In the bright light it is lovely. It tries to swim in the air.] Aquaculture is five thousand years old, gentlemen. It's not a new idea. [Flips fish gracefully up toward the tank and camera follows it high in the air. It arcs over the lip of the tank. A splash is audible.] But we are at a historic oppor—[Static. A new scene. Dark. The interior of the 537 elevator, from eye level. The left side of Caroline Crowley's face appears.]

Caroline: —don't like it, Simon.

Simon [out of frame]: It's atmosphere. [Arm appears, slides door shut. The shaft wall is visible through the cage as the elevator rises, each floor number sinking past.]

Simon: This building is due to be demolished soon.

Caroline: That's why there are no lights?

Simon: Yessiree, Bob.

Caroline: How does the elevator work?

Simon: Old Simon has mucho trickeros up his sleevo.

Caroline: Old Simon's dad was an elevator repairman.

Simon: That, too. Matter of fact, I consulted him earlier today on certain technical questions, like how to get another man's tongue out of your wife's cunt.

Caroline: This again?

Simon: Here we go. [Elevator stops at seventh floor. His arm pushes the door open. Simon and Caroline exit the elevator into what appears to have once been a small lobby area. She is as tall as he. She is dressed in a loose yellow dress. He is wearing a baseball cap, red T-shirt, and jeans.] People lived here once. [Directly in front of the elevator door is a bed, freshly made. The space is lit only by a strange apparatus next to the bed: a light connected to a car battery. A cardboard milk carton is on the floor. Behind the bed is gloom, the suggestion of paint flaking off rotten plaster.]

Caroline: Very lovely.

Simon: It's our kind of place.

Caroline: Why are you so hateful toward me? Why?

Simon: You resist me.

Caroline: I'm just tired, Simon. These little experiments don't interest me anymore.

Simon: You know all that you need to know?

Caroline: I know you're full of shit, Simon.

Simon: I'm full of truth.

Caroline [sitting on bed heavily]: Shit, truth, whatever. [Looks up.] What are you doing? [Simon has carried a small table over to the bed. There are several objects on it, but the camera angle is such that they cannot be identified.] What is this stuff? My horse? You took it from the apartment? [Picks up small figurine.]

Simon: These are items of marital interest.

Caroline [puts figurine down]: I'm getting out of here. [She rushes into the elevator. Face is toward camera, eyes anxious. She looks back at Simon, who has not moved. The control panel is below camera.]

Simon: That won't work. There's a code. You have to push in a code, and then hit the down button. Otherwise nothing. [She rushes out of the elevator, past the bed, and out of the frame. Banging.] That's not going to work. They're all locked. [She rushes past him. Banging.] Caroline, I said all the fucking doors are locked!

Caroline: What? What do you want?

Simon: Come here.

Caroline: Fuck you.

Simon: Come here.

Caroline: No.

Simon: I'm your husband. You married me.

Caroline: You—

MY OFFICE PHONE RANG. It jolted me. I froze the tape; the image showed Caroline shaking her fist in anger, her face a bright smear.

"Hello?" Silence. "Hello?"

"Hi."

"Caroline?"

"I've been missing you."

"You just saw me."

"I didn't feel good about how we said good-bye."

"Maybe we'll never say good-bye."

"Why aren't you home?"

"I'm on a story."

"Is it a good story?" she asked.

"Very complicated."

"Is there a man and a woman in it?"

"Don't most stories have a man and a woman?"

"Yes."

"Usually one of them is bad."

"I don't believe in stories like that," said Caroline.

"No?"

"I think everyone is bad. Some are a little and some are very."

"That's probably accurate."

She sighed. "So, in your story, which is the *very* bad one, the man or the woman?"

"It's unclear."

"Still?"

"Still."

"Porter, I'm lonely. I know that's silly, but I'm lonely." She was quiet. I could hear music in the background of her apartment. "Will you come back?"

"I'm afraid I can't."

"Could we have breakfast?"

I looked at my watch. The sun would be up in about three hours. "I'd like that," I said.

"An early breakfast?"

"Eight early enough?" I asked.

"Yes."

I told her to meet me at the Noho Star, at the corner of Bleecker and Lafayette. "I keep trying to eat there," I said.

"Eight?"

"Yes."

"You won't forget?"

"No," I said. "You're forgetting that you're unforgettable."

I RESTARTED THE TAPE. Caroline's furious face melted into movement.

[Continuing.]
    Caroline: —asked me, Simon.
    Simon: I asked you because I wanted to know what it was like to be married.

Caroline: This is not marriage. This is some weird arrangement where you go off to L.A. and fuck girls at parties and I sit at home with my thumb up my ass. Your parents were *married*.

Simon [picks up figurine]: Tell me about this little horse, Caroline. Tell me why Hobbs gave you this. This thing is like a thousand years old. This little fucker was pretty expensive. Even for a guy like that.

Caroline: It was a present.

Simon: Commemorating what?

Caroline: I told him a stupid little story about when I was a girl, about how I wanted a horse, and he sent me a present. That's *all*, Simon.

Simon: Tell me the story.

Caroline: No.

Simon: Tell me, I want to hear it.

Caroline: No. It's just—

Simon: It means something. You wouldn't have told it if it didn't.

Caroline: Tell me what the elevator code is, Simon.

Simon: The story.

Caroline: No.

Simon: The story, and then you can go.

Caroline: I will never tell you the story, Simon, never. [He throws the horse at Caroline. It flies past her into the elevator. A breaking sound.] What is your fucking problem?

Simon: Fucking is my fucking problem! Don't you realize that there is one thing that I require? I require sexual fidelity. Is that too much to ask? I am a busy, busy guy, and I have quite a lot of pressure on me, right? I need to have you *there*, waiting for *me*. Is that too much to ask? I'm the one who found you sitting on a bar stool! You were sliding fast, baby, and I found you and picked you up. You'd think that I could then hope for some *fidelity*, since you are, in fact, my wife! But when I called two nights ago, where were you? I know all too well where you were—you were with that fat fuck! How can that be? How can my wife prefer a fucking four-hundred-pound pig when she has me?

Caroline: It's not like that. We just talked, we were only— [Simon holds up his hand, as if to strike. She winces. He does nothing. She relaxes. He hits her with an open hand.]

Simon: The fuck you think I am, an idiot? Dead in the skull, lady? We're talking about Hobbs! This man is buying up Hollywood and New York and China. He doesn't eat food, he eats *people!* He eats you! And you love it, you can't get enough, right? I saw the man's mouth. The man has a tongue like some kind of farm animal! I know what you two do. I know that he talks to you and makes you feel safe, like you have a real *daddy*—

Caroline [with bitter scorn]: That hurts, Simon—you really, really hurt me with that one.

Simon: Here, take this knife. [Tries to hand Caroline a knife from his pocket. She won't take it. He grabs her fingers, thrusts the knife into them, closes the fingers.] Here, stab me. Go ahead. I'm asking you to do it. Do it! Do it, you fucking cunt! You don't have it in you, you can't do anything! Come on, do it! What? What do I see? I see your mind working, Caroline, I see your mind working! Within those blonde tresses, the little wheels turn! What are you thinking? You're thinking I have to get the elevator code out of him! That's right! You need that to get out of here. No problemo! The code is your birthday. February twenty-first. Two-two-one. Kill me, Caroline, and you will think of me on your birthday the rest of your life! Now *that* is a wrinkle, wouldn't you say? I specialize in wrinkles, sweetie. Now then, where were we? Oh, you were killing me. I'll give you a hint—get on with it. Do it sooner rather than later, because maybe I'll decide to switch things around. Oh, do it, huh, huh, huh. Wait, wait! We have forgotten the key! *You* have forgotten the key! [He holds up a small key.] We needed a key to get into the sidewalk doors, remember? If you kill me and leave without relocking the padlock, then somebody could come up here right away and find me. As long as I'm not found for a few days, it's all cool, baby, 'cause they're gonna tear the shit out of this building and your pal, your husband, will flop around in the rubble like a rag doll. Not a bad plan, don't you think? Except for one problem. Watch. I've practiced this. [Drops key into mouth, grabs cardboard milk carton of water, spilling a little water, throws head back, takes an extended drink, throws carton to floor, brings head forward, opens mouth. Key has been swallowed.] Am I evil incarnate or what? No, that is too grandiose. I do not aspire to evil, I aspire to truth, I aspire to push at you until you give me your guts, Caroline. Give me them, I want them. I want the little-girl story. I want to know how the little girl who hung out in L.A. fucking pro basketball players and then wound up in New York getting picked up in a bar by the most brilliant young movie director since Scorsese, how did she survive? She won't tell me, her husband? Did she tell Hobbs? No, I expect not. I expect that she was too busy enjoying his oral charms. But you know what? The answer is with Hobbs. Your husband figured it out. Yes! How did she survive? It's easy, folks. She wants to be loved! She goes where she thinks the love is, and when she figures out that it's not there any-more, she moves on. She is very good at getting men to fall in love with her! But something, something inexplicable, makes men begin to find her revolting! How can this be, my beautiful wife, the woman with a golden ring in her singing cunt? She has moved on from her loving husband to Sir Hobbs. And how long will this last? Oh, per-haps not long. He will glimpse something in you and he will turn away, or perhaps you will see his revulsion before he himself does and you will leave. You will then tell your same sad little story to someone else. Woe and grief! Et cetera, et cetera. You're good, lady. *Good.* You fucking fooled me! You had me going. I was signed up. I believed, yeah! The artist had found a muse! Then the muse checked the fuck out. Well, fuck you, baby. This is where *I* check out. This is where the rubber leaves the runway. I'm gone. But first—yes! Yes, of course my intention is to kill you, of course I must, don't you see? What's the alternative? Say good-bye, let the lawyers work out the de-tails? No, no, no, flibbertygibbet! Flibbertygibbet! Poor Tom! *Lear*, a play you never read! It's the muse thing, babe, the American muse thing. You're very special! My American babe. Look at her, look at those teeth and hair and blue eyes and breasts. Corn-fed! Can't be killed by evil American men! They should make a movie about her!

Make a fucking movie! She's all-American. Corn-fed! The *Playboy* pinup. Grew up on the wrong side of the train tracks! Why, her fucking cunt is made out of Cheerios! Sings along with Willie Nelson! Only she's updated, she's ready for the millennium! The postmodern American babe! Been sunburned on both coasts! Can drive a Chevy made by Toyota in Mexico! Seen a thousand channels! Fucked a superstar! Opened her legs for a billionaire! That's who she is! *But it's not good enough.* She wants love, more and more and more love! She never had enough! Her mother worked for Visa, and her father came from ARCO money. She's got capitalism in her very genes! Don't you see the tragedy of it? You are tragedy incarnate! You have everything America can give you and still you are hungry! Still you go unloved, my American babe! Oh, please end this, sweetie, stick this knife in me, stick it right in my fucking throat or stomach or nuts or someplace to shut me up. Do it! Hey, American babe! Come on! Come on come on come on! Do I have to order you? Kill me. Do it. I dare you. Take a stab at it. Wait! [He scurries into the corner of the room and picks up something. Comes back, a manic expression on his face.] I have a gun, yes! Did I show you this? Did I show you that I have a gun? After you kill me, I suggest you take it with you and dump it in the river—that's the typical thing. Or wipe it down and throw it in the street! Give it to the nine-year-old boy on the corner. He can use it. He wants it. Now, listen to me, sweetheart, there are bullets in every chamber of this gun, and I am going to blow a culture spout in your skull if you don't stab me. Come on, see if you can take the pressure. Can you get out of this one, American babe? Here, come on, push, hold with both hands, push, push back! So many men pushing at you, dicks and fingers and tongues pushing at you in your mouth and cunt and asshole! Push the knife. [Lifts the gun.] Do it. Do it now. I'll pull the trigger. Now, okay? I'll fucking blow you to John F. Kennedy International Airport, sweetie. I'll count backward. Get your Cheerio molecules lined up, American babe, muscles in your arms, five, four, my finger muscles are on-line, sweetie, three . . . two . . . not much more time to see if— [He seems to have a new thought and lowers the gun. They stare at each other. He exhales. It is then that Caroline thrusts the knife directly into Simon's neck.] Ha . . . aaah. [Simon stands straight up, the knife stuck deep in his neck. He pulls it out. Blood spurts sideways out of his neck for three or four feet, and then he staggers backward. His hat falls off. The knife clatters to the floor.] Oh, Jesus. [He points at the gun, fumbling with it to show that it was empty. Then he falls over, one hand on his neck. Blood is puddling quickly across the floor. He looks up at Caroline. She stands back.] Caah . . . Caah! [She begins to move toward him, but he spasms, a wet sucking sound coming from his neck. He has lost so much blood that he cannot get up to his knees. Now he rolls onto his back and in doing so the force seems to drop out of him; there is a slackness to his body and no longer does he groan or twitch. She kneels next to him. His eyes are open. Her shoulders shake. She sits this way for minutes. The room is quiet. There is a squeak and she tears her head around. The shape of a rat runs through the foreground. Minutes pass. Simon is still, hands and legs splayed out. She cries and then stops, then cries some more. She sits with her knees drawn up, rocking on her haunches. Finally she stands.]

Caroline: Oh, the key. [Her words come out a whisper. She picks up the knife, lifts up Simon's red shirt. She is weeping. She pushes at his pale belly a little bit. Then she stands again and moves her hand down her throat, between her breasts, and then right under the diaphragm. She pokes there experimentally, probing, feeling. Then she kneels down next to Simon. She places the knife in his stomach, perhaps an inch. It sticks straight up. She stands abruptly and walks over to the bed. There she kicks off her shoes, then lifts up her yellow dress and lays it carefully on the bed. There is a colored shape on her shoulder blade, a butterfly. She takes off her bra, then her panties. These, too, she lays down on the bed. Then she takes Simon's baseball cap off the floor and tucks her hair up into it. Her naked bottom rests on her heels. A naked woman in a baseball cap. Then she returns to Simon. The knife is still sticking out of his belly. She leans over the body, looks away, then sets her weight above the knife. It goes in with a bellowing whoosh of air and blood. Now she is wet. She looks at it and sighs. Then she saws at the flesh, cutting a flap.

Holding the flap back with one hand, she cuts deeper. Now blood seeps upward as she presses down on the body, seeping up out of the wound and across Simon's belly and down his sides, at first painting stripes down his ribs, then covering them completely as she pushes around with the knife. She pulls out her hand and violently shakes a piece of flesh off her hand. Then she reaches her hand into the cavity and fishes around. Nothing. She sighs. She is slick with blood across her belly and arms and knees. There is blood on her nipples. Now she cuts a larger flap. Then she sits back to one side of Simon and rolls him onto his stomach. There is an audible dribbling as the contents of his stomach come out. She rolls him onto his back again. She pushes around in the stomach contents with the knife, looks up. Rats have appeared in the shadows.] Get away from me. [She returns to the task. She puts her hand back into the cavity and then suddenly pulls something out, looks at the bloody object in her hand. The key. Now she stands, puts the key on the table, and moves back to the bed, where she removes a pillowcase and wipes her hands and belly carefully. There is a bit of blood on her thighs, her knees. She rubs each place vigorously. She checks her pubic hair for blood, sucking in her belly, both hands pressed against her hipbones. Then she wipes off her fingers and hands and looks at the back of her legs, her ass. She steps back into her panties and shoes, then slips on her bra and yellow dress, buttoning it behind herself with the awkward grace that women have. She takes off the baseball cap, inspects it, shakes it, inspects it again, then tosses it onto the floor next to Simon. She slides the key off the table and puts it in her purse. She picks up the empty milk carton and drops the knife and gun into it. She looks around, checking. Now she notices something out of the frame of the camera, something small on the floor, closer to the camera. She picks it up. It is a piece of the green figurine. She goes back to Simon and stands above him, her face seeming to hold both remorse and victory. She kneels down, rubs the piece against her dress, slips it into the breast pocket of his shirt, then wipes one finger in the blood on his neck and touches her tongue. She stands up quickly, picks up the carton by the top, and walks straight into the elevator.

Caroline [facing camera but looking down, apparently at the elevator buttons]: Two-twenty-one. [Her voice is a whisper.] Two. Two. One. [She looks around.] Down. [Nothing happens.] Oh, shit. [She notices that the cage door is open, pulls it shut.] Down. [The elevator begins to grind downward. The corpse of Simon Crowley, and the floor upon which he rests, begin to rise. The number seven appears on the elevator shaft and then darkness. Then, in the faint light of the elevator, a six, then five, four, three, two. Now she breaks, suddenly coughing and choking out little sobs. When the elevator reaches the first floor, she thrusts the cage door open and races down a hallway, her footsteps receding. The cage door slowly expands, stopping halfway shut. In the corridor of shadows, nothing moves. There is the sound of a heavy door opening, a quick flung brightness, indistinct, refracted off several walls, the last messenger of light, and then all is dark. The door is not slammed shut. There is no sound. Only dark. There is no sound. Only dark.]

MORNING IN MANHATTAN. Excellent and fair. Washed yellow taxis speeding downtown. Mexican men trimming tulips outside Korean delis. The early walkers to work, pleased with themselves. Subways flashing like information. Brightness unfurling almost perceptibly down the faces of buildings. In the back of the bars and clubs and restaurants, a hundred thousand conversations are swept up, hosed down, hauled off. A mother brushes her daughter's hair. Millions to be made today, pal. The city's Greek chorus reads the op-ed page. A street-cleaning machine passes, whisks up an empty wallet. Sunlight penetrates the irises. The pleasure of blinking. A man looks at his stomach, sees a pile of ruin. A woman is pleased by her lipstick. What shoes will she wear? Coffee dreams of sunlight and redemption. Battered vans full of fish speeding uptown. Formation and decay. I'm losing money here. Get to the office early. This could be the day. This is not the day. FedEx it. A Chinese woman sits at her industrial sewing machine. A stack of models' photos blow down an alley behind the agency. Somebody robbed the corner deli, took two stale bagels with him. I'll fax it to you. Smoke condition at Forty-ninth Street. Woody Allen is washed up. Bicycle messenger hanging on to a city bus going forty down Broadway. They raised the rent on me. Rikers Island guard issues instructions to the night's catch: "Lift your arms, show your pits, open your mouth, show your tongue, lift your nutsack, then bend over, spread your ass, and cough five times hard." Please hold. I'm going to try a new antidepressant. An account executive looks at the business card a woman handed him last night. Fire in Harlem, six dead, five children. I'll put you through. Ewing is getting old, man. Please go see a doctor, Harry. What credit card will you be using for this transaction? This is Sal from Brooklyn calling. The ferry from Staten Island bumps against the piling. There's no respect anymore. In the big lot off the West Side Highway, a man puts air into the tires of garbage trucks. Don't forget your lunch box. A woman sits on the edge of the bed, remembering that yesterday's AIDS test was positive. I'm telling you the MTA wastes millions. The methadone clinic has a line out the door. Times Square ain't the same. We got serious racial problems in this city. The president is in town; traffic will be a nightmare. You owe us the money. It didn't make any money. It's not about the money. You can have the money. I don't have any money. It costs a lot of money. Tour buses full of Midwesterners. They moved to New Jersey. The medical examiner pulls on his plastic gloves, turns on the radio. I'm not gay, I'm queer, explains a man to his mother in her apartment on Riverside Drive. The cocaine is safely delivered, and today Spanish Harlem looks like paradise. I'm watching too much television. A beautiful apartment in this price range. Please sign here. It's not really a democracy anymore. In an office in Midtown all the doors are closed: the boss was fired. Call and get tickets, why don't you. Outside the Plaza Hotel, a cabbie shortchanges his customer, smiling. I'm going to get liposuction. A man briskly walks south on Lafayette, feeling a key in one pants pocket, a stone fragment in the other, then steps into a corner restaurant, the first patron. He is not shaven. He is befouled with dried mud. He carries a small package. A waiter is folding the fresh linen.

"Good morning, sir."

"Good morning." I made a show of checking my cash. "I know I'm dirty as hell."

"We'll let it go."

I sat watching the world go by, a few patrons coming in. Breakfast is the most optimistic of meals, and you could see it on the faces of the men and women. In the restroom I looked into the mirror. The dirt was in my hair, in the creases around my eyes, in my ears. My gums were receding, my teeth turning brown, my hair going gray. There's only one direction.

Was it murder? Caroline had stabbed Simon in the neck as he lowered an unloaded gun. That wasn't self-defense. No doubt the moment was one of extreme agitation, with Simon screaming and acting strange, but I wonder why she did not walk to the elevator and use it, since Simon had told her the code that would make it work. Or perhaps she could have hollered out of a window. The swallowing of the key must have been for effect. Simon must have had another way to get out of the building. All he would need was a pair of bolt cutters secreted somewhere. If he had gone to the trouble to have the water in the milk carton and the bed and the electric battery and the light and the videotape device, it would not have been much extra effort to have a pair of bolt cutters. Billy Munson had said that there was all sorts of equipment in Simon's father's van. Caroline could not have been expected to think of all these things right then, but neither could she have been expected to stab Simon simply because he was raving. I had replayed that moment ten or twelve times in my office. There was a pause, a long beat, between the moment that Simon lowered the gun and the moment that Caroline lunged with the knife. It was a pause during which each looked at the other to see what came next. It was also a pause in which he was vulnerable, and she took advantage of the opportunity. That is how I saw it; that is what she had always done.

And what had happened next? I imagined that she had waited as long as she could in the dark vault beneath the sidewalk doors, waited until the hour was late and few people were outside. Then, when she heard no sound, she had clicked the lock with the key, opened one of the doors, and silently sprung up the stairs carrying her little milk carton with the gun and knife in it, locked the doors from the outside, and then darted around the corner. You could do it in under a minute. This had transpired either in the last hours of August 6 or the early hours of August 7. If the time had been late enough, it was possible that no one had noticed her or remembered that they had noticed her. After all, Simon's body was not discovered until August 15, and that interval was certainly long enough for someone to forget what they had seen. But Caroline's immediate actions were not the only indication of her guilt. She had gone to elaborate lengths to cover up what had happened. She had lied to the police about the nature of Simon's disappearance. She had told them that she didn't recognize the little piece of the jade figurine. She had the cleverness to hire a private investigator to try and determine what had happened to Simon. That was smart, for the investigator might unknowingly report to her information that might implicate her, allowing her to anticipate problems. Even more ingenious was that such an arrangement, should it come to the attention of the police, would seem to indicate that she was not the culprit. The investigator found no useful information, of course, because if he had checked the ownership of 537 East Eleventh Street, he would have found out that a Korean owned it, not the Segals. If, like the police, he had talked to the Korean owner, the owner would have been able to tell him nothing, because, being unfamiliar with the building that was about to be demolished, the owner did not know about the quirky sidewalk doors. Nor did the foreman from Jack-E Demolition, who was obsessed with a piece of rope he'd found. The detectives had no reason to seek out the Segals, and Mrs. Segal, because of her questionable deal with the Koreans, had what she believed to be a good reason not to seek out them. The police did talk with the superintendent of 535, but their conversation had centered on access to the roof door of 535, not on the sidewalk door to 537. It was true that if the police had looked through the paperwork to Simon's estate, they might have been led to Mrs. Segal, as I had been. But I had been looking for a singular item, namely the Hobbs tape, when I found her and not, as the police would have been, for information about how Simon had entered a building. It was a logical contraption of chance and intent. No one had acted with full knowledge; no one had planned on the events as they occurred, including Caroline. So was it murder? In my mind, yes.

A beautiful woman in a mink and jeans walked in through the sunlight. One black lizard cowboy boot crossing in front of another, she smiled confidently at the world, at the waiter, at me. "Hey, baby," she said, presenting her cool cheek, and this I kissed with great interest, having never knowingly kissed a murderess before, and the softness of her skin seemed even softer for the hardness of the woman. I cannot report that I was filled with revulsion. No, I cannot say that at all.

"You've been rolling in the mud?"

"I'm a dirty guy, you know that."

"What happened?"

I fingered the head of the broken figurine in my pocket. "It's a long story."

"Can I hear it?"

"Sure."

The restaurant was starting to fill up. "We'll order breakfast first."

We sat, and I watched her gladness. I had liberated her from Hobbs yesterday, and she was leaving for China today; it was the first time since we'd met that she believed she had nothing to worry about. Her eyes were bright and her lips ready to smile. She didn't need me anymore; she needed only to close it off with no trouble. The music from the back of the restaurant was Vivaldi, bright and clear, and I knew we both were going to be different only minutes hence, and so I simply watched her. It was no small pleasure as she talked about this, about that, leaving a bit of lipstick smudged on the rim of her water glass, and while she talked, my mind imagined itself to be a silver pool of lust at her feet, a pool that morphed into a moving film of desire that flowed up her shoes and ankles and over her knees and thighs and between her legs and right up deep into her, plunging deep and deep and deep again, and then, withdrawing, brushing the tiny secret scar, then continuing upward past her hipbones and belly button and along the contours of her back and stomach, lingering helplessly at the heavy crease of her breasts against her rib cage, and then flowing out and up and over them, rubbing the palms of my imagination over her nipples, and then, upward to the delicate bones of the neck, out to and around the shoulders and down the arms to the fingers that had held the knife. To the tips. To the lovely, clean, manicured fingernails. And then, sweeping back up the arms, cupping her chin and jaw and pressing deep into her mouth past her pink tongue, which itself had touched me, and then, withdrawn from her mouth, sliding the bright film of my desire slowly up over her cheekbones and eyes—her eyelids blinking, lashes brushing softly—and then up past the forehead and like fingers through the sweet thick length of blonde hair, and then up, my desire for her flowing up and away forever, letting go of her forever. This I did as I looked at her there. I would miss her. When I was an old man, I would miss this woman.

"I've got something to show you," she said.

It was one of those glossy brochures that the real-estate firms in the better neighborhoods have printed. "I was just looking at it in the taxi." She flopped it open. "Look at that." It was a color photo of a big white house with a long lawn, a lot of windows, porches, eaves, gables. It looked like a yacht, or maybe a wedding cake. "Charlie will like it," she noted. "The real-estate agent says it's a seven-minute walk to the train station."

She continued to study the photo, and as I looked upward to her face, I saw that time was starting to accrue around her eyes. I didn't really believe that she wanted to end up in a big white house or that she wanted a life with Charlie. I think that the idea of these things represented a kind of oblivion into which she could become lost for a while. But appetites always return, and if there was anything I understood about Caroline Crowley, it was that her appetites would continue to carry her away from, not toward, what safe white houses still exist in this society. On the other hand, I understood now how desperately she might desire a new life; here it was, in front of her, and I could see that it seemed almost close enough for her to touch, and that perhaps she truly believed her long, strange journey to be over. It is not fashionable for a young woman to depend completely upon the support of a man, and for a woman such as my wife, who has been the beneficiary of a premier education, the idea of such dependence understandably smacks of a kind of existential death. But if Caroline harbored a desire for a career or work, it was subordinate to a more basic drive to be delivered into a life discontinuous from the one she had long inhabited, a life in which, for the first time, she might be safe—from others and from herself.

"I've got some things to show you, too," I said.

"You do? Are they as interesting as what I showed you?"

"Tough call."

"Let me see the first one."

I slipped my hand in my pocket, pinched the fragment of jade. I could stop it right here, I could say I was kidding and it would all just drift away. I put the jade fragment on the table. The ears were broken, but the eyes and mouth were still perfect.

She frowned, then picked it up. "It's beautiful," she said. "What is it? I mean, where's it from?"

I looked at this lovely face, these blue eyes, this mask, and I felt that I had never known her and never would.

I whispered, "Don't lie to me now, Caroline."

She looked down and then away.

"It was the gift," I said. "To you, I mean."

"Yes."

"From Hobbs."

"Yes."

"Very valuable."

"I guess. He'd owned it for a long time."

"Simon found out and got pissed off."

"Yes. I told you that."

"You wouldn't tell Simon the story you told Hobbs because it was something you could keep from him, something that was yours."

"Yes." She nodded. "We talked about this last night, Porter."

"He threw it in your direction in the building on Eleventh Street, and it smashed against the wall of the elevator, and you didn't bother to pick this piece up."

She was looking right at me now, and there was everything in her eyes: fear, hatred, amazement, and even, I think, something like love, because I knew her, finally. "Yes," she said.

I held her gaze then, saying nothing. Then I paid great attention to my omelette, pushing little pieces of green onion onto my fork. Around us came the scrape of silverware on china, the talk and society, the great stage set of Manhattan life.

"Porter?"

I looked up. Then I slid the key across the table.

She stared at it. "A key?"

"The key."

She stared straight into my face. Blue eyes. Then she touched it with one fingernail, then pinched it between forefinger and thumb, picking it up.

"Hobbs returned this key to me," I said. "His men had—"

"I know, I know."

The waitress brought me a glass of tomato juice.

"Did you know there was a videotape?" I finally said.

She ate a bite of eggs. "Of what?"

"He wired a little camera into the panel mechanism of the elevator. The actual lens was hidden behind the floor indicator."

She was just on the edge of figuring it all out.

"On the seventh floor of the building, the elevator stopped, and with the door open, the lens aimed directly into the adjoining space. This was the room where—"

"What are you saying?"

"The whole tape is there, Caroline, the whole thing." I leaned forward so that the people around us would not hear. "Second by second. The argument, the knife, the key."

She nodded, this time more heavily.

"I believe he asked his father how to wire it, it being an old elevator."

"I see."

"I think it was all an act on Simon's part. To see what he'd get on tape."

"Fooled me."

I looked at her. "You sure?"

She didn't answer. There was no answer.

"There is the original tape," I said, "and now, one copy. The original is in a place you do not know about and the copy is here." I slipped my hand under the table. Her eyes watched carefully. I put the tape on the table and slid it across to her. "Here, this one is yours. You can watch in the privacy of your own home."

Caroline's fingers touched the videotape.

"All this is a surprise," I said.

"It was a surprise for me, too."

"So what's the story?" I asked.

"What?"

"The story Simon wanted so badly to hear."

"Oh, it's just a story I told Hobbs. About when I was a kid."

"Why?"

"He wanted to know."

"I don't get it."

Her face went screwy. "He just understood me—it was the strangest thing. In some kind of way no one ever did. That was what Simon hated so much. You saw the tape, you saw how it drove him crazy." She looked out the window at the people passing by, and I could feel our whole affair falling away now; it was a matter of half an hour, perhaps even less. "I don't know—it's not really much of a story really. He just wanted to know what made me strong, and I told him about when I was a little girl." She had longed for a horse as a girl, she said, but Ron was not interested in giving her one, and her mother was useless at arguing on her daughter's behalf. They had one of those blighted marriages that is a tissue of hatreds. Ron, moreover, was far along in his fixation on Jackie Onassis and had amassed a not insignificant collection of books and magazine articles about her. There was even a small collectors' market in Jackie memorabilia, and he was an avid buyer, promising his wife that the stuff would be worth a lot of money someday. When she protested, he sometimes hit her. There was more to all of it: drinking, a failing trucking business, a bleeding ulcer. It was conceivable the man had quietly gone over the tapered edge of sanity. And yet the ten-year-old Caroline badgered Ron for a horse, asking that she get it for her birthday in February. He hit her a few times, but he didn't really mean it, she decided, not compared with what he had done to her younger brother the summer before—thrown him straight off the motorboat, so that he pinwheeled before hitting the water at thirty miles an hour, breaking his arm. A horse, she wanted a horse. Every day she asked. And so one cold February morning Ron told her to get in the station wagon, we're going for a ride. They drove across the frozen Dakota prairie, saying nothing, a defeated man in his forties in an old black coat that came past his knees and a blonde little girl who was already troubling to look at, and fifty miles and forty minutes later they pulled up to a paddock and a stoved-in barn in the middle of nowhere and Ron got out, slamming the door and crunching across the snow. She followed, and ducked her head under the rail of a fence and kept after the black bulk in the snow in front of her. There were hoofprints and frozen horse shit on the ground, and she saw an old nag off to one side, lifting her feet and trying to stay warm. This was a good sign, she decided, but where was her horse? The nag was too old and broken down for any-one to ride and suffered a disease that was eating away the hooves, yet Ron was walking toward the horse, and so she followed, catching up with him as he reached the horse, who looked too cold even to move. They stood there a moment. She didn't understand. "Happy birthday, Caroline," Ron said. "This is your horse." Then he withdrew a large old pistol from his coat, cocked it, and shot the horse in the head. And then again, before she fell. Caroline jumped back as the weight hit the ground, red spreading across the frozen grass.

"That's it," Caroline told me now. "That was the story." Her eyes were clear; she was beyond the moment.

"That was what Simon wanted to know?"

"He had taken everything from me already, Porter. I had told him all my stories."

"You killed him over a story?"

"I don't see it that way, exactly."

"It's all there on the tape."

The waitress brought me the bill, and I paid it with cash. There would be no record of our breakfast, ever.

She played with her spoon. "Why did you look for it?"

"I think you wanted me to, Caroline."

She said nothing.

"You wanted to tell somebody." Her head was down; the part in her hair was perfect. "Sometimes things happen and people have to tell some-body. You never really needed me to find the Hobbs tape. You knew where it was. Basically. All it took was seeing that the estate was paying for some-thing odd. You certainly didn't need me for sex. You needed me for some-thing else, Caroline, and fuck me for not understanding it from the beginning. Jesus, Caroline, you just needed to tell somebody before you married Charlie."

When she looked up there were tears in her eyes. I didn't believe them.

"I don't want any more of this, you understand?" I told her.

She nodded.

"I have a certain—I felt a certain . . . but now I can't do that anymore.

You never cared for me, but you saw that I might be useful. You could involve me and then let out the story a little at a time. Hobbs was just part of
the whole thing."

She took a regular cigarette out of her purse.

"Miss," a passing waiter said. "There's no smoking. They made that
new law."

"Yes, yes," she said in agitation, waving her hand. "I couldn't tell Charlie, you see, and if I married him without straightening it out . . ." She
didn't have to finish. I understood that Charlie would leave her, like *that*, if
he were to know of such a thing; not only would he rightly despise her for
not telling him, but he would also fear that her past would somehow taint
his career, and if there was anything he would protect, it was this. And
once she married Charlie and took his name, her problems became his.
The fact that Hobbs's company received some of its financing through
Charlie's bank meant, Caroline figured, that Hobbs could have Charlie removed from the account, perhaps even fired. I understood now why she
had chosen Charlie. Here was the perfect man, perfect in his handsome
emptiness, his dependable blandness.

"So how could you go to the party that Hobbs threw?"

"I went because I wanted the chance to tell him one more time. I was
going to swear to him that I didn't have the tape. That Simon must have
done something with it . . . but I couldn't get to him. All his people were
around him. They had people for him to meet and everything. I stood
with Charlie but I kept watching . . . actually, I saw you introduced to
Hobbs, I saw them get you and bring you over to him . . . I recognized you
from your picture."

Looking across the room, Caroline admitted to me, she had seen
someone who snooped around in people's lives, though the last thing she
wanted was to induce a newspaper story about the video that Hobbs
wanted. If she was going to have me try to find the Hobbs tape, then it
would have to be because I wanted to do so personally. All this she understood as soon as she glanced up and saw me looking at her. Then she
had excused herself from Charlie and his little group of executives and
walked over toward me. Within a minute or two of our conversation she

knew that she could sleep with me if she wanted. After all, she might have made colossal mistakes, but she knew how to hook a man. Perhaps, she allowed, perhaps she was also attracted to me as well. Not that she had meant to be. She liked the way I gave it back to her in that first conversation, hard, even as I was completely losing what rationality I might have had. She also liked the fact that I was married; it gave her an added measure of control.

Our waitress brought more coffee.

"You want to know if I'm going to give a copy of this tape to the police."

She looked at me, her eyes haunted. "Yes," she whispered.

"Here's my answer. If, in any way, you let my wife know what has happened between us, then the police get the tape. God knows what they'll make of it. Did you murder Simon? That's a tough question. Certainly he threatened you. Was it self-defense? Very difficult. That's *very* difficult, I would say. You *could* have walked into the elevator, tried to get away. You could have refused to kill him—"

"He was going to kill me."

"No, he wasn't. He was taping a scene. A sick scene. He wouldn't have gone to the trouble of hiding the camera in the elevator panel if he hadn't—"

"I swear he was going to kill me, that very moment."

"Look at the tape, Caroline. He drops the gun down. There's a long pause. Then you stab him. There it is, on tape."

"No, that's not—"

Suddenly I was very tired of myself. "Good-bye, Caroline."

I stood up and put a few bills on the table for the tip.

"Don't just go. Say something to me."

I looked at her, and I knew that she didn't care really what I thought, just that when I left she would be alone with herself again, as she always had been. I leaned down and kissed her gently on the cheek. "Be well," I told her. "As well as you can."

And then I left, shouldering past the other patrons, not looking back, glad to be leaving, ready to get back onto the street, ready to go at it again. I had a column to write, about the Fellows tape. At the door I thought about looking back and even wanted to, to see Caroline one last time, but I didn't, and when I had turned the corner, I told myself that I felt much better about things.

THE UGLINESS OF IT, of who I have been and who I am now, is strongest when I am with my wife and children. As they play at the beach, as we eat dinner together. As I touch Tommy's scar. I could tell my wife about my affair with Caroline and she would, I think, forgive me in time. Hers is a genuine and true heart. But if she believes in anything, it is family, and, like a teacup that has been repaired, the fracture would always show, would always be there. Perhaps I am only a coward, but I would rather hold my own guilt close to me than force my wife to deal with it.

I have tried to be smart about all this and figure out what could go wrong in the arrangement that Caroline and I have. We both hold a card. We could both destroy each other's lives. I have asked myself if, by not turning her in, I am betraying those who once and still loved Simon Crowley. The question is a difficult one. Mrs. Segal had loved him as only a surrogate mother could. She still ached at his death and would until she died, but, I surmised, perhaps conveniently, the fact of his death seemed not to have surprised her, given the way he lived. What would be gained by telling her that Simon had been killed by his own wife? She seemed old enough that all sorrows had melted in the deeper burden of being human, and I doubted that knowing would have added to her grief, which was already, in itself, complete.

As for Simon's father, I have no answer. The man I met was ebbing away; what would be gained by attempting to explain it all to him? He had struggled to provide a single clue to his son's death—is he owed a recognition of this? Or should he be left in peace? He will die any time now, today or tomorrow or next week—it will be a mercy, if not for him, then for me.

And, as I go over all this, I find I can't determine where the story begins or really ends. Is it Simon's story? How a boy became a brilliant filmmaker who became a corpse? Is it the story of what happened because a Korean businessman sued an old Jewish lawyer and his wife in Queens? Is it the story of a hand surgeon who went to the trouble of putting a tuxedo into her husband's car so that he could go to a business function? The story of a dull boy from Bay Ridge, Brooklyn, who grew up to work for a "security" outfit and who, because he shot a bullet through the biceps of an eighteen-month-old boy, the son of the hand surgeon, was—as I eventually learned—kicked down some stairs by the police three weeks later, breaking both arms and some teeth? (How oddly wretched this made me feel.) Or is it the story of Officer Fellows's widow, who, after the call came from the detectives telling her they got the man who killed her husband, stood in the kitchen and wept? I know that because I wrote a column about it. Or, last, is it the story of an aging, obese billionaire who confessed his heart to a ravishing woman one night in a hotel room in New York City and came to regret it?

In the words of that old drunk reporter I once knew, it's all one story, and I suppose it is, but the strand I cannot let go of is Caroline's, of course, and having reconstructed it in sequence, it still remains mysterious to me; how, I wonder, does the young girl standing in a South Dakota field over a dead horse become the teenager being raped by Merk, then the woman riding down the elevator in a building about to be destroyed, key in hand, and then the executive's well-dressed partner on a plane to China? The same question could be asked of me, of course, and although my life is comparatively undramatic, I can't help but wonder how the quiet boy fishing in the dark hole of a frozen lake came to be, twenty-five years later, the man kissing a murderess good-bye in a Manhattan eatery—the man who let her go unpunished. Caroline and I passed through each other's lives with crazy speed, with—as Hal Fitzgerald would put it—unmanaged velocity.

Why haven't I turned Caroline in? It's not that I care for her, not exactly. It's that I cannot bear to think of her in prison. Nonetheless, I keep that tape in a safe-deposit box in an obscure New York City bank. I have instructed the bank not to bill me annually; instead I arranged to pay for the next forty years in one sum. The bank clerk thought this odd, but I pointed out that I was effectively lending the bank a considerable amount of money at no interest, and they found this observation convincing. So the tape of Caroline Crowley killing her husband, Simon, inside 537 East Eleventh Street sits in the Seventh Avenue branch of the Greater New York

Savings Bank in Brooklyn, which I chose not because I have my accounts there but because I do not and because I happened to notice, while on a story not long ago, that it was a brand-new bank, and therefore unlikely to soon be torn down or sold; two plastic spools, one spun with videotape, both in a black plastic box, one side labeled, in Simon Crowley's hand, TAPE 78 (REUSED), the cassette itself wrapped in a plastic bag from a Korean deli, the whole package inside the small metal space. And where is the safe-deposit-box key? Where did I put *that?* I had to think about this at some length. It's small—perhaps an inch long, an eighth of an inch thick, and made of brass. I needed to be able to get at it someday, quickly perhaps. But I didn't want it to be in the house; not only could Lisa or one of the kids find it, but it would be something of an obscenity to have it there. Yet where to put it? I wondered. (Where has Caroline put *her* key?) Not in another safe-deposit box, of course; that creates another key. And not at the office; it could be stolen or, more likely, I would lose it. I considered burying it in the garden outside the house, perhaps connected to a piece of copper wire or something, but again I could not bear seeing my children playing in the grass above it. No, the garden was too close. I considered hiding the key somewhere in Manhattan, under a rock in Central Park, perhaps, but this plan didn't appeal to me either. The island of Manhattan is washed by a human tide each day; anything can happen, and anything does.

It was only by accident that I figured out what to do with the key. One Saturday I was inspecting the gate at the end of the tunnel and noticed not only that the gate needed repainting but that the key might fit in a small gap between two welded bars near the bottom hinge. I retrieved the key and tried it. It wedged between the bars perfectly. *Perfectly.* Almost as if that old ironworker had known that I might someday need such a tiny space. From any angle the key was invisible. I shut the gate forcefully half a dozen times. The key stayed put. Then I slammed the gate as hard as I could. The key didn't move. I told Lisa I was going out to the hardware store, and there I bought a quart of Rust-Oleum brand black paint, thick and glossy, and repainted the entire gate, right over the key. When the paint dried, I painted thickly over the key again, such that now, even upon an unlikely close inspection, it would appear to be part of the gate itself, an imperfection of metal and paint and rust. I check it from time to time; always still there. It has become part of the apparatus that keeps the world out, or, rather, keeps me inside mine.

If all goes as planned, at some point in the far future, perhaps when I am in my fifties or sixties, I will retrieve the videotape and destroy it. It will be interesting to see if I want to view the tape again, assuming that I am able to procure a by-then-antiquated videotape player. I will have wondered if Caroline has kept her copy, and where, and whether she has looked at it ever or more than once, or has shown it to anyone; these are questions that presumably will be unanswerable. A lot of other things are going to happen in the future, and some will not be good. There will come a time, of course, when my family will leave our little hidden apple-tree house. We will move, and our bed will be dismantled and movers will take the mattress and box spring down the stairs. The photos on the mantel and the children's things will have been packed away, along with the dining-room chairs and everything else. I dread such a day, because it will mean either that calamity has befallen us or that a lot of time, *our time*, is gone. The house will be empty again, quiet again, until someone else stands there, looking at the windows and walls and floors, mindful perhaps that the last occupants, my wife and children and myself, were only passing through.

PASSING THROUGH. Those words were to have been my final contemplation of this affair. I wrote them a few months ago, when I was sure that the matter had settled in my heart. But it had not. And so here is my last confession, not as bad as the ones that have gone before it, but indicative, I fear, of the basic weakness in my character, a rotted sentimentality, an inability to let things have their end.

It was just this September, and the story I was working on was, sadly enough, a forgettable triple killing in Spanish Harlem. Two guys with guns holding up a delicatessen. The twist was witnessed by an old woman sprawled on the floor: after emptying the register and executing the deli owner, one of the gunmen fired at the deli's glass door, thinking the police were coming in. They weren't—he'd seen his own reflection. Instead he hit his fellow gunman—his brother—killing him instantly. The first gunman, distraught, watched his brother die, then pushed the muzzle of his semi-automatic against his own heart and fired. I logged a good interview the next morning with the grandmother, who listened to Tito Puente records and kept parakeets and remembered the two men as boys. The column was due that afternoon, and as I was driving back down Fifth Avenue with the windows open, I passed the green-and-white-striped awning at Sixty-sixth Street. The remembrance of Caroline came back to me with merciless clarity. I missed her with foolish desperation. The mind is cruel this way. I pulled over next to a fire hydrant and sat in the car, glancing up into the rearview mirror from time to time. I had little doubt that Caroline was no longer living in the apartment house; she was probably married to Charlie now and had moved out of the city. I picked up the new phone in my car and, remembering the neighborhood where Caroline had shown me the picture of the three-story white house, called information and asked for her. There was no Caroline Crowley listed, but there was a listing for Charlie and Caroline Forster, and I got the address.

In a little more than an hour I was there, and I eased along the leafy streets, stopping twice for school buses. Each house sat grandly on its plot; each was beautiful or magnificent. An occasional service van passed, green or red, with the name of the tradesman neatly lettered on the side. I found the house; it was as it had been pictured: two ancient copper beeches flanking a glassed-in porch, the drive curving up around one side, the lawn a great long rug of grass that ran fifty yards to the street. I stopped. There was a big car in the driveway, but I did not see anyone. Of course I would not drive up to the house. I sat thinking how foolish I was, how idiotic my sentimentality, how dangerous my curiosity. The wind pushed against the leaves of the beeches, shaking them, a sight that would thrill children.

I do not know how long I sat there, musing. The story was large and heavy inside me, and always would be. But then, I told myself, this was something that I had brought upon myself. What an asshole I had been, not even telling Lisa the truth of things after she returned with the kids from California, instead letting the bad time drift downward into the mud of the marriage, hidden beneath a surface of children and work and days.

Many evenings Lisa had looked at me waiting for the conversation to begin, and once she had even seemed to start it herself, but I think she finally decided that whatever was in me now was dark and ugly and better left where it was. In this way, for the time being, the marriage is damaged.

Now the wind gusted about me, whirling leaves into the air, and, suddenly desiring the sensation of motion, thinking about the return drive and the column due later in the day, I eased the car forward, and that was when I glimpsed the figure by the rhododendron bushes around the far side of the house—a woman, her blonde hair pinned up, kneeling in gardening clothes with a trowel and a basket. I'd almost missed her. Oh, Caroline. She was intent on her work and did not notice the car. She dug at the earth, plunging the trowel into it, and then reached in her basket. I could only imagine that she was planting bulbs for the next spring. She worked for a few minutes, then sat back and wiped her brow. I could see by the cast of her shoulders that she felt safe and unknown there. We learn more about other people when they don't realize that we are watching. This was what Simon Crowley knew so well. What a nest of ironies; in his attempt to study his wife and learn who she really might be, Simon Crowley created arguably the best record of who he himself was. It was his final creation and he didn't even get to see it. Now his former wife, the one who had killed him, the one whom I also had loved in my own foolish way, pulled her gloves back on and set herself to her task; her motion released mine, and as I let my foot rise from the brake, the wheels rolling, I wished then, with a final sweet pain, that despite Caroline's hard soul, she might yet attempt some act of redemption, that despite my own betrayal of those whom I loved most, I might yet prove worthy of their affections. Better then, I thought, that our respective confessions go unheard, that they fall away into time. There would, I knew, be other questions to worry about, other dark crises of heart and hope; sooner or later life brings to all of us some form of suffering. Would that we were equal to it always.

But perhaps such a thought was merely a sentimental lie. Perhaps we are a society of murderers now—murderers and their accomplices.

ACKNOWLEDGMENTS

I AM INDEBTED to Michael Daly, the columnist at the *Daily News*, Peg Tyre and Paul Moses at *Newsday*, Karen Van Rosen, former librarian at *Newsday*, and Mark Lasswell; Kristin Juska and Pat Friedman, authors of the note on page 56; Rahul Mehta, Nora Krug, and Hilary Davidson; my colleagues Susan Burton, Clara Jeffery, and Ben Metcalf; Babo Harrison, Jack Hitt, Don Snyder, John Bradford, M.D., Mark Costello, Greg Critser, Tony Earley, Earl Shorris, and Richard Zacks; Kris Dahl, Karen Rinaldi, and Ann Patty.

And to Kathryn.

THE STORY ON PAGE 349 was told to me by a French-Canadian woman as I lay sick on a bed in a cheap hotel in Cozumel, Mexico, in January 1986. She was about thirty, blonde, and wise beyond her years. I remembered her story but not her name.

Read on for an excerpt from

THE FINDER

Available now in hardcover from

Sarah Crichton Books,

Farrar, Straus and Giroux

THREE GIRLS IN A CAR AT NIGHT, on their way to the beach in Brooklyn. Two are Mexican, about nineteen or twenty, young and pretty—like a lot of Mexican girls you see in New York City. Straight black hair, soft faces, a sweet-eyed optimism not yet destroyed by labor. Dressed in identical blue service uniforms with CorpServe patches on the breast, they are nestled in a Toyota two-door subcompact as it flies along the Belt Parkway. The rattling, uninsured car is fifteen years old, carries expired Georgia plates, and has a market value of $125. In New York City you can always buy a car like this and you can always sell one. Who cares about the paperwork? That's for people who have big money to lose. These Mexican girls have no money. They work cleaning offices in Manhattan. Their day begins at seven P.M., so the hour now might be five in the morning, just before dawn. They go out afterward almost every night, a way of saying this work is not yet destroying us. A few minutes sitting in the car at the beach, then they'll swing back to the house on Avenue U, where they live with nine other people. Why drive? *The subway, it don't go where we live.* And the bus, it takes *like forever.* So the girls drive. Often they will smoke a little pot some boys gave them and giggle. Open the car's cracked sunroof, let the smoke drift upward. They are enjoying their freedom, their few hard-won dollars, their provisional American identities. They smoke, maybe drink some too, listen to the radio. Giggling and sweet, but tough—tougher than American girls. In the country illegally. Each carrying some kind of fake green card that she bought for $150. They've made the journey and are not yet beaten down, not yet burdened with children and husbands. They have cookouts and volleyball in one of the Mexican sections of Marine Park. And they have guys, when they feel like it, know what to do to make their men feel *bien*. Sex yet another kind of labor. Their mothers back home don't know—don't know a lot. *Be careful!* they beg, *Nueva York is dangerous for girls like you*. But that's wrong. Mexico is where girls get found in the desert, legs wide open, hair dragged with dirt, dead eyes already eaten out by bugs. New York City is big and safe and filled with rich, fat *norteamericanos*. Maybe the girls won't even marry Mexican men. Why should they? They talk about the office guys. The tall ones who look so good in a suit. You want to do him, girl, I know you do. *No, no, es muy gordo*, too fat. They laugh. They see a lot of powerful people leaving their offices at the end of the day. Men and women in business clothes. Nice haircuts, good watches. *White ladies who think they's better than us*. A corporate world so close they could reach out and touch it with their cherry-colored fingernails. Yet given the stratifications of American society, it is a world they are unlikely ever to know from within. They are like Nigerians in London, Turks in Paris, Koreans in Tokyo, Filipinos in Riyadh—outsiders in their new homelands. Their only advantages are their youth and willingness to suffer, but they will lose these advantages, as eventually they will lose everything, including their lives. Come to think of it, they will lose everything a lot sooner rather than later.

Tonight, in fact. Before the sun is up. Minutes from now.

The third girl in the car, sitting in the back, is older, and not really a girl anymore. She's cute, slim, and Chinese. Yet fluent in English. She's learned to speak a little Spanish, with a Mexican accent. She is the Mexican girls' boss. They were afraid of her at first but now they like her, although they can barely speak English to one another, because of the accents. You speak Chenglish to us, they laugh. Her name is Jin Li, and they call her Miss Jin, which comes out *MeezaJin*. She's very pretty, in that

Chinese way. Slender, with a beautiful face. But so *nerviosa*! Always checking on everything. Telling people where to put the full trash bags for the
service elevators. What's she so worried about? They work hard, they do a
good job. You need to relax, they finally told her. You ever go out? She
shook her head and they could see she wanted to. So now, every week or
so, she'll go out with them. Keeps things friendly. MeezaJin is studying
them, they know. She's quiet, she watches everybody. They are outsiders in
America but more at home than MeezaJin is, though she makes a lot of
money and reads English. She even has a white boyfriend—or used to,
they are not sure. MeezaJin doesn't say much about herself—like she
might be hiding something, like she might be some kind of *criminal*, girl,
you know what I'm saying?

The work shift has come and gone, as it does each night. The offices
need tidying and vacuuming. The trash cans need emptying. There's precious little conversation between the girls and the office people—a few pa-
tronizing *thank-yous*, sometimes a perfunctory nodding of the head on
the way out. Nobody pays much attention to the cleaning people in a corporation. Why should they? They're *cleaning people*. Occasionally the girls
encounter office workers eating pizza and pulling all-nighters. But for the
most part all they see is just big-time corporate calm, the hushed rush of
money moving through the wires and across the screens. And there is
plenty of money, millions and billions, by the look of it. The marble lobby
floor gets buffed at night. The elevators get wiped clean, even the steel-
walled service elevators that the girls are required to use. The carpeting is
washed. The vending company guy refills the free coffee machine with
twenty-four kinds of coffee and tea. The Indian computer guys go through
like mice, fixing firewalls, loading spam blockers, cleaning out viruses.
Every activity is about money. A way to make more money. The windows
are washed, the computers are new. *Money*. Being made in every office.
You can almost smell it. The girls like being near the money. Doesn't
everyone?

To what degree do they realize that the trash they empty out of the offices each day is in fact the paper trail of deals, trends, ideas, conflicts,
sensitive issues, and legal wars—some of which, set before other eyes, may
have enormous value? The answer is that they have no actual awareness of

this. They are only barely literate in Spanish and more or less illiterate in English. This is expectable. Indeed, it has been purposefully expected: They have been hired by MeezaJin for their distinct inability to read English, their unknowingness about the ornate structures of capital and power through which they lightly pass each night. Industrious as they are, their naïveté also has value. Much of New York City depends upon such people. The ones who know nothing. The city needs their labor, compliance, and fear. You could question these girls in a court of law. *Exactly which proprietary documents were you removing, Miss Chavez?* They could never answer.

Jin Li likes these Mexican girls, though. They work hard, they do not complain. She knows that they do not suspect her of anything other than an eagerness to exploit their labor. She knows too that the building services managers who contract with CorpServe, tough guys with keys and beepers and walkie-talkies, see in her a pretty Chinese girl whose English is not so good—she purposefully makes it worse when she speaks to them—and they think she will be a little cheaper. They are right, too. The Chinese are always a little cheaper, when they want to be. They figure out how to do it, how to undercut everyone else, and then they become indispensable. Jin Li's customers are eager to exploit her eagerness to exploit others. People expect the Chinese to be brutal to their workers when they need to be, even in America, and most of the time they are not disappointed.

Tonight the two Mexican girls have worked hard stuffing blue plastic bags into the service elevator of a building near Fifty-first Street and Broadway, with Jin Li supervising. CorpServe is contracted for nine floors of the building: the sixteenth through nineteenth floors, commercial loan processing offices for a bank, and the twentieth through twenty-fourth floors, the national management offices of a small pharmaceutical company. Jin Li runs seven crews at different midtown Manhattan locations each night and floats among them. The office layouts are all roughly similar, with a service elevator that drops into a street-level truck bay where CorpServe's immense mobile shredding vehicle is parked. There an older man in a blue uniform matching theirs tosses the bags into a sucking orifice that shreds them into confetti. This man is Chinese, like Jin Li, and at times she comes down to the truck bay with certain piles of bags, issues specific instructions to him, then watches to see that he complies. The roar of the shredders drowns out their speech. They both know that they are always being watched by ceiling-mounted security cameras, some of them remote-swiveling, and they also both know how easy it is to work around them. You just have to know the angles. The cameras can see the CorpServe truck but not into the truck. You can set aside a few bags marked by hand with a special inch-high Chinese character and the camera doesn't know.

But that was hours past and now the night's work is done and the girls laugh and listen to the Latino radio station and feel the salty mist off the water. The beach parking lot is usually empty at this hour. Nobody bothers the girls, but if someone does—some cracked-out motherfucker, some drunk-ass wannabe punk—they have pepper spray in their purses. Tonight they drink a little cheap jug wine in plastic cups, dance in their seats to the radio. The Mexican girls ask MeezaJin about her white boyfriend. I liked him! So macho for a white guy! What happened? one of the girls asks, wriggling in a seat patched with duct tape. Oh, you know . . . Jin Li laughs but is quick to look toward the water. It wasn't going to work out. But she doesn't elaborate, barely admits the real reason to herself. She was forced to end it. Listened to his phone messages asking her to call. Hated herself for not calling him back. What he did to her in bed—thinking about not getting *that* will just upset her. She's had relationships with *gweilos* before—British, German, Italian. She likes them, much better than Chinese men, and this one was best of all. And maybe that's why she's here tonight, just to forget him.

Now Jin Li feels the wine in her bladder and slips out the passenger-side door to go pee in the sea grass. She has a bit of toilet paper folded in her purse with her and steps over the lip of the parking lot toward a dirt path that leads to a private spot. Private and disgusting. People hang out down there lighting up crack pipes or having sex, and so she is careful before she disappears into the grass. You have to watch out for broken bottles, used condoms, tampons, rotting chicken wings. The girls in the car can no longer see her, so she listens a moment—is anyone lurking down there in the grass? She hears nothing, though the wind is blowing now, rain in it. She braves the dark path and finds a place where she will squat down.

She is just pulling up her pink panties when she hears a low diesel vibration nearby. What is it? She walks halfway up the path and crouches in the grass below the parking lot. Two trucks are pulling into the lot, one a big pickup, tricked out with fog lights and custom chrome parts, and the other a huge commercial vehicle, big as a municipal garbage truck but shaped differently. It's too dark to know what colors they are. The trucks brake to a sudden stop next to the little Toyota. The pickup sits directly behind the car, pinning it against the curb of the parking lot, and the other truck has slipped up on the driver's side, an inch away, so tight the door can't be opened. What are they doing? What do they *want* to do? Two burly men get out, one from each truck, and rush around to the unblocked side of the little car.

Standing in the weeds, the rain making her blink now, Jin Li can see that the two Mexican girls have rolled up the windows and are screaming inside their little car.

One of the men shatters the sunroof of the Toyota with a hammer, then keeps his foot on the front passenger door, in case the girls try to push it open. Meanwhile the second man hooks something on the back bumper of the car—a chain, she thinks—then starts a motor on the bigger truck. Moving quickly, he pulls a huge hose off a spool on the truck and drags it around to the broken sunroof. He shoves the nozzle of the hose downward into the car, releases a lever, and holds the thick hose as it sends its gurgling contents inside onto the girls. The hose bucks and kicks, the flow inside sloshy and heavy.

Behind the windows the screaming intensifies.

What should she do? The car is filling quickly, a line of dark stuff rising against the windows. The only way out is across the parking lot, where Jin Li will be seen. Behind her is the sharp sea grass and sand. Her cell phone is sitting in her apartment in Manhattan, charging. She never takes it to work, on purpose: Cell phones give law enforcement a perfect record of your movements. She has an untraceable walkie-talkie in her purse that she uses to call the other CorpServe crews. But its effective range is only about a mile, good enough for midtown Manhattan but no good in Brooklyn. . . .

One of the girls is pushing on the driver's door now, banging it against the big truck pulled up tight against the car. But the door will open only a crack, no more. Then a hand shoots out of the passenger window, wildly firing pepper spray. The man holding shut that door slaps the hand and the spray can flies to the pavement.

"Richie!" the taller man calls through the rain. "That's enough!"

Jin Li fumbles in her purse for the walkie-talkie and clicks it on. Nothing but windy static. "Hello? Hello?" she tries in English. Nothing.

Now the lights of the car go on and the engine starts. The car lurches forward to the lip of the parking lot, jolting the truck behind it. But the chain on the bumper holds. The car's back wheels spin violently, burning rubber, the smelly smoke drifting over the sea grass. Then the engine slows, as if in capitulation. Inside the car the girl's foot is slack now. Something is oozing out of the passenger window, dripping down the glass.

"Richie, you fuck, let's go!" the man screams.

The man holding the hose doesn't move.

"Turn it off!"

The man named Richie pulls the lever and withdraws the nozzle. More stuff pours out lumpily from the broken sunroof. The car is full. He replaces the hose onto the truck, then removes the chain.

"Go faster!"

The little $125 car doesn't move against the lip of the parking lot, even though its lights are still on and the engine putters. The taller man removes his boot from the front passenger door, jumping back as it opens just enough to release a torrent of ooze. Then he does a strange thing. He reaches around to lock the door and uses all his weight to slam it shut, then does the same thing with the driver's door.

He locked both doors, Jin Li thinks. Why?

"Get out of here, man!"

The men hurry now into their respective trucks. The whole thing has taken perhaps six minutes. The big truck reverses in a half circle, then shoots forward out of the lot. The pickup truck backs more tightly, swings around, and follows the big truck. They drive without lights, fast.

In ten seconds they are gone.

Jin Li runs toward the car. The wet wind has shifted, and the smell has alerted her. She knows that smell from China, would know it anywhere. The public pit latrines in the smaller towns. The holes in the ground next to huge construction sites in Shanghai where the workers squat over cutout boards. The raw sewage spewing into the rivers. Yes, she knows this smell.

She hurries up to the car and pulls on the doors just to be sure they are locked. Does she see movement inside, a hand flailing through the dark liquid against the glass? She looks around for something to break the window and flies over to the edge of the lot, where she frantically scrabbles around in the grass, her hands raking through plastic bags, old newspapers, beer cans, anything but what she needs. Suddenly she finds a heavy chunk of asphalt. Too much time has gone by! Right? How could anyone—? She awkwardly carries the asphalt back to the car and after three tries breaks the front passenger window. Wet, thick muck streams out, spatters her, the smell horrific. Fecal gases. Fetid urine. She gags, bile burning her throat. She hits the safety glass again and again to make a hole large enough to reach through. Finally. She drops the asphalt and thrusts her arm into the cold, lumpy wetness and feels around for the door lock, the broken glass rasping against her wrist. She finds the lock, pops it up, pulls on the door—it flies open, a great thick black tongue of filth spewing out across the lot.

"Come on!" Jin Li shrieks in Chinese. The stench is sickening, burns her eyes. She reaches in and finds one of the girls. No movement! Too much time has gone by! Seven or eight or even nine minutes! She pulls an arm, and the body of the girl falls limply out to the pavement, covered in muck. Jin Li wipes at the girl's face. Her mouth is filled, black hair tangled and wet with the stuff. She is not breathing. Jin Li rolls her over, clears the mouth, pushes on the back. Nothing! She runs to the other side of the car, breaks the glass there, soaking herself, opens that door, the sewage gurgling as it empties from the car. The girl is deadweight, slumped against the steering wheel, but Jin Li pulls her free and tries to get her breathing. She doesn't respond. Jin Li is weeping in fear and frustration. Come on, come on! she says, pushing on the girl's back, wiping the stuff out of her mouth. Nothing. Jin Li can't even look at her eyes, which are mudded over with gunk. The girls were scared, they hyperventilated, they inhaled the wet muck deep into their lungs. As they lost consciousness, the stuff oozed down their throats, suffocating them. Same as being held underwater for long minutes. Now the girls both lie on their stomachs on the pavement, still as death while the tongue of filth spreads across the parking lot as the car empties, the rain coming faster now and forming rivulets that travel toward the storm drains at the end of the lot.

Jin Li hears a woman's voice talking excitedly in Spanish, and she freezes. Who? She looks at the girls. But the girls appear to be—yes—*dead*, bodies already sinking softly into themselves. Yes, it's true, she tells herself. Dead! Now comes Latino dance music. The radio is still on in the car and the muck has drained below the dashboard speakers. *"Yo te voy a amar hasta el fin de tiempo!"* wails a singer's voice.

The first light of day is on the horizon, showing the rain gusting across the lot.

Jin Li understands now. Someone knows. Someone knows what she was doing. They saw her get into the car in Manhattan and followed. They wanted *her*.

She runs. Fleeing over the pavement, wet black hair streaming behind her, eyes wide, she runs for her life.